The Fifth Seal

"*And when he had opened the fifth seal, I saw under the altar the souls of them that were slain for the word of God, and for the testimony which they held . . .*"

THE REVELATION OF ST. JOHN THE DIVINE, VI, 9.

THE
FIFTH
SEAL

By *Mark Aldanov,* pseud-
Mark Aleksandrovich Landau

TRANSLATED BY

Nicholas Wreden

NEW YORK · CHARLES SCRIBNER'S SONS

1 · 9 · 4 · 3

AUTHOR'S NOTE

I left Russia a long time ago, when the liberal, republican, democratic form of government was overthrown there. The men connected with that government, whose political beliefs I shared and who were my personal friends, had attempted to build in Russia a free social order, based on respect for human dignity and similar in conception to that which exists in the United States. Like most of them I chose to live in a free country, where I could work without being subject to anyone's orders.

This novel was begun in 1937 and parts of it appeared in Russian in pre-war Paris. I have made virtually no changes for the American edition. When parts of the novel were first published in Russian one of the critics on a large New York paper, in a much too flattering article about it, pointed out that, in spite of my anti-bolshevism, I portrayed individual bolsheviks as impartially as I portrayed other characters. May I be permitted to say that I concur with the observation just as wholeheartedly as I believe that this is a natural thing for me to do. Following the tradition of letters, I am concerned only with artistic truth. There cannot be two Russian literatures—one Soviet and the other exile. Both spring from the same sources, both were created by the same great masters, and they constitute one integral whole.

A storm broke, on June 22, 1941,—a terrifying storm which in its fury and in its destructive violence has had no equal in Russian

v

history. It seems almost superfluous to say that this storm has aroused in the exiled writers the same emotions that it has aroused in the writers who continue to live in Russia. Just as strongly as they, I hope for victory—a total victory—for Russia and for her allies; just as strongly as they, I hope that every possible assistance will be rendered to Russia by her allies; just as strongly as they, I hate Hitler and Hitlerism. And I allow myself to believe that among the Russian people, who are fighting so heroically for their country, there are many characters out of this novel, beginning with General Tamarin and ending with the self-effacing secretary.

Mark Aldanov

New York
1943

Book One

1

THE MAN who called himself Wislicenus always had the same dream. During the recent years the nightmare repeated itself more frequently than ever; shots, blood, chase, underbrush, forest, a hand tightly gripping the cocked gun—in those days a gun still had to be cocked—all those things which happen only in moving pictures, but which actually had happened to him during his strange life—a life that unfolded as an incredible, third-rate thriller. The men came nearer and blew their whistles; he grasped the gun tighter than ever; he was resolved not to be taken alive. Even in his dreams he remembered the dime novel which had on the cover a picture of a man with a smoking Colt in his hand over a caption in blurred ink: "He was determined to sell his life dearly." The huge, red-haired giant with a bestial face who was leading the others was brandishing a dagger. Something that looked like a yellow wooden box crossed his vision. Wislicenus stirred and opened his eyes; his heart was beating fast; the train compartment was in semi-darkness. He could not realize at once that all of it lay in the past, that now he was traveling through Germany, that the moanful sound assailing his ears was the whistle of the engine, and that the dull metallic glitter which caught his eye was merely the spigot on the washbasin, and not the barrel of a Colt. His right hand which had been gripping the arm rest, relaxed. He felt a surge of relief, but also a trace of disappointment that it had been only a dream. Laboriously he tried to reconstruct the details of the vision; among the absurdities of a dream were buried certain involved combinations of circumstances with which he was familiar, though they never occurred to him when he was fully awake. Something inside him kept thinking about those things without any conscious effort on his part, without any apparent purpose of reason. It was weird and unpleasant, like wandering through a deserted house.

The piercing sound of the engine whistle was lost in the clatter of the wheels. He turned on the light. All his bags, including the one that was important, were in their proper places. The glare of the electric bulb hurt his eyes. He stood up, raised the shade, and following the impulse of a man accustomed to economize, immediately turned off the light. Outside, the morning was a dismal grey. The train was pulling into a station. He glanced at his watch—no, they were still a long way from Berlin.

Wislicenus took a comb out of his pocket, smoothed his hair and irritably ran it through his greying beard to which he could not get accustomed. Ever since he had let it grow in Moscow it had added ten years to his age. "I can still be recognized, and besides there is no longer any reason for disguise. Just a stupid game of hide-and-go-seek," he thought absent-mindedly as his eyes followed the rows of neat stone and brick cottages which slowly dragged by the window.

There was a shout outside and Wislicenus lost his balance as the train came jerkily to a stop. Pushing a wagon along the platform a boy was calling, "*Kaffee . . . Br-rödchen! Belegte Br-r-rödchen . . .*" He had a disagreeable way of rolling his "r's." Wislicenus motioned him to stop, took a paper cup filled with coffee, and in order to test his German pronunciation—it had been a long time since he had had an opportunity to speak German—asked the name of the station. "*Frankfurt-am-Oder,*" the boy seemed puzzled and emphasized "*am-Oder*" as though he resented the question. "*Frankfurt-am-Oder!*" "*Was macht das?*" Wislicenus asked, carefully counting the unfamiliar coins paid for the coffee, and trying to sound German, said, "*Stimmt.*" No, he was still able to get along . . . "*Danke sehr, danke schön,*" the boy sang out and gave his wagon a push. "*Kaffee. Br-r-rödchen!*"

A detachment of stormtroopers appeared from around the corner of the station. They marched with heavy, firmly resounding steps along the platform. The people on the train watched them curiously through the car windows. Aware of their audience, the men stepped with a swagger as though they were on parade. "They march well," Wislicenus conceded. He was a competent judge; as a young man he had served in the army, though few people knew when or where. The pleased, self-satisfied, dull expressions on the stormtroopers' healthy, energetic young faces suddenly filled him with such intense hatred and disgust that his heart skipped a beat. But inwardly he had to admit that the other young people, who marched around Moscow, had the same general appearance and even wore the same expressions—only these looked a trifle stronger, healthier, and neater. The platform, the uniforms, the swastikas, the white jacket of the boy who sold coffee, the waxed paper around the sandwiches—everything here shone with a cleanliness as peculiar as the appearance of German coins. The detachment disappeared into a subway at the end of the platform. "I suppose I should hope that the constructive influence of our propaganda will bring these misled young men into the communist camp," he thought, resuming his seat. But it was so much simpler to hope that they would all be dead. He remembered how in Moscow, many years ago, a kittenish young woman had asked him whether he would like to strangle Lord Curzon with his bare hands. To teach her a lesson he had opened his eyes widely and had answered that it was awkward to strangle people with one's hands; "Usually I use my gun, but if it is absolutely necessary to strangle a person why not avail oneself of the services of the comrade executioner?" The effect of his answer, especially the mention of the comrade executioner, had been everything he had hoped for. The girl had become paralyzed with fear. Wislicenus knew that behind his back speaking in diffident whispers people associated him and his past with the most horrible acts of brutality. "In the smaller towns I would have been lionized by the ladies, but as a matter of fact I had told the truth to that girl . . ." He felt no special hatred for Lord Curzon, though it went without saying that hanging him would have made the world a better place. "Why should he have the privilege of dying in his bed? Besides, it is so much easier to name the men who do not deserve the noose . . ."

In a ringing voice the conductor called, *"Einsteigen!"* The train was moving again. Wislicenus washed his face and hands and at the same time curiously examined the mahogany washstand which occupied the corner of his compartment. "Yes, they love comforts," he thought, remembering how he had traveled in the old days. Luxury irritated him—so did almost everything else. If he were free to do as he pleased he would have traveled third class even now. But Wislicenus was accredited to the embassy; the nature of his work and the suitcase he had with him made it imperative that he travel everywhere, and especially in Germany, on a diplomatic passport. To avoid inquisitive neighbors the embassy staff was traveling in a special car. "I am sure the porter is a Gestapo agent anyway," Wislicenus thought indifferently. Having finished his morning toilet he picked up the book which was lying on the floor. Without any good reason he had brought with him a volume of Dostoyevsky letters. Lazily flipping the pages he began to look for the place where he had gone to sleep the night before.

Wislicenus did not feel like reading. He dropped the book in his lap and staring out of the window sat for a long time thinking about a variety of things; about Hitler, about the coming war, about Nadia, about his assignment, about his asthma—or was it asthma? The Moscow doctor whom he had called in to the Hotel Luxe had looked worried. In an evasive way he had said that present-day medicine did not consider asthma a disease in its own right, but rather a symptom of certain pathological conditions; he had advised a more settled mode of life. Wislicenus had smiled and the doctor had understood that his advice was impractical. "Have I heard someone say that he is a Macedonian? Or has he merely worked in Macedonia for a long time? In any case Macedonian adventures don't make for longevity, but he may last another three—four years." These thoughts had raced through the doctor's head, but aloud he had said, "There is no immediate danger. However, if the opportunity will present itself it would not do you any harm to take a rest." "I will see what I can do, Doctor. I'll see what I can do, thank you," Wislicenus had answered. They had parted looking at one another with derision. "It's none of my worry. It's up to him," the doctor had dismissed the whole thing from his mind.

The sound of voices and subdued laughter reached Wislicenus from the passageway. Members of the embassy staff were getting up. The secretary walked by his door and erasing the smile from his face, coolly said, "Good morning, Comrade Dacocci." He was also known as Dacocci—in reporting the meetings of the Communist International the newspapers referred to him sometimes as Dacocci, sometimes as Dacozzi, sometimes as Dakochich. Only the veteran members of the party knew his true history. As far as names were concerned he had had so many of them that frequently he could not remember what name he had used under what circumstance. He chose his aliases without any serious thought, just as they occurred to him; he had been known as Ney, as Chatsky, as Kirdjali, as Ouralov. He had come across the frivolous sounding name of Wislicenus in some book on chemistry and its impressive vagueness had appealed to him. His real name he had used only in his youth, long before that nightmare, and by now it had become less real than Wislicenus or Dacocci. The fact that he did not discuss his past created an aura of mystery around his reputation. It was whispered that by birth he was a Macedonian, a Slovak, a Dalmatian, or whatever they call these people, but that he had received his education in a military academy in Russia; as the legend grew, the military academy became the Imperial Page School. "That also helped, just as the noble antecedents for which we persecuted other people had helped create a halo around Lenin's name. . . . So much the better. . . . After all, nine-tenths of Prince Kropotkin's prestige depended on his title and on his long beard. . . . If his name had been Petrov or Rosenberg, and if someone had shaved his beard, who on earth would have paid any attention to him?"

Wislicenus' thoughts were interrupted by Nadia, who with an overnight bag in her hand and a towel over her shoulder slipped unobtrusively past his door on her way to the washroom. He smiled at her and for a fleeting second felt happy. Almost immediately, however, he realized how ridiculous it was; there was something hopelessly stupid and trite about his smile and the nonsensical feeling of happiness. "At the sight of the young girl a gentle smile softened the stern features of the old soldier. . . . Old soldier, my eye," he said to himself, and for the hundredth time made a halfhearted effort to consider his relations with Nadia. "Actually, there is nothing to consider—there are no relations. . . . But there could be and they would make everything extremely unpleasant; not just senseless, but disgusting. It is bad enough to deceive others, but there is certainly no necessity for an old man to try to deceive himself. After all, I am sixty and then some . . ." his mind seemed to wander. "And she plays the part of a devoted youngster at the feet of a hero who belongs to an older generation. It's a good performance, and I shall tell her so." An unaccountable irritation brought him to an abrupt decision. "What right have I to tell her such things? None whatever, but I may as well give vent to the nasty cantankerousness of old age. It does not bother me any—it's no fault of mine that I'm getting old. . . ." That part of his being which with such determination controlled his inward and outward self seemed to relish the fact that there was no escape from this situation. "Why isn't there a way out? There should be some escape from every situation. How childish to console oneself like that! Certainly there are situations from which there is no escape."

Wislicenus remembered the volume of letters, picked it up and forced himself to read a page, but Dostoyevsky was as unbearably dull as ever. "Such a righteous and well-meaning person. . . . Just listen to him—a veritable paragon of righteousness. . . . They kept a man [he almost called him a "young fellow" in his thoughts] for four years in prison and he came out a different person, ready to serve them faithfully for the rest of his days. And

still he and his kind could not bring themselves to believe in the
effectiveness of brute force . . . God forbid! . . . Well, it's nice
to know that he was righteous and well-meaning, but why should
I worry about him, or about all those people, or about the fact
that he found everything so dirty in Germany—I suppose he
found everything clean and comfortable in Siberia! Why should
I be bothered with his 'satanic' encounters with his landlady or
with his 'satanic' gambling loss of ten guldens which made it necessary for him to pawn his wife's skirt! And he wasn't simply
embarrassed about it; instead he was filled with self-abasement!
. . . Why should anyone publish stuff like that? Who on earth
could be interested in the traveling impressions of such a lower
middle-class mind? He is our enemy and to hell with him! He is
the kind of man who tried to strangle us. . . . A great novelist?
Well, then go ahead and publish his *Crime and Punishment*. . . ."

Nadia once again slipped past his door, this time without looking in his direction. "Her towel is spotless and she has a smart
overnight bag. It's written all over her that her father was a professor and that she belongs to a 'nice' family. Perhaps that's what
I like about her. . . ." Not to make it too obvious he went on
with his reading for another fifteen minutes, then put the book
away and walked out into the passageway.

II

In the large drawing-room compartment Ambassador Kangarov,
his wife Helen, Nadia and the young secretary were finishing
breakfast. The ambassador was in very good humor, though he
complained that he had not slept well. The night before he had
played bridge until two in the morning, and after that he had
dreamt for a long time about brilliant plays and crushing slams.

They had played the game the way Kangarov enjoyed it most; with animation, with amusing asides and with explosive zest, but without unnecessary rudeness and without long arguments. After a particularly bad mistake he always asked the guilty partner where he had learned to play. Over breakfast the ambassador and the secretary were still discussing one of the more dramatic incidents of the night before.

"The father beat his son not because he kept losing, but because he kept arguing about it," Kangarov was saying smilingly. He invariably smiled when he spoke, as though he knew some secret of which the others were not aware. His smiles were always sweet and always different; the degree of their sweetness depended on the subject under discussion and on the person whom he was addressing. But his brown eyes never smiled, instead they were filled with constant uneasiness; at times they turned a bright yellow and became angry and mean. This lack of coördination between his smile and the expression of his eyes was the distinguishing characteristic of his face, and it made observant people uncomfortable in his presence. "Certainly you should have finessed the queen! Any child could have told you that, my dear secretary!" Adding "my dear" to words which he chose at random was a mannerism of speech which he had developed over a period of years. "If you had made the finesse, his Excellency would have gone down three." Kangarov pronounced the words "his Excellency" with a playful emphasis which seemed to intimate that after all they were among friends. He was referring to their traveling companion, the distinguished military expert Tamarin, who was not a member of the embassy staff, but who was on his way to Paris on a special assignment.

The secretary upheld his end of the argument softly and politely, as became a diplomat. He tried to avoid the air of undue diffidence and solicitude in the presence of his superiors, but after all an ambassador was an ambassador, and the very manner in which he defended himself seemed to concede that he was not altogether right. Actually, he was not subservient to his superiors;

he was a decent, kindhearted person, incapable of obsequiousness. But ever since the secretary had been assigned to the diplomatic service he had been walking on air; his face constantly reflected a state of inward bliss and of delight with his own attainment. Toward Kangarov, who was responsible for including him in the embassy staff, he had a deep and sincere sense of gratitude; he considered the ambassador a statesman of the first rank and admired him without reservation. To assert his independence he sometimes argued with him about politics, or about bridge, but he was always ready to acknowledge the superiority of the ambassador's judgment. Besides, Kangarov really played an excellent game of bridge. Now, having proven his point, he laughed and gently patted the secretary on the shoulder.

"You need intuition in everything you undertake," he said. "As a bridge player you are a good shoemaker, but let us hope that you will use your intuition in your diplomatic career."

Kangarov took the view that he had to combine within himself two entirely different personalities. At work he was a stern, exacting, almost austere official. But off duty they were all equals, they were all party comrades, and a tone of gay familiarity was permissible among them, though naturally within reasonable bounds; off duty he was no longer a personage, but a charming, intelligent, attentive human being, beloved by all the underlings —no, underlings was the wrong word; by his colleagues was much better. That was the line of behavior which Lenin had followed and that is why he was known affectionately as "Ilyich." The degree of informality in Kangarov's case, however, depended on circumstances, on his mood, and on the people with whom he was associating. He allowed himself the greatest latitude with Nadia, the favorite member of his staff.

"The train is traveling awfully fast!" Helen Kangarov, the ambassador's wife, remarked. "Our trains are much slower. . . . Oh, please, please! Close the window! Cinders!" she exclaimed. The secretary had opened the window to dispose of the papers which cluttered the table after breakfast. The paper sacks, caught by the gust of wind, pitifully hugged the side of the car. "Cinders, cinders!" the ambassador's wife repeated in a horrified voice.

Kangarov shrugged his shoulders and turning to Nadia began to tease her about something or other. The secretary, who lacked intuition, attempted to join in the same playful vein, but not meeting with any encouragement, as became a diplomat, engaged the ambassador's wife in a suave and respectful conversation about the theatre; she was an actress.

The entrance of Wislicenus introduced a marked chilliness into the atmosphere. The ambassador disliked him personally and, besides, his very presence reminded him of a recent and extremely unpleasant experience. In the early stages of his political career Kangarov had been a moderate socialist and at the time of the first revolution, during those days of violent upheaval, immediately after the suppression of the Moscow rebellion, he had written for publication abroad an article about the bolsheviks, entitled; "Come to Your Senses, Renegades!" That had happened a long time ago. Kangarov's party record began officially with 1911. He was considered one of the best economists within the party, he had occupied a succession of important posts, he was never known to deviate from the party line or to have any contacts with the opposition, and he had every reason to believe that his unfortunate past had been forgotten. He had received the offer to be transferred to the diplomatic service quite recently. As an expert he had taken part in numerous international conferences, where his ability and his knowledge had been appreciated by his superiors and by the foreign experts. At one of the conferences no less a person than Schacht had said about him; "it is a pleasure to do business with a person like that. . . ." When diplomatic relations had been resumed with one of the smaller and less important Western kingdoms Kangarov was offered the post of ambassador. He had accepted the offer with alacrity, but having an exaggerated opinion of his importance and lacking experience and inside information, he had made his acceptance subject to one condition; no one was to interfere with his work and no one was to stick spokes in his wheels. By "no one" he meant the

Comintern. Kangarov's immediate superior, who also detested the Comintern, gave him a puzzled look, sighed, but refused to commit himself in any way. At the farewell audience Kangarov quite unexpectedly learned from the dictator that Wislicenus was to be one of the members of his staff. Overcoming the physical fear which Stalin's presence instilled in him as well as in all the other members of the party, Kangarov with great dignity and with his sweetest smile reminded Stalin that he had made his acceptance subject to a condition and proceeded to expound his point of view. But Stalin had immediately interrupted him and, transfixing him with a heavy, sardonic stare, had said that he was not in any position to discuss conditions, and that in the future he could confine himself to carrying out orders he was given. At the same time Stalin had hinted broadly that his unfortunate past was not entirely forgotten, and that his article, "Come to Your Senses, Renegades!" was kept on file in the proper place. At that point in the interview the dictator had become quite affable, but though his familiarity carried comradely implications it was altogether one-sided, and Kangarov left with the most unpleasant impression of the audience.

Now the ambassador gave no outward indication that he was displeased by the appearance of Wislicenus. Anger may have flashed for a second in his eyes, but the sweetness of his smile, if anything, became even more marked. Greeting him he half-rose from his seat—a courtesy which he reserved only for important people (he stood up only for a chosen few).

"Have you slept well? Have you had breakfast?" he asked (the two questions indicated that he did not expect an answer to either one of them) and immediately turning to Nadia, resumed the interrupted conversation; "And so, my child, just remember my words! They will seize us and throw us in a dungeon."

"How can they do that? How about our diplomatic exterritoriality!" Nadia asked pretending to be frightened. They had a tacit understanding that Kangarov considered her a naïve child and derived a certain amount of pleasure from teasing her.

"'Diplomatic exterritoriality!' What big words you use! And

who was it who flunked the exam in political literacy? And who was it who did not tell me about it? If I had known it, I never would have brought you along."

Kangarov had no reason to assume this tone with Nadia; she was almost twenty. But it had come about in the most natural way; the first time he had addressed her as "my child" he had done it unexpectedly, prepared for immediate retreat if she showed any sign of resentment. But she seemed to have no objection and so he used the name more and more frequently. He enjoyed it. Once or twice he even had patted her head, but he had made it a point to do so in public; no one was to be given any grounds for gossip —it was a perfectly natural, fatherly gesture.

With artless warmth Nadia responded to the mention of the examination in political literacy which she had failed to pass; there was nothing she could do about it, it was simply her bad luck that she had drawn such a mean instructor, she had had no trouble with dialectics and things like that, she even had done well with the tactical opinions of the group known as "Free Labor," but when he had asked her what the essential difference had been between the newspapers *Worker's Thought* and *Worker's Task*—"I simply gave up. I just told him I did not know. It turned out that the *Worker's Task* was in favor not only of strikes but of demonstrations too . . ." The ambassador laughed.

"I swear by everything holy I did not know the answer myself!" he said, the tone of his voice implying that their conversation was on the same level with the stories about the teacher who had marked with a "D" a composition which had been written for a boy by Turgeneff, or about that problem in algebra which baffled Henri Poincaré who tried to solve it to help his nephew with his school assignment. "So the *Worker's Thought* was in favor of both strikes and demonstrations?"

"No, no! That was the *Worker's Task*." Kangarov apologized, his laughter indicating how unimportant it all was. "It's the most ridiculous thing I ever heard! Have you heard it, Helen?" he asked his wife, who he felt too pointedly avoided speaking to Nadia;

some people might consider such behavior a discrimination against the younger comrades.

"No, I was not paying any attention to your chatter," Helen Kangarov answered coldly. She was not jealous of her husband, but neither did she like him to address Nadia as "my child." "She is a long way from being a child. Besides, it's just an act. . . . It's really his manner that annoys me—it is so obnoxious. . . ."

Helen Kangarov disliked almost everything about her husband. A daughter of a former landowner, deep down in her heart she felt that she had married beneath her. She deliberately turned away ("yes, he is right, I have not spoken to her for a long time, and what's more I don't intend to!") and once again addressed the secretary.

"Yermolova was simply marvelous in her part, but I still feel that she butchered the scene with the nurse on the lawn. She lacked the spontaneity, the lightness! Do you remember the lines? 'Let me enjoy my freedom! Come, let's be children! Look at the luxurious carpet which nature spreads at our feet!' That's the place where I whirled and danced, just as in real life I danced on the lawn when I was a girl going to private school. . . ."

"I will never forgive myself for not seeing you play Mary Stuart," the secretary said respectfully.

"That would have been impossible," the ambassador cut in, suddenly exasperated by his wife's manner. In the presence of Wislicenus the least she could do was to shelve her society airs and refrain from mentioning that she had attended private school, even if it were true. "That would have been impossible because she never has appeared as Mary Stuart."

Once again he considered the desirability of parting ways with his wife in the least painful manner. "Why should we continue to fool ourselves? I feel indifferently toward her, and she hates me. I am not accusing her of anything, but when sensible people see how things are going they should do everything they can to simplify matters. . . ." His eyes were a brighter yellow than usual.

"The date for the opening was already set," Helen Kangarov answered icily. She usually took tragic parts and she loved royalty. Before the war only a behind-the-stage intrigue prevented her from playing the part of Lady Macbeth. During the war days she rehearsed the parts of Mary Stuart and of the Maid of Orléans, but this time a combination of intrigue and revolution interfered. "If they had not changed the repertoire," she began, stifled a yawn, and did not finish the sentence.

"I suppose they will meet us at the Friedrichstrasse Station," the secretary said, tactfully changing the subject. He had graduated from a Berlin technical school and was familiar with the city.

"That is, providing anyone takes the trouble to meet us," Kangaróv answered casually. "The people at the Berlin embassy are too lazy to get up so early in the morning."

Wislicenus walked out of the compartment. All these people with the exception of Nadia irritated him. And he was even angry at Nadia for her behavior with the ambassador. "She has no feeling for him. She can't even respect that old shopkeeper with the soul of an executioner and the manner of a grand seigneur. As a matter of fact the damned girl has no real respect for anyone," he decided. Of all those people Kangarov irritated him most. Wislicenus believed that the vast majority of mankind were scoundrels, but he was inclined to be much more tolerant with those who were willing to admit it; if Kangarov had been willing to concede this point, Wislicenus would have felt much more kindly disposed toward him. In his eyes Kangarov was simply a scoundrel who had not been exposed. "With all that, he still is a useful person," it was his habit to consider all the good as well as the bad traits of the people with whom he had to work. "Intelligent? Maybe. At least he is shrewd and not at all stupid. He knows his business—finance is duck-soup to him. He is malicious, despite his smiles which are a thousand times sweeter than sugar. His benevolence, his jokes are all a front; the OGPU is staffed with benevolent people like him. He eternally is saying nice things to everyone, but most of his compliments have a sting in them. . . . All in all he is not any worse than most of the others. At least he is a good worker. To call him a shopkeeper is not quite fair. After all, he has proven that he is a man of convictions. . . ."

It occurred to him that during the thirty-five years of his revolutionary career he was never able to conquer in himself an instinctive dislike for the Jews, which he had inherited from a long line of ancestors. "A vain people. . . . However, Kangarov is not typical. His mother was not a Jew and vanity is not one of his weaknesses; besides, nationality has nothing to do with it. . . ." Wislicenus disliked the Jews, but he hated any trace of anti-semitism.

He paused in the passageway; where should he go now? A long journey on a train had something in common with a prison; there you paced the cell, here you paced the car, always conscious of the fleeting time. He took a folding chair and sat staring absent mindedly out of the window. He was thinking about the same thing again; only two or three years of life remained, five at the most if he took a vacation and went for a rest to the Caucasus or to the Crimea. There would be no difficulty about getting a leave of absence. Quite a few people would be delighted to see him retire and vacate his position without a struggle, without unnecessary intrigues or bitterness. For a second he wondered who would replace him, but he preferred not to dwell on that subject. He pictured himself in a house of rest or in a sanatorium with only the thought of how to prolong his life uppermost in his mind. The picture was absurd. It did not upset him in the least, because it was so palpably impossible. "Then along will come the last illnesses—if I am lucky they will not last too long. The very end will be accompanied by speeches, 'let's close ranks over the grave of an old soldier,' a guard of honor around the casket, and another urn in the Kremlin wall. . . . The urns with the ashes of the old soldiers form a background for Lenin's mausoleum, just as the graves of the generals form a background for Napoleon's tomb in the Hôtel des Invalides. Stalin, if he is killed and if those who kill him don't win, or at least if he dies at the right time—everything has to be done at the right time—will be placed in a special mausoleum. . . ."

Lazily he paused in his thoughts and tried to visualize the appropriate design and the exact place for Stalin's mausoleum in the Red Square. "Two mausoleums in one Square will not look well. Just as a second tomb would look out of place in the Hôtel des Invalides. . . ." Once again he returned to the main current of his thoughts. "Yes, an urn in the Kremlin wall, and the band playing the 'International' . . . In the old days it would have played 'You Have Fallen a Victim' . . . Which of the two is more impressive?" Again he paused in his thoughts trying to decide which of the two he liked better. "It does not make much difference. If one dies at the right time there will be a certain number of newspaper obituaries, a memorial meeting in honor of the 'old revolutionary leader,' and lots of orations. Later, they even may find a biographer, simply because there was a moral in the life story. Well, lots of others will not receive even that much." Wislicenus thought about it without any trace of bitterness. After everything he had lived through he still with a minimum of effort could work himself into an exalted state of mind. "Disappointed? No, I have no reason whatever to be disillusioned. 'Oceans of blood?' Our accusers did not seem to mind spilling oceans of blood in the world war! Intrigues, squabbles, hatreds behind the mask of loyalty? If the truth were known I doubt that Napoleon's marshals loved him as a man during his lifetime, even though they surround him with such soldierly devotion in the Hôtel des Invalides! It always has been like that. . . ." The chain of syllogisms worked out by Lenin in 1918 and accepted by everyone with such enthusiasm still remained unchallenged. The great work, the tremendous work of liberating all the working masses of the world, was progressing; what difference did it make that a part of this work was done by scoundrels and renegades, or by such inarticulate persons as "my dear secretary." "If he ever says 'my dear Comintern' to me again I will hit him in his pudgy, white face!" Wislicenus flared up in a sudden onrush of cold fury, but immediately took himself in hand. "I must be going insane. Pretty soon they will have to muzzle me. . . . Men like that will attach themselves to any great movement—that's inevitable. In a tremendous undertaking of this kind, noble, unselfish people have to work side by side with fortune-hunters. But only a petty and distorted mind can draw from this the conclusion that the undertaking itself is not any good. Hangers-on like that can be found in any camp, but the very cause of our enemies is rotten. What else can we be charged with? Terror and brutality? The ruling classes never would have surrendered their power or their money—the comforts of these sleeping cars for instance—without a bitter struggle. Only a rule of terror could break their resistance. Without 'oceans of blood' we never could have remained in power for more than six months. At best we would have been remembered in history as weak, well-meaning and impractical dreamers, at worst—as German hirelings and traitors. And those who would have destroyed us would have been the first to ridicule and laugh at our weakness! No, it is better to be accused of spilling 'oceans of blood' than to be known as ineffective intellectuals!" he thought with another flash of anger. The chain of syllogisms remained unchallenged, but it no longer was vital to him. That was the saddest part about it.

Nadia came out of the drawing-room compartment into the passageway. Wislicenus had a fleeting impression of displeasure on her face when she saw him there. He felt a sharp pain in his heart. "What sort of foolishness is this? What can she possibly mean to me," he argued with himself, but his attempt at self-discipline was not reassuring. "She is very attractive. . . . If I had more time than just two or three years, perhaps . . ." "Nadia, dear, are you very tired of traveling?" he asked and immediately was aware that his "Nadia, dear" sounded exactly like Kangarov's "my child." No, at least he had no intention of fooling himself by pretending that he had a fatherly feeling for her. She answered him in an entirely different tone from the one she used in talking with the ambassador. Her voice was a mixture of tenderness and admiration. "I wanted to get my book," she said. Reluctantly he rose from his chair to let her by. The car swayed and she was thrown against him. "What are you reading?" he asked, his nerves tingling from the contact of their bodies. "The new novel by Vicki Baum," she mentioned the first name that came into her head. He did not know, or perhaps he did not recognize the name, but her manner made him feel that he was being put in his place. "Serves me right. . . . I am old enough to know that every dog has his day!" Nadia entered her compartment and closed the door behind her. Slowly Wislicenus strolled the length of the car, sat down, picked up the volume of Dostoyevsky letters and glanced at his watch. They were still a long way from Berlin. "I may as well have a talk with Tamarin," he decided, struggling against hopeless boredom.

III

RED ARMY commander, one time Major-General in the Imperial Army, Constantine Tamarin was trying to kill time in his compartment by working on a crossword puzzle. He enjoyed this form of relaxation and considered it useful for people engaged in intellectual pursuits: like chess, it required a degree of concentration (always a valuable form of training) and at the same time it provided a change from the usual thought channels. However, Tamarin never worked crossword puzzles in the mornings and now he felt a trifle self-conscious about it. Traveling completely disrupted his life. The night before, he and his traveling companions had played bridge much too late. In the old days in Petersburg he always had stopped around midnight, and then had had a light supper and two glasses of sherry. Everyone knew his habit of drinking sherry before retiring; the waiter at the club served the bottle without being told, and Tamarin was proud of it, just as he was proud of the precise regularity of his life and of the fact that he slept well after eating supper: many men of his age made it a rule not to eat anything before going to bed.

Tamarin played a masterful game of bridge and had been the recognized authority at the club. Because of this distinction he frequently had been invited to fill in at tables occupied by the highest personages. On the train the night before, they had held an unusual hand which had been played as a little slam in no trump—a hand almost identical with the one he had played years ago at the Yacht Club: he had a remarkably good memory, but especially so in cards. His partner, Kangarov, had played his hand just as the Grand Duke had played his in Petersburg. This coincidence had amused Tamarin, though the awkwardness from which he had suffered during the first few years of service under the bolsheviks had left him a long time ago. "There is no use being narrow-minded: all the Dukes were not angels, and all these are not scoundrels. Occasionally you come across a very decent person among them. . . . They even play bridge the same way," he had cheered himself up, dealing the cards.

They had finished playing very late and then, to be polite, had sat talking for a while. While the score was being added they had exchanged good-natured jokes: what was the proper currency to use in settling—Russian or German? They had not played for high stakes, but the secretary had succeeded in losing more than he should, considering his salary and his daily travel allowance. To cheer him up the ambassador had been exceptionally sweet to him. "Unlucky at cards, lucky at love, you handsome fellows," he had said. (The secretary had rather ugly features). "Just imagine: three women have committed suicide on his account. . . . My dear secretary, altogether how much alimony do you pay out each month? It really is about time for you to settle down . . ." "We have laughed enough for one night," the secretary had answered quite appropriately with a bashful smile. "Act quickly and press the advantage! Courage conquers all things," the general also without success had tried to keep the conversation going. "Well,

that's about the way they talked at the Yacht Club," he had ex-
cused himself absent-mindedly in his thoughts. "I realize that the
short suit came in very handy, but I must say, you played that
slam to perfection, my dear commander," Kangarov had said at
that point. Over the card table they frequently exchanged compliments with the air of Napoleon paying his respects to Archduke
Karl. Each appreciated the game played by the other, and
their admiration for one another extended beyond cards. "This
one, for instance, is not altogether a scoundrel, though in the old
days the very idea of him as an ambassador would have been
ridiculous," Tamarin thought. "His Excellency will never set the
world on fire, but he is a decent person who has taken to heart
the lesson history has taught him and who recognizes the inexcusable blunders made by his class," was Kangarov's opinion. The
general had returned to his compartment at a quarter past two. He
had long ago given up his habit of drinking sherry, but he had
wanted something to eat: as usual the meals in the dining-car
were expensive and none too good.

As was his custom before going to sleep Tamarin read a chapter of *Hinterlassene Werke*. He owned a fine Dümmler edition of
Clausewitz with which he never parted: he was more likely to go
on a journey without his passport or without his toothbrush than
without these small volumes in their ancient bindings of polished
yellow leather. Their very appearance, the dried paper, the last
word or the last syllable on each page repeated in the bottom right-
hand corner, the small "e" used instead of an "umlaut" over "o,"
"u" and "a" had a soothing effect on him. Usually he read one
chapter before turning out the light. But being hungry he had
not been able to settle for the night and, besides, he had happened
to strike an interesting chapter. First of all he had come across one
of those brief, clearcut aphorisms, which sound like a command
and which have endeared Clausewitz to military men all over
the world. *"Der Krieg hat freilich seine eigene Grammatik, aber
nicht seine eigene Logik . . ."* "How very true and how lucid!"
Tamarin had relished every word. He had been delighted with

the realization that he did not remember this chapter too well, just as other readers are delighted when they realize that they have forgotten Gogol's *Dead Souls*: they know they have new pleasures ahead of them.

The passage was interesting. However, at three in the morning Tamarin could not concentrate on what he had read and he had been certain that if he tried he would not go to sleep. For a second he had been tempted to mark the place by folding the corner of the page, but he had decided against it: he liked the book too much, it was better to remember the number of the page, 148. "One hundred and forty-eight," he had said aloud and had wondered whether there was some mnemonic formula for memorizing this figure: eight equals twice four, but the first digit . . . "To hell with it! I will remember it anyway: one hundred and forty-eight," he had decided and had fallen asleep. He had not slept as soundly as usual and his dreams had been crowded with absurdities: the Grand Duke was playing bridge with Clausewitz and Peter the Great was looking on. Against a bid little slam Clausewitz made a brilliant play which set his opponents down three. "You played this hand to perfection, my dear Clausewitz!" Peter the Great exclaimed with glee.

Just then Tamarin opened his eyes and smiled at the absurd fragments of the conversation which still rang in his ears. "I wonder why I should dream about Peter the Great? I haven't thought about him for a year!" (Two days later he remembered that in the card room at the Yacht Club there had been a portrait of Peter the Great on the wall.) There were lights outside the car windows. The train was standing in a station. The general glanced at his watch: it was six o'clock. "I wonder if this is the border?" Glancing out of the window, under the dim station lights he caught sight of an officer in a German uniform, and gave a low whistle: Germany! He hurriedly slipped on his clothes, raised his overcoat collar, and filled with a strange excitement went outside.

Tamarin had not been abroad since the war. During the preceding day they had traveled across Poland, but it was difficult for him to think of Poland as a foreign country and of Warsaw, where he had been stationed as a young officer on the staff of the governor-general, as a foreign capital. "This is really being abroad. Though it is not the way I had planned to enter this country twenty-two years ago. . . ." Men in strange-looking uniforms were checking passports, while others were inspecting baggage. No one came near the Soviet diplomatic car with the exception of an official who exchanged a few words with the pleased and somewhat nervous secretary. The official saluted and walked away without changing the expression on his face. Controlling his excitement the general paced up and down the platform. Everything about the station excited him, especially the appearance of the German army officer. The German watched him out of the corner of his eye, apparently recognizing in him a fellow soldier. Tamarin noticed at once all the changes which had been made in the German uniform since he had seen it last. He felt that he had done wrong to leave the car without shaving and without putting on a collar. He wanted something to drink: coffee, or still better, some Danzig vodka, but it was too early in the morning and the restaurant was still closed. Only the news-stand was open for business. The general looked around hesitantly: his position was well established, there was no reason for him to have any fears, but perhaps it would be more discreet not to buy any German newspapers, especially at the first stop, as though he could not wait any longer. Suddenly he became angry with himself, bought the paper, folded it, stuck it in his pocket and returned to his compartment. "Actually, now that we are across the border, I could stay here forever and no one could touch me," the wild thought unexpectedly occurred to him. "I could become an émigré like the others. . . . How ridiculous! . . . Why should I even think about it? . . . We led one kind of life before and we are leading a different life now. . . . The others, too, had to change their mode of living. . . ." The compartment was warm, but he was still shivering. "Yes, I made a mistake: I shouldn't have left the car until I was fully dressed. . . ." Casually he glanced at the change which he had received from the news-stand. He even found the appearance of the German coins exciting. A long time ago he had spent a year in Germany on a special assignment and it had been one of the most pleasant experiences of his life. "No, I shouldn't have left the car without a collar . . ." he reprimanded himself again.

The train gave a jerk. Tamarin took off his coat, hung it on a hook, stretched out on the berth and lay shivering under the blanket. He felt that there was no sense in going to sleep again, but he dozed off in spite of it and did not awaken until he heard the whistles and noise outside the windows when the train reached Frankfort. He had no desire to leave the car again, instead he decided to shave while the train was in the station. Tamarin had no use for safety razors; from the better days he had saved a special set consisting of seven excellent straight razors made in England. There was a special razor for every day of the week and the words: "Monday, Tuesday, Wednesday"—were engraved on the handles. After using it the blade was put away for a week's rest, which was supposed to keep it in good shape. During the first years after the revolution people who had been cleanshaven had begun to grow beards as an economy measure, while those who already had beards proceeded to shave them off for hygienic reasons. Tamarin's face had been adorned with old-fashioned sideburns, styled after Alexander II—even before the revolution only one person in a thousand could permit himself the luxury of wearing sideburns like that. They answered neither a hygienic, nor an economic purpose. During the days of turmoil Tamarin's chin had been always faultlessly smooth, and his sideburns neatly combed. There had been something counter-revolutionary about his sideburns and people he met in the streets, especially those belonging to an older generation, frequently had followed him with eyes filled with surprise mingled with fear. He had shaved his sideburns only when the days of poverty and hunger had reached their climax. It had seemed ridiculous to wear them any longer and, besides, they had begun to turn very grey. His life was

divided into two distinct periods: with the sideburns and without them. After the sideburns were gone he never had the same
respect for himself.

His days in Russia always followed the same routine. After
shaving he took a bath, whenever that was possible; even during
those winter days when people had sat in their houses wearing
overcoats he had doused himself daily with cold water and had
changed his underclothes. The cook, who had served him for many
years and who had stayed with him after the death of his wife,
kept house for him. He had no children, and no near relatives.
Tamarin's entire life centered around his work. After bathing he
made his own tea according to a special formula: he put a dash
of boiling water over three teaspoonfuls of tea, wrapped the teapot in a towel, let it stand for a couple of minutes and then filled
the pot to the brim with boiling hot water. He carried the teapot
to his study, where over his work he drank three glasses of tea
with one lump of sugar each and ate a piece of dry toast: he
avoided bread because he was inclined toward stoutness. That was
the part of the day he liked best. Between seven and nine in the
morning he wrote dispatches, reports and articles for the military
and technical publications. First, he jotted down the outline in
pencil, then, without any further corrections, he wrote the final
draft on his old Underwood, which in spite of its age was still in
perfect condition. The work, the strong tea, the clear light clatter
of the typewriter which with such pleasant preciseness recorded
his thoughts (after they were down in type they always were so
lucid and clear)—all this blended in one and became the one great
joy of his life. At nine sharp he stopped his work with a sigh,
gently covered the Underwood and went to the office. There he
listened to reports and read dispatches written by other people. He
did not like most of them, but he did his best to consider them
impartially and he expressed his conscientious opinion about
them, unless circumstances made it imperative to conceal the
truth.

On a train there was nothing for Tamarin to do. He remembered the newspaper he had bought at the border. The very first thing he saw was a leading article, headlined: *"Die jüdischen Bluthünde."* It referred to the bolsheviks, toward whom his own feelings were rather mixed, but he was working for them now— he was working for them faithfully and to the best of his ability— and he resented this appellation: indirectly it cast an aspersion on him.

Tamarin glanced over the newspaper. The news was not very pleasant: there were reports of major Italian victories in Africa. Personally, he wanted to see Italy win: he considered Mussolini a great statesman—"we did not have a man like him and that's why things have happened the way they have." But the general was convinced that the Italians would have great difficulty in conquering Abyssinia. In one of his best articles he had proven conclusively that the Amba-Aladji mountain range was invulnerable to attack. Quoting him as a foremost authority a Soviet newspaper had expressed an editorial opinion that the imperialistic aggressors had bitten off more than they could chew in Ethiopia (this reference to his professional opinion had been a great feather in his cap). Now, judging by the latest dispatches not only the Amba-Aladji, but even the Amba-Aradam line had been taken. "Maybe this has not been confirmed?" Tamarin tried to reassure himself. But those barely perceptible indications which ordinarily accompany exorbitant claims in a headquarters communiqué were lacking—apparently the report was true. Once again he rechecked his reasoning. To storm a steep mountain range in the face of fortified positions held by an army under Ras Desta seemed a difficult, almost impossible, undertaking. "And while they are attacking the range Ras Sayum will not be idle: he most certainly will hit them along the line Makale-Adua," he thought, wishing from the bottom of his heart success to Ras Sayum, despite his own secret political sympathies and his admiration for Mussolini. Somewhat reassured he threw the German newspaper out of the window and opening the volume of Clausewitz on page one hundred and forty-eight (which he had remembered without any mnemonic formula) he began to copy certain excerpts into his notebook. But the train was traveling fast, the pencil skipped and jumped all over the paper and the results were illegible. "No, it's impossible to work on a train . . ."

He reached into his suitcase and extracted an illustrated magazine with some crossword puzzles. At first everything went along smoothly. But after a while the definitions began to sound like riddles. "These will not turn back a determined man . . ." "Bullets? No, that's too short. Fortifications? No, that's too long . . ."

At that moment Wislicenus entered the compartment. The general was slightly embarrassed. He put the magazine aside and after twirling his silver pencil for a few seconds, unobtrusively stuck it in his pocket. He had known Wislicenus very casually in Moscow (they had met occasionally around conference tables). The general believed that he should deal with him as he would with a dancing dervish, or with a being who had just descended from the moon: probably he was a good person, but anything could be expected from him and he should be watched constantly. Just before his departure from Moscow Tamarin had been advised that Wislicenus might need his assistance while they were abroad. This bit of news had disturbed the general very much, despite the fact that his chief had tried to reassure him by saying that assistance meant "advice and technical opinions." "Is it possible that he already needs my advice?" the general wondered uneasily, but his misgivings were unfounded. Wislicenus was simply lonesome and looking for someone to talk to. Besides, he had been wondering what sort of a person the general was. He liked Tamarin instinctively. He had a weakness for the army and for everything military. As a boy he had dreamt frequently about becoming a great military leader.

"How did you sleep?" he asked. "How did you rest?" the general asked at the same time. They both laughed. Tamarin said that they had been up too late playing bridge. "What pleasure do you get out of it?" "The ambassador plays a very good game," Tamarin countered. "Does he, really?" Wislicenus asked, the tone of his voice indicating that he held no exalted opinion of such accomplishments. "Yes, everyone says that he plays a good game of bridge. Every man must have something real in him, and in Kangarov's case it must be bridge," he thought. "I have heard that he is an excellent bridge player," he said caustically. The general was immediately on his guard. He loved to watch quarrels and fights between these people (he had frequent occasions to do so at the meetings of the various commissions on which he served, where these people invariably were much more polite with him than they were with one another). However, Wislicenus did not pursue the subject any further. Instead he began to discuss Germany and the German neatness and orderliness. "Yes, that's their strong suit," Tamarin said and recounted some episode out of his own experiences in the last war. There was nothing unusual about this episode, and Wislicenus waited patiently for the end hoping that there would be some point to the story. His expectations were not realized: the story was pointless. Trying at random he asked Tamarin what school of military thought he considered best: German or French? The general answered that the Germans were more solid, they had *"Gründlichkeit,"* but on the other hand the French had more imagination, or perhaps what the French called "élan." Wislicenus nodded sedately as though after this explanation by a recognized authority he at last understood the fundamentals of the two schools. In developing his thought the general quoted Clausewitz: *"Die moralischen Hauptpotenzen sind: die Talente des Feldherrn, kriegerische Tugend des Heeres, Volksgeist desselben,"* and immediately translated: "The military abilities of the leader, the fighting qualities of the army and its national spirit . . ." As soon as the words were out of his mouth he began to wonder: maybe it was safer not to mention things like that. "Then we must be quite strong," Wislicenus thought sadly. "Yes, Clausewitz: *'Der Krieg ist eine Fortsetzung der Politik',"* he said, indicating that in talking to him it was not necessary to translate German. "Lenin, too, had a great admiration for Clausewitz. That made me want to read him, but I gave it up: I found his generalizations quite boring." Tamarin looked at him with the expression of a tolerant but faithful Mohammedan talking to a man who had mentioned the name of Mohammed without showing proper respect. In a few minutes they were lost in a heated argument.

". . . Yes, that is true to an extent," Wislicenus said in answer to the general who had repeated verbatim the quotation which had excited him so much the night before. "But only as far as it goes. It is perfectly natural that you military men find opinions like that to your advantage. If you are victorious, you get the honor and the glory. And if you are defeated then politics are to blame. You couldn't do anything about it: 'unmöglich'—isn't that right? That's why you like Clausewitz so much. No, the whole crux of the matter is technological development, not politics. You people in the army visualized the war with Germany as another war with Japan, and from 1905 until 1914 you were preparing for another Japanese war. And now you visualize the coming war as another war with Germany, and once again you are one war behind. When it comes it will be entirely different from anything you expect. Why? Because some civilian named Mayer or Sidorov, or some civilian bastard fooling around with a chemical set, will invent something or other that will throw all your calculations on the junk pile."

"That's absolutely wrong and it is not borne out by well-established facts," Tamarin said, trying to control his irritation; after all, he could not argue seriously on military matters with a civilian. "In the first place it is wrong because all these things invented by Mayer become known to us, and we always can put them to our own use. . . ."

"You don't know a damned thing about them because in peacetime Mayer never gives any thought to the possibility of war. He begins to think about it only when war is already under way, when the daily papers whip him into a state of white heat, when his sons, his grandsons, his nephews are being killed. That's when he begins to think in terms of destroying those 'foreign friends' with whom only a year ago he had toasted the brotherhood of man and guzzled beer at the various scientific conventions. And because Mayer has more technical knowledge and more grey matter in his head than all the generals put together [Tamarin shrugged his shoulders] he is the one who pulls a white rabbit out of his hat. Only then you generals appear on the scene and 'put it to your own use.' That's what happened in the case of poison gas, that's what happened in the case of tanks. . . ."

"The tanks were invented by a general! Your examples seem to contradict your own arguments!"

"Are you sure? I bet some civilian engineer attached to a staff did the inventing and the general merely claimed the credit. But in the case of poison gas I am sure I am right; it was some civilian professor named Haber, or Haver, or Hager, or something of that sort."

"But if science is the deciding factor what happens to your economic determinism?" the general asked. His face was pale and wore a changed expression. "What guides the destinies of the world? Circumstances or free will?"

"That has nothing to do with it!"

"Oh, yes it has! Basically it is the same question. I ask you; is it free will? If it is, pardon me, but your determinism is nothing but balderdash . . . !"

He became aware of what he was saying and stopped short. Wislicenus laughed. He appreciated the general more and more; he liked the fact that his expression had changed while he talked about a subject that was near to his heart ("that's the real thing in him"), he approved of his furbished civilian suit which looked new and trim, he enjoyed the odor of toilet water that filled the compartment, he liked everything about him. "Appearances are not important, but in certain respects both of us belong to the old world," Wislicenus thought. To his great surprise he found nothing unpleasant in this extraordinary discovery.

"You have flanked me from the left," he said laughingly, trying to show the general that he had nothing to fear. "I suppose you already have noticed that I am a poor Marxist." Tamarin was immediately on his guard. "This can mean one of two things; 'I have a poor understanding of Marxism' or 'I have little faith in Marxism.' Is he trying to draw me out?" he wondered. The engine whistled and the clatter of the wheels changed its rhythm, abruptly bringing to an end the intimacy which had sprung up between them. Wislicenus glanced at his watch.

"Time is dragging very slowly . . . Did I interrupt you?" he asked, picking up the magazine and handing it to the general. "I believe you were working on a crossword puzzle?"

"Yes, I enjoy them on a train," Tamarin answered with a bashful smile, and after a moment's hesitation pulled the silver pencil out of his pocket.

IV

LIKE THE OTHERS Nadia had a compartment to herself; there was more than enough room in the car. The porter had finished cleaning a long time ago; there was not a speck of dust anywhere. She looked at herself in the mirror; her face was in order, there was just a barely perceptible shadow from the cinders around her nostrils. "Does not look too bad . . . What a peculiar man, this Wislicenus . . ." she thought and felt sorry that she had been rude to him; he had not said anything out of the ordinary, he had merely spoken to her in a fatherly tone. "It is amazing how many old men assume a fatherly air with me. But there is nothing disgusting about it, on the contrary. Why 'on the contrary'? After all, I will not marry an old man! How perfectly preposterous!"

Nadia settled by the window and took a book out of her overnight bag. Outside, the day was grey and dreary; neither winter, nor spring. In weather like that traveling was both cheerless and comforting. "It is a little boring to travel with them. . . . Soon we shall be there and then what? We will get settled, we will visit all the points of interest, and then what?" There was nothing beyond that. "Take dictation and translate letters and state papers? I am not complaining. It's useful work and someone has to do it, besides, I have no reason whatever to expect anything better. My entire equipment consists of shorthand and three foreign languages. It all has worked out for the best; I have been sent abroad, I will see the world, I will meet interesting people. This hope of meeting interesting people may be somewhat exaggerated. Probably I will not see a soul except myself and the secretary. That's too bad, because there is every reason for people to like me," she thought and immediately reprimanded herself; this sounded too conceited. "Yes, shorthand as a makeshift is not too bad, though I have no intention of spending the rest of my life writing somebody else's letters. But if I have no special talents, what else can I do? There are certain occupations that are neither arts, nor professions and that do not require any special talents, nothing more than a reasonable aptitude. I could be an interior decorator. I could do leatherwork or make pottery. Even people who don't like me concede that I have pretty good taste. . . . I could learn anything of this sort within a couple of years. . . . All I have to do is make up my mind. . . . No, I have nothing to fear, I will find something. . . ."

Nadia had every reason to think of other things, but those were unpleasant thoughts and she did not want to be bothered with them at the moment. "No, I will think about all that later. . . ." She gazed out of the window studying the unfamiliar scene. It was her first trip abroad and so far she had not made any worthwhile observations. "When we were in that other station something rather entertaining did occur to me, something I would not mind repeating in front of a whole gathering. Perhaps it will be wise to make notes. . . . To be perfectly honest I can't see any difference; the girls, the young men and the older people look very much like the people at home, only they dress a little better. That couple at the station was obviously in love. . . ." She gave a deep sigh. "Their stations are arranged differently, they have restaurants. Their small towns have things which we see only in the capital. I wonder what Berlin is like. . . . Naturally, at home everything is much better." Outside, something dirty and grey began to fall out of the skies, something that stuck to the windows and melted almost immediately. She laughed; "I hope they don't think this is snow!" She felt happy and gay; no, everything was so much better in Russia. "That's what they call winter, that's what they call frost!"

The train blew for a station and Kangarov peered through the door of the compartment. "This is Berlin, my child! Schlesischer Bahnhof!" he announced, his voice charged with excitement. "Berlin? Already?" Nadia answered, finding his excitement contagious. Hurriedly she glanced at the mirror once more and without any conceit felt pleased with what she saw. She had very nice features. "A beauty, a positive beauty," the young men who knew her in Moscow said about her. "She can't be called exactly a beauty, her nose is a trifle long, she has large feet, and there is something lacking in her face, but she is quite good-looking, almost very good-looking," the girls said about her. Nadia straightened her belt and walked out into the passageway. Everyone else was already there. Wislicenus glanced at her quickly and without a word shifted his eyes back to the window. Helen Kangarov stifled a yawn.

"I am bored, I am terribly bored," she said.

The huge form of a policeman slowly glided past the window. The train came to a stop and the conductor, saluting with one hand, respectfully threw open the door. A slightly bent, tall, thin, exceptionally smart-looking elderly man, wearing a monocle and a top hat, climbed the steps to the car. Kangarov was barely able to hold back an exclamation. This was a titled diplomat, an important figure in the German Ministry of Foreign Affairs. For many years, while it was still permissible, German caricaturists had tried to draw the likeness of this man, but without success; the result was always a portrait rather than a caricature, because the man himself was a living caricature of a diplomat. "Just look at that! Wilhelmstrasse has sent an official representative!" Kangarov said to the secretary in an excited whisper (whenever he spoke about the various ministries of foreign affairs he always referred to them as Wilhelmstrasse, Downing Street, or Quai d'Orsay). In accordance with diplomatic usage the government was not in any way obligated to send a representative to greet an ambassador accredited to another country, merely passing through Berlin. But apparently in this case the Ministry of Foreign Affairs wanted to show special attention—there was also a small business matter to be discussed—and if there were any criticisms from any important officials it could always be blamed on diplomatic etiquette. Nevertheless the diplomat felt somewhat embarrassed. While he stood waiting on the platform he looked around self-consciously and he climbed the steps more quickly than was his usual custom.

A ripple of excitement ran through the car. The secretary's face wore an exalted expression; "even in this barbarous country!" Kangarov gleefully stepped forward to meet the diplomat; they had met before at various international conferences. He introduced the guest to his wife and to the secretary, at the same time casting a worried glance at Wislicenus—"one can expect anything from those people!" Leading the diplomat to the drawing-room he glanced into Nadia's compartment and said "pardon me"—though it was empty except for the overnight bag.

They took seats opposite one another, the train moved, and Kangarov made a motion to get up, but the diplomat reassured him; "I wanted to have the pleasure of escorting Your Excellency as far as the next station." "I almost forgot that through trains stop at several different stations in Berlin," Kangarov answered, beaming with the sweetest smile in his repertoire. Outside, crowding the track, large, new, freshly painted houses, showing no evidence of smoke, rushed past the windows. The diplomat asked whether they had had a pleasant journey, inquired about the health of the people's commissar of foreign affairs, and expressed his opinion about the weather. He spoke with all the mannerisms used in a leftist play by a leftist actor portraying a diplomat of the old school. Kangarov answered with great dignity, as if to say: "yes, we are enemies, but we play the game according to the rules, and we will never forget that we are professional diplomats. . . ." In his excitement he almost asked about Hitler's health, but he checked himself in time and instead inquired about the minister of foreign affairs. They said only a word or two about business, but that was enough; it was not a momentous matter. Once again the train entered the darkness of a gigantic station shed. The diplomat took leave of the ambassador and on the way out his thin figure bent low before Helen Kangarov.

Wislicenus watched him with contempt. He too had met the diplomat before and he even had been introduced to him (he had been unable to avoid it) in Geneva at the Café Bavaria, which was the meeting place for the delegates to the League of Nations, newspapermen, and curious people, who liked to be seen in the same room with celebrities—you could never tell when a press photographer would happen along. The diplomat did not recognize him, but to be on the safe side Wislicenus looked at him with eyes which discouraged any move toward recognition. "There is no sense in shaking hands with these gentlemen. . . ." He remembered that several years ago the same diplomat had been bowing and scraping before the liberal and radical German ministers. The huge, fat, crude Stresemann with his bloodshot eyes and his swollen veins bulging on his forehead, with the typical manner of a natural leader of men, a people's tribune and a "Napoleon of the peace" (a sobriquet under which without any apparent reason he was known at the Café Bavaria), had treated the diplomat in a cavalier fashion. "Now he bows and scrapes before the others," Wislicenus thought with a hatred which bordered on a feeling of personal triumph. "Back home we call it serving the country regardless of political convictions. Keep on serving and you will keep on getting a salary. . . . God willing, you will get another promotion. . . . And our ambassador is not much better: they are two of a kind. . . ."

For the second time the diplomat said: *"Gute Reise, Exzellenz,"* and reached for the handle of the car door. At that very moment the door was pushed from outside and Tamarin entered the passageway. At this station their car had stopped opposite the restaurant; as soon as the car door had been opened Tamarin had walked across the platform and hurriedly had drained a cup of coffee—there was no Danzig vodka at the restaurant, and when he had asked for it the waiter had given him a puzzled look and had offered a glass of cognac instead. The general was dumfounded when he saw the diplomat. For several seconds they looked at one another in silent amazement and then both burst into laughter. *"Alle Wetter!"* the diplomat said in an entirely different voice from the one he had used in talking to the ambassador and with unexpected heartiness slapped the general on the shoulder (he never had been known to behave like that before.) *"Donnerwetter!"* the general answered, finally recovering from his surprise.

A long time ago, in the prehistoric days, they had known each other well and had had frequent occasions to meet in entirely different surroundings. Now they were pleased, amused and a little embarrassed. *"Das heisst: 'vingt ans après',"* the diplomat exclaimed and his eyes seemed to add: "So they have you working for them too! . . . Well, here I am serving the same kind of bastards, and there is nothing I can do about it. . . . Our days are over. . . ." There was nothing more they could say to one another.

To their relief just then the conductor called: *"Einsteigen! . . ."* The diplomat gave a quiet chuckle, shrugged his shoulders as though he wanted to repeat that there was nothing they could do about it—it was fate—warmly shook hands with Tamarin, looked back at the smiling Kangarov and for the third time hurriedly said: *"Gute Reise, Exzellenz. . . ."* The ambassador glanced out of the corner of his eye at his entourage: "It is silly to be called 'Exzellenz,' but just the same, I hope you remember it!" "An old friend?" he asked Tamarin with an air of unqualified approval. The secretary was watching the diplomat, trying to memorize everything about him: the cut of his coat, his gloves, and his top hat. "What an amusing old German!" Nadia thought gaily. Helen Kangarov looked like Mary Stuart in the big scene in which she is confronted by Queen Elizabeth.

V

THE EVENING MAIL brought a letter from the publisher: *memento mori*. At first glance it contained nothing actually unpleasant. The publisher was not in the least curt or impolite: Louis-Etienne Vermandois occupied a position in French letters which made it impossible for publishers to be impolite to him. On the contrary, the letter was extremely complimentary; if anything it was too flattering. As usual it began with *"Cher Maître et ami,"* and ended with *"Croyez, je vous prie, cher Maître, à mes sentiments admiratifs et cordiaux,"*—everything was as it should be. The publisher did not reject the idea suggested by Vermandois for a novel with a setting in ancient Greece. He merely refused to make an advance of thirty thousand francs, suggesting rather vaguely and indefinitely that only a much smaller sum could be considered. That in itself was not peculiar, or unusual: publishers always wanted to drive a hard bargain and he was prepared to bargain with them. But there was something annoying and suspicious in the fact that the letter did not suggest any definite figure, merely saying that it would have to be "much smaller." True, the publisher used business conditions as an excuse and mentioned that there was not an author whose books were selling at present. However, Vermandois did not like the words "there was not an author": it seemed to imply between the lines that there were other authors who had greater claim on popularity than he.

Dispassionately and impersonally Vermandois considered the entire situation over the hurried and uninteresting dinner of a lonely old man. The publisher definitely wanted his novel, but

he was not over-anxious about having it. The letter made it clear
that the novel was well worth publishing but that neither the publisher nor the reading public would languish without it. "A
much smaller sum" indicated fifteen thousand francs; possibly he
could get him up to twenty thousand, but not another penny
over. It would have been much pleasanter if he had begun by
asking twenty thousand, but in that case the publisher would
have offered him ten. There could be no denying that a twenty-
thousand advance against a full-length novel was highway robbery. . . . "Well, not exactly highway robbery, but he is a bastard just the same—he could advance the thirty thousand just as
easily. What is he afraid of? Does he think that I will die? True, a
writer at sixty-nine can die easily enough without finishing a
novel. But the bastard has published seven of my books," Vermandois became more and more irritated as he thought about it.
"If I die he will make such an event of my death, he will make
the critics shed such bitter tears that in three days the seven old
books will sell enough copies to cover any miserable amount I
might owe him. . . ."

The dinner was very light,—no meat, no wine, nothing Vermandois really enjoyed—the kind of a meal that had become fashionable during the last five years among middle-aged and old
Parisians who were in the habit of carefully watching the latest
developments in medicine. There was nothing definitely wrong
with him. Ever so often Vermandois went to see a famous doctor
just as all civilized people go to see a dentist once or twice a year:
the teeth were in perfect order, but it seemed better to let a dentist
look them over. The last time he had been to see him was just a
week ago. The doctor had given him a minute examination and
had found nothing wrong with the possible exception of a barely
perceptible weakness of the heart. The deviation from normal,
however, was so small that he had mentioned it only to display his
thoroughness: after all, the patient was sixty-nine years old. His
stomach, his lungs, his liver and his kidneys were in perfect shape.
"A young man could not hope to function any better," the doctor

had said gaily and with a playful smile had mentioned another matter. "*Les femmes, cher Maître, les femmes. . . . J'ai vaguement entendu dire que vous menez une vie de bâton de chaise. . . .*" "*Voyons, docteur, voyons, on exagère,*" Vermandois had answered, feeling very flattered. "*C'est que vous n'avez plus vingt ans, ni même cinquante. Je ne vous dis que ça . . .*" the doctor's voice had been stern, but his smile most sympathetic. His advice was to eat less, to drink less, not to go out for late suppers, and to take pills; his blood pressure was one hundred forty-five—it would be better to bring it down to one hundred thirty-five. It was quite clear to Vermandois that there was no absolute necessity for taking pills: as far as a human mind could foresee eventualities nothing disastrous need be expected if he did not take them regularly. "How pleasant life was before you doctors learned how to measure blood pressure! People lived without knowing anything about their pressures and they did not worry about them," Vermandois had said with a laugh. After he had learned that his health left nothing to be desired he felt that he could show that he accepted medical science with a grain of salt. The famous doctor had shrugged his shoulders: what else could he say? "*Mais oui, mais oui,*" he finally had answered, as though he were talking to a precocious child much too well informed for his age.

Avoiding any further discussions the doctor had taken a seat behind his desk. Reaching for a memorandum pad he had torn off a sheet of paper which was imprinted in the upper left-hand corner with his name and with his scientific degrees. In a neat hand he had written out the instructions in detail: no dark meat, no game, no spices, nothing strong to drink. . . . "How about wine?" Vermandois had asked in a sudden panic. "You may have wine but in small quantities," the doctor had given permission and, after thinking it over, had added: "Red wines . . . No white wines." Several other questions had occurred to Vermandois. "Would it be better if, instead of dieting, I should go to a watering-place and take a course of treatments?" he suggested, subconsciously drawing an analogy with the option exercised by a court in imposing sentence of a fine or of a prison term. "No, there is no need for you to go to a watering-place; your heart irregularity is barely perceptible; there is nothing wrong with you," the doctor had answered. With an inward relief Vermandois had become convinced that the whole trouble was in the doctor's manner of referring to his age, and that there was no real necessity for any specific prescription: black meat, or white wine would not spell disaster.

This was very reassuring. Before his visit to the doctor Vermandois had felt an occasional vague uneasiness. Just the other day, sitting at the table, he had dropped a book on the floor, and had bent over to pick it up. Suddenly he was struck by the thought that at his age, especially after dinner, it was better to avoid the strain of brisk movements: no telling what could happen. Now it was clear that his fears had been groundless. Vermandois believed, and was in the habit of saying, that he was tired of life. But the one thing did not exclude the other: being tired of life did not prevent him from fully enjoying the doctor's words. "Here, my dear doctor, are three hundred francs. I know this is the regular charge for your valuable time, which I see now you could have spent much more usefully." He had known what the answer would be beforehand. "The charge is one hundred and fifty and not three hundred," the doctor had said, observing the rules of the game. "But why only one hundred and fifty?" "Just because . . ." the doctor had answered with a gentle gruffness.

In discussing business affairs with Vermandois, people usually spoke with an apparent assumption that he had an inexhaustible supply of money on deposit at the bank. They seemed to take for granted that the financial returns of his fame were in direct proportion to the fame itself. On the other hand, because of that very fame a number of organizations and enterprises, including some hotels and stores, offered him special rates. He paid part of the price with the satisfaction which people were supposed to experience in rendering a service to the cause of French culture.

Vermandois had made a gesture with his hands which was intended to convey that he was touched, embarrassed, and disappointed, but that he had no choice except to submit to the wish of
an admirer. Having pressed the doctor's hand a little more firmly
than the degree of their friendship warranted and having paid
one half of the fee with the prestige attached to his person, he had
left the other hundred and fifty francs on the corner of the doctor's
desk.

"Now I will not have to see him for another two years," Vermandois thought absent-mindedly, for the moment forgetting the
publisher. Lazily he ate the soup and a piece of some fish which
was supposed to be exceptionally light. An old, querulous *femme
de ménage* performed an indifferent, listless task of cooking for
him. She was a woman who hypnotized him by her irritability
and who, whenever he made any complaints, invariably reminded
him with a perverse pride that she was not a cook, or a *cordon
bleu.* Her tone implied that she had consented to cook for him and
to serve him generally only because of his urging: in contrast to
the doctors and the hotel managers the old woman apparently
found no pleasure whatever in her association with him. She
worked for him from early in the morning until eight in the evening. For the same wages he could have had a smart, young
maid waiting on him. There were moments when Vermandois
seriously considered making a change, but the very idea of having
to confront the old woman and of having to make an explanation
made him feel desperately tired and bored. "What difference does
it make? At least she does not steal. . . . It does not matter
whether I have this fish or a lobster, a pheasant or a Strassburg
pie. . . . The thing that really counts is good wines."

Wines had become one of the genuine pleasures in his life
only since Vermandois had passed middle age. He had tasted some
perfectly amazing Château Haut-Brion 1918, just a few days
earlier at a very select dinner given in his honor by a wealthy
financier. "Only here, in France, can we hope to find such heav-
enly wine," the host had said. "Its perfection, its mellowness and

its bouquet remind me of your prose. . . ." Vermandois had
answered with a modest smile—at dinners given in his honor a
good part of the time was spent on his professionally modest
smiles. But his mind had not been idle. It had occurred to him that
with certain changes the words of his host could be incorporated
in that scene in his new novel where Anaximander and his
wealthy host drink Falerno: the wine reminds the host of the
third book of the Iliad. However, this idea had not worn well. It
had left a bad taste with him from the time it had made its appearance until the dessert had been served—only much later he
had realized that the sound of such words as Falerno and Anaximander was responsible. "Yes, they do not sound well." Even now
he frowned when he thought about them. "Maybe the reason this
idiot of a publisher is afraid of my novel is because its setting
happens to be ancient Greece?" Vermandois found such a possibility pleasant to contemplate. The whole difficulty was in the
subject matter and had nothing to do with him or with his age.
These days and times who on earth cared about the life in ancient
Greece? A tidal wave of primitive ignorance was inundating the
world. "But who and what will be destroyed by this wave of
ignorance?" Vermandois immediately asked himself. "The Louvre
and the Bibliothèque Nationale will remain. Only this ultra-
refined banker will disappear, and, as far as I am concerned, this
would not be such a great loss. . . ."

At dinner the host had made a studied effort to keep the
conversation on a high plane. In the room where the guests had
been seated—until the entrance of a manservant in knee-breeches
who had announced: "Madame est servie,"—the walls were covered with books from the floor to the ceiling. Over a beautiful
writing-desk hung a Matisse, which according to a modest aside
by the owner, had been bought in the days before it had become
necessary to pay "today's perfectly insane prices." He had shown
them his collection of first and rare editions in fine old bindings
and, while his fingers were caressing the volumes, his face had
beamed with such a benevolent, satisfied, Anatole France-like

smile that Vermandois suddenly had felt a sharp pang of hatred toward this man who every day of his life drank, or at least could afford to drink, Château Haut-Brion 1918. He could have borne it better if the financier had been fat and bloated, or if there had been a thick gold watch chain suspended from his vest, or if his conversation had been that of an ignorant parvenu. But there was nothing of this kind about the financier. Though he had acquired his wealth quite recently and, some said, not quite honestly, his appearance, his clothes, his manners and even his Anatole France-like smile were very presentable. "Devil take the old bastard! Perhaps he is really fond of his old books. . . ."

One could not pass a law prohibiting bankers from appreciating the fine arts. But at that dinner the necessity for a social cataclysm had become more than ever apparent to Vermandois. When an occasion had offered itself, jokingly he even had said aloud: "Long live Comrade Stalin!" A toast of this kind coming from someone else could have had a depressing effect at a banker's table. But the great writer had chosen the appropriate moment, his tone had been so carefree and so pleasant, and his appearance so far from terrifying, that the guests merely had exploded with laughter. "My dear Vermandois, please don't frighten us like that," the host had said and everyone had had a second laugh. "I notice that he already is becoming quite familiar and calling me 'my dear Vermandois'. . . . Well, I suppose after serving Château Haut-Brion he is entitled to it," Vermandois decided magnanimously. From a sense of duty he had said a few words in defense of communism—to be more exact, not so much in defense of communism as in defense of communist ideals; he had not denied that everything in Soviet Russia was far from being perfect; but he had insisted that in that young country a new life was in the making. His statements were supported by a lady who only recently had spent a whole week in Moscow: everyone who knew her could vouch that she was not a communist—that sort of thing did not fit the French people—but the Russian people were happy and unanimously in favor of the new regime, that much she could say without any fear of contradiction. Their host had argued that communism was utopian in its very conception, that one by one its tenets were being discarded in Russia, that with each day pan-slavism was occupying more of the thoughts of the Russian people, just as it had under the old regime—and he had made a reference to the last will of Peter the Great: *le testament de Pierre le Grand.* The manservant in knee-breeches had served the turkey. The conversation had lagged temporarily, but it had been renewed over the salad. The approximate line which Vermandois had taken was that though the old order was toppling or, in any event, beginning to topple, there were individual representatives of the old order who were charming, highly cultured people. They had done much for society by gathering amazing art collections. This definitely had to be taken into consideration, and, besides, "to our great regret" France would not reach a breaking point for some time to come. This reasoning had made even the Château Haut-Brion 1918 somehow acceptable. "We may as well enjoy as many things as we can before we are stricken by the divine revolutionary fever."

At that moment, while Vermandois was still thinking about the turkey, the old woman served him stewed prunes. She did it with a flourish, as if to say: "Yes, you had stewed prunes yesterday and you will have stewed prunes tomorrow. . . . You ordered them and now you can eat them, whenever they are served. I don't happen to be a *cordon bleu.* . . ." "Perhaps the diet could be modified slightly," Vermandois toyed with the idea. A great deal had been said about stewed prunes at the last gathering of writers belonging to his generation. He had known every one of them for at least forty years and one of the chief consolations of his old age was the knowledge that all of them were aging as rapidly as he. Émile had described in detail how little he ate and what a moderate life he led. Vermandois had listened to him with a dis-belief mixed with envy. "Probably he is lying. . . . Even if he is telling the truth it's a lot of nonsense: probably the banker with his Château Haut-Brion will outlive them all. And if that old fool,

Émile, should live another hundred years and should write forty more books it will not make any difference to a damned soul." Nevertheless he had not relished the idea that foresight, moderation and stewed prunes would allow Émile to outlive him, and he had given orders to the old woman to serve stewed prunes oftener. Her face—much more frankly and openly than his thoughts—had reflected what was in the back of his mind: stewed prunes or not, you might die tomorrow and no one will consider it a calamity. On this occasion her expression was even more provoking than usual: "just try and say one word about it, and you will never hear the end of it!" Vermandois refused to accept the challenge. Obediently he finished the stewed prunes—they were not so terribly bad after all—and told her to bring the coffee pot to his study. The old woman's face showed clearly that she would not be held responsible for the coffee.

After dinner Vermandois changed to a velvet bathrobe, soft bedroom slippers and a skull cap. He luxuriated in the thought that the pleasantest part of his day was about to begin: from now on there was not a chance that anyone would disturb him. Entering his study he rolled back the top of his desk. There were no valuable pieces of furniture in his workroom—everything was arranged to provide a maximum of comfort and efficiency. After glancing over the radio programs in a magazine, he turned the dials of the radio which stood on the mantel. They were having a Beethoven festival in Munich. Vermandois liked to work to the accompaniment of gentle, soft, distant music. He adjusted the volume and stood listening. The old woman entered the study and displaying contempt for music opened the window. The rattle of the closing shutters drowned out Beethoven. "That's just like life," Vermandois said to himself and immediately became ashamed of the triteness of his metaphor. "Am I getting as silly as Émile? . . ." He sighed and silently gave the woman her daily wages—this was his last trial of the day. A deafening round of applause reached him from Munich.

Vermandois made the coffee, which he had not mentioned to

the doctor, in a new and recently perfected contraption consisting of two glass containers and a connecting pipe. In doing this he followed a routine established since the war by the best restaurants in Paris where coffee like that was made by dark, Eastern people wearing strange costumes. The ritual and the process itself seemed to lend a special flavor to the coffee. Enjoying each successive step he lighted a small alcohol lamp under the glass container and stood for a long time staring at the water. At first only a few tiny bubbles rose to the surface, then everything was in motion, something began to vibrate in the pipe, and a torrent of brown liquid poured from the upper into the lower container.

The publisher's letter no longer worried or irritated Vermandois. Undoubtedly the subject matter was to blame for everything. That was the reason why at their last meeting, while he had given a brief and casual outline of his novel, the publisher had listened to him with such a hopeless expression and had constantly repeated: *"Très intéressant, Maître. . . ." "Vous allez créer un chef-d'oeuvre, Maître. . . ."*

Vermandois read the letter once again. *". . . Vous devinez, cher Maître, que ce n'est pas l'envie qui me manque . . ." ". . . la situation empire tous les jours, et je ne vois décidement pas comment . . ." ". . . la crise m'impose donc la tâche pénible de . . ."* "Yes, this means fifteen thousand. . . ." Obviously he had the choice of going to another publisher. But if he, too, refused to make a better offer it would be more embarrassing than ever to have to return to the first one. In some mysterious way publishers invariably learned about the most confidential negotiations between their authors and other publishers. Most important of all, to begin negotiations all over again was terribly boring, even more boring than to have to argue with the querulous old woman. "There is nothing I can do about it," he decided. "I will have to write to him and tell him that I will accept twenty thousand. . . ."

Out of his desk drawer Vermandois took a ledger and quickly added some figures. In this ledger he kept a neat and exact record of every penny he earned. He did not bother to put down his expenses because this was pointless. There was never anything left over, which showed that his expenses equaled his income and, at times, even exceeded it, inasmuch as he had certain debts. They were not personal debts, but advances he had received from publishers—he never resorted to borrowing from friends. The figures in the ledger were not reassuring. There was nothing he could count on, except the royalties on his books and the money he received from the newspapers for writing articles which he detested. This year it seemed impossible to make ends meet. "Unless I can sell the moving picture rights to one of my books, but that sounds like a pipe-dream. . . ."

Some of his friends and contemporaries insisted that Vermandois made money hand over fist: *"Des mille et des cent, cher ami: les Américans lui payent des sommes folles! . . ."* Others were just as certain that he lived in strained circumstances and that on occasion he even went hungry: *"La dèche, vous dis-je, la dèche noire! . . ."* Actually his average annual income was in the neighborhood of one hundred thousand francs. Out of this amount, however, Vermandois had to pay his first wife eighteen thousand, and his second wife, with whom he had parted after he was already a person of considerable means—twenty-four thousand. This expenditure could not be reduced in any way.

It was next to impossible to curtail his personal expenses any further. Vermandois was economizing in every way he could without endangering his standing. At first glance it would appear that his position in society did not in any way depend on money, and that it rested entirely on the fact that he was a famous writer— one of the five or six men whom any educated Frenchman was certain to mention in enumerating the great living writers of France. Wealthy people, not in the least concerned with the amount of his income, considered it a great honor to have him as their guest. But even invitations made it absolutely necessary to spend a certain minimum. A more penurious mode of living in no time at all would undermine his social position, and, no matter how absurd that seemed, also would decrease the value of his literary output. Editors and publishers gradually would assume an entirely different tone with him if they did not see an occasional news item on the society pages mentioning that he had been entertained by an ambassador or by a duke, or that he had spent several weeks at one of the more expensive resort hotels. That was the only reason why he continued to go out into society which bored him to distraction and that also was the reason why every August he spent two weeks in the most expensive hotel in Deauville, continually swearing at the terrific amount of money it cost him despite the discount he received from the management. All this was extremely stupid, but Vermandois no longer was amazed by the stupid things in life.

"How else can I economize? Move to a cheaper apartment?" he sullenly asked himself and shuddered at the very thought. After twenty years a habit was difficult to break, and as for moving a library of six thousand volumes it would be a veritable catastrophe. He no longer owned a car. He had disposed of it at the very beginning of the depression and his social position had suffered a telling blow to which he mockingly referred as: *"capitis deminutio."* As for entertaining guests he very rarely gave even an inexpensive but universally accepted cocktail party. "I suppose my friends are beginning to call me a miser. . . ."

Secretary? Recently these duties had been performed by a young man who came every day for a few hours. Vermandois paid him such a pittance that at times he did not have the courage to meet the eyes of the young man who probably went for days without eating a square meal. "If I sell the moving picture rights, I will have to give him a bonus: a thousand . . . no, five hundred francs," he vaguely reassured himself, though he knew that the chances of the secretary getting a bonus were very slim. "And for all of that he is a disagreeable and abnormal young man. . . ." The expression "and for all of that" had no real meaning. Vermandois simply was irritated by the secretary's acerbity, which exceeded his own. "One should not, however, pay any attention to his way of expressing himself. Whenever he calls someone a blackguard or a son of a bitch it simply means that he does not find that particular person congenial. . . ." The young man had a habit of referring frequently to people as: *"crapule," "sale crapule," "canaille,"* and *"vieille canaille,"* but these epithets were in his case merely a manner of speech. "I suppose he calls me a *'vieille canaille,'* " Vermandois wondered and was about to become angry, but changed his mind: he felt too sorry for the hungry-looking young man.

For a while he dwelt on other possible measures of economy. No, there was nothing else he could eliminate from his budget with the exception of some very trivial things. "I suppose I could persuade Marie to come for only six instead of eight hours, providing I should be willing to listen to her complaints. Maybe I should change tailors? But as long as I order only two suits a year the saving will be negligible and it would be another case of *capitis deminutio*" . . . Vermandois emitted a deep sigh. Sixty thousand a year was the minimum on which he could live in Paris. "If the publisher gives me an advance of twenty thousand I cannot hope to go through the year without a deficit. . . ." He looked in his checkbook. The balance was nine thousand francs and this amount represented his entire capital. "There is not a soul anywhere who has spent money as stupidly as I have and who has not saved something out of fifty years of work. . . . Yes, it is positively disastrous. . . ." There were only two possibilities which could enable him to make ends meet: a sale of the moving picture rights, or the death of his second wife who had poisoned five years of his existence. He wished no harm to his first wife, on the contrary he had retained nothing but pleasant memories of her. "Oh, hell! I suppose the other fool can keep on living too, as long as she stops writing those idiotic letters. . . ." Then he became ashamed for allowing such a thought to enter his head. With a new sharpness he felt the hatred accumulated during many years for a society which, despite his important position, despite the select dinners in his honor, despite the Château Haut-Brion (even though it belonged to someone else,) despite his six thousand books, could be so cruel to a famous, old man who had spent his entire life at work.

The flame of the alcohol burner flickered and a black, velvety spot appeared in the glass container. Vermandois turned down the wick and put out the light. The clear water which had been drawn into the upper container now returned as an absolutely black liquid. The coffee was so strong that it was undoubtedly bad for the heart, but why should he take care of himself when he had to continue living under a social system of this kind? Nevertheless, it was nice to remember the reassuring words of the doctor: "There is nothing wrong with you: a young man could not expect to function any better. . . ." "As a matter of fact I am not conscious of any signs of old age. My memory is as good as ever. My creative ability has not dwindled, or at least not perceptibly so . . . Women?"

Women were now his chief interest in life. Vermandois was a little ashamed and secretly pleased that he no longer craved honors, fame, or a literary reputation. His only craving was women. Whether he was in the street, in a bus, or in the theatre, his eyes never missed a young girl, and ideas occurred to him which never had entered his head before, or at least it seemed so to him. "Only now can I understand what it is all about. . . . Only now can I appreciate the full meaning of life. . . . Only now when there is so little left of it. . . ."

Probably he should plan to spend the brief remainder of his life in a sensible way. Once or twice every year Vermandois made a resolution to turn over a new leaf: to get up every morning at six, after a light breakfast to take a daily stroll through the Bois de Boulogne, to work steadily after that, to read worthwhile books in the evenings, and to go to bed every night at eleven. It also would be nice to have a house somewhere in the country—even if it were only a three-room, dilapidated cottage. How pleasant it would be to accumulate a reasonable sum of money in the bank, instead of the pitiful balances which he left for the sake of appearances and so he could be on the safe side whenever he drew a check. How delightful it would be if, instead of the old woman, a young good-looking maid would wait on him—he could call her "my child" and she would look at him with dog-like devotion.

But invariably these plans for a new life came to naught. When he arose early he found that his shoes had not been shined, that there was no fresh bread for the morning coffee, and that it was impossible to go to the Bois de Boulogne because it was raining and, besides, there was nothing worth seeing in the Bois anyway. He worked whenever he could find time, most frequently in the evenings, keeping himself awake with coffee. He went to bed very late and he arose around noon. "I doubt that there is another man in France who leads such an unhealthy and stupid life. . . ."

Every week Vermandois received anywhere from twenty to forty new books. Those of them that were written by notoriously bad authors or by unknowns ("If the book were any good, I would have heard about it.") were placed in one stack. The secretary carefully tore out the flyleaves bearing the authors' inscriptions and carried the books from this stack to a second-hand bookseller. This small additional income was earmarked for donations to charity: the money was given to a succession of women wearing semi-monastic attire, who continually rang his doorbell —it was amazing how many useful, charitable institutions in Paris counted on him for assistance. To the authors the secretary sent Vermandois' card with a few words wishing them success. In the second stack were books which Vermandois intended to look over (probably without cutting the pages). Most of them also were not worth reading, but because of the reputation of the authors an acknowledgment with a mere card was not sufficient in their case. Instead, the secretary typed an individual letter and gave it to him for signature. The books in the third stack had to be acknowledged by Vermandois in longhand, and that was especially boring because it made it necessary for him to cut the pages (he would have been embarrassed to delegate such a task to the secretary).

On this occasion the third stack consisted of two books. There were a few famous writers still alive belonging to his generation. Vermandois decided to save the second book for tomorrow: perhaps, for once, there would not be any new arrivals! He cut the pages of a fat volume and after flipping them for a few minutes hurriedly jotted down a letter. . . . "The sixth chapter is wonderful, and so is the characterization of Antoine! I would consider it a sacrilege to attempt to analyze the ending: it is a masterpiece—a masterpiece even for you, my dear friend! . . . It would be presumptuous for me to wish you success—how could it be anything else? . . ."

"I don't believe I ever have written this to him before," Vermandois hesitated for a second. The fact that he had praised the characterization of Antoine did not worry him—he knew from long years of experience that in writing things like that he was on safe ground. Extravagant praise heaped on any chapter, or on any character, could never surprise the author. It would have been easier to read the book than to have to lie about it. But Vermandois felt that he did not have the energy to read even good new novels, unless it was absolutely necessary. He only refreshed his memory about the books he had read in the past, just as ladies, reconciled to old age, continually try to fix and re-arrange treasured possessions, which they have acquired in their youth and which are not completely dated.

The possibility of not acknowledging the receipt of a book inscribed to him never even occurred to Vermandois. Politeness was an integral part of his nature. He could not bear arguments in newspapers; he particularly disliked literary feuds, which differed from political feuds in that no one ever derived any direct benefit from them. Vicious criticism usually irritated and puzzled him. Reviews of this kind never accomplished anything useful. They did nothing for the standard of literature—time alone tested and evaluated all books, regardless of reviews—or for the public —readers watched such squabbles just as urchins watch a street fight—or for the author, or for the critic who had written the review. Sooner or later all critics wrote books, and sooner or later all writers had occasion to write criticisms. Openly or in some roundabout way, every vicious review inevitably and invariably provoked another return review just as vicious as the first—this seemed to be an immutable law of nature. It seemed incredible that otherwise brilliant and intelligent people should engage in such absurd and useless literary feuds which benefited no one. An argument over a question of principle always could be conducted in a gentlemanly way. "After all, we were not created in order to spoil one another's lives, which even without that are so short and so filled with troubles. But even if we are created that way, we should fight against it as we would fight against a vice—I doubt that it is a result of a biological weakness in the human race . . . I, for instance, never enjoy it in the least. . . ." His verbal, his written, or his published praises were never taken seriously because no one had any faith in them, except the person to whom they were addressed. But that was the very thing he wanted.

Vermandois sealed the envelope and was annoyed to discover under the paperweight some other letters, which had been left for him by the secretary. He glanced at them. There was a questionnaire from a not well known but very enterprising magazine with a small circulation. People always expected him to give them free material for which he was entitled to be paid in money, or at least in advertising. To do this was just as inconsiderate and as indecent on their part as it is to ask for legal advice from a lawyer who happens to be a friend and whom you casually meet in the street. Questionnaires arrived, not as frequently as books, but there were a good many of them. The young secretary even had the impudence to suggest that he prepare a specially printed form such as used by Courteline. "*M. Georges Courteline a reçu votre enquête sur*. . . . *Il a l'honneur de vois informer qu'il s'en f* . . . *complètement.*" On the margin of the questionnaire the secretary had written in longhand: "*Formule 2, n'est-ce pas, cher Mâitre.*" There was something very impudent in the secretary's question, in his handwriting, and in the way he used the words "*Cher Mâitre.*" Nevertheless he was right: there was no need to antagonize magazine editors. Vermandois jotted down: "*Mais oui.*" This meant the secretary would answer that because of Monsieur

Louis-Etienne Vermandois' absence from the city he was unfortunately unable to fill out the extremely interesting questionnaire.

Underneath there were two other sheets of paper held together by a clip. Vermandois glanced at them and emitted an oath. This was a reminder that he was expected to take part in an indignation meeting protesting against the outrages that had been sanctioned by some South American Government. As a matter of fact he had promised to speak at the meeting, but it had never occurred to him that his promise would be taken so literally. The people who were arranging the meeting should have known that he simply had loaned them his name, so that they could use it in their advertising. Attached to the letter was a typewritten draft of an answer prepared by the secretary. Vermandois read it over hurriedly. It advised the committee that he had been taken suddenly ill, that to his great regret he would be unable to be present, that he was sending his greeting to all the comrades, and that he was joining them in decrying the barbaric acts of the South American Government. The answer was written quite passably, but again there was something insolent, presumptuous and brazen in its tone, in the expressions used, and most of all in the fact that the young whippersnapper took for granted that *cher Mâitre* would not attend the meeting. Nevertheless the secretary was right again. Vermandois picked up a pen and made several minor changes. Instead of "*flétrir ces actes abominables*" he wrote down: "*flétrir ces actes que la conscience du monde civilisé ne saurait accepter.*"

For the evening this brought the mechanical tasks to an end.

VI

Vermandois took out of the drawer a fat cardboard file stuffed with small notebooks and with sheets of paper covered with corrections and notations and held together by clips, with extra pieces pasted to the margins. This was the material he had assembled

for his novel of life in ancient Greece. To the publisher he had
said that the novel was "for all practical purposes finished," but
he had said so with a smile which indicated that he meant it in
the same sense as Racine's famous words about "Phèdre": *"C'est
prêt, il ne reste qu'à l'écrire."* Inwardly, however, Vermandois
realized how little was accomplished, though the characters had
been carefully outlined, and all the necessary historical references
collected. Worst of all, possibly for the first time in his life, it was
not clear to him how he should begin—this was his first experience
with a historical novel. He knew the Greek language well and he
had read at least a hundred books on Greek civilization—his difficulty lay not in a lack of knowledge of the period. "How terrible
it will be if the result is a forced, synthetic book. . . ."

Only the central thought was clear. For three thousand years
the world had been in a state of barbarism and during those three
thousand years it had only a vague understanding of its shortcomings. The world could not now and was never able in the past to
change itself, because of the natural weaknesses of the human race.
But in all the ages the best and the most fastidious human minds
had tried to find justification for a point of view which would put a
different face on barbarism, or which would consider it only as a
passing stage in the evolution of man. For many centuries humanity patiently had borne the absolute rule of evil, because it had
considered earthly existence only a temporary and miserable
stage preparatory to a state of eternal bliss. This faith began
to disappear about a hundred or, perhaps, two hundred years ago
and it was hurriedly and fumblingly replaced by the shallow and
unsatisfying belief in science. Now, since 1914, this school of
thought had also demonstrated its bankruptcy and its stupidity.
The world was entering a new period of catastrophes and had
returned or was returning to a condition of primitive barbarism.
During those three thousand years apparently there had been only
one exception: a small race of men in the Eastern Mediterranean
—the Greek people, who had disappeared soon, but who within a
short period of time through some inexplicable biological acci-

dent had produced a disproportionate, unreasonable, almost supernatural number of men with a spark of genius. Long before the
others these men had carried out quickly all the social experiments
known to a subsequent world. They had carried them out so
brilliantly and with such concentration in space and time that
even now it was best to study the basic problems of human society by analyzing their experiments, their history and their myths.
Here began an exposition of a new interpretation of these problems—it seemed to Vermandois that he had acquired a completely
new understanding of ancient Greece.

The sound of fate knocking at his door reached him from the
radio. Vermandois smiled with satisfaction at the realization that
the strains coming from the outside world synchronized with his
thoughts. "I should always work to the accompaniment of
Beethoven's music," he decided, but immediately with a disturbing sense of reality answered himself that at sixty-nine it was
much too late to acquire new habits of work. "And there is no
sense in seeking new forms of expression—that is the worst possible form of snobbism." Every time he began a new book he
always wanted to write in some new way—in a way in which
neither he nor anyone else had ever written before. Nothing came
of it: everything new turned out to be very old—"and there is no
new thing under the sun." Progress in art was nothing more than
pushing along a path things which had been created by generations of men who had worked before you. The greatest innovators
always followed this formula. And those who wanted to be known
as startling innovators among their contemporaries were invariably forgotten within twenty years and even within ten years
became absolutely unbearable. "In this book I shall just barely
push along a path the art of the historical novel. But what exactly is a historical novel? . . ."

Before beginning his work Vermandois had collected a certain
number of books which were considered the best in their field.
By his desk stood a revolving rack filled with books to which he
might have occasion to refer. There were serious studies of Greek

history, philosophy and daily life, but there were also famous historical novels which had nothing to do with Greece. "Perhaps I should look them over?" he thought and at random picked up a volume of "War and Peace." "No, I better not try it. . . ." For a number of reasons he made it a point to avoid Tolstoy, but whenever he happened to read him he always finished in a mixed state of exaltation and depression. "I will never be able to write like him. . . . Why should I read books which kill in me the desire for literary work? . . . Besides, why should 'War and Peace' be considered a historical novel?" he asked himself. "His father took part in the Battle of Borodino, and he merely described the experiences of his own family in the form of a historical novel. . . ."

Vermandois picked up another book; this time it was *Ninety-Three*. "Let's see what papa Hugo can teach me? . . . This may be much more to the point. Though his father also took part in the events he describes. . . . It seems to me that I have bad luck with fathers. My father never had the pleasure of meeting Alcibiades. . . ." He immediately regretted that he was getting himself into an ironic frame of mind: nothing could be worse for the quality of his literary effort. He opened the book at random. "*Audessus de la balance il y a la lyre. Votre république dose, mesure et règle l'homme; la mienne l'emporte en plein azur. C'est la différence qu'il y a entre un théorème et un aigle.—Tu te perds dans le nuage.—Et vous dans le calcul.—Il y a du rêve dans l'harmonie.—Il y en a aussi dans l'algèbre.—Je voudrais l'homme fait par Euclide.—Et moi, dit Gauvain, je l'aimerais mieux fait par Homère . . .*" Vermandois yawned and laughed trying to recreate these people in his memory. "Yes, Cimourdain was a fanatic, and Gauvain—a humanist. The fanatic kills his disciple, the humanist. And, if I remember correctly, the trial should come before that. . . ." He glanced at the chapter describing the trial and read the speech for the defense. The fact that in this speech, supposedly made in 1793, there was a reference to the Battle of Fleurus which took place in 1794, amused him. "I don't believe the critics ever noticed it. . . . Papa Hugo was pretty careless about his facts. . . ." He flipped a few more pages. ". . . *Et la femme qu'en faites-vous?—Ce qu'elle est. La servante de l'homme. —Oui. A une condition.—Laquelle?—C'est que l'homme sera le serviteur de la femme.—Y pense-tu?* s'écria Cimourdain, *l'homme serviteur! Jamais. L'homme est mâitre. Je n'admets qu'une royauté, celle du foyer. L'homme chez lui est roi.—Oui, à une condition.— Laquelle? C'est que la femme y sera reine. . . .*" He felt happier. "No, my dialogue could not be any worse than this. The only difference is that his people could have talked like that—though they most certainly never did. . . ."

Vermandois had difficulty with the style. In the first draft his conversations of the ancient Greeks sounded hopelessly artificial, or hopelessly cheap and in most cases both cheap and artificial. Vermandois wrote down a sentence used by Anaximander and it seemed to him that this ancient Greek had already appeared in hundreds of third-rate novels, in which he had used the same Attic sentences that sounded so trivial and so flat. He knew that he was a victim of a psychological trick which was a result of the difference between the spoken and the imagined words: one's own writing always seemed so much worse than anyone else's. In a novel written by another person he never would have given this sentence a second thought. "But how can I possibly understand the minds of a people who lived two thousand years ago? I don't understand the mysteries of our own government; Bulgarians and Danes are as foreign to me as are the Eskimos; and here I have the nerve to claim that I have found the answer to the 'mystery of ancient Greece!' Any new answer is no better than the old ones, besides, there is no special mystery attached to ancient Greece. They were simply foreign, exceptionally gifted men whom it is very difficult to understand because we are separated from them by such a long span of time. . . . What shall I do? Shall I give up this novel?"

So much effort had been expended on the study of the period, so much mental energy had been spent on thinking about the novel, that Vermandois could not bear the idea of giving it up. "Should I take a trip to Greece, and gather some local impressions? . . ." For a moment this seemed like the right solution. Though he did not have the necessary money, a trip to Athens could be engineered. He could have a talk about it with the government officials. The fact that Vermandois had communist leanings would not stand in the way of some minor mission. On the contrary the minister of foreign affairs might welcome the opportunity to display his impartiality, his knowledge of the fine arts, and his ability to appreciate men like Vermandois, regardless of their political affiliations. On his side Vermandois, too, would not feel the least uncomfortable about it. "Perhaps I could make arrangements with some newspaper. . . ." The wealthy newspapers would accept his offer gladly, though they would continue to blast the communists in their editorial pages. But the very thought of new articles, of new obligations to the newspapers, of new advances which would have to be covered by a stipulated number of lines previously agreed upon aroused a feeling of horror and disgust in Vermandois. Newspaper articles were the bane of his existence. "Well, what if I do go to Greece. . . . Dirty hotels, exotic rich foods, poor wines, a matter-of-fact provincial people living on the most sacred ground in the world. . . . Suppose I am not taken ill and nothing unforeseen happens, how would my novel benefit if I were to see on the spot the huge joke which has been played by history? . . . Yes, but at least I shall see the same sun, the same skies, the same yellow rocks. . . . But I already have seen all that years ago. . . . As was the fashion, forty years ago I recited Renan's prayer in the Acropolis. Probably it would be better not to read it now, just as it would have been wise to have left *Ninety-Three* alone. . . ."

In his memory Vermandois tried to reconstruct the hill topped with the Acropolis, the rocks bathed in the bright lucid light, the fresh breeze blowing from the sea. Everything had been so beautiful. . . . But now, forty years later, it was frightening and depressing to think about it all. From the mantelpiece Beethoven's music kept repeating the same thing over and over again: you will die, you must not die, you should retain a grip on life, you must make yourself a part of the minds of other people. . . . "No, I should not allow myself to think about things like that!" Of late he more and more frequently repeated to himself: "No, I should not allow myself to think about things like that!"—for the same reason that he went out of his way to be polite when he was in the company of others. He did not want to give any indication of the disgust, the irritation and the anger that most people generated in him.

Vermandois put *Ninety-Three* back on the shelf and this time deliberately picked up *The Gods Thirst*. There was nothing he could hope to find in this book: he did not like Anatole France. "The worst possible thing that could happen to me would be if unconsciously I were to succumb to his influence and build my true, serious, and probably last book around epigrams, quotations, witticisms and a literary style. In that case it would be better if I were to devote my time to the writing of articles about Anthony Eden and Mussolini. . . ."

The realization so familiar to Vermandois that art was false, superfluous and unnatural, now that he was working on the Greek novel became almost unbearable. "But this 'being natural' is only an illusion. When one is twenty it is natural to write poetry, and still, even at that age, I thought a great deal about discovering useful new tricks that had not been used by Mallarmé, or by Verlaine. And that's what all great artists do—Beethoven thought about it all the time. While those painters, writers and musicians who don't think about it, who generally are not interested in the nature of art and who create only on the strength of divine inspiration, are the shortest-lived among us. But now that I am old, to think about it all is *corruptio boni pessima*. . . . What is natural? The experiences of a Greek, "N," may be natural, but to write a novel about them is embarrassing, useless and foolish. . . . I should write at least one real book about real things; write it without thinking about the public or about the critics."

In the very beginning Vermandois had called his chief character Anaximander. But as the first draft continued to grow Vermandois realized more and more clearly that he could not call his hero Anaximander any more than he could call him Rhadames. There was no real reason why he should have felt that way: obviously there had been a good many Anaximanders in Greece and, besides, no matter what name he chose, it still would sound as melodramatic as Rhadames. Nevertheless, in his more recent notes, and in the special dossier of the central character, Anaximander had disappeared and had been temporarily replaced by an "N." It was depressing to realize that art, every form of art and his art in particular, had to be melodramatic. "And how about this?" A miracle, which had become commonplace and everyday, brought to the room over certain mysterious waves from Munich a Beethoven scherzo. "I wonder what it was that suddenly cheered up the old man? Had he forgotten fate?"

With a sad smile Vermandois listened to the music which he knew so well and thought of the different ways in which it had been interpreted by numerous commentators. "The great struggle of humanity—struggle against what? If these divine sounds had a definite meaning how could there be such wild transitions from despair to ecstasy, and from ecstasy back to despair? These absurd, stupid, illiterate program notes! 'Sorrow over a lost penny expressed in a caprice . . .' 'Wellington's victory or the Battle of Vittoria . . .' 'A difficult decision: does it have to be? . . .' Beethoven had written music inspired by Goethe, but he also had written when he was inspired by Kotzebue, which proves that he did not understand a thing about literature. But he would find it just as ridiculous and just as offensive that I should dare to criticize his music. However, all of us, great and small alike, are considered servants of one master—art, and it is assumed that we have in common a general esthetic gift or understanding not possessed by other people. . . . This scherzo, for instance, is supposed to represent the eternal triumph of good. At least, he thought it would be better if it represented the eternal triumph of good rather than merely the first appearance of trombones in a symphony in the entire history of music. No, this is also melodrama, tinged with genius, but not any more true to life than my Greek Anaximander. . . ."

Vermandois pushed back the chair and began to pace the floor. "Yes, all of it is pretense! For almost fifty years I have been deceiving readers by concealing in every possible way the technique of my tricks, by passing off melodrama for life, by inventing people who never existed, and by being satisfied with the thought that my Rhadames and their adventures were not in the least like the Rhadames who had been pulled out of hats before my time by other magicians. True, that was not the only thought that guided me, but it, too, played an important part. If Tolstoy's Austerlitz repeats Stendhal's Waterloo I suppose Tolstoy also tried to avoid an obvious resemblance. And they, too, had their share of Rhadames. There was a Rhadames in Fabricius, and in Julien Sorel, and even in Prince Andrey. All of it had some of the poison of melodrama in it, even though it was only a drop. But they firmly believed in human rights and in the tricks of art. They even lived like their heroes. Tolstoy had his roots in his land, like an oak; he wrote organically because he lived organically, and, most important of all, he loved what he wrote. When he did not love it, then the results were caricatures like his Napoleon. Without earthiness, without joy of life, without the love for one's subject, there cannot be any art. If I should undertake to write organically my chief character would be an old, tired, bored Parisian, who at the age of seventy is fed up with his work, with his life, with the comedy of fame, with the comedy of society, with the comedy of politics, and whose only remaining interest in life are young women who have no desire to look at him. Perhaps this would be true art, but the further one is from art like that the better. Probably when I conceived my tired Greek Anaximander this was the very thing that was subconsciously in my mind. The result would be mediocrity and there is little to choose between mediocrity and melodrama. To hell with this whole damned novel!" Vermandois felt a sudden burst of anger. He knew no one with whom he could talk about it: young writers, he believed, had an inadequate understanding of art and were generally ignorant; most of the older writers read only their own things and, occasionally, a classic.

The last strains of the symphony came to an end on some completely incomprehensible notes, which had nothing in common with anything that had preceded them. They were followed by an endless, stormy clatter of applause. "Just as though Hitler had finished a speech. . . . But how can they reconcile things like that in their stupid heads? . . . Old Beethoven, who was an honest radical-socialist, would turn in his grave if he could see the people who are applauding him," Vermandois thought as he sat down behind his desk once again. "Should I burn the whole thing?" he asked himself with bitterness and irritation. "No, this would be more melodramatic than the novel itself." He never destroyed any of his manuscripts; even in the worst of them there was always some good sentence, word or expression. "Why burn it? I can simply put it away. At least I will have the consolation of thinking that the novel has not ripened yet; the period of gestation is not yet completed."

Carefully Vermandois closed the file, tied a string around it and put it away in the drawer of his desk. The swollen file which had grown fatter and fatter did not go in easily, the corners caught against the top, and Vermandois became more and more irritated. "What should I do now? Should I try an article? Why not? They have asked me to write about Eden, and why shouldn't I?. . ." He pulled out another drawer and took out a thin, unprepossessing-looking file. It contained a number of newspaper clippings and a sheet on which he had jotted down some ideas for the article. Not without pleasure Vermandois looked over what he had written; his thoughts were expressed in terse, strong sentences. "This at least is absolutely true; there is no Rhadames or any other kind of deceit about it. Besides, five hundred francs for two hours' work is not so bad. . . ." He sighed, tore a sheet of paper from a pad, turned back a corner and began to write.

VII

On the day set for the presentation of credentials the building occupied by the embassy was permeated with excitement. New difficulties continued to arise until the very last minute. In the morning Wislicenus had announced that he had no intention of being presented at court. "You do what you want, but I will not play the fool!" he had said somberly to the ambassador. "But why didn't you mention it until now?" "I thought you would guess as much." "I have no way of reading your thoughts, and no wish to do so," the ambassador had answered drily. "Believe me I have no more desire to participate in this stupid ceremony than you have. But you are a member of the embassy staff and I have included your name in the list. If you did not want to come, it was your duty to warn me ahead of time. Now, your absence will draw special attention to your name. [He tried to place an emphasis on the last words.] It would seem to me that this would be highly undesirable. Nevertheless, you can do as you please—you are supposed to know what you are doing."

Wislicenus knew that Kangarov was right even though he lied when he said that he did not want to go. "Actually, it is nothing more than an empty formality," he thought, leaving the room. Just outside he met Nadia.

"No, there simply is no justice in this world," she said with a laugh. "I would give my right arm to see the whole ceremony, and no one even offers to take me. While you receive a polite invitation and refuse to go! And, besides everything else, you place the ambassador in a difficult position. . . ." "The ambassador can tell them that I am ill," Wislicenus answered hesitantly. Nadia gave him a quick, appraising glance. "So that's it! He wants to be coaxed!" she thought. "Why don't you go ahead?" she said aloud. "I am being selfish about it: if you don't go who will describe everything to me—all the others seem to be half-blind." "You have too much curiosity for your own good!" Nadia immediately went to the ambassador. "Why don't you ask the old man once more—I am sure that he wants to go," she volunteered her advice smilingly. Thirty minutes later Kangarov came to her and with ill-concealed triumph in his voice said: "Well, our prima donna finally has consented! It was just a pose: 'I will not stain my snow-white revolutionary vestments!' As though I enjoy mixing with the flunkies at the court! But when in Rome do as the Romans do. . . ." "I don't see why it should be such a terrible ordeal. Certainly I should not mind in the least seeing the court flunkies . . ." Nadia thought.

From two o'clock on, the secretary remained glued to the window. The entire embassy staff had gathered in the first-floor drawing-room adjoining the entrance hall. The room smelled of paint and moth-balls. Kangarov was not present because he was involved in an unpleasant conversation with his wife. Helen Kangarov insisted that she had to be presented at the very first opportunity. "I hope you realize that it does not depend on me. We have no choice except to follow the prescribed custom," Kangarov said to her in an effort to restrain himself.

The mood in the drawing-room was gay and exhilarated. Bazarov, the first counselor of the embassy, a middle-aged man, was in a sarcastic frame of mind. "The ambassador is simply superb," he whispered when Kangarov walked through the door. Their appearance brought a benevolent smile to the ambassador's lips. "We have no choice in the matter: in Rome do as the Romans do," he repeated. "I have asked those gentlemen to simplify the procedure as much as possible, but they were so horrified they almost suffered strokes. However, I expect all of you to do your part without any unnecessary levity," he added sternly, addressing himself chiefly to Bazarov. "Certainly, certainly," Bazarov spoke for everyone.

The secretary standing by the window emitted an exclamation. Three gilded carriages with footmen wearing court liveries stopped in front of the embassy. They were followed by a cavalry escort. "Wonders will never cease," Bazarov whispered. The ambassador glanced at him out of the corner of his eye and hurriedly went to meet the marshal who was entering the hall. The marshal was a very ancient and somber-looking man who moved with apparent difficulty. His facial expression did not change in answer to Kangarov's welcoming smile and he made no attempt to explain the purpose of his call, which was obvious anyway. Kangarov said that the weather was very pleasant; the marshal did not agree with, or contradict, this statement. "Perhaps he is the Mute of Portici?" Bazarov whispered in Russian. The secretary giggled nervously and immediately became frightened by his behavior. Kangarov fixed a stern gaze on them as if to say: "Yes, the old man is about as stupid as they come, but this is no excuse: we must not forget that we are diplomats." "We can proceed to the palace," the marshal said curtly. "We are ready," the ambassador answered and addressing his staff, added: *"Allons, Messieurs. . . ."* His "messieurs" sounded playfully apologetic, but in the presence of the gold-braided old man he felt he could not address them as comrades. *"Allons, enfants de la patrie,"* Bazarov whispered again.

A small crowd had collected on the sidewalk. Seeing the cavalry escort, Kangarov frowned as though to say: "What is this for? But if it's the accepted custom, there is nothing I can do about it. . . ." They took their seats in the carriages and moved on, accompanied by the escort. The ambassador rode in the first carriage with the marshal, whose face remained absolutely void of any expression: looking at him one had as much reason to believe that he was attending a bridegroom on his way to the wedding, as one had to imagine that he was taking a prisoner to the gallows.

"Your capital is a beautiful city!" the ambassador said. "What amazes me most is how it combines majestic vistas with a feeling of coziness. . . ."

"Yes," the old man answered, apparently considering it superfluous to carry on a conversation: silence would accomplish just as much. Kangarov was somewhat puzzled and hurt by this show of a complete lack of interest in the Soviet Embassy and in the occasion itself which he considered historical: after all, it was a meeting of two contrasting worlds. Later he learned that the marshal had been performing the same duties for almost thirty years. In court circles he was criticized as being too unbending and lacking in cordiality. But nothing was done to replace him because he had occupied his position for such a length of time, because he belonged to one of the leading families and, chiefly, because he did not know how to do anything else. During his lifetime the old marshal had escorted to the presentations at the palace no less than two hundred embassies and delegations, among which there had been Chinese, Negroes, and Hindus. With an impartial lack of interest and amiability he had accompanied British lords and Malayan princes. There was nothing about the appearance of the members of the Soviet Embassy staff that could have startled him; probably he would have taken it as a matter of course if he were to see the ambassador wearing a quiver full of arrows at his belt. The marshal was even less impressed by the fact that the ambassador represented the first socialist republic in the history of the world. Unconsciously Kangarov caught his mood and remained silent. Fortunately, the distance between the embassy and the palace was very short. The carriages slowed down, the distinct clatter of the hoofs of the escort's horses became less rapid, and the huge gilded gates were thrown open. They entered the palace grounds.

The band was playing the "International." A guard of honor presented arms. Walking between two rows of soldiers, Kangarov, not too sure of himself, lifted his top hat. On the steps stood several men in uniforms embroidered with gold. "There is no way of telling who among them is a courtier and who is just a flunky, but for that matter there is little real difference between the two," Kangarov thought, trying to down his nervousness by affecting a polite contempt. He was afraid that he would make some glaring mistake. "But, in the end, what difference will it make? I have never pretended to be a prince of the blood, and there is no reason why I should know anything about their silly etiquette. . . ." Wislicenus watched him with a sardonic smile. In the immense reception hall a handsome, distinguished, middle-aged man, also wearing a gold-braided uniform and carrying a baton, stepped for-

ward to meet them with a kind, friendly, welcoming smile. This
was the chamberlain.

"I am very happy," he said and warmly shook the ambassador's
hand.

That day the lunch at the palace had been most unpleasant.
The king was very modern in his views and he considered that
while he was on the job (when he spoke about himself he always
jokingly referred to his "job"), regardless of his own feelings in
the matter, it was his duty to receive all kinds of people, to shake
hands with them and to tell them pleasant things. But when the
queen had entered the dining-room her face had been covered
with red blotches. Apparently she had been crying and the king
had felt rather uncomfortable. To make matters worse, they had
as their guest for lunch the old prince, who was known for his
difficult disposition, his outspokenness and his lack of tact. As the
oldest member of the reigning family he did not hesitate to express
his opinions to the king, whom he did not particularly like
anyway.

The prince detested everything new, beginning with socialist
cabinet members and ending with cocktails and grapefruit. He
was convinced that real life had existed only before the war, and
that decent history had come to an end, giving way to the heyday
of scoundrels and louts. That day at lunch, without any apparent
reason, he deliberately had spoken at great length about the
Russian Imperial family, about his pleasant meetings with them
in the old days, and about the horrible crime that had been committed in Yekaterinburg. Toward the end of the lunch, also without any apparent reason, he had asked the minister of foreign
affairs, who was present at the table, whether it was true that this
gentleman (he did not deign to mention the gentleman's name,
but everyone knew whom he meant) was a member of the central committee—or whatever they call it there?—which had issued
orders for the execution of Emperor Nicholas. Very curtly the
minister had answered that he was unable to answer the question.
The old prince had emitted a vicious cackle.

"Apparently our newspapers are also unable to supply this information," he said. "But I have read in the *Figaro* . . ."

Just then with inward joy the prince had remembered how on one occasion he had asked Clemenceau's opinion of this particular minister. The old man had answered: *"J'ai le plus grand respect pour ses fonctions et la plus vive amitié pour lui. Mais avec toute l'admiration que je lui porte, je dois dire en toute sincérité que c'est un vieux c . . ."* Whenever Clemenceau had opened his mouth, everyone had waited with joyful anticipation: you never knew what he would say! This answer had transported the prince into perfect ecstasy: he loved the peculiarities of the French language and he prided himself on being able to understand French idioms, but he seldom had the privilege of hearing such pungent words.

"It is unfortunate that you are unable to answer this question," the prince had said and, without addressing anyone in particular, had imparted the information that his late friend and cousin, Franz-Joseph, until his last day on earth had refused to receive the Mexican ambassador because his brother, Maximilian, had been shot in Mexico. "In our days everything was different, and people saw things in a different light," the prince had added. This time he was no longer merely disrespectful, he was being rude. However, the prince could permit himself to say things like that because of his age, because of the reputation he had established, and because he was not in any way dependent on the king, on the government, or on the parliament.

The blotches on the queen's face had become redder than ever. Hurriedly the chamberlain had interjected some remarks about the recent heavyweight fight, and about the amazing skill that had been displayed by the winning champion. He was very much pleased with the lunch. Every day he conscientiously worked on his memoirs, which were scheduled to appear in print twenty-five years after his death. This day seemed to hold in store some extremely lively pages.

The old prince had listened skeptically even to the mention of the heavyweight fight: what kind of champions could there be this day and age? Jeffries or Fitzgerald could have knocked either one of them out in the first round. Leaving after lunch, he had asked the chamberlain, in a loud voice, to warn him ahead of time whenever "this gentleman" was to be entertained at the palace. The chamberlain had bowed with a smile and had closed his eyes. Without worshiping them and without any undue obsequiousness he loved the royal family and considered himself a part of it. He was not interested in politics and did not presume to criticize the actions of the king. But it seemed to him that at least in one respect the old prince was right: something had changed in the world. In any case, the lively picturesqueness with which the prince said and did things fitted nicely into the memoirs.

After lunch the chamberlain retired to his apartments where he rested, contemplating with relish his memoirs and the old prince. He found it slightly disappointing that the book would not appear in print during his lifetime. Within a circle of close and dependable friends he had read aloud some excerpts taken at random and they had met with great success. Over a cigar he worked for a while on his stamp collection which now was the most important thing in his life. He was wealthy and not over-ambitious—he had accomplished everything he had wanted to accomplish. Society and what it had to offer bored him to death. He had a habit of repeating a saying which is ascribed by some to Palmerston and by others to an obscure French statesman: *"La vie serait très supportable sans les plaisirs."* As the years went on postage stamps absorbed more and more of his time. He had some fine items in his collection: the rose-colored stamp from Bagdad with the value omitted, the purple American twenty-four cent stamp which had not been released for public use, the blue "Lady Macleod" from Trinidad with a yellowish spot in the upper left corner, and the British Guiana imprinted *"patimus"* instead of *"petimus."* For obvious reasons he did not have in his collection the British Guiana, 1856, described in the catalog as "black on magenta, the famous error." He only dreamt about it in his wildest moments, and in the hope of getting it some day he had begun to save three thousand dollars yearly out of that part of his income which was set aside for stamps. In connection with that afternoon's presentation the chamberlain glanced casually at the part of his collection devoted to Soviet stamps. He had virtually all of the new issues, but so had most of the other collectors who belonged to his circle. "Perhaps I should try to get through 'this gentleman' a consular air-mail stamp at a reasonable price?" he wondered. It had been offered to him for fifteen hundred; he knew that by bargaining he could get it for five hundred dollars, but even that seemed too much.

Closing the album, the chamberlain put on his court dress, picked up the long gold baton (even after all these years he still felt self-conscious whenever he had to walk with the baton in his hand), glanced into the throne room and, reassured that everything was in order, exactly at three o'clock descended into the reception hall. While he was coming down the stairs he heard the strains of the military band and, though he was not familiar with the tune of the socialist anthem, he guessed that it was the "International." "It is fortunate the prince has left: he would have suffered a stroke if he had heard this music," he thought with a smile.

Wearing his customary official expression of welcome the chamberlain greeted Kangarov and firmly shook hands with all the members of his staff, who did not look as though they belonged in the palace. His gaze met the eyes of Wislicenus. "This one looks more interesting. He has character," he thought about him, almost in the same terms in which he thought about the prince. "The others are not much. . . . The young one looks like a penguin who has encountered the *Normandie* on his first venture from the home island. . . ." With inward pleasure the chamberlain made a mental note of this comparison for his memoirs. "Probably, after shaking hands with his excellency, Kangarov, and with the rest of us, the old fool with the gold stick would like to wash his hands in eau-de-Cologne. But I am even

more disgusted than he is," Wislicenus thought angrily, looking
around at the beautiful rooms through which they were being
shown. Watching him out of the corner of his eye the chamberlain felt his polite queasiness disappearing. "He is the real thing,"
he decided, leading the embassy into a tremendous hall in which
on a dais under a canopy stood a gilded armchair covered with
silk. "The throne!" the young secretary whispered ecstatically to
Wislicenus who stared at him with contempt.

With smooth unobtrusiveness and a gentle smile the chamberlain placed them in the proper order of precedence (once again
his eyes rested with strange uneasiness on Wislicenus) and asked
the ambassador's permission to leave them for a few minutes. The
moment he was gone another man covered with gold braid who
had been escorting them walked up to Kangarov and asked him
whether he had found the journey from Moscow very tiring.
"Tiring? Not in the least! Not in the least tiring," Kangarov
answered, speaking considerably lower than usual. His voice
almost cracked with excitement. He began to say something else,
but he did not have time to complete the sentence. The doors of
the throne room opened wide and a loud, strained voice called:
"His Majesty!" Accompanied by the minister of foreign affairs,
the chamberlain and several other men in uniforms, the king
entered the room. The ambassador and the members of his staff
made a deep bow, as they had been instructed in Moscow. Along
with the others Wislicenus bowed his head feeling a familiar
tightness in his chest as though he were about to suffer an attack of
asthma. "It would be worth it, just to make them all uncomfortable," he thought. Hurriedly the king walked up to the ambassador and quickly, as though he wanted to get the most unpleasant
part of it over, shook hands with him.

The ambassador asked permission to present his colleagues to
His Majesty and one by one called their names and positions.
Kangarov had gotten a grip on himself and he spoke louder than
was necessary. Silently the chamberlain looked on, beaming with
the smile of a proud parent. The king bowed acknowledging each

introduction and said something pleasant, using virtually the same expressions without actually repeating the same words. However, he did not shake hands with anyone except the ambassador. Later, Kangarov learned that this was considered a sign of lack of cordiality. The king deliberately remained within the limits of the required minimum of politeness.

With a bow the minister of foreign affairs handed to the king a large sheet of paper. Placing himself immediately in front of the throne the king stood waiting for the ambassador's speech. Reaching in his pocket Kangarov produced his sheet of paper and began to read. He had rehearsed the speech a number of times and his voice was clear and loud. He pronounced even the most difficult French words without any trouble, only his French *"eu"* sounded occasionally flat. Having finished reading, with an air of being pleased with his own performance he took two steps forward, handed the paper to the king with a respectful bow, and immediately stepped back to his original position. "He behaves like a duke," Wislicenus made a mental note. For a few seconds the king looked at the ambassador's speech as though he were trying to decide how to answer it. Then he handed it to the minister of foreign affairs and in turn read his own speech, his manner lacking the impressiveness of Kangarov. "He does not like it any more than I. He, too, must feel degraded," Wislicenus consoled himself.

Everything moved ahead with majestic ease. Both speeches expressed deep hope that between the two countries cordial and friendly relations would be established, in keeping with the interests, the feelings and the desires of the two nations. Both contained a solemn assurance that each country would scrupulously refrain from interfering with the internal affairs of the other. The minister of foreign affairs listened to them very attentively, as though the contents of the speeches were entirely new to him. Actually, he had spent a great deal of time studying one, and he had written every single word of the other. Besides interest his face expressed a deep conviction that each word spoken was

absolutely true. The chamberlain was very pleased, but for some
reason or other he decided that it was entirely out of the question
to broach the matter of the "consular air-mail stamp" to the ambassador.

Once again Kangarov stepped forward, with a bow took the
speech from the hands of the king, and, stepping back, handed it
in turn to Bazarov, fixing him with a stern glance, as if to say:
"You can think what you want, and inwardly I may agree with
you, but while we are acting in our official capacities, you will
have to do everything that is expected of you." At that point the
less important but the most difficult part of the ceremony was
about to begin. In accordance with court etiquette the ambassador and his staff had to retreat toward the door without turning their backs to the king. "I hope I shall not step on someone and
fall down," Kangarov thought anxiously. Nervously he glanced
over his shoulder like a fencer who looks over the ground just
before fighting a duel, and sternly gave a sign to his staff:
"whether you like it or not, that's the way you will have to do it!"
"We know all about these tricks and we'll do our part," Bazarov's
face seemed to answer with amused resignation. The chamberlain
looked forward to the next few seconds with pleasant anticipation: he was certain now that he would have to read this particular chapter to some of his closest friends. To his great disappointment, however, the ceremony of retreating toward the door
never materialized. Whether because of his absent-mindedness, or
whether because of his desire to make the embassy staff more
comfortable, the king made a quick bow, shook hands with the
ambassador and was the first one to leave the room.

The minister of foreign affairs approached Kangarov and
asked him whether he was happy in his new post. Shining with a
smile as though he just had passed with honors a difficult examination, the ambassador answered that he was extremely happy
indeed. "Your capital is a beautiful city," he said. "The loveliest
part about it is a combination of a feeling of coziness with such
magnificent vistas. . . ." He wanted very much to add that he

thought the king a delightful person, but behaving with great dignity he refrained from saying anything superfluous.

Just then an aide informed the ambassador that His Majesty would like to have a private conversation with him. Kangarov took leave of the minister and without a trace of his former nervousness hurriedly followed the aide. "He will be calling him 'my dear king' before very long," Wislicenus thought watching him.

The aide led the ambassador to an adjoining, small drawing-room. The king was seated in an armchair and with a friendly gesture he invited Kangarov to join him. These informal receptions which supplemented the official ceremonies were extremely trying for the king: by nature he was a most retiring person. Ordinarily, beforehand he outlined in his mind suitable topics for conversation with foreign ambassadors. Most frequently he asked about the health of the monarch whom the ambassador represented and about the members of the royal family, then he remembered and inquired after people whom he had met in the ambassador's capital, and next he mentioned in most cordial terms the ambassador's immediate predecessor. This type of conversation occupied ten minutes—the exact length of time required. In most instances the mention of political subjects was avoided. But in Kangarov's case there was no one about whose health he could ask, the ambassador had no predecessor and it was very doubtful that they had any mutual acquaintances. The king mentioned Moscow. He said he had visited there when he was a much younger man and that he had retained most pleasant recollections of his visit: it was a beautiful city.

"Your capital is a magnificent city, sire!" the ambassador said, using the word "Sire" with evident enjoyment. "I am constantly amazed by its majestic vistas which somehow blend with a feeling of coziness. . . ."

"I am very glad that you like it, Monsieur l'Ambassadeur. I hope you will be happy here. . . ."

The king wanted to say a few more words about the necessity for establishing cordial relations between the two countries and to mention that his government would do everything within its power to further this objective. He even began a sentence, but he let his eyes wander away and he never finished it. Quite unexpectedly for him, he suddenly felt that he could not go on with this conversation: he was likely to do or say something that he would have reason to regret.

"Yes, I hope you will be happy here," the king repeated hurriedly and arose, though instead of the customary ten, only three, minutes had elapsed. "It was very pleasant to see you," he said, shook hands with Kangarov and walked out of the room.

Not more than thirty seconds later the chamberlain joined the somewhat bewildered ambassador in the drawing-room. Engaging Kangarov in a polite conversation he led him into the large room where the members of his staff, the minister, the aide and the somber marshal were waiting for him. "You wanted me to remind you about the calls," the secretary said to Kangarov in a worried whisper. "Thank you," the ambassador answered and turning to the minister said: "I intend to make a number of calls in the next few days. . . . Members of His Majesty's family and cabinet ministers I presume. . . . I wonder whether you would be kind enough to indicate the order which I should follow?" Evading an immediate answer the minister promised to send him a list. "He should begin with the old prince who is perfectly capable of having him thrown out by the servants," the chamberlain found the thought amusing. The mental vision of the expression on the face of the prince when his butler should bring him the tray with the ambassador's card put the chamberlain in a mood of irrepressible gaiety. He decided to go back to his memoirs at the first possible moment.

The councilor, the secretary and Wislicenus took their seats in the second carriage. Bazarov was laughing: "What damned fools! But I must say we are not much better. . . ." "Speak for yourself, comrade," the secretary said in a hurt tone. Wislicenus gazed at the guard of honor standing at attention and had a vision of an armed mob storming the palace. "Perhaps we shall not live long enough to see that day," he absent-mindedly said aloud. "What did you say, comrade?" the secretary asked. "I said: he was determined to sell his life dearly," Wislicenus answered. The secretary opened his eyes wide. The carriage entered the square. "Long live the Soviets!" someone shouted from the sidewalk. Uncertainly several other scattered voices joined in the cheer. "A demonstration!" the secretary exclaimed with horrified delight and pushed himself further against the back of the seat: diplomats were not allowed to take part in political demonstrations. From behind, constantly increasing in tempo, came the soft, pleasant clatter of the hoofs of the escort.

VIII

TAMARIN arrived in Paris in the evening. He had never lived in France for any length of time and he was not as much at home there as he was in Germany where he had served several long assignments. It was twenty-five years since the last time he had been in Paris; before that he had visited there three times. In 1900, the year of the exposition, he and his wife had gone there on their honeymoon. It so happened that on his previous visits he always had arrived in France in the spring, in the midst of bright and balmy weather. Partly as a result of this he carried with him a permanent impression of cheerful, gay and carefree life and of an endless round of entertainments, traditionally associated with Paris by all foreigners and especially by Russians. This time it was a cold winter evening.

At the station Tamarin bought an inexpensive city guide and, waiting for his turn in the custom house shed, he glanced over the list of hotels. He and his wife had stopped at the Hôtel de Bade on the Boulevard—a better than average but not too expensive hotel: they never had had too much money. On his last visit when he already was a general and was aware that the center of the city had shifted to the Champs-Élysées, he had stopped at the Élysées-Palace. But the Hôtel de Bade and the Élysées-Palace no longer appeared in the city guide and he found this disturbing, as though a part of life he knew had vanished along with the hotels.

He saw no reason why the pleasantly stagnating backwaters of Paris should have undergone a change. It seemed to him that in the old days one had not waited quite as long at the custom-house, that the officials had been more polite and the porters more respectful. He tipped the porter three francs but he barely thanked him.

"*Chauffeur, êtes-vous libre?*" Tamarin asked. He spoke French like all educated Russians of his class and generation. Not too well, but never at loss for a word—at times he even permitted himself such expressions as "*Oh, la-la!*" or "*Tu parles!*" or "*Et ta soeur!*" Uncertainly he inquired about the Hôtel de Bade and the Elysées-Palace. The chauffeur laughed and in his turn said: "*Oh, la-la!*" but with an entirely different inflection: no one even remembered the Hôtel de Bade and the Elysées-Palace any longer. Tamarin at once decided that it would have been unbecoming for him to stay at such hotels anyway. He was working for a proletarian state and, besides, he could not afford it: his daily traveling allowance was not large and he wanted to save enough for a new suit. He told the taxi to take him to the Latin Quarter—a part of the city with which he associated pleasant memories. The hotel he selected did not look too Bohemian, but it was without any pretensions. The servants carried his suitcase to his room, drew his bath, and kept saying: "*Oui, Monsieur,*" and "*Monsieur désire?*" He could not become accustomed to being called "Monsieur"—it seemed to him that they were addressing someone else. In the bathroom were three normal-sized towels and one towel the size of a sheet. Tamarin had an odd feeling that he had never stopped in a hotel before. He put on his other civilian suit, the better one of the two, which had not been furbished and which had been made only three years ago. He had ordered it when quite unexpectedly he had received some royalties for the second edition of his book: *Some Thoughts on the Use of Motorized Infantry in the Light of Present-Day Tactics.*

The first thing Tamarin had to do was to report at the embassy. He studied the map of the city in an effort to find what bus would take him there, or what would be the shortest way to walk, but it was too involved and he decided that during the first two or three days he would have to spend some money on taxis. Leaving the hotel he walked down the street with the same feeling of unreality: he was in Paris! . . . The sound of voices, laughter and music reached him from the numerous cafés—there seemed to be a café in every building. "No sign of the Gay-Pay-Oo here! Don't kill, don't rob, don't steal, and for the rest you can do as you please. That's bourgeois morality for you." (Expressions like that had become with him a matter of habit.) The air was filled with the odor of automobile exhausts—a smell which in his memory he always associated with Paris. The traffic was heavier than ever: it was almost impossible to cross a street. He noticed a few innovations: metal markers on the pavement—very clever idea, he decided, as soon as he realized their use. Horses had disappeared. There were no top hats anywhere: that was too bad—he wondered what had happened to them? What else had changed? . . .

At the embassy Tamarin met with a very cordial reception. They talked for a while about work, but apparently there was no rush there. Cautiously, without ever becoming too pointed, they asked him for news of Moscow and he answered in the same vein. They jotted down his address without voicing any disapproval about his choice of a hotel. Just a few words of advice about where he could be comfortable if he should have to stay in Paris any length of time, but without any attempt to force their opinions on him—he had been afraid of this. He was asked to drop in, everyone was extremely polite, they even saw him off to the door. "Over here they behave like Europeans," he thought, very much relieved to find himself in the street again.

Tamarin walked back to the Latin Quarter. On the way over

he had made note of several landmarks and to his great satisfaction he had no difficulty in finding his hotel. There was no sense in going up to his room: what could he do there? He was in a very pleasant frame of mind. "Certainly nice to have this opportunity to be in Paris again. . . ."

Noticing everything about the windows, the people and the signs, Tamarin went for a stroll. "They live well . . ." He walked down the Boulevard, recognized the Panthéon, and was pleased that he had not forgotten it. "And that, over there, must be the Sorbonne. . . ." On his right was a dark garden. He could not remember what the garden was, but its somber winter sternness appealed to him. He made several turns and was delighted with the old narrow streets. For a second the headlights of a speeding automobile illuminated a dark, narrow passage in the wall of an old house. At the end of it was a bookstore. "How charming! The building must be at least two hundred years old . . ." Tamarin thought. He even was tempted to walk in and browse among the books, but the store was closed already. "I will have plenty of time to do it. . . ." Immense, solitary nose-glasses shone with deep-red light over the door of an optician—they certainly did not economize on their lights! The showcase in a drugstore was crowded with thousands of jars, boxes, bottles and cases—there was everything there one could imagine! In the window of a liquor store there were at least a hundred different bottles of every conceivable shape, flanked by clay jars and pitchers—how well and how cleverly displayed! Two huge posters hung on a shabby wall under a street light. "*Non, tout de même!* . . ." was printed in large letters at the top of one. "*En prison les bandits!*" shouted the other. All honest people, who still obeyed the dictates of their conscience, were invited to attend a large meeting of protest against the arbitrary and infamous acts of the South American Government. Among the speakers was the name of the famous writer Louis-Etienne Vermandois, which was headlined in big letters. Tamarin read the poster with a vague uneasiness. This was the first time he had heard anything about the outrages committed by this

Government. When he had almost finished reading he saw that the invitation was signed by the communist party. "There is no sense in coming to Paris for that sort of thing. . . ."

At the end of a wide street Tamarin saw a café aglow with lights of every color in the rainbow. The glassed-in terrace with a roasting pit at one end was filled with people. These roasting pits seemed also to be a new and practical invention! Outside, on a bench by the door stood a row of baskets filled with oysters, shells and all sorts of sea monsters. *"Clams," "Claires extra," "Armoricaines," "Oursins,"* Tamarin read and found pleasure in the very sound of the words. Suddenly he felt that he was hungry. He looked at the menu card displayed in the window and his eyes ran eagerly over the various *"Sole au Chablis," "Rognon de veau flambé à l'Armagnac," "Pied de Porc Ste. Ménehould," "Faisan cocotte aux truffes . . ."* Cautiously he glanced at the prices. A good dinner would come to about forty, or possibly fifty francs. Quickly he added in his mind what he had spent during the day: the lunch on the dining-car, the porter, the taxis—a lot of money. "The first day is always more expensive and I cannot hope to stay within the allowance. . . ."

Tamarin entered the café—it was wonderful! Probably if an establishment of this sort had opened in Petersburg or in Moscow in the old days, Tamarin would have been horrified. The walls were in three shades of yellow, with uneven, unsymmetric mirrors and with something greenish in the recesses. Apparently the only objective the decorator had had in mind was to arrange things so that no one could guess where the lights originated. For that reason all the lighting fixtures were carefully concealed, and the few that were visible looked like soup plates, containers used for developing films, or hothouse glass roofs. But mixed with these bashfully hiding rays were other green, red and violet lights which glared brazenly out of projectors shaped like long glass tubes: the only conceivable purpose of these was to spoil the eyesight of the patrons. Instead of a ceiling there was a cupola reminiscent of St. Peter's. The café was so crowded that Tamarin found it difficult

to push his way in. "Perhaps there are some seats upstairs," he
thought walking up the stairway. Under his weight each step
seemed to repeat the same, nonsensical word: pergola, pergola,
pergola . . . "Stop that!" he tried to brush aside this peculiar
impression as he took a seat by the railing overlooking the main
floor.

A bus boy in a white jacket approached the table at a trot.
Two soup plates resting on metal shafts—one on each side—
exploded with light, and with a pleasantly contrasting glow a
small lamp with a shade which did not pretend to be anything else
came to life on the table. "How very comfortable!" Tamarin
thought, finding special charm in the humble, unassuming table
lamp. A wildly dressed woman—he was not certain whether she
was Albanian or Mexican—walked over and took his coat and hat.
A boy in a green uniform came on the run offering newspapers.
A more dignified but extremely obliging man dressed in a plain
dark suit approached him, straightened the table a little and
presented him with the menu and a wine card. The seat was not
too good—it was too close to the bar. "Perfectly satisfactory . . ."
A lady dining with a young man at a neighboring table glanced
quickly at Tamarin. "She is beautiful . . ."

Tamarin looked downstairs at the main floor. "Good Lord!
Not a single empty chair! And they say that their entire social
system is collapsing in this crisis. . . . No, it looks as though
capitalism will be with us for some time to come. . . . But in the
old days the crowd looked smarter. . . . Our girls are prettier, but
these look much more civilized! . . ." All the ladies were wearing
furs. "Some have a single black fox, others have two. I suppose it
denotes rank, as in the Red army: a division commander has two
bars, a corps commander has three . . . This one must be an
army commander—she has a whole cape of black foxes! Four
bars! . . ." He felt gay. Everything delighted him: the ladies, the
bourgeois civilization, the murals picturing naked women with
snakes—"who knows? maybe that, too, is very good,"—the lobsters
which stood out like bright, recklessly colorful spots on the white

tablecloths below, the serving table next to him on which there were at least ten different kinds of mustard, the fact that his neighbors were being served some dish which was burning with a pale blue flame, and the fact that on their table there was one bottle standing in a bucket and another one lying in an elongated basket.

The dinner Tamarin ordered did not denote a gourmet, though once upon a time he had known how to eat. From a lack of habit his eyes could not rest long enough on any one item on the menu. He ordered only half a bottle of wine which he did not know by name. He was not a heavy drinker. The wine was good, and the food: an oyster cocktail, some sort of Navarin de Homard, and kidneys—excellent. He had not dined like that in twenty years! In recent times Tamarin had not been hungry in Moscow,—"but they have no conception what such dishes are like —they don't even understand what they mean! Just reading the menu makes me hungry. Almost as good as it was at Donon or at the Praga in the old days. . . ." An orchestra began to play a medley of tunes from "Carmen." Tamarin laughed aloud from sheer joy of hearing melodies with which he had been familiar since childhood. He was sorry he had not ordered sherry. "Papa, God bless him, always drank sherry with his meals. . . . But, I suppose that as long as I am in Paris I should be drinking French wines. . . ."

When the orchestra reached the toreador aria, however, Tamarin's mood underwent a change. Around him people hummed and sang the familiar tune as well as they could. They all seemed proud that they knew the aria and swinging back and forth in time with the music they kept repeating one word over and over: "To-re-a-dor . . ." For some unknown reason Tamarin remembered once again his meeting with the diplomat in the Berlin station: this memory had bothered him ever since. He remembered a state ball at which William II had charmed everyone with his hospitality, he remembered a hunting meet at some castle with an unpronounceable name, he remembered an actress to whom the diplomat had introduced him years ago: they had spent several gay months together. This had happened thirty-five years ago, no, it had been longer than that: thirty-seven or thirty-eight.

Tamarin's memories went back to his wife. Their marriage had not been a happy one, chiefly on his account, though at the time he had believed that she was to blame. "We never did understand each other until the very end. . . ." With amazing clarity he remembered that night, the Marinsky theatre, the unpleasant conversation on their way home, and the absurd, hysterical quarrel, which began over the way in which the tenor had sung his part. "I told her . . . No, what's the use of thinking about it now. . . ." The orchestra began the overture to the fourth act. The young man at the adjoining table put out the table lamp but promptly switched it on again at the request of the lady who slapped his hand. "We had a lamp like that on the piano in our drawing-room. . . ." Tamarin remembered every detail of that small room the walls of which had been covered with dark brown paper, and the lamp which had stood on a lace center-piece. "We were always so terribly afraid of scratching the piano! . . ." They had quarreled in that very room. He had wanted to separate, to get a divorce. She had threatened to kill herself. . . . "Was it worth quarreling about? Where is she now? No one except me remembers her, and when I am gone nothing will be left, just as there is nothing left of the lace center-piece, or of that brown wallpaper, or of the oyster cocktail I have eaten. . . ."

In this café where several hundred people had gathered and were enjoying themselves Tamarin suddenly felt as lonely as though he were in the desert: no one, not a single person, not a single soul anywhere near! "I, a senior officer in the service of the world-socialist revolution . . . Pergola, pergola, pergola . . . How did it happen? How is it possible? What is the reason for all this nonsense? Not only for this but for all nonsense? Why did my life, which now undoubtedly is drawing to a close, have to follow such a strange pattern? Pergola . . ." "Ta-ra, ta-ra," a lady who had a little too much to drink was trying to sing the first strains of the overture. Tamarin wanted to get up and leave, but he knew that in a new place with thoughts like that on his mind he would not be able to go to sleep. At home, in Moscow, where the walls had a quieting effect on him, only work, persistent work, saved him from them. "What should I do?" he wondered, with an effort trying to control his rapid breathing. "Why did it have to be that way? And in spite of it all we did scratch the piano. . . ." The music stopped, followed by a burst of applause, and from the main floor came the spirited buzz of voices determined to make up for the time which had been lost to chatter. "I like only good music," the young man at the adjoining table was saying. "If someone does not know how to play I would rather not listen. . . . Don't you think I play well?" "Certainly, you are a wonderful musician, but you are also getting very impudent," the lady answered, interspersing her words with laughter.

IX

THE GUN was a good one—a five-round automatic with etched steel facings on the stock, with a safety and with a front-sight blade shaped like a half-moon. A Browning would have been too expensive and, besides, it was not a question of long-distance shooting. Unfortunately the gun had no name; sonorous, double-name trademarks are pleasant to the ear: Forey-Lepage, Webley and Scott, Holland and Holland. In describing the gun the clerk had been vague: "It is of a very fine quality. A Belgian make of the Smith and Wesson type. You will like it, Monsieur." Alvera was pleased with his purchase. The Belgian gun did not bulge in his pocket. At least, on the train from Paris to Louvécienne no one had given him a second look.

At dusk the forest was deserted. "The air is really wonderful. It certainly is clever of them to live in their own houses in the country, outside of Paris. . . . If I ever become rich, I shall follow their example. . . ." With curiosity Alvera looked all around him. During his entire lifetime he had been in a forest only three or four times and that had been in the days of school picnics. He did not know the names of the trees and he could not tell them apart. "I believe this is an oak. But it may be a maple or a chestnut. When I have time I will improve my education in this field and take a regular course in natural history. I will do that as soon as I have a suburban house. . . ." He thought that they would consider it "cynical" on his part to buy a house in the very village where he intended to commit murder. "I suppose that to hold target practice in the same village is also 'cynical.' But if they consider it cynical that is the very reason why I am going to do it."

Alvera looked over his shoulder: there was no one in sight. During the fifteen minutes he had been walking through the forest he had not seen a single, solitary soul. But he pushed on farther into the thicket, walked another hundred feet and began to choose a tree. There was no reason why he should prefer one tree to another. He chose a large oak (he made up his mind that it was an oak) and only then remembered that he had nothing he could use for a target. "Why didn't I think of it before, damn it!" He went through his pockets in search of something colorful and bright, but there was nothing there except a pocketbook and his *carte d'identité*. He certainly could not use that as a target!

In the inside pocket of Alvera's overcoat was a book: *Crime and Punishment*. He carried this book with him on purpose, to spite them. But he loved books, and it seemed a shame to tear out a page. The yellow cover would not be a good target; something white would stand out so much better. The book opened on a page with a turned-down corner: "*Raskolnikov se laissa tomber sur la chaise mais ne quitta pas des yeux le visage d'Illya Petrovitch qui semblait fort désagréablement surpris. Tous deux pendant une minute s'entre-regardèrent et attendirent. On apporta de l'eau. —C'est moi . . . commença Raskolnikov. —Buvez une gorgée. Raskolnikov repoussa d'une main le verre et doucement, avec des pauses et des reprises, mais distinctement, il prononça:—C'est*

*moi qui ai assassiné à coups de hache la vieille prêteuse sur gages,
et sa soeur Elizabeth et qui les ai volées . . ."*

In the margin, opposite these lines, was written: *"Un fameux
crétin, celui-là!"* Alvera always was amused by this passage. "Yes,
he is absolutely a cretin!" he thought, meaning both the Russian
author and the confessing student. It occurred to him that the note
in the margin could be used as evidence and he tore out the page.
The end of the volume containing advertisements and announce-
ments of new books had not been cut. Absent-mindedly Alvera
tore the pages apart with his finger, looked with displeasure at the
ragged edges, and tried to even them by tearing off tiny pieces of
paper. He strode over to the oak and tried to fasten the sheet to
the trunk approximately on a level with his eyes. Fumblingly
he pinned it under a loose piece of bark, but the first gust of wind
blew it down. With a curse Alvera took out of his pocket a narrow, cheap ebony-covered penknife and frowning at the effort—
he always was afraid of breaking a fingernail—opened the single
blade. Then, holding the sheet of paper with one hand against
the trunk, with a strong thrust he drove the knife through the
paper into the tree. The sheet remained hanging there, its edges
stirring gently in the breeze. There had been something pleasantly
final about the thrust of the knife—a touch of Gustave Aimard.
He felt that he still was something of a boy and smiled. There had
to be a black circle on the paper. Alvera reached into his pocket
for his fountain pen and was annoyed to discover again that the
thin, inexpensive clip had become loose and that the pen was
buried in the depths of his pocket. That was bad: the top would
be filled with ink and there would be smudges on his fingers. . . .
He was not surprised to find the end of the pen above the small
point of artificial gold entirely covered with ink. Holding it carefully by the other end he tried to draw a circle, but the bark under
the paper was rough and the ink was dry. He gave it a shake, the
last drop of ink fell to the ground and the pen was empty. Angrily
he pulled down the sheet of paper, rubbed its center against the
point and tried to pin it back with the knife. But this time the

thrust was not a success, the blade snapped shut and nipped his hand. He winced and dropped the knife—no, thank God, there was no blood! Without any more flourishes Alvera cautiously attached the sheet of paper, with an ink-smudge in the center, to the tree. Then carefully following the clerk's instructions he loaded the gun. He carried the ammunition in a separate box. On the way down he had wanted to avoid any possibility of an accident on the train.

With his thumb Alvera jiggled the safety catch. He was not sure when the gun was on safety: when the button was up or down? "I believe it has to be up, but I better check it. . . ." He unloaded, tested the catch and reloaded: now he was certain how it worked. With precision Alvera measured off five paces—this he found pleasant; it made him think of a duel. For the last time he took a quick look around—no one was in sight. Planting his left foot a little farther back than the right one he flexed the knee— he had heard that some guns had a strong recoil. He stretched out the right hand with the gun, closed one eye, took aim—the front sight blended with the ink smudge—and fired. The sound was much weaker than he had expected, and he did not even notice the recoil. Once again he glanced around, stuck the gun in his pocket and walked over to the tree. He was disappointed to find that there was no hole in the ink-smudge, or, for that matter, anywhere in the paper.

Once more Alvera measured the distance, again counting off five paces, but this time taking shorter steps. He was shocked to notice that he had put the loaded gun in his pocket without placing it on safety. This proved that he was not sufficiently calm. "I will have to take myself in hand. I am not the same person I was a minute ago. I have told myself that I am not afraid of anything. At any moment I can kill myself, a few seconds of suffering and then everything will be over, so there is nothing to fear. Certainly there is no reason to have any regrets about this life or about them." He began to shoot again, this time feeling calmer and more sure of himself. Altogether he fired ten rounds (the little box held twenty-five rounds of ammunition). He hit the paper three times: twice in the edges and once very close to the ink-smudge. The results satisfied him. The main thing was to learn how to shoot and how to handle the gun.

Having finished everything he had set out to do that day, Alvera with a feeling of relief stuck the gun in his pocket and while putting away the book in his overcoat pocket came across a crumpled piece of paper. "Damn it!" This was a sheet he had spoiled while copying a manuscript for his client. Before leaving home he had by mistake included it with the others, and noticing his error on the train he had put it away in his overcoat pocket. "Too bad I forgot about it. It would have made a better target and I would not have had to tear the book. . . ."

Alvera returned to the main road and started in the direction of the railroad station. "Yes, the whole secret is to make the murder a perfectly natural part of the daily pattern. I must acquire the habit of firing the gun, but that alone will not be enough. . . . For the sake of experience it would be a good idea to shoot a dog. The sensation should be essentially the same—the only difference is the fear of the guillotine. It is a simple matter to kill a man. Granted certain habits, it is just as easy to murder without any trivial qualms, without any self-explanations, and without pretending to be a Napoleon, as it is for a butcher to slaughter cattle. During the Middle Ages executioners had all the necessary habits and they got along very well without any philosophy. I suppose the Vampire of Düsseldorf in the end also acquired the necessary habits, but in his case there was a sexual motif which to me is filthy and incomprehensible. People like that are a living insult to the philosophers who believe in the divinity of nature."

The forest began to thin out and houses became more frequent on both sides of the road. A woman walking in the opposite direction looked at Alvera, glanced around and began to walk faster. Consumed with curiosity he read the signs with the names of the houses and of their owners, as well as the occasional posters on the fences. Two lions in a circle stood on their hind legs above two crossed keys and an inscription: *"La Vigie mobile. Propriété guardée."* He wondered whether it was a profitable enterprise and what steps they took to guard their property. A black arrow pointed the way to the church and to the town hall. On a square sign decorated with black and yellow triangles—"how ugly and how stupid!"—was a drawing of two little girls walking hand in hand—"nasty-looking brats and it certainly would not be any great loss if some reckless driver should run over them." Just then a car appeared in the distance. Deliberately Alvera walked on heading straight for it and stepping aside only when he was a few feet away. The man behind the wheel shouted something highly uncomplimentary. "How strange that we should feel so safe in our daily lives. One wrong move by this cretin, a moment's lag of attention, an extra glass of brandy at lunch, and I would be dead. There are thousands of drivers in Paris, and this means that the life of every Parisian depends on millions of such trivialities. This means that my chances of survival are no worse than anybody else's. . . . This means . . ." He was tired of these eternal, boring thoughts. "If you want to kill, go ahead and kill, but don't try to fool yourself about it," he said to himself. He laughed as he read a sign on the fence: *"Défense de déposer et faire des Ordures sous peine d'Amende."* The fact that *"Ordures"* was spelled with a capital struck him as being especially funny. Absent-mindedly he glanced at his watch: there were still eighteen minutes left until train-time. His watch was four minutes slow. It was early.

From the crossroads a footpath led toward the house. Alvera was tempted to stroll that way, but he decided against it. It would not contribute anything as far as habits were concerned and it would involve a certain risk. There was always a chance of meeting the idiot. "He would be very much surprised and would ask: 'Why haven't you left yet?' Then I would have to tell him that I had forgotten the number of the last page I had given him, and did not know what number to use on the next one. Very likely this would make a good impression. Perhaps he would even be so moved that he would offer to pay me for the short lines. 'Young man, I never pay for short lines as a matter of principle. You should not expect monetary rewards for things which do not involve work.' I suppose it is also a matter of principle with him not to pay me for the paper, or for the railroad fare, or for the time I lose, as though it is a part of my duties to bring the work to Louvécienne." "Young man, you could have sent it to me by mail," he said aloud, imitating his client's voice, though his client had never said anything like that to him. The question of lost time had never been mentioned. "I could not tell him that I came here to look over the ground because I intend to murder him," the very thought seemed ridiculous. "If I am caught I shall say that I murdered him because he refused to pay me for the short lines. This will be proof that I am a 'moral idiot,' and it is useful to be a moral idiot when one is accused of murder. . . ." Lazily he thought about Jacqueline: she was a charming girl.

A train whistle blew in the distance. Alvera exclaimed: "I am late! Now I shall have to wait another half-hour!" He glanced at his watch—he still had twelve minutes. "This must be a train going in the opposite direction. . . ."

Alvera stopped in front of a huge white billboard with a green border around it, and with a picture of two exceptionally vigorous-looking green figures of a boy and a girl. An athletic society was inviting young people to enroll. "*Pour une jeunesse saine, forte, joyeuse, le sport c'est la joie et la santé* . . ." "If they are so healthy and gay already, why in hell should they want more gaiety and health? How idiotic! '. . . *La fédération sportive et gymnique du travail vous accueillera dans un de ses clubs* . . .' What does '*gymnique*' mean? I never have heard such a word. Apparently this invitation is addressed to me too. I am what they call '*jeunesse saine, forte, joyeuse*'! . . ." He laughed again and read every word, including the information about applications and yearly dues. Applicants under eighteen were entitled to special rates. "Too bad it does not apply to me: I am past twenty. . . ." It occurred to him that in the criminal courts also he would not be entitled to special rates. He was familiar with the legal definition of a child and of a person under age. "Twenty is just nice and ripe for the guillotine. . . ."

With malicious delight Alvera imagined the amazement of Vermandois when he should read about the murder in the newspaper: "His secretary! His secretary and such a sordid affair! He will be particularly horrified because he will have to be a witness, first during the preliminary investigation and, later, in court: how boring and what a loss of time! And the reporters! They are paid so much a line and they will gather like vultures to ask questions: one good, decent murder and they can enjoy life for two weeks! But publicity, even in connection with such an affair, is still advertising, and there is no such thing as bad advertising. . . . Later it will occur to him that I could have killed *him* just as easily, and then he will pant and be covered with cold sweat from fear. And why shouldn't I kill that third-rate maniac? Only because suspicion immediately would point in my direction: I am the only poor man who visits his apartment. . . . Vermandois is a communist or something of that sort, but he cannot stand poor acquaintances. Besides, the police would make a special effort to find the murderer of a famous writer. On the other hand, if I kill him I can count on a permanent place in the history of literature. I don't believe there ever was a case like that. That also would be the only thing that would perpetuate his fame: his present immortality will last exactly one year after his death, until his successor is elected to the Academy. No one reads him now, anyway: he has been a 'cher maître' for thirty years. But when he calms down a little he will make it a point to display his generosity. Probably he even will find a lawyer for me—someone who is so-so, not too expensive. Though at his request even the most expensive lawyers will be glad to take the case without a fee—they all like advertising. . . . Perhaps he will even come to see me in prison and bring me a quarter of a pound of sliced ham. . . . No, he will not bother to do that—it would bore him too much. But I can depend on seeing him in the court-room and on hearing him say a few tearful words—something about modern youth and about the disintegration of ideals. He will never pass up such an opportunity, knowing that every daily paper will devote at least twenty lines to him. They will call him *'le grand écrivain,' 'le célèbre écrivain,'* and *'l'illustre écrivain.'* The jury will listen to him with tears in their eyes, and then they will find me guilty without any extenuating circumstances. First of all because I shall be guilty of robbery and to them this will mean that I could have robbed *them* just as well, and secondly because I am a *'sale étranger,' 'un de ces étrangers indésirables qui viennent chez nous et qui . . .'"*

Seven minutes remained until train-time: it was still early! Alvera stopped in front of another old, weather-beaten poster. The local branch of the communist party invited everyone to attend a meeting: *"Pour . . .* (several words were illegible) *. . . liberté! Pour . . . blique des Soviets en France!"* Alvera read the poster with distaste: he had no use for communists.

The low, yellow-grey railroad station loomed in the dusk. A number of people were hurrying across the square. "No one will notice me in this crowd. . . . Why should they look at me and, besides, this time it does not make any difference. . . . They can stare at me if they like. . . ." There was no guard at the door and no one asked to examine his ticket. "This is a fine state of affairs!" He tried to think of ways in which a dishonest passenger could take advantage of the department of railroads. "They will ask for the ticket at the exit in Paris, but there is nothing to prevent me from getting off the train at the last station before Paris and buying a ticket there. That would be much less expensive. Haven't these idiots thought about it?"

Alvera strolled along the platform continuing to read the signs with the same absorbed interest. "Danger! Beware of third rail. . . ." "This is an electrified railroad. If I stand with one foot over here and place the other one on the third rail, it will be the end. A painless death . . . Very much like the electric chair. . . . Often it is the fate of a perfectly innocent person to suffer a much more painful and violent death than the deaths of the so-called criminals. . . ." He wondered for a while which was better: the electric chair or the guillotine? "They say that in Sing Sing it lasts for several minutes. Flyers say that when there is an airplane accident the fall also lasts two or three minutes. On the other hand, a cancer of the tongue takes years of torture to kill a person. . . ." This brought to his mind a whole series of unpleasant words: *"la kératite interstitielle, l'hépatite diffuse, les convulsions épileptiformes, le retrécissement mitral* . . ." "I suppose that degenerate piece of humanity will die sometime of some rotten, painful disease, without any help from me. . . . If they chase me I always can jump on the third rail. Then I will be glad to give them a welcoming hand. It will mean one less bastard in this world."

With a nervous yawn Alvera reached the end of the platform, turned around, and stopped in front of a huge thermometer on top of which extremely gay-looking men dressed in red and white were carrying a tremendous bottle. "Saint-Raphael Quinquina." He did not remember ever drinking any, at least he did not remember the taste. . . . As a rule he drank very little: " '*Jeunesse saine, joyeuse* . . .' What was the third word?" It worried him that he could not remember the other adjective.

A cock crowed in the distance. Alvera was surprised. He always had believed that cocks crowed only at dawn. Only now he noticed that the entire village of Louvécienne was submerged in a sea of green. On both sides of the station, as far as the eye could see, there were trees, shrubbery and flowers. "I would not mind buying a house and living here . . . I might even buy the very house—probably it will be sold at auction. That would be very amusing and it would do away with any suspicions that might linger. What murderer would ever buy a house where he would be haunted by his victim's ghost? A good point to mention to the lawyer. If Vermandois comes to see me in prison I shall tell him that I committed murder to spite Dostoyevsky. He will be delighted and he will use this brilliant paradox in his next novel. 'The novels of the great Slav moralist have only the effect of stimulating the criminal tendencies of the unfortunates.' "

A passenger strolling along the platform looked curiously at the short, emaciated, ugly youth whose face was disfigured by an expression of suffering and horror, as though he just had experienced a major tragedy. "He even can call the novel 'The Crime in Louvécienne' . . . No, this would sound too vulgar to him. It will be a psychological novel filled with brilliant conversation and that will bring him an advance of thirty-thousand francs. Someone should warn him: '*Défense de faire des ordures . . .*'" Alvera laughed, and saw in the distance a slow-moving green train consisting of a few cars. He was surprised that there was no sign of an engine or of smoke. Then he remembered that it was an electric railroad. "I was thinking about it only a few minutes ago," he sighed deeply and took a seat in a second-class coach. "They call it second-class to make fun of us. Actually, it is at least fourth-class. They have done everything they could to make traveling uncomfortable and disagreeable. But, then, any man who does not have the money to buy a more expensive ticket must be punished. . . ."

X

DARKNESS HAD settled when the train reached Paris. Absent-mindedly Alvera headed for the exit. His ticket was collected at the gate. "No, I suppose these highwaymen know how to go about it. Their entire lives depend on routine. If it were not for the routine, they could not exist." The street lights were on already. The stores were closing their doors. He began to walk faster: with the exception of some butter and eggs—two to be exact—which were left from the day before, he had no food in his room. Food was cheaper in the section of town where he lived, but he had a long way to go. He had to do his buying now. Mentally he added the money at his disposal. He had left the house with fifty-five francs, he had received eighty-four for his work, the return ticket had cost him eight, and he had bought some bus tokens for six francs. This left one hundred and twenty-five. He stuck his hand in his pocket. The fountain pen was loose again and he could not find the hundred-franc bill. For a second he was chilled with fear. "Good God! No, no, there it is!" The change was also there, his calculations had been correct. "Day after tomorrow I will receive two hundred from Vermandois. This should see me through. . . ."

Turning into a side street Alvera stopped in front of a meat market. A huge, bloody carcass was hanging by the door. For three francs he could buy a steak, take it home and fry it. But the sight of blood seemed even more revolting than usual. The butcher, almost as bloody as the carcass, came out of the door carrying a two-pronged stick. While Alvera was watching him he deliberately went through the motions of closing the store, as though he guessed that the customer was about to buy a steak and intended to show him that he could get along without his three francs. Next door Alvera bought some ham. "Three francs' worth—sliced. And two francs' worth of sausage without garlic." The salesgirl sliced the sausage with evident impatience—perhaps she too wanted to display her contempt. He watched each move of the big knife and it occurred to him that an executioner must have the same agility, steadiness and precision of movement. "This ham guillotine is very much like the real one. . . ." He bought some cheese and a couple of apples, all the time relishing the thought that the flippant salesgirl had to wait until he was through with her. For once, the established custom was on his side. With a pleasant realization that he had not exceeded his budget by a single penny, he paid for his purchases.

The bus which Alvera intended to take stopped right in front of the store. His favorite seat inside was not occupied: it was the one by the window, in the two-passenger section. This was very lucky. He dropped the packages in his lap, pressed his feet against the wall, and leaned heavily against the back. His head touched the hat of a woman sitting behind him and she angrily mumbled something unintelligible. A lady was sitting next to him, but he did not even look at her. He felt the light touch of her body when she arose, at the bridge. Only then he noticed that she was young and quite good-looking. He was surprised that he had not been aware of her presence until then.

The bus route went past the court-house. With a lazy indifference Alvera tried to picture his own trial. "In which room will they hold it? Which way will the windows face? Maybe these are the very ones?" He had a mental vision of the judge and of the prosecutor. The jury will retire to their room. He will be left alone with the gendarme who will try to avoid his eyes because, according to the great humanitarian writers, as a true man of the people he will feel sorry for him. "*A Dieu dans ses pauvres . . .*" "It must be a joke to call the poor, 'His poor': if they were His, He could make them rich. . . ." The bus turned down the Boulevard Arago. "They usually erect the guillotine between those two trees. . . . *'Du courage, Alvera, l'heure de l'expiation est venue. . . .'* I shall have to force a smile, but I don't imagine that it will look very cheerful, though if I try hard enough probably I will be able to oblige. 'I have been ready for a long time. . . . And, besides, if I were not ready what difference would it make?' I will try to avoid the parting embrace by the lawyer. Instead I will take a cigarette and a glass of rum, and I will say: *'Merci, Monsieur, bien aimable . . .'* Then the first glimpse of the machine and the usual galvanizing, nervous shock . . . No, it will not be so terrible. At least by constantly thinking about it I can train myself to feel that way. Strangely enough, even in the matter of death habits play an important role. It is difficult to shoot or to hang oneself because one is not accustomed to handling guns and ropes. Poison is much easier because swallowing is something we do every day. . . . Actually, murder can be considered a complex form of suicide. . . ."

Absorbed by this interesting thought Alvera got off the bus at his usual corner. He walked up to the seventh floor, where he rented a servant's room without the privilege of using the elevator: "this also is a punishment for being poor." There was no running water in the room, but otherwise it was comfortable and well furnished. He had gathered the furniture gradually by shopping in second-hand stores. The mahogany-finished desk was quite nice. Everything was in perfect order. Neatly arrayed on the desk were an inkwell, a reading lamp and a container for pens and pencils. Every book had its own place on the shelves. According to the numbered catalog which he painstakingly had compiled he had two hundred and ninety-six.

Once again regretting that he had torn a page out of it, Alvera put the book in its proper place, and absent-mindedly stuck the paper he had used as a target in the middle drawer of his desk. He kept everything of importance there: the notebook, his lyceum diploma, letters of reference and paid bills. Then he took off his collar, hung his necktie on a ribbon which was strung on the inside of the cupboard door, slipped on his soft slippers and was irritated to discover that his big toe had made a hole in the right sock. He placed the food supplies on a small, unpainted table, went into the corridor for some water, made tea over an alcohol burner, lighted a second lamp on his desk and saw a bill from the electric company. Yesterday he had forgotten completely to send them their money! This was the first notice, there was no way for them to turn off the current, but he became excited nevertheless. He made it a practice to pay his bills promptly: the laundress, the bakery, and the newspaper woman. In his pocket notebook he put down a reminder to send the money off the very first thing in the morning. "I have enough money right now."

His secretarial duties and the copying brought Alvera at least eight hundred, and sometimes a thousand francs a month. He seldom experienced any actual need. During the winter months he had even managed to save a little, but now the money had gone for underclothes, a suit, and shoes. He had to be presentable to keep his secretarial position with Vermandois. "That bastard orders his clothes from the best tailor. I bet his red bathrobe alone cost more than I make for an entire month's work. . . . By New Year I should be able to save another thousand. . . ." He was amazed at himself: what was the sense of thinking about savings and the New Year if he intended to go through with his plan? With a thousand francs the lawyer would have difficulty in claiming that he was destitute and hungry, especially in view of *"ces étrangers qui viennent chez nous . . ."* The only evidence that Alvera was a foreigner was his passport. His father, who had escaped from South America after some revolution, had brought him to France before he was three. He spoke only French, he did not know and did not want to know any Spanish, and he was embarrassed by his long name: Ramon-Gregorio-Gonzalo. The Gonzalo part seemed particularly vapid and ridiculous, and it annoyed him most. In the lyceum he had been known as Raymond Alverá, with the accent on the last syllable. "But the police will be certain to dig up the Gonzalo."

In the cupboard which Alvera had bought for fifty francs and which was worth at least two hundred (he had most pleasant recollections of this transaction), just to the right of a neatly stacked pile of folded towels which formed a boundary for the section devoted to linen, stood a jar of cherry preserves. He felt that this jar was a symbol of something shameful and at the same time cozy. Hungrily Alvera ate his supper, drank a glass of tea, filled a second one a third of the way with preserves and placed it on the desk, put away what was left of the food, and rinsed the dishes. Then he took out of the drawer a fat notebook handsomely bound in cloth. It contained his great work: *The Energic World Conception.*

Alvera had planned this work while he still was in the lyceum, soon after learning that energy can be expressed as a product of which the multiplicand is the mass and the multiplier the intensity, and that physical equations change with the decrease of the multiplier. This thought had interested him then, and he frequently had returned to it. Gradually it had occurred to him that it was possible to create a social-philosophical system based on a mathematical formula. He imagined a large, beautifully made book in which every word flowed logically from one source. He bought a notebook and in an uneven line, which tended to bend upward at the right margin, wrote on the first page: $A = U + T\frac{dA}{dT}$ Now, he no longer remembered clearly what these letters were supposed to designate in physics. The basis of his system was the development of the multiplier which represents intensity. Twenty blank pages were set aside for the mathematical part of his work; he could fill these out later when he was more familiar with physics and mathematics. On page twenty-one began pure sociology—there were thirty-seven pages of it. Opposite page two hundred was a marker. Here he copied the final versions of his poems, each line having a seemingly irresistible urge to curve upward. Alvera dipped the pen in the inkwell and at once felt that his work would not progress today. Lazily he drew an obscene figure in the margin and immediately regretted it—why should he deface his own manuscript? Angrily he put the notebook back in the desk drawer.

The room was cold, much colder than the outdoors. "Is it possible that I am catching cold?" The warm blanket on the bed looked very inviting to Alvera, but it was ridiculous to go to bed at nine o'clock. As a compromise he could lie down for a while and cover himself with the overcoat. But he also knew if he were to take a nap for a couple of hours that he would not be able to go to sleep again until morning. Nevertheless he decided to compromise, took the first book he could reach on the shelf—it happened to be number sixty-four—and stretched out on the bed twisting his body so as to avoid the sag in the mattress. But like everything else in the room the sag in the mattress was comfortable and his own. Sounds of music reached him from below. On the sixth floor the daughter of the landlady was playing the piano. "If she does not stop at ten o'clock I will make a complaint: she has no right . . ." He strained his ears, but could not recognize what she was playing. "It's something very hackneyed and familiar. They certainly should change the entire conception of music. It cannot go on like this. The public has no appreciation whatever. If the pianist hits the keys like a blacksmith and puts his entire weight on the foot pedal they are impressed with his power. If he plays pianissimo they like his soulfulness. . . ."

The music stopped. Alvera read the book mechanically, almost without thinking: he knew that whenever it should become necessary he would concentrate on it and form an opinion. The pleasure he was deriving from the book at the moment was automatic, the kind he derived from walking or relaxing. Once again his thoughts turned to his philosophical work. "Perhaps in considering the multiplicand of mass I place too much emphasis on habit?" A new idea occurred to him and he knew that he should write it down at once, but he did not feel like getting up and sitting at the desk. "I believe I really have fever: the room cannot possibly be as cold as this in summer." Shivering with a chill and with excitement he turned over the pages. "*Le coeur débordant de passion, la tête forte d'un enthousiasme raisonné* [Alvera laughed aloud], *les yeux perdus dans la contemplation des splendeurs qu'elle entrevoit, l'humanité se dirige, irrésistible, vers la Terre promise où chacun pourra vivre dans la paix de son coeur et de sa conscience, aimant et aimé, sans contrainte et sans haine, sans envie, sans entrave, dans le rayonnement bien-faisant des passions satisfaites, dans l'affinement vigoureux des facultés décuplées dans l'épanouissement fécond des originalités et des caprices* [he laughed again], *dans la suave caresse des rêves et des aspirations vers le sublime et l'idéal, les sens apaisés par des fêtes de la chair réhabilitée, le cerveau élargi par la science fortifiée, l'oreille bercée par l'harmonique vibration des choses, le coeur gonflé de l'amour d'autrui . . .*"

Alvera was very much amused. The anarchists were even sillier than the communists. This one realized clearly that it is possible to kill and to rob, but he was afraid of killing and robbing, so he invented all sorts of subterfuge. "Individual acts of murder and robbery corrupt and degrade a human being." "But isn't it just as corrupting and degrading for me to have to beg all kinds of bastards for work as though I were asking them for a favor, or to

have to be ingratiating with people whom I despise and hate?
This gentleman, like all the rest of them, makes a career out of
beautiful words. There were no openings among the socialists, so
he called himself an anarchist, which also happens to be a beautiful
word. Just wait! I will show you *l'harmonique vibration des
choses!'* " he thought in a sudden fit of fury. "As though people
live for the sake of an ideal, or for any other plausible reason!
They live because they are alive, and when they die they are
dead!"

The light hurt Alvera's eyes which always were red and
slightly swollen. A medical student and a former classmate of his
at the lyceum had warned him: "Be careful! It's a chronic condition of the conjunctiva." Alvera lifted his hand from under the
coat and turned the switch. The pale glare of the street light
penetrated the room. It became more restful than ever. "I suppose
even a rat is fond of his hole and finds it cozy. . . . Until I have
broken their laws no one can enter here and no one has the right
to disturb me. Tomorrow I will go to a café and order hot coffee
and rolls. My lunch and my dinner are assured, unless Vermandois fires me, but he would not have the nerve. Everything here
is mine. . . . Are these mere appearances, or is this real human
independence? At the meeting the anarchists squawked that
France was a land of slavery and of flag-waving fascists, and on
that score I was inclined to agree with them. But at the door stood
a detachment of police who were there to protect them in case
they were attacked by fascists or by communists. Are these mere
appearances? Perhaps, after all, my entire plan is nothing more
than monumental stupidity?" Dispassionately he went over all the
arguments against it. "Well, I still can change my mind, there is
plenty of time!"

The possibility of a delay appealed to Alvera. At that moment
he felt certain that he would change his mind. "Yes, this is a cozy
rat-hole. . . . In daylight the curtain on the window is especially
inviting. It looks like a dispersion spectrum." The comparison
with the drawing in the textbook pleased him, as well as the fact

that he remembered it so well. "Come what may, this night is mine, even though it will last only five or six hours. Human life consists of parts, of tiny, very tiny parts, and each part has to be considered and evaluated separately. For this part I am grateful, though no one in particular is responsible for it. There is a possibility that the most valuable part of my life will be spent in prison, perhaps the five or six hours in the cell just before the execution. But the sum of all these parts is always the same: zero. . . ." He remembered that on the way from Louvécienne something else pleasing had occurred to him, something that concerned someone else. He no longer evaluated his own and other people's thoughts by their content, but only by the effect they had on him, whether they produced in him a sense of satisfaction or irritation. "What was it? Oh, yes . . ." The thing that had pleased him so much on the train was the mental picture of Vermandois' amazement, horror, and embarrassment when he should read in the paper about the Louvécienne murder. Alvera laughed happily and immediately fell asleep. In a faraway, ancient land a shepherd had a quarrel with the sun. To punish him the sun made a law—a charming law, which benefited the descendants of the shepherd: *jeunesse saine, forte et joyeuse* . . . That was the third adjective, thank God! All this was followed by a nightmare. A maid in the adjoining room awoke, cursed and angrily decided that tomorrow she would complain to the landlady about the young scarecrow who screamed at night, and who like an idiot disturbed working people who had to get up at six in the morning.

XI

"Am I becoming sentimental in my old age?" Wislicenus wondered irritably. He could not control his excitement. This was the street and it had remained virtually unchanged. Only on the right side, directly opposite the house where Ilyich had lived, was a

long new red building. Before, in the same spot, there had been
a garden belonging to a convent or to some other church institution—he never had been certain about it nor sufficiently interested to find out. But with the exception of this offensively new
building everything else in the tiny street remained the same. On
the left was the same monotonous mass of tall, narrow houses.
His heart began to beat faster. During the quarter of a century
nothing had changed about the house. The balconies on each
floor, the quaint metal ornaments on the central balcony, the glass
door in the deep recess of the dark entrance. In the evenings they
had stood there, some dubiously, others with more self-assurance,
forever repeating: "*Cordon, s'il vous plaît* . . ." Ilyich always was
deathly afraid of any arguments with the janitress; he had been
forced to move from his previous apartment because of this:
"*Cordon, s'il vous plaît.*" The low door leading into the cellar—
that was the door he had used in the spring when with a feeling of
exhilaration he had brought out the bicycle. Suddenly Wislicenus
had a vision of Lenin standing by that door, looking like a country
bumpkin in his shirt sleeves rolled above his elbows. In those days
you could come out into this street looking like that—probably
people still did it in warm weather. "Oh, it's you! How are you?
Why don't you ride a bicycle? If you want one we will get it for
you on the installment plan. It will be useful in your work, you
will enjoy it, and it will be good for you. . . ." "He always was so
amusing. . . . I don't remember seeing these signs before: '*Pi-
qûres. Ventouses. Massages médicaux.*' No, I am sure they were
not there in those days."

Someone peering out of an open window on the third floor
stared curiously at the strange, lanky man who, without moving,
with his feet spread wide, stood like the Eiffel Tower directly in
front of the house entrance. "This is so stupid. There always is
something weird and stupid about any pilgrimage. . . ." Wislicenus had an irresistible desire to walk up to the second floor,
ring the bell and find some pretext to look inside. Who possibly
could be living there now with no notion of who his predecessor

had been? What possibly could occupy the right corner of the study in place of the low, wide divan with a cover over it and with a chessboard on the arm-rest at one end? "It's so weird, so stupid, and so enervatingly sentimental. . . ." Wislicenus turned away from the door and walked in the direction of Avenue d'Orléans.

The lights were on now. From somewhere in the distance came the sound of music. Their entire lives had been spent in this quarter, between Lenin's apartment and the printing press. They very seldom had ventured into the city (they always had referred to it as "the city"). Wislicenus' memory was bringing everything back: he was touched by the sight of the familiar street signs, and he was surprised that they should affect him so: after all, there was no reason for the names of the streets to change. "Here I bought tobacco. I never had money enough to buy cigarettes and, besides, the mechanics of making my own were restful for my nerves. Even then my nerves were on edge," he thought with satisfaction; "if they had been on edge then, they could not be so bad now. Here at six o'clock I bought the *Temps*. The news-stand is still there. And here I could get sausage on credit. . . ." Suddenly a savage anger stirred in him at the recollection of how on one occasion, when his bill had reached the amount of thirty francs, the owner had given orders not to let him have anything more on credit. The salesgirl had been so embarrassed when after wrapping it she had had to put back the package which contained the sausage with the meat-jelly center: "exactly like the sausage they have in the window now. . . ." Certainly there never had been anything pleasant about hunger and the necessity of finding ways to earn a few pennies; there was no reason for him to feel nostalgic about it. Prices had changed—he remembered clearly what he had had to pay for everything. He experienced an old man's delight in these trivial recollections and in the fact that everything then had been so much cheaper. "But if there is nothing left except the joys of old age, probably it is time to quit! . . ." From a *rôtisserie* a block away an aroma reached his nostrils. He could not see or remember what it was, but with sudden vividness the odor brought to him memories of his youth and of Paris of the old days.

Nothing had changed about the house where the printing press had been. The same second-hand store had a display on the sidewalk; colorful things of all kinds: linoleum, brushes, handkerchiefs, pieces of wallpaper,—beggarly luxuries to tempt the poor. Wislicenus emitted an exclamation: the same owner in a black skull cap was sitting behind the counter, but now he looked very ancient. "The French are a people who cling to life and abhor changes. . . ." There was not any more for him to do here than there had been in front of Lenin's house. It was silly to stand there gaping: life was the same, but it was strange and foreign, even more so than it had been in the old days. The sound of music became stronger, he saw a merry-go-round. Some sort of a public celebration was getting under way. "For some reason even then they were always celebrating something. They are a people who enjoy life. . . ." The sight of other people's gaiety was disagreeable to him.

The unpleasant appointment was set for seven-fifteen in their café. Wislicenus did not know the address of any other café in Paris and that was why he had chosen this one. He knew that the conversation about the important political matter would be extremely unpleasant and he intended to be through with it within thirty minutes. At eight o'clock he was scheduled to have dinner in a restaurant with Kangarov, who recently had arrived in Paris.

Wislicenus had parted with him some time ago. At work their relations had remained cool and correct, as before. They both tried to avoid talking to one another unnecessarily. Whenever they met, Kangarov began to smile at a distance, but his eyes turned yellow. On occasion, in the course of their conversations, they exchanged some disagreeable remarks, but this usually was done in the form of friendly advice proffered out of the best-intentioned party considerations. Soon after he had been presented to the king, Wislicenus had received orders to go on a special mission to Spain. He had remained there longer than he had foreseen. He had run into Kangarov quite unexpectedly at the Paris embassy. While he still was ten feet away the ambassador had begun to smile sweetly; he shook his hand with warmth and invited Wislicenus to join him for dinner in the restaurant.

"With all the trimmings, if you please," Kangarov had said and in the way of an explanation had added: "Siegfried Mayer—you know, the German émigré?—wants to meet you. He has been on my trail about it. Instead of making a separate appointment with him, why don't you come along and have dinner with us? . . . That is, unless you have some very important secrets to discuss?" he had said with an inquiring smile. Wislicenus had not answered, and Kangarov's eyes had become yellower than ever. "At the same time you will have a chance to see Nadia. She also has been asking about you." "Is she here, too?" feeling the blood rush to his face, Wislicenus had asked, though a moment ago he had intended to refuse the invitation. "Yes, I brought her with me because I need an interpreter. I don't seem to be able to master the finer points of the French language, and when it comes to languages she is tops," the ambassador had answered with affected indifference. "Thank you very much. I shall be glad to come. I really should take a look at this Mayer," Wislicenus had accepted, also affecting indifference. "How is she?" "Who?" "Nadia." "Nadia? Fine. She is blossoming. She has taken to Paris like a duck to water. We shall expect you at eight sharp. Better make a note of the address." "Thank you." They both had been embarrassed. "Blushing like a damned fool!" Wislicenus had cursed himself inwardly and had taken immediate leave of the ambassador. "Certainly he noticed it. How could he help it? . . ."

In the café Wislicenus hurriedly took a seat against the wall: suddenly he felt very ill. His chest hurt as though someone were driving a stake into it. The pain spread to his shoulder and then down in his hand. "Strange. This never has happened to me before. Could this also be the result of my asthma? No, there is no use in fooling myself, it's the heart. No sense in being afraid and trying to evade it with words like 'weakness' or 'neurosis.' What difference does it make? The important thing is that it looks pretty bad. . . ." A waiter brought him a glass of milk. A young man sitting at an adjoining table looked with condescension at his glass. From somewhere in the back came the inviting, clear sound of clicking billiard balls. As usual the chess enthusiasts of the fourteenth district were playing at the same tables. Exchanging remarks in lowered voices, onlookers crowded around the tables of the best players . . . "Don't you want to move your castle? Why bother with the bishop?" "Don't count your chickens before they are hatched!" "Who is counting chickens? Just listen to him! You should be playing in the sand-pile instead of trying to play chess! . . ." Wislicenus' excitement was bordering on hallucination. "I know that people have hallucinations simply because I have read about it in books, or because I have seen it in some old-fashioned melodrama on the stage. Now I should be seeing Ilyich taking his seat behind the middle table over there, behind his table. . . ." And almost at once he saw Lenin at his table, surrounded on all sides by people who answered his unpretentious jokes with respectful laughter. All these half-starved, funny, futile men, who almost had turned the entire world upside down. Now nearly all of them were either in their graves or in prison. The most famous among them had been executed only a short while ago. "I suppose before their death they too remembered this café, the public celebrations in the street, the two-room apartment, and our printing-press . . ." "C'était une erreur! Il ne fallait pas sacrifier le pion!" "Vous n'y entendez rien, mon vieux." "C'était une erreur, vous dis-je. La combinaison était fausse! . . ." an angry voice reached his ears. "Yes, yes, that's it. La combinaison était fausse . . ."

"No matter how you look at it, the error in our combination was due to the fact that our theory was built on faith in man, on faith in his dignity and in the possibility and necessity for his moral improvement. In practice, however, everything had to be based on the assumption that man is stupid and foul, and because of that— temporarily, only temporarily of course!—he had to be made even more stupid and foul for the sake of the ideal and of ultimate success. Lenin had developed this line of thought, but he had concealed it from us until the time came to carry out some of his decisions. We, a band of political outlaws, followed him just as we always followed him. Like all great generals, by the grace of God and by the use of some very simple methods he had succeeded in developing soldierly qualities in us and in winning our love, our respect and our loyalty.

"The experiment was carried out. It proved that a human soul cannot exist under the terrific pressure to which we exposed it. Under such pressure people turn to slime. We were depraving them in the name of a socialist ideal, but they became depraved without any aim or objective. Step-by-step, without being aware of it, we created a society never before known to the world. We offered no correctives of our own for the traditional, bottomless human baseness, but at the same time we did away with all other, old and tried methods of restraint. Then something happened that even the most practical among us could not foresee. The cancer which we had introduced into the souls of the governed soon spread to the rulers. We discovered that force, which always has triumphed in history for its own sake, in order not to cease being a force requires resistance within the surroundings in which it exists. As soon as the governed ceased to resist we also turned to slime. We had contaminated them with a form of moral syphilis, but they in turn contaminated us, and we became depraved, crippled human derelicts, who had lost respect for everyone and for ourselves.

"If there was any subject which had been overlooked by Ilyich it was the one of human happiness and of the moral qualities of humanity. To him it was shallow and boring, just as the ennobling influence of chess and all sorts of vague references of this kind are shallow and boring to the chess-player. Actually his entire power of concentration was centered on the game itself. If Ilyich had given frequent, precise, and imaginative thought to the human being as such, he never would have accomplished anything. Part of his strength was due to the fact that he never gave him any thought. He played his great game, the game of misanthropic, inhuman socialism, by building on the eternal hatred of the poor for the rich. No one before Lenin had appreciated with such clarity the potentialities of this force which had given us victory and power. We gave this hatred an outlet such as it never had received anywhere before in all world history. But this release was not enough to sustain even the older generation. And as for the younger generation they cannot understand it because they never have been in contact with the rich. It is impossible to live on hatred for something that no longer exists. They see the rich only in the movies, and when they see them their feeling is one of envy rather than of hatred. In the West, democracy destroyed and continues to destroy socialism by serving as its substitute. It feeds the people a spoonful at a time of that substance which socialism always promises and never supplies. Because of their short-sightedness socialists of the tame variety defend democracy without being aware that it slowly is gnawing at their vitals and in time will devour them. But by contrast with us they enjoy one opportunity. Without seeming to appear Machiavellian, cautiously, without taking any undue risks and with advantage to themselves, they can wave the red rag. That is something we no longer can do. We, ourselves, have become the red rag, though the bull has learned to bide his time and to control his instincts. For their privations, for their hunger, for their enslavement and debasement, for the crippling of their souls, for their own cowardliness, for their inability to resist, they pay us back with a savage, brutal hatred. And being aware of their dull, concealed and inarticulate hatred we cannot afford to change our methods. We are responsible for this vicious circle. We have led them back on the path to medieval gangsterism, and now the only kind of leaders they recognize are gangster leaders. During recent years our entire history has narrowed down to the hunt for potential gangster leaders,—a hunt without any pretense at ideology or, at most, justified by an ideology invented on the spur

of the moment to fit the circumstances. That is why rivers of blood
have flowed, are flowing and will continue to flow. It is something
that Lenin had not foreseen. Life has turned out to be even more
misanthropic than Lenin, and it has led us haphazardly no one
knows where or why—there is no compass and the Pole Star is
hidden. As is usual in such situations the leader of the gang turned
out to be the most ruthless and fearless individual. But twenty
years like that could not fail to leave a mark even on him. The
clever, unfaltering, crafty leader has been inventing crimes against
the state and throwing criminals to the mob for so long, that now
he has come to believe in them himself. We are living in an age
of police mythology, and that only increases the dull hatred for
us throughout the country. The people cannot understand why
some of us are worse than others as long as we, ourselves, cannot
understand it. No one knows who will be right when history
makes its final appraisal: perhaps it will be Trotsky, perhaps—
Hitler . . .

"Without adhering to our ideals, at times completely forgetting them, we, in our blindness, ascribed some inner force to them.
Now it has become apparent that they never had any inner force,
that our victory was due entirely to our methods, and that we
could have achieved as much or more with any sort of ideology,
no matter how ridiculous or absurd. We failed to make an allowance for the irrational nature of hatred. Far away, beyond the
boundaries of our jurisdiction, people appeared who had understood that our strength was due to our methods and that we had
nothing else to offer. Very quickly they assimilated the lesson in
irresponsibility, in lack of restraint and in mental self-indulgence,
which we had taught the world. They created a force of their own,
camouflaged in a different color, but which just as easily, just as
successfully, and just as surely turned people into dirty slime.
Erring in our application of the law of great numbers we had
assumed that in every society we could incite the millions of poor
against the thousands of rich. It has been proven that it is just
as easy to incite one million against another million, simply by

changing the approach, the bait, and the slogans. In the formula take what has been taken from you' the psychologically dominant factor turned out to be the word 'take.' We tried to persuade the German worker to consider himself the salt of the earth because he is a worker. Instead, he has gone insane with the joyful realization that he is a German. And if their philosophy is just as capable of providing people with happiness, why should anyone prefer our brand? . . .

"Two human herds are facing one another. So far, the leaders have been held back by the fear of making a wrong decision. There is no reason why they should want to exchange their assured position as generals for a gamble in which the stakes are a marshal's honors against the executioner's noose! Their doubts are the doubts of inveterate gamblers who all their lives have been playing for large stakes and who are about to place everything they have on the line. The entire fate of humanity depends on when and how these extremely determined individuals will overcome their final doubts.

"Well, let it come! We cannot survive a war, and for that matter neither can the others. There is always a remote chance that we may be overthrown, but with a war this chance becomes a certainty. All these things have to be brought to an end, and the quicker the better. A delay of a few more years is conceivable, but a delay of another ten years will bring with it a complete moral ruination of the human race. No matter how horrible our experiment it will have to be tried all over the world. The fact that moral syphilis is inherited does not prove anything. An immunized generation still can create a society which the best and the most stupid among us had dreamed about in this very café. . . ."

A tall red-haired man wearing a grey overcoat appeared in the café door. Wislicenus took one look at him and became taut. "Where have I seen him before?" he anxiously asked himself. "What a disgusting face! . . ." There was something gross and predatory about the stranger's features. He stood for several seconds in the doorway, letting his eyes roam over the café as though he was looking for someone. His glance reached Wislicenus, rested on him for a mere fraction of a second, and Wislicenus immediately realized that he was there to see him. For some reason his heart began to pound. Squinting his eyes unpleasantly the stranger walked past him to the far end of the room, looked around and shaking his head returned to the door. A piece of paper was lying on the table in front of Wislicenus. "Good work," he thought. He had no inkling of how or when the note had been placed there. "But why should he go to all this trouble?" The man in the grey overcoat was no longer in the café. For a full minute Wislicenus sat without moving. Though no one was watching him he did this automatically, as a matter of habit. Then he unfolded the note and read it. The appointment he had made for seven-fifteen had been canceled.

XII

NADIA was delighted when unexpectedly Kangarov told her (he purposely had saved it as a surprise) that he was taking her to Paris. "You will be my interpreter, my child. Thank your papa and mama for making you study foreign languages," the ambassador said with a gay and bustling air. Now he openly addressed her as "my child," and whenever they heard him the members of the embassy staff merely assumed expressions of forced innocence. The secretary especially was punctilious about showing his sentiments in the matter: "Why not? It's perfectly understandable; I don't see anything wrong with it." Nadia knew that her trip with Kangarov would serve as a target for gossip and questionable jokes, but she did not care. Her attitude toward her colleagues was one of cool indifference. "If they want to gossip, that's their privilege." The prospect of spending two or three weeks in Kangarov's company was not very enticing, but when would she have

another chance to see Paris? Everyone insisted that next to Red
Moscow, Paris was the most wonderful city in the world. Besides,
she had no choice in the matter: she had her orders from her
superior.

Before their departure Kangarov had another scene with his
wife. Helen Kangarov assumed the tone of a martyr, taken from
the last act of "Mary Stuart": "Earl of Leicester, you have kept
your word. You have promised me your hand to lead me out of
prison. And you are here. . . ." Because of the revolution Helen
Kangarov never had had an opportunity to play the part of Mary
Stuart. But the manner in which she intended to play opposite the
Earl of Leicester the brief last scene before the execution was sensational. The audience was to be shaken particularly by the pause
which she planned in the middle of the sentence: "And you . . .
are here." She tossed the words "are here" in a throaty, clear voice
and with her head lifted high retreated to the back of the stage,
while the crushed Leicester stood with his face buried in his hands.
For several seconds the bewitched audience sat silently, then there
was a deafening burst of applause, and for a long, long time the
auditorium resounded with shouts and screams of delight. Helen
Kangarov was especially touched by the tribute of silence which
preceded the outburst. Though situations of this kind are impossible and never have been known to arise since the creation of the
world, she had read about such moments of triumph in a biography of a great actress. She fully intended that it should appear
in her biography which was to be published at the right time,
illustrated with numerous photographs and with her name in gold
letters on the cover: "Helen Zapolski." She did not like the name
Helen: it would have been so much better if her name were
Ariadna, or at least Irina.

Whenever his wife assumed the tone of a martyr Kangarov
was driven to a state of cold fury. He tried to be very curt and
told her that he was going to Paris on a matter of state and that
he was leaving her, thank God, in most comfortable circumstances: "you have never lived like that before, my dear." He met

with little success, and Helen Kangarov's tone became even more haughty—the tone from the third act: "What words I'm forced to hear! If the crown on my head does not command respect, then, Sir, my suffering must. . . ." A recent examination by a doctor had revealed that Helen Kangarov's blood pressure was one hundred and fifty and any excitement was bad for her. Their parting was very cold. Nadia was not in any way to blame for their quarrel, but the departure took place under most unpleasant circumstances. "The temperature is ten degrees below absolute zero. The ambassadress is out shopping for sulphuric acid," Bazarov announced cheerfully. "I don't understand exactly what you are trying to imply," the secretary answered coldly.

On the train Kangarov bored Nadia to distraction by telling her stories, by his fatherly attitude, and by calling her "my child." His jokes never varied and he always repeated them at least twice in succession. If they were appreciated he made it a point to shout with laughter and to repeat the last line for the third time. Usually he began laughing even before he told the story: "this makes me think of something I heard. . . ." But, all in all, their journey was quite pleasant: when the train made long stops they walked together along the platform, they took their meals together in the diner. Though Kangarov had been brought up in a poor family he knew good food. Unconsciously Nadia envied him: he had something to say about each dish and he ate with such obvious pleasure and appetite: "I have dined in the finest restaurants in the world, my child," the ambassador held forth. "But let me tell you: anchovies, chopped herring and salted cucumbers are better than the rarest delicacy. Believe me, the mark of a true gourmet is the appreciation of simple dishes as well as of fancy things. That is the difference between a gourmet and a snob. But despite this we will visit some of the finest restaurants in Paris. They know how to cook!" "I have never been in a famous restaurant, but I still think that they eat better in Moscow than they do in Europe," Nadia said. Kangarov looked at her appraisingly out of the corner of his eye.

They discussed everything except politics. With a great deal
of enthusiasm the ambassador talked about love, casting sweet
glances at Nadia (this always amused her), about the people he
had met, and about his tastes. To her great amazement Nadia discovered that he was genuinely fond of farming, vegetable garden-
ing and flowers. He was full of technical information about tulips
and he rattled off scientific terms which Nadia never had heard
before, such as *Tulipa pubescens* and *Rex rubrorum*. The lore of
the tulip fascinated him. He told her that the origin of the word
"tulip" was connected with the Turkish turban, which it resembled, that in Holland the *Semper augustus* had been responsible for a state crisis, and that in the language of flowers a tulip
stood for pride (here he gave Nadia a significant look). He was
so carried away that he even drew a luxuriant tulip on the back
of the menu. It was rather a nice drawing. "How strange!" Nadia
thought. "I would have sworn that the only things that interested
him were his career and women. . . . This is a very attractive
trait in him. . . . Apparently no person is entirely bad." Becoming confidential Kangarov confessed that he always had dreamed
about a piece of land of his own: he wanted a small place (he
almost called it a villa) somewhere (he did not say where) so he
could plant trees and flowers and keep dogs. "You are positively a
bourgeois at heart," Nadia said with a laugh. "Why bourgeois?
Socialism believes only in the common ownership of the tools of
production. I should be happy to stay out of politics." "I wonder
who is stopping you?" Nadia thought and to add zest to the conversation said: "I bet your little place in the country, your apple
trees and your dogs would bore you in no time at all!" "Bore me?
Never! You don't know me, my child!" the ambassador exclaimed
with a great deal of feeling and was on the point of adding: "If I
were there with Helen probably I would hang myself from sheer
distress, but if you were along! . . ." But he stopped short, and
heaved a deep sigh instead.

In Paris they stopped at a very good hotel. The ambassador
chose a suite of two rooms with bath for himself, and a small

but nice room for Nadia on a different floor so as to avoid any unnecessary grounds for gossip. "Well, my child, now we will have to part," he said. "We can clean up after the journey, take a bath, call up a few people, and then we can have dinner together. If you feel like it you can have a look at dear Paris before dinner. It's a lovely town, even though August is a bad time of the year to see it." He wanted very much to be the one to show Paris to Nadia, but he could not expect the child to wait until he was free. "But be careful! Don't get run over! That's strictly against orders." Nadia pretended that she was frightened and immediately disappeared, delighted to be rid of him. "Now I can enjoy myself! . . ."

In the best of moods Kangarov sent the bellboy for a morning paper and was undressed by the time the paper was stuck through the half-opened door. With a sense of well-being he settled into the tub full of water: he loved to read while sitting in a hot bath. There was plenty of time: it would be a whole hour before he could call anyone. He glanced at the headlines and for a second his heart stopped beating. A number of persons who only recently occupied some of the most important posts in the Soviet government were accused of the most unbelievable crimes and scheduled to go on trial. The news was so important and so sensational that even the foreign newspapers had devoted to it huge headlines on the front page. According to the story the accused had made a clean breast of it and confessed. But Kangarov barely took time to read that part of it: the accusations were so absurd. "Good God, what is he trying to do?" the ambassador whispered. "These men were Lenin's right hand!" He knew well the men who apparently were doomed to execution; he had worked, dined, joked, and exchanged thoughts with them for a great number of years.

Quickly Kangarov scanned his memory for recollections of associations with these men in recent times and during his entire career. "No, there was nothing there that could be misinterpreted," he thought with relief. But these days it was impossible to say what could and what could not be misinterpreted. Kangarov's governmental and party career had followed different roads at different times. On occasions it had taken a path which now was obviously in disfavor. Horrifying thoughts occurred to him: "They will dig out of the files my old article: 'Come to Your Senses, Renegades!' They will relieve me of my duties and recall me to Moscow! Whenever anyone is relieved of his duties it means prison. If they showed no mercy to the others, prison is the best I can expect. Maybe I should tender my resignation and refuse to go back? . . ." For a second he tried to imagine the attitude of the White Russian emigration toward him. "They have no special reasons to hate me personally. . . ." He considered the state of his finances—how could he possibly live abroad? Then he was struck by the absurdity of these thoughts. His face was a deathly white; he sat for a long time in the tub thinking. "What should I do now?" There was nothing he could do. The character of the Moscow events did not require any action on his part. "The party! There is always the party!" he thought and tried his best to get himself in the soldierly frame of mind, reminiscent of 1918: the party is always right, the party needs, everything for the party. . . . But he immediately was aware that the rôle of an old sergeant, which never had suited him, was now less convincing than ever.

Suddenly Kangarov remembered Nadia. At once it was clear to him that everything else: the party, his career, the receptions at the palace, the inner satisfaction derived from successful diplomatic moves—everything was of secondary importance. Only one thing was real: Nadia. "Yes, I am in love, absolutely in love! I am willing to throw away everything for her! I cannot live without her! I don't want anything else: I only want to be where she is. . . ." By comparison, all considerations connected with his career and all fears of what awaited him faded into insignificance. "If they should recall me I would go back! But they are certain to separate us at once. . . ." Moved by his own sincerity he thought that the finest form of happiness he could wish for would be to live with Nadia on a small piece of land, where they could build a cottage and grow flowers. "How futile all this superficial glitter, these diplomats, these speeches, these receptions! I may have yearned for them before, but now I have had enough of them. There is nothing more I can expect in the way of a career and there is nothing else I want!"

Though the water in the tub was hot Kangarov's teeth were chattering. Once again, this time in greater detail, he mentally went over all his associations. "No, there is nothing to fear, even if they should dig up 'Come to Your Senses, Renegades!' The only thing they can have against me would be his desire to get me out of the way. But that is nothing new! Others have incurred displeasure before, and so far they have left me alone. . . ." One of the important questions was the effect which the Moscow events might have on the standing of the commissar for foreign affairs. It could be one of two things: on the one hand, judging by the combination of his party, office and, most important of all, personal ties, it would appear that everything in the case of the commissar was in order; then again, because of certain other combinations, you never could be sure. Kangarov thought about his other colleagues in the department. The position of some of them was much more vulnerable than his. This had a calming effect on him.

Kangarov climbed out of the tub and, wrapping a towel around his middle, picked up the telephone. He spoke in an unusually mettlesome voice as though nothing had happened, and he was answered in an unusually mettlesome voice, also as though nothing had happened. There was no mention of the Moscow events. Casually Kangarov asked about the health of the commissar and at once felt that just then it would have been more judicious to refrain from asking questions of that kind. But it seemed that the commissar's health left nothing to be desired. The conversation had a reassuring effect on Kangarov. "Why should it affect me?" he decided and began to dress. From another telephone conversation he learned that there was a great deal of work to be done and that probably he would have to go to Amsterdam. This too was consoling: apparently no one considered that there had been any change in his position. By the time Nadia returned, Kangarov had regained his composure. As soon as he saw her he felt at once that nothing else mattered. Just so long as she stayed here, by his side, and continued to chatter: "A lovely place! A lovely city! But our Moscow is better!" He affirmed every word she said with an enthusiastic nod.

Life settled into the usual routine of work, business lunches and receptions. Nothing of a disturbing nature happened, apparently the storm had blown over. Within their own circle they cautiously discussed, in passing, the recent events. "Who would have imagined that any of them could have sunk so low?" A few days later Kangarov had to go to Amsterdam. This time he could not take Nadia with him and before leaving he entrusted her to Tamarin's care. "She will be safe with him; at least he will not permit himself to take any liberties," Kangarov thought, while aloud he said: "Be stern with her, Your Excellency! If she misbehaves, my dear commander, just make her stand in the corner!" Nadia pretended that she was pouting. "I shall have no trouble handling him," she thought.

And it seemed that the commander could be handled without kid gloves. To Nadia's great delight he immediately told her that he was busy in the mornings, but that after seven he would be at her service. Nadia spent entire days sightseeing, looking at the various quarters of Paris, and visiting famous historical sights and museums described in the city guide. Every few steps she paused in front of a store window, sighed, prepared new estimates for her budget and hesitantly went inside. But the more things she bought the more obvious it became that she needed others. "It's a bottomless pit. I could spend hundreds of thousands like that. Too bad!" Nadia was discouraged. She had only a very limited amount of money at her disposal.

Everything about Paris appealed to Nadia: the streets, the buildings, the museums, and especially the Galeries Lafayette. She resented the fact that most things were better than they were in Moscow, and she was extremely happy whenever she found something that was not as good. The fact that the walls of the Paris subway were not paneled with marble pleased her, but it would have been even more pleasant if Paris had not any subways at all. "Their mileage may be ten times greater, but that's only because our socialist construction began so recently," she thought. Invariably, whenever she met Tamarin, with a challenge in her voice (he made no attempt to argue with her) she said: "There are lots of interesting things here, but everything is so much better at home!" Tamarin hastened to agree.

Everything seemed better in Russia because it was part of Nadia's life—it was gayer even though it was not quite so nice. In Moscow four men had been seriously in love with Nadia and seven others had been on the verge. Young men pursued her with the pointless persistence of flies who know that they will be shooed away as soon as they light on the nose, but who persist just the same. Nadia, herself, had been in love twice—not too seriously, but definitely in love. "If I wanted to marry I would not have to think twice about it. All I would have to do would be to give a wink and Sasha Pavlovski would go insane with happiness." Abroad no one except old men fell madly in love with Nadia. All of her colleagues happened to be either unpleasant, or physically repulsive like the secretary. Repeating other women's words Nadia hesitantly said that good looks were not important in a man. Actually, only handsome men appealed to her, but she was careful to conceal this, as though it were something shameful and abnormal. Nevertheless, the secretary did go too far with his male prerogative of being ugly. Nadia had not met many "Europeans" and her dreams had not been realized: they had not fallen at her feet. "No, they are a cold lot! They suffocate themselves with their riches, while we are building a new life." She bitterly regretted that she had been so determined and so successful about getting a foreign service appointment. Time hung heavily on her hands. It seemed to her that she was losing her freshness. Without any reason she spent one entire night crying. Life was passing her by—any place without people was dismal.

She would not admit even to herself that she was bored by the famed attractions of Paris.

Usually Tamarin stopped for Nadia at seven o'clock. They had dinner together and then went to a theatre, or to a movie, or to a café. The commander's conversation was not exciting, but it bored her in a comfortable way. Besides, she was not under any obligation to answer. When she answered at random he never was offended like Kangarov, who demanded that his audience hang on his every word. He even was not offended when in the middle of one of his stories she mused aloud wondering whether the seal coat worn by the lady at the adjoining table was real. At the same time it was much more convenient to visit cafés and theatres in the company of an educated, distinguished-looking, elderly man. Nadia was under the impression that everyone mistook them for father and daughter. This amused her. Unconsciously she began to treat Tamarin as though he were her father. Only she insisted on paying her own way. Nadia had established this rule the very first time they had visited a café. On that occasion Tamarin's face had turned very red. "Please! Are you trying to embarrass me?" But Nadia had insisted. She felt more at ease that way and, besides, she had guessed that the commander had no money to spare. By the second day they had established a regular procedure. Tamarin paid for everything and later Nadia reimbursed him for her part. In accepting her money he was always self-conscious and tried to arrange it so that her share would be a little less. "No, you have not included the tip. I owe you at least one franc more." "How silly! Aren't you ashamed of yourself?" "Not in the least."

At first, obeying a habit formed during eighteen long years, Tamarin was extremely cautious and reserved in his conversations with Nadia. Later, he became much franker, especially after he had learned that Nadia's father was a professor, that he had owned a country estate and that he had been a nobleman (she had referred to it as a joke). Naturally this was not an absolute guarantee. But Tamarin's general impression of Nadia was such that he became more and more comfortable with her. At first he mentioned his superiors with an appropriately serious expression; later—with a smile which could be interpreted in different ways; still later he became almost outspoken with her. It was obvious that she would not denounce him.

When Kangarov returned from Amsterdam, Nadia with exaggerated warmth told him that the commander had taken care of her like a father. "He is an exceptionally charming old man!" As a token of his appreciation Kangarov invited Tamarin to the dinner. "He is a distinguished man and an outstanding non-party specialist. . . ."

XIII

IN HIS turn Tamarin was charmed with Nadia. Before her arrival there had been days when he did not have a chance to speak to a soul except to waiters and to the clerks in the stores. But this did not bother him. He had not for years been as contented as he was in Paris. Every day he gave thanks to God for the foreign assignment and the very thought of returning to Moscow horrified him. Though ordinarily he was an honest and conscientious worker, without being aware of it he did everything in his power to prolong the special work he was doing.

Tamarin arose at six in the morning and worked for an hour and a half on an empty stomach. Without a kitchen he could not make tea according to his formula, and, besides, in France coffee was the customary morning drink. Usually he had breakfast in a café, partly as a matter of economy—the hotel was too expensive —and partly because he derived a great deal of enjoyment from the early morning strolls through Paris. Around seven-thirty he left the hotel and walked to a stationery store located in a side street. There were places much nearer where he could buy a paper, but he preferred the stationery store. In addition to the French papers he bought a daily published by Russian émigrés and he felt safer buying it in a store than asking for it at an outdoor news-stand. He stuck the papers in his pocket, folding them in such a way that only the French papers showed, and always went to the same café. He already was known there. After welcoming him with a cheerful *"Bonjour, Monsieur,"* an exceptionally pleasant garçon did not even wait for his order. Without a word he brought a pot of coffee and a basket of hard rolls and proceeded to pour, knowing exactly how much cream Tamarin liked in his coffee. While he was busy pouring he always said: *"Fait beau aujourd'hui, hein?"*—or something else like that. Tamarin was fully aware that no one knew his name, his position, or his nationality and that if he were to die suddenly neither the pleasant owner of the café nor the pleasant garçon would be stricken with grief. At most they would be sorry to lose a client. But in their manners, in their pleasant smiles, in their *"Fait beau aujourd'hui"* there was a human cordiality which he had forgotten in Moscow. People in Paris were indifferent to one another, but they did not try to poison each other's existence, they did not denounce one another, and they were not secret police agents.

Breakfast occupied half an hour of Tamarin's time and the garçon was always fascinated watching him manipulate the paper while he was reading it. Only a small portion of the paper appeared above the table and no one possibly could read even the headlines. Tamarin never had had any unpleasant experiences, he never had met anyone he knew in the café, he had no grounds for thinking that he was being watched, but he believed in taking sensible precautions.

Having finished his coffee Tamarin left the money on the corner of the table (during the first few days he was amazed that this could be done without fear that it would be stolen). Then he took a stroll along the Left Bank or through the Luxembourg Gardens and only when absolutely necessary went to see someone on business—most of his work could be done in his room. Around ten he usually was back in the hotel. He still was staying at the same hotel where he had stopped on the day of his arrival in Paris. His room was cleaned early and as soon as he returned he settled at the typewriter. A very light lunch consisting of a slice of ham and toast was brought to his room—he was careful not to gain weight. Bringing his workday to a close at five o'clock he took another walk, relishing the feeling of a growing appetite. He had a good dinner in some medium-priced restaurant and always drank a half bottle of good Bordeaux. This and the purchase of books on military subjects were the only luxuries Tamarin allowed himself. "One cannot find wine like that in Moscow and stuff that tastes like vinegar costs ten times as much there." Very often he went to the movies or else to see some light, entertaining play. "Something unpretentious, gay, amusing, and typically French."

More frequently Tamarin spent the evenings at home. For about half an hour he worked on a crossword puzzle in the émigré paper. Though he spoke French reasonably well, he found French crossword puzzles too difficult. Often he played a game of solitaire, pretending that the result would tell him how much longer he could stay in Paris. There was no one with whom he could play bridge and he missed it. Occasionally, instead of playing solitaire, Tamarin read something besides Clausewitz. He decided to re-read the classics while he was in Paris. Furtively he stopped at an émigré bookstore and purchased a six-volume émigré edition of Pushkin. "There is nothing wrong about buying Pushkin anywhere! But they certainly make ugly-looking Russian books abroad! . . ." he thought with a trace of the satisfaction so frequently experienced by Nadia. He liked most of Pushkin's things, but even those he did not particularly care for he read with gratification, remembering how he had read them half a century ago. "I don't believe I have read them since. . . . That is the greatest charm about the classics, not to mention their intrinsic merit. . . ."

Over a book Tamarin thought about his work and about many other things. If there was any way of determining how much longer his Paris stay would last he could rent a room with a kitchen and a bath, and buy a radio and a new typewriter. If only he could spend the rest of his days in Paris calmly engaged in work useful to the Russian army, without having to take part in intrigues, without signing obsequious telegrams, without any bootlicking (though a certain amount of bootlicking had to be done even here). And only when he had nothing more to fear, a week or two before his death, he would return home so he could die in Petersburg, where he had been born.

When Kangarov had asked him to take his young secretary under his wing Tamarin at first did not relish the idea. He had become immersed in the routine of his Paris life and he was not anxious to make any change. But the girl turned out to be extremely nice and soon she aroused in him a kind, almost tender feeling mixed with pity. "Her whole generation has no conception of real life. God has deprived them of their heritage. And she is such a clever and capable girl!"

On the day set for the dinner Kangarov at the last minute had to see some Frenchmen on business, so he asked Tamarin to stop for Nadia and bring her to the restaurant. "The poor thing should not have to come by herself! Please, Your Excellency, bring her in a taxi and permit me to reimburse you." "I shall be delighted to bring Nadia," Tamarin answered with a blush.

The general appeared in Nadia's room wearing a white tie and tails, which was too formal for dinner in a restaurant. After his life in Paris had become adjusted within a definite budget Tamarin figured out that he could afford to spend in the neighborhood of three thousand francs on clothes. He ordered a good suit, a topcoat which was sufficiently heavy for year-round wear in France and a full dress. There was not enough money left for a cutaway and a dinner jacket. The realization that he was well or at least passably well dressed gave Tamarin no little satisfaction. Before the war in Russia he had worn civilian clothes only when he went shooting. But he had several suits and a full dress for travel abroad, and with a smile he remembered how on the way to the railroad station instead of taking off his hat he always, as a matter of habit, had given the military salute. After the revolution he had become accustomed to civilian clothes, but in Moscow he had not worn the full dress on a single occasion and he doubted that he could get into it. He called it antediluvian and thought that in this instance the word could be used in its literal meaning. Before his departure he had hesitated whether or not to take the full dress with him. He had tried it on and had given a deep sigh—it was even worse than he had feared, it was impossible. The antediluvian full dress had been sold in Moscow. His new one—the second and probably the last one in his life—which had been made to measure in Paris, he decided to wear for the first time to Kangarov's dinner. A couple of days before, afraid that after twenty-five years he would make some mistake, he made it a point to go to the opera and examine other people. Then he bought everything new: shirt, cuff links and tie. He discovered that people were wearing some kind of new, complicated ties which had not existed in his day. Though he had listened carefully to the condescending explanations of the salesman in the store he had a great deal of difficulty in tying the new-fangled contraption. When he had finished dressing Tamarin stood in front of the mirror on the rickety dresser and filled with self-pity smiled at his own satisfaction. "I am behaving like a boy!" Half a century ago he had stood just like that admiring himself, when for the first time he had worn the resplendent uniform of a guard regiment.

In the new full dress Tamarin's mature figure looked well groomed and very distinguished. "Good Lord! I am completely overcome! It is terribly becoming! Terribly! It's just a joy to look at you!" Nadia exclaimed. "Why look at me? You are the one who is dazzling!" he answered, smiling bashfully. Nadia looked very smart, or at least it seemed so to him. He had no inkling how much worry and excitement her appearance had cost her. In Paris there was not a soul whom she could consult. In warning her Kangarov merely had said: "Better dress up, my child! Be sure to wear all the prescribed frills and doodads! Remember, it's the

best restaurant in Paris, and that means in the whole world!" And
with a superior air the ambassador had added: "Vermandois will
be there—you know, the famous French writer? If something is
not just right he will notice it at once. Before you know it, he
will be making fun of you in one of his novels." Nadia had
assumed a naïve and frightened expression. Of late her conversations with Kangarov always ended in this simple art of making
faces. She thought that her expressions must seem awfully silly.
"But they are so convenient!"

That day, after a long and painful period of hesitation, Nadia
plucked her eyebrows. Now she was a little ashamed of herself,
and besides, she was not quite sure whether she would be criticized. When Tamarin failed to notice this startling innovation
she was considerably annoyed. After restraining herself as long
as she could she finally called it to his attention and he became
extremely apologetic. "Certainly not! I am not in the least angry.
You have more important things to think about, commander,"
Nadia said laughingly in answer to his abject amends. "I do hope
you aren't angry with me! But why on earth did you do it? You
had such charming eyebrows!" "Is that so? I suppose after this
you still expect me to believe that you have any idea what I look
like? But I did something else insane! They really should keep me
in chains. . . ." "What else did you do?" "I bought this . . ." she
took a small enameled box out of her bag. "What is that?" "That's
what they call a vanity case." Tamarin laughed. "That's the way
it always happens. Some practical joker invents a queer expression. Gradually the word acquires the full rights of citizenship till
no one notices how queer it sounds. That's what happened with
the expression 'infernal machine.' A hundred years ago. . . ."
But Nadia was not interested in infernal machines.

Unaccustomed to travel in taxis they miscalculated the time
and the distance and arrived in the restaurant a full half hour
before dinner. A man in uniform rushed forward to meet them.
Quivering with excitement Nadia stepped out of the taxi.

Tamarin glanced at his watch and suggested that they wait in an adjoining café, instead of sitting in an empty private dining-room. Nadia immediately agreed. The delay suited her: she felt terribly self-conscious.

They took a table in the café and sat engaged in their usual pleasant and unpretentious chatter. The commander told her about his work (it had progressed especially well that day) and he repeated word for word a quotation from Clausewitz. Nadia nodded without listening, occasionally interjecting an "Is that so?" or a "How terribly interesting!" and, at random, opening her eyes wide to show her attentiveness.

XIV

THE OWNER of the merry-go-round shouted at the top of his lungs trying to drum up trade. Excited children sat astride horses, pigs and lambs with long protruding tongues. Mothers and nurses gave the final word of warning to their charges: to hold tight and not to leave their seats. A determined-looking boy took a seat in the gondola of a balloon. A tiny girl, obviously his sister, watched him with horrified admiration. The sound of music came from somewhere inside and the merry-go-round began to move. Floating past Wislicenus the children with set and preoccupied expressions held on tight to the reins and the steering-wheels. Two boys astride lambs were riding side by side: when one of them was up in the air, the other was close to the floor. To the accompaniment of shouts and shrieks the merry-go-round reached the peak of its speed and began to slow down. The music ceased. The merry-go-round stopped. The shouting came to an end. Some children looking very proud, others with disappointment written on their faces, climbed down from their horses, pigs and lambs. All that remained before Wislicenus' eyes was a row of black, shabby monsters.

XV

KANGAROV'S dinner had come about accidentally. To the people who evinced an interest in the occasion he explained that he had to entertain a certain international financier. "In Rome do as the Romans do" (of late he had been forced to fall back on this expression more and more frequently). The Roman, alias the financier, was conducting negotiations on a very important matter. Kangarov had no direct connection with it, but another government department had asked him to do what he could to help. That was the reason for his presence in Paris. Abroad all important problems were considered, discussed and settled in expensive restaurants. The financier had fed Kangarov in Paris, and in Amsterdam and now it was the ambassador's turn to reciprocate with a dinner. In the financier's house the ambassador had met Vermandois and, relying on the element of surprise, immediately invited him. He had no choice about inviting Cerisier, the famous lawyer, who was looking after the legal side of the negotiations. Along with the others he invited a well-known count and his wife. The other guests were not as impressive. Kangarov invited Nadia because he wanted to give the child a treat. "Besides, it will not do for that fool to be the only lady at the table!" he reassured himself, thinking about the Countess. He felt that he was under obligations to Tamarin for the attention the general had shown Nadia during his absence. The commander was a distinguished man who spoke French well, who had been a general in the old days, and who, therefore, could not possibly spoil the tone of the dinner. As far as Doctor Siegfried Mayer was concerned he had actually invited himself, also relying on the element of surprise. This man had occupied a number of important and influential positions in old Germany. In the past Kangarov had been on the best of terms with him, had met him at numerous conferences and had visited in his home. Now Siegfried Mayer was an émigré and quite obviously in financial straits. Kangarov considered it indecent not to ask him—"one cannot behave like a hog!" Besides, Doctor Mayer had some business to transact. He was extremely anxious to meet Wislicenus who, he had heard, had recently arrived in Paris.

At the mention of Wislicenus Kangarov had been on his guard at once. He had no desire to invite "one of those people" to the dinner. On the other hand he could not very well avoid it. "If they have some business to talk over, before I know it they will be saying that I had blocked it! . . ." Various rumors circulated in Moscow about Wislicenus. Some said that he was one of the most trusted men, others claimed that his career was virtually at an end. Both situations were within the realm of possibility. Judging by certain hints dropped by exceptionally well-informed people, Kangarov was inclined to think that the position of Wislicenus was not as secure as it had been in the past. "It would be more politic not to ask him. This dinner is spreading like a weed," the ambassador thought angrily, but after hesitating decided to accommodate Mayer. "But not another solitary person. That's enough. . . ." He pretended that he was giving the dinner solely for business reasons. As a matter of fact, Kangarov by nature was an extremely hospitable person. In addition, after the recent, well-remembered perturbations he looked for opportunities to relax. "To forget things," he had said to Nadia without giving her any indication of the cause for his nervous strain. The preparations for the dinner occupied his mind. He was not in the least disturbed by the strange assortment of guests. A long time ago he had become convinced that there was no reason to show special consideration for people like the Countess. He even liked to repeat the words which he had picked up in some magazine and which were ascribed to Lord Kitchener: "I have had only two terrifying enemies in my life: African mosquitoes and society ladies."

When the restaurant manager showed him the tentative menu Kangarov said with satisfaction: "Ça va, ça va." The only change he made was to cancel the cocktails and instead to order out of special stock a fifty-year-old sherry of devastating price and quality. "At least it will make them gay." From personal experience he

knew that at the most serious business and political dinners the
progress and the success of the negotiations—naturally not of the
main issues but of the essential details—frequently depended on
whether a benevolent mood had been created by pleasant surroundings and especially by good wines. In this instance no further negotiations were scheduled to take place at the dinner.
Everything had been discussed and settled with the financier
beforehand. It was merely a matter of strengthening already existing friendly ties.

Kangarov arrived at the restaurant about ten minutes ahead
of the appointed hour just in case one of the guests should put
in an early appearance. Accompanied by the manager and by the
maître d'hôtel he entered the private dining-room, inspected the
table with a proprietary air, and was pleased with what he saw.
Everything was as it should be. On a serving table champagne
and Rhine wine were cooling in buckets filled with ice. Instead
of being black, the caviar was grey and large-grained—just exactly
the way he liked it. The bottle of sherry was so covered with dust
and cobwebs that it looked as though it had been excavated after
being buried underground for at least fifty years. The manager
and the maître d'hôtel received their last instructions, respectfully answering: *"Oui, Votre Excellence," "Oui, Monsieur l'Ambassadeur. . . ."* The door opened and Nadia accompanied by
Commander Tamarin entered the room. She appeared indescribably beautiful to Kangarov. "I am in love—in love like a school-
boy!" In contrast to Tamarin he at once noticed the revolutionary
change in the girl's face, his heart skipped a beat with delight,
and he shook a finger at her. But Nadia was too frightened to give
him even an answering smile. "Afraid of the capitalists!" she
angrily took herself to task in her mind. Her eyes darted over
the room. The long, narrow table, as well as the entire dining-room,
exuded smartness. "Where will I sit? I hope next to someone I
know. . . . I wonder what's beyond that other door? . . ." Adjoining the private dining-room were a coat-room and a small
sitting-room with a divan, behind a curtained doorway. "That's

where they hold the orgies!" Nadia thought with avid curiosity. The walls were covered with mirrors. Passing through the coat-room Nadia had looked at her reflection. "Everything seems to be in order," she decided, pleased with her eyebrows, with her dress and with the vanity-case in the bag.

"Beautiful! Very beautiful!" Kangarov said, affecting a tender indifference. "I knew I could depend on you! . . . Glamorous, smart and elegant! Allow me to thank you, my dear commander. . . . Well, how are things in Spain?" Tamarin began to air his views, but at that moment the financier and Cerisier entered the room. "My dear commander, you can tell us about it at dinner. . . . But please speak French. . . . Russian is strictly forbidden . . . " the ambassador said hurriedly before leaving them.

Kangarov performed the introductions and in presenting Tamarin added: "one of our finest generals." The financier glanced curiously at the commander. "We were just discussing the situation in Spain." "After the rebels took Badajoz," Tamarin began and stopped short: "who knows what kind of people they are?" "It will be extremely interesting to hear the opinions of an important Soviet specialist," the famous lawyer said encouragingly. The financier's face remained expressionless, but there was nothing indefinite about his thoughts: "They took Badajoz, they will take everything else, and some day they will hang every one of your kind, thank God! But until that day comes there is no reason why we can't transact business and dine, especially in a place like this!" Concealing her excitement Nadia tried to get another glimpse of herself in the large wall mirror and to do it so that no one would notice her childish gesture. "What a poseur! What a bastard!" Kangarov thought angrily, looking at the new arrival standing in the doorway. Wislicenus was wearing an offensive, unpressed brown suit and an equally offensive, soft, striped collar. "What a lout! What an animal! What a son of a bitch!" the ambassador repeated in his thoughts, as he met Wislicenus and greeted him with a warm, comradely handshake.

XVI

AT THAT moment Louis-Etienne Vermandois was just leaving his apartment. That day his work had taken a remarkable turn. His novel of ancient Greek life suddenly had assumed a new direction. One of the characters met Lysander under different but much more appropriate and probable circumstances. The meeting came about in a perfectly natural way, but in order for it to take place this character had to do certain things which he had not done until then. In retrospect his action seemed reasonable and absolutely in keeping with his personality. The character became much more lifelike, the story moved faster, and the entire novel was greatly improved. All this could be considered as a flash of inspiration and for several minutes Vermandois had known true happiness. "But why hadn't it occurred to me sooner? Though, I suppose, I cannot act as a free agent in this matter. Apparently characters in creative fiction have a life of their own. Things said about Flaubert, Stendhal and Tolstoy in this connection are not mere figments of imagination put forth by their admiring biographers, by perspicacious critics, or by themselves."

During the last month Anaximander's name in the novel had changed to Lysander. In the final draft the new name not only had been substituted in every single instance, but the old name had been carefully scratched out. For some inexplicable reason Vermandois was ashamed of the fact that Anaximander had become Lysander—ashamed before his young secretary, who had copied the manuscript. "How can I ever explain to him that Lysander is merely inadequate, while Anaximander is both horrible and impossible?" In the presence of others Vermandois most of the time felt awkward and embarrassed because he persisted in writing novels, regardless of their merits or shortcomings. He was not certain whether he was more self-conscious in the presence of other writers or in the presence of inarticulate people, and he believed that musicians and painters never could experience a sensation of that kind.

After the changes had been made Lysander's thoughts became even more depressing than they had been before. Also, it unfortunately seemed as though Lysander were thoroughly familiar with the events which had occurred in Europe during the twentieth century and particularly since the war. Hurriedly Vermandois jotted down in his notebook the necessary changes along with some new thoughts—unless they were down in black and white they were so easily forgotten. He became so absorbed in his work that he forgot to look at his watch. When he had finished at last he had only twenty minutes before the time set for dinner. Inwardly cursing himself he began to dress hastily. "Why in the hell did I promise the man to be there at all?"

Recently a rumor had been circulated in Paris that Vermandois had joined the communist party. At moments when he was more than usually disgusted with the world, with publishers and with what along with others he termed "bourgeois literature," Vermandois was in the habit of saying that within the next few days he definitely would link his future with the communists. On such occasions his tone seemed to imply a threat, though he was well aware that in the literary world his enemies and friends alike would remain completely indifferent to such an action on his part. *"Avez-vous entendu la dernière de Vermandois? . . . Elle est bonne, n'est-ce pas? . . ."* And as far as politicians were concerned (he was well aware of that too) despite an outward show of respect they never had taken him seriously. Frequently they asked him for a foreword to a collection of their articles and speeches, but they did it because *"une préface de Vermandois"* was still highly prized by publishers: it meant at least five hundred extra copies. Ordinarily he never refused to write a foreword. People who did not know him personally merely shrugged their shoulders in bewilderment when they read the exorbitant praises he heaped on collections which disgusted him, while before long other politicians in their turn came to him for a foreword.

But despite his outbursts Vermandois had not joined the party. There were too many arguments "for" and "against." Before audi-

ences Vermandois was known to say: "In these times a lone individual is completely helpless. At present there is only one vital
struggle in the world and everyone has to choose the side on
which he will fight. Shades of opinion have no meaning. Anywhere from ten to fifteen political parties bearing all sorts of ridiculous names participate in our elections. The most reactionary
party calls itself the party of the Republican Left—that's nothing
but an empty word! We know that the best street in Paris is called
a field, but that does not mean that it is used for growing wheat,
or for grazing cows. But, actually, there are only two parties fighting each other in France: the party of progress and the party of
reaction (he involuntarily made a wry face when he used such
clichés). This means that in the great struggle which is being
fought today in a world passing through a period of social revolution and social catastrophes, it is absurd to allow oneself to be
influenced by words and shades of opinion. If a man wants to
be useful he has to join the party. . . ."

This was the official "for." But the unofficial "against" also
had its points. It was not based on the reign of terror in Russia,
which probably,—who could tell?—was justified by circumstances
and which at a distance of a thousand miles did not fill Vermandois with horror. The execution of people unknown to him could
not excite any more feeling in him than an earthquake in Mar-
tinique, or a cholera epidemic in China. What bothered him most
was that the communists had certain dogmatic teachings which
had to be accepted not only by the rank and file—he could have
resigned himself to that—but which also were acclaimed as a work
of genius by the élite of the party. With an effort Vermandois
read several books elucidating these teachings, refreshed his memory about several others, and with a sigh admitted that it was a
philosophy intended for cooks. "Probably a cook needs a philosophy as much as anyone else. . . . Perhaps the entire purpose of
political life is a process of selection from among a number of
uninspiring systems of one that is least dull and most catching?
But I am not a cook and, besides, there is no assurance that their

system is less dull than the others. If it is a question of quickly smothering intelligence so that everyone should reach the intellectual level of cooks and waiters, then the present German philosophy is even more effective: Germans are unsurpassed masters at that sort of thing. . . ." Also, he knew that if he joined the party he would have to appear at least three times a year on the platform at their meetings. He could not hope to get by forever on letters of greeting and, besides, he would have to send various telegrams and be present at the burial of distinguished persons. "No, it's better to wait. . . ." Vermandois communicated with the proper people and told them that he did not feel sufficiently ripe for so important a step. He was careful to assume a heartfelt, profound and somewhat mysterious air which suited the occasion, and his words made a very deep impression.

The collar button slipped through the tight collar without any difficulty, the laces on the oxfords were most docile (of late he had found it more and more difficult to tie his shoes) and at eight sharp Vermandois found himself in the street. He had plenty of time to take the subway: there was nothing inexcusable about being fifteen or twenty minutes late. But to reach the restaurant he would have had to change trains, and underground travel with its long corridors and endless staircases exhausted him. No, there was no choice, he would be forced to spend the money on a taxi. Vermandois stopped to buy an evening paper and quickly glanced at the headlines. It was always the same old story! . . . France was suggesting to the other great powers that they discuss the matter of non-intervention and of localizing the conflict in Spain. The newspaper went on to say that this suggestion "was being eagerly discussed by political circles in all the capitals of Europe. . . ." "No, it is really better to have dishonest men at the helm of the state. There is a certain breed of noble-minded individuals who are responsible for the destruction of societies and who can be charged with all the great catastrophes in history."

The news-vendor, making change, stared with hostility at Vermandois' immaculate dinner jacket. A young man standing next to him said: *"Non, vous avez beau dire, c'est un fameux type, ce Hitler!"* "I suppose in their own way they are right. If Lysander and I cannot offer them anything better than elegant pessimism and if the interpretation placed on the declaration of human rights benefits only men like Stavisky they have a good reason for admiring force, coarseness and brazenness, and for spitting at everything else. . . . 'The people joyfully rushed into servitude,' *'ruit in servitium,'*" he remembered the words of Tacitus and angrily thought that his memory, which constantly prompted him with quotations, was poisoning his existence. "It's not my fault that everything has been said already. Besides, if my memory was not functioning well, I should be sharing with the ignorant the illusion of 'new words.' As if there is such a thing as a new word under the sun!" He glanced at the skies. The sun had disappeared. The fading sunset amazed him as though he never had seen it before in his life. "How inadequate is the language of the greatest masters! When I was young I was convinced that it was possible and necessary to invent new and exact comparisons, word-pictures and epithets, and I drove myself to the verge of insanity searching for new ways to describe a sunset, a forest, or the sea. Just like a maniac! I have been a maniac all my life! . . .

"This Spanish war, and everything else that is reported in the newspapers, has no more significance for me than the dinner with this gentleman who in addition to caviar and pineapples wants to have the 'glitter of Vermandois' sparkling words' (that was the cliché used by friendly critics). There are only two or three years left of life, at best—or at worst, five or six. There is nothing new I can possibly expect. No matter how stupid or how idiotic, the rest of my life will mean nothing more than 'sparkling' at dinners given by dull, ignorant people (right then he decided that tonight he would not speak about anything but the weather). Despite the sense of happiness I experienced today, I could get along very well without the sparkling Greek Lysander, and without the thirty-seventh sparkling novel, especially since no one seems to have read the thirty-sixth which preceded it—at least, not more than one Frenchman in five thousand. Three hundred years ago the few books which appeared at great intervals were read by people for the sake of their souls. Thirty years ago, when I was one of the most fashionable writers in Europe, my books were read by people so they could quote me in smart society and earn an approving smile from the ladies. 'Vermandois says . . .' Now one person in five thousand hurriedly glances through my books as a matter of habit. Something to read out of sheer boredom when one cannot go to the theatre, or play bridge. But my 'admirers,' just as my unfriendly critics, know that in my case the 'author already has said everything he has to say and now merely is repeating himself' (this was the cliché used by unfriendly critics, who on the whole were few). No one seems to notice that I write much better than I wrote when I was young, that I am wiser, more mature and more experienced, and that my sentences are firmer, clearer and more precise. And there are none, except a few maniacs like myself, who read my books with malicious anticipation so they at last can say with a clear conscience: '*Il est fini, Vermandois!*' Though they have been saying it already without bothering about their conscience. To hell with them! Before I die I will say what Lord Holland said when a bitter enemy wanted to call on him while he was on his deathbed: 'If Mr. Selwyn calls, let him in; if I am alive I shall be very glad to see him, and if I am dead he will be very glad to see me.' "

Vermandois made a mental note to use this quotation on some suitable occasion before an audience, though not tonight. Actually, he had no real enemies among the critics. There were some critics who did not show a sufficient respect for him, or at least not as much respect as they showed for other famous writers. He heaved a deep sigh: "Obviously all of us would enjoy an existence such as was known in Versailles when it was forbidden to bow to anyone except Louis XIV when he was present. . . ." There were some critics who were gay and familiar and who in summarizing the contents of Bergson's, France's, or his books, referred to the author as "our philosopher," or "our novelist." There were other critics who suffered from nervousness and who constantly, without any apparent reason, changed their attitude toward him from cordiality to rudeness. Of late there were some critics who outwardly were extremely polite, but who never failed to mention in passing that his books no longer enjoyed the popularity which they deserved. Finally, there were a few intelligent and conscientious critics who always had a word of praise for him.

Classifying the critics was so entertaining that it was some time before Vermandois returned to his original trend of thought. "Why should I go on living in such surroundings and among such people? Goethe told Eckermann that periods of social retrogression and of moral disintegration were especially conducive to thought and inner life. A means of making a living? I could move to some out-of-the-way spot where living is cheap and where there is a lake and a forest. There is no reason why I should have six thousand books—that, too, is a mania,—but I could take with me a hundred good ones, those which have what people call a 'lasting' quality. I could live there until the end of my days. I could spend the last years of my life without talking to snobs or men of good taste, to fools or wise men, to enemies or admirers, and so I could commune with a hundred men who were fortunate enough to be the first to tell the eternal, everlasting, forceful truth about life and about humanity. Perhaps I would even give up writing and merely live, for the same reason that made Rabelais want to be king. '*Affin de faire grand chere, pas ne travailler, poinct ne me soucier, et bien enrichir mes amis et tous gens de bien et de scavoir. . . .*' Except that I could get along without enriching friends and '*gens de bien*' . . ."

Inwardly Vermandois doubted that he ever would move to the country. He was afraid that in the wilds, despite the forest, the lake and the communion with the great men of the past, he would begin to yearn for less distinguished society. It seemed to be his fate until the very end, until those last horrifying days, weeks, or months—it was better not to think about them!—to continue living just as he had lived for the last twenty years. Once again it seemed to him that civilization was coming to an end. Probably a new one would replace it, but it would be pitiful and incalculably worse than the present one. There was only one chance to stop a new cycle of civilization and that was for science to step in and provide savages with weapons which would enable them to destroy everything, including themselves. The destructive force of science was so incalculably greater than its constructive force. At that moment he felt especially vividly that savages were all around him, savages within and without, that he was hemmed in by savages on all sides, and that the streets of this beautiful, this most civilized city in the world now, with the descent of darkness, were lurking with shadowy, mysterious, horrible beings who were plotting terrible crimes. In paying the taxi he noticed that the chauffeur had a brutal face, and so had the doorman who wore a uniform as badge of a subservient class and who ran to the curb to meet him, and so had the maître d'hôtel who with a special show of respect led him to a private dining-room which he had visited so many times during the last forty years. He was almost in a state of panic when he found himself shaking hands with a strange man in a brown suit. With a sweet and embarrassed smile he apologized profusely to the other guests and gently reprimanded them for not going ahead with the dinner without him. "Not another word, cher Maître! Everyone arrived only a few minutes ago. You are not at all late," Kangarov insisted politely as he introduced those present to the famous guest who knew only the financier and the Count and Countess. "You are being too kind. Once again, please, accept my apologies. . . ." "*Akademische Viertelstunde,*" Doctor Siegfried Mayer remarked and immediately translated his words into terrible French. "There is nothing brutal about the girl. On the contrary, she is charming and that is the only thing that matters in this world," Vermandois thought listening with disgust to Mayer's accent (he realized, though it was unfair, that he detested all Germans: radical, conservative, or any other kind). "Let us sit down, my friends! Let us sit down!

I believe I can honestly say that you will like the sherry," Kangarov said gaily.

XVII

THE MURDER was set for nine-fifteen. Alvera had worked out the schedule carefully: under the circumstances the time element was extremely important. That particular train from Paris to Louvécienne was usually crowded, and so was the return train which carried back to Paris many of the late visitors to the country. The train arrived in Louvécienne at nine sharp and it was a seven-minute walk from the station to the villa. Approximately as much time had to be allowed for the preliminary conversation: he could not very well open fire as soon as the door was opened. Another quarter of an hour to search the house for the money, a ten-minute reserve for emergencies, and seven minutes for the walk back to the station. The suburban trains on that line were always on time.

Later, Alvera would be surprised when he remembered that on that day on the whole he had been quite calm. To all outward appearances it was just another day. The preceding night he had gone to bed at eleven o'clock. Before dropping off to sleep, with a sudden tenseness he had asked himself: "Should I change my mind? A month ago, though difficult, it would still have been possible. Now I can't! And why should I change my mind? Do I feel sorry for him? The old man is a miser who deducts a few pennies because there is an extra blank line at the bottom of a page, though I must admit that he never has been particularly mean to me. . . . Darwin would say that the old man should be singled out for destruction because he is a degenerate: the nervous twitch is sufficient proof." Monsieur Chartier was afflicted with a nervous twitch of the facial muscles around the left eye. Apparently he was self-conscious about this affliction: at least he always turned away in an effort to conceal it. "It's curious to learn the type of thing that preys on a person's mind. . . ." These thoughts had occurred to Alvera in an offhand, impersonal manner: only the technical details connected with the plan seemed pertinent and real. He had considered everything: there was nothing he had overlooked. With hurried precision, almost mechanically, he had gone over every step once again. "It's much too late to change my mind," he had repeated to himself. He would have found it difficult to explain why it was too late or when the turning point had come, but he knew it was so. In bed he had forced himself to read a few pages of the memoirs of Lassenaire. Though Alvera held the man in utter contempt, when he had reached the sentence: "At that moment my duel with society began. I made up my mind to become a social calamity,"—he had been deeply moved and transported with delight. His last doubts had vanished. "Everything is settled." Immediately he had dropped off and had slept more soundly than usual.

In the morning Alvera awoke in a cold sweat. He sat up in bed and with wide-opened eyes remained there for several minutes without moving: "This is the day! . . ." He knew that nothing could induce him now to change his mind. He even felt that he no longer had any control over it. From early in the morning he was troubled with yawning, as though he had spent a sleepless night. Alvera washed his face, shaved without once cutting himself—"this means that my hand is steady"—dressed and while buttoning his shirt thought that he would have to wait for another twelve hours. For a moment his strength forsook him. Taking himself in hand he decided firmly not to allow himself to deviate in any way from his usual routine; any deviations could later be construed as circumstantial evidence against him. "Though if it ever comes to a matter of evidence, I will not have the ghost of a chance. . . ." Alvera drank his morning coffee; he did not feel like eating and the yawning was bothering him. He scribbled a note to his tailor. The letter was a double-edged weapon. "On the one hand, a man contemplating murder would not spend his time arguing with a tailor over twenty francs; on the other hand, if anything were to go wrong, it would be a dangerous, psychological factor: 'what a hardened, cold-blooded criminal!'"

At ten o'clock he went to Vermandois' apartment. Contrary to custom the old man seemed to be absorbed in his work. Without leaving the table he absent-mindedly greeted the secretary, casually said: "yes, yes, that's the thing to write them, my friend,"— and made it very plain that he did not want to be disturbed. On the desk before him was the file with the material for the Greek novel and he was scribbling something with unusual alacrity.

Later, Vermandois could not forgive himself that on that morning he had not paid any attention to his secretary. It had been his only opportunity to talk to a man who intended to commit a murder that very night. "Is it possible that I, a trained observer, did not notice anything unusual about him?" But there was no sense in deceiving oneself. He had not noticed anything out of the way; all his thoughts had been centered on Lysander and on the meeting in Corinth. Alvera watched the old man with contempt. To his amazement his decision gave him a sense of moral superiority over people incapable of violence. Once again he was amused at Vermandois' amazement when tomorrow the police would appear unexpectedly and advise him that his secretary had robbed and killed a man. He almost regretted that this scene would never take place: the crime would have to remain unsolved.

Having discharged his secretarial duties, Alvera, yawning nervously, took a stroll along the streets, and stopped for lunch in a cheap restaurant. He made himself eat a normal meal (he knew the calorie count of everything on the menu), he did not order any wine—"alcohol is an additional hazard under the circumstances"—but he drank a great deal of water. Having bought some sliced ham for his supper he returned to his room. Time hung heavy on his hands: usually he spent these hours typing and reading. He tried to read, but he found it impossible. Hurriedly he glanced over the paper, thinking all the time about the news

item that would appear tomorrow right there, in that column.
. . . Sitting at his desk, unable to do anything else, he once again
went over the entire sequence, which he had reduced to a series
of concise formulas.

Only four things could lead to the capture and conviction of
a criminal: confession, testimony of witnesses, direct and circumstantial evidence. "Confession is out of the picture—I will leave
that to the idiots of Dostoyevsky. Testimony of witnesses? On the
average there are from eight to ten people who take the train at
the station. If each one remembers the appearance of all the others,
suspicion will be divided evenly among four or five people. Probably it is reasonable to assume that for one reason or another the
others will be eliminated. But why should the trail lead necessarily to that particular train? The murder will be discovered next
morning, providing it is one of the days on which the char-
woman cleans for Monsieur Chartier. If not, no one will learn
about the murder until much later. The autopsy can show only
the approximate time of death. . . . Let us assume that they
decide that the murder took place between seven and ten in the
evening. During those hours at least ten trains pass through
Louvécienne. This means that the suspicion can fall on forty or
fifty people. It will be much more serious if someone recognizes me in Louvécienne. But who could identify me? I have
yet to meet anyone on the walk leading from the main road to
Chartier's villa. Is it possible that tonight I shall meet someone
there for the first time? That certainly would direct suspicion in
my direction. Along the main road, on the other hand, on a summer evening, one always can meet a large number of people, but
the very fact that it is used by many local residents as well as
Parisians makes that part of the journey reasonably safe. The
most dangerous moment will be when I emerge from the private
walk into the main road. But the street light is quite a distance
away, it is dark, and, besides, I can choose a moment when no one
is near, so I can step out unobserved. As far as police go, they
cannot have more than three policemen in the entire village.

During all the months I have been going there I have met a bicycle patrol only once, and I believe even they were on their way to Saint-Germain. . . ." He went into the hall, filled a pitcher with water, gulped down a glassful and returned to his thoughts.

"Let us suppose that for some reason someone does notice me. Suppose that after reading about the murder this person communicates his suspicions to the police. As a rule, people don't like to volunteer such information: being questioned and appearing in court is too much trouble, and there is always a chance of drawing suspicion on oneself! It will be different if I am arrested. Then my photographs will appear in the papers and I shall be recognized by people who never have set eyes on me before. But suppose that someone notices me and reports me to the police. What description will he be able to give? A young man wearing glasses and a dark suit. . . . But I shall not wear a dark suit for months to come, and the glasses will be a false clue which only will get them further off the scent. . . . Besides, first of all they are certain to look for the criminal among the residents of Louvécienne. . . ."

Once again Alvera tried on the glasses. He was developing the knack of handling them; he no longer felt as awkward and as strange as he had the first time he had worn them. But he had blundered in buying them. The optician had suggested that he see a doctor. "I believe you have a chronic condition of the conjunctiva." "Yes, I have seen a doctor and he told me to wear reading glasses. . . ." "What number?" "I don't remember, but I am not very near-sighted." "The doctor did not tell you what number?" With a shrug of the shoulders the optician had seated him on a chair facing a board covered with letters of all sizes. Alvera had pretended that he could not read the last two lines. He had bought the glasses, but the transaction had left him with a dimly unpleasant sensation. It had been carried out in a clumsy way, and in a perfect crime every detail had to be considered carefully. He felt awkward wearing glasses and, besides, they had introduced another element of surprise. He had feared that he would find it difficult to see things through the lenses; instead, quite unexpectedly, he saw everything better and with new clarity; men, trees, things—everything looked different. Still, he had decided against wearing glasses when he entered the villa because with them on he was not sure of his aim. "Besides, Chartier's suspicions might be aroused. . . ." All in all, the glasses were the weakest link in the entire chain and they did little to change his appearance.

Yawning continually, Alvera paced the floor of the room, drank another glass of water and pushed into its place a book which was out of line on the shelf. He wondered whether he should do some work on the "Energic World Conception. . . ." To work as though it was just another day would be a great triumph of the will! But he did not attempt it. He knew it would not be worthwhile, and instead, he went back to the subject of evidence. There would be no fingerprints. That was the most dangerous evidence of all and he intended to wear gloves. "An elementary and foolproof precaution, and the fact that criminals don't use it oftener only shows that the technique of crime is on a very low level. There are a few Sherlock Holmeses on the detective force, but their task is comparatively easy. They do not kill, instead they hunt without infringing on the man-made or on the so-called divine laws. In contrast to the detective, the murderer's hands are tied: laws, fear, conditions, time element, lack of equipment, 'pangs of conscience,'" Alvera laughed. "Perhaps mine will be the first perfect crime in history! . . ." He had trained himself to wear gloves: the last time he had fired at the target in the forest he had worn gloves, and he had practised handling papers with gloved hands in the desk drawers at home. To avoid suspicion in his client's mind, the night before last he had worn gloves in delivering the work to him. He had explained it by saying that he was suffering from a skin irritation and immediately had regretted his words. "What if he is one of those people with a phobia? He might become frightened and not give me any more work! . . ." But at that moment Chartier's face had begun to twitch: he had turned away quickly and had not mentioned the subject again.

There could not be any question of circumstantial evidence. The old man did not know his name. Alvera had answered a newspaper advertisement and since then he had been bringing the work to Louvécienne in person. Only at their first meeting had he mumbled something that resembled a name. The strange sound with which Chartier accompanied the word "Monsieur" in addressing him made it obvious that he had not the slightest notion of the copyist's name. "How could he know it? . . . I doubt whether a businessman would tell anyone that he gave his business papers to be typed outside. They are chiefly documents pertaining to his business, and people don't like to talk about things like that. But even if he has mentioned it to someone, what is there to connect the copying of business papers with the murder? Suppose the worst has happened and he has told the charwoman that a copyist brings work to his house in the evenings. There are thousands of people in Paris who are known as professional copyists and my name is not among them. No one knows anything about my work: I am Vermandois' secretary, and that's all they know about me. Let the police search among the professional copyists—that's only one more thing to get them on the wrong scent. True, every typewriter has its own characteristics, but they can learn about my Remington only after they search my room. That would be an important bit of evidence, but if it ever came to that any additional evidence would not matter. . . . Why, as a general rule, are most criminals caught? First of all, because they lack experience and are scatter-brained: they are incapable of thinking a thing through ahead of time. Next comes gossip; most criminals belong to a milieu where the police have many informers. Next are fingerprints. A crime scientifically committed should remain unsolved nine times out of ten. In my case the most dangerous part is getting rid of the loot."

This was the weakest part of an otherwise perfect plan. Alvera heaved a deep sigh. He assumed that his client was a man of means. The business papers he had been copying indicated as much. But there was nothing pretentious about his mode of life. True, a villa in Louvécienne must have cost him around a hundred and fifty thousand francs, but he kept no servants. A char-woman came in several times a week. He ate breakfast in Paris where he spent the morning and the early part of the afternoon. Apparently he ate supper at home alone. "Is he a bachelor or a widower? Probably a widower . . . All his friends live in Paris. But even if Chartier is rich why should he keep large sums of money around the house? Usually, when he pays me for my work his pocketbook is bulging with money. And they are not hundred-franc bills; night before last I noticed he had some big ones. Perhaps it will be empty tonight? But why should it be empty to-night, if on the last three times it was bulging? He also must keep a certain amount of money in his desk drawers. In addition to the cash there must be some negotiable securities. . . ." Alvera had only a hazy conception of the term "negotiable security." "Will I be able to sell them? Are their numbers recorded anywhere? In any event I am assured of several thousand, and with the negoti-able securities it may come to as high as fifty thousand. . . ."

With a crooked smile Alvera remembered that in France, ac-cording to criminal statistics, the average crime netted the criminal forty francs. "But mine is not an average crime: everything else is different and the results, too, will be different. . . . I have never seen a safe in the villa. But there is no way of telling what hiding-places an old bourgeois is likely to use. His diamond ring alone should be worth six or seven thousand. Probably he has some other valuables. . . . Yes, that's the weakest part of the plan . . . According to the laws of probability it is logical for me to expect a minimum of ten thousand—that makes it worth while! The maximum expectation can be somewhere between fifty and a hun-dred thousand, provided I use my head in disposing of the loot." He had worked out a detailed plan for selling, but he did not feel like bothering with it now: it was too early to think about that. "In any case I will not make the slightest change in my mode of life for the next six months. That's how most of the boys get caught: they kill, rob, and immediately run to a bawdy house, where the police are waiting for them. Later, I can tell Vermandois, the janitress and everyone else that I am moving to the country. The Paris climate and the city air are bad for my health —any reputable doctor will bear me out on that point. After living in the country for another six months or so I should be able to dispose of everything, and then I can start a business of my own. . . ." There was another weak link in the chain. "What's the use? Why should I try to fool myself? In the end the guillotine is almost a mathematical certainty. . . ."

And again, but this time without the previous zest, Alvera imagined the arrest, the prison, the court, the wait for the guillotine, the execution with all its details which before excited him so much; "Courage, Alvera! The hour of retribution is at hand," the last glass of rum, the encouraging smiles and the parting words. "There is nothing particularly terrifying about it, but neither is it very pleasant. Even if the occupation of a criminal is less hazardous than that of a coal miner the degree of difference is so negligible that the choice should not be made without seriously considering all the factors." Impersonally he asked himself: "Does this make sense? Or is it merely an obsession of a man who is losing his mind?" But he at once dismissed such a supposition. "Whatever it is, it's too late to think about it," he said aloud with a yawn and suddenly became frightened. "I must break this bad and dangerous habit of talking to myself."

Though food did not appeal to him Alvera believed that he should not start out without eating. "Suppose I have a spell of dizziness and faint, or something of that kind—then everything will be lost!" He forced himself to eat a piece of ham. Then, glancing at his watch with a feeling of relief, he yawned, stretched, checked the gun, slipped on the gloves and went out. In the street he paused in front of a bookstore window and, pretending that it was difficult for him to read the titles, took out the case and put on the glasses. No one paid the least attention to him. "I did that very well. . . ." This pantomime was a slight improvisation. Even in a carefully thought-out plan one had to rely on resourcefulness for certain minor details. He was very pleased with himself. Feeling slightly awkward with the glasses, to which he could not become accustomed, he started on his way to the station. Except for the yawning which bothered him, Alvera was calm. He found comfort in the realization that no one among the endless number of people in the streets could sense his feelings or know his intentions. "I am about to break all the human and divine laws and not a soul among you knows about it. I have the same contempt for you that a wolf must have for a flock of sheep. . . ."

XVIII

". . . If that is so, my dear Vermandois, perhaps you can tell us the exact date on which the world will come to an end?" the financier asked. "An event of such magnitude is certain to have an effect on the stock market."

"Which, incidentally, has been rather weak today," Cerisier put in casually with an inquiring note in his voice. With a smile the financier shrugged his shoulders and raised his eyes to the ceiling. He always referred to business as though it did not concern him in the least and was merely a form of amusement. The impression he conveyed was that his business career was a joke, or an act of God, or a matter of accommodation for others. "Sherry is a wonderful wine. You can enjoy it with every course."

"I wonder why you people don't believe that the end of the world is at hand?" Vermandois asked with a playful smile which was in keeping with the tone he had assumed. A private dining-room in a restaurant was not a suitable place for a serious discussion. "For obvious reasons science avoids commitments on this subject. They could jeopardize its maintenance. But some time ago I remember a debate in the pages of a scientific journal between two of my friends who are both reputable physicists. One of them, basing his arguments on the gradual exhaustion of solar energy, claimed that the earth would perish from cold. The other, referring to the works of the great Clausius, insisted that it would be destroyed by excessive heat."

"Such a lack of unanimity is encouraging," Cerisier interrupted. "In order to reconcile the opinions of the two distinguished scientists, perhaps the temperature of the earth will remain more or less normal."

"Of the two I much prefer the cold. I love winter sports and I never feel better than when I am in Saint Moritz," the Countess de Bellancombre remarked. "How about you?"

"In general, the so-called exact sciences, or rather the sciences which are less inexact than others, foresee a good many sad possibilities which could completely destroy life on our charming planet," Vermandois continued. "The loss of oxygen from the atmosphere is one; the sinking of continents is another; the collision of two suns is still another; the collision of the earth with a comet is a fourth. At the moment I cannot remember any others. . . ."

"Don't strain yourself, cher Maître. The four are more than enough to ruin our appetites."

"In that case I must put in a word of protest," Kangarov said. "We have a duck stuffed with oranges on the menu."

"O-o-oh!"

"Let us hope that the earth will not collide with the comet until we have finished with the duck."

"Why doesn't someone try the Rhine wine? In the matter of white wines I am definitely pro-German," Kangarov announced. "Please! Please, don't smoke before you taste the cheese! . . ."

"I am afraid you will find me smoking at the moment of the world's destruction."

"All joking aside, I refuse to believe in all these horrors!" the Countess said. "God would never allow this to happen!" She placed her hand on the sleeve of Kangarov's dinner jacket. "I know that you are an atheist. In politics I am with you at least seventy-five percent. Everyone calls me a bolshevik. But nothing will induce me to part with my God! Nothing!" she said with a smile.

"My dear Countess, I should never dream of asking you for such a . . . My dear child, how do you say 'sacrifice' in French?" the ambassador said in Russian to Nadia, who was sitting opposite him at the other end of the table.

For several minutes after the Count and Countess had entered the dining-room Nadia had felt depressed. The Countess was a middle-aged woman—"of mediocre beauty"—but she wore a black dress and a cape of black fox. "Mine is also black, but God! what a difference," Nadia thought with a sigh. On her neck the Countess had a *sautoir* of unbelievable length shining with numberless pearls. And she wore so many bracelets that Nadia almost emitted an exclamation when she saw them. On the wife of a banker Nadia would have ascribed such a number of bracelets to lack of good taste. From books she had read and from moving pictures she had seen Nadia knew that in contrast to aristocrats, bankers' wives dressed in bad taste. "But she is a real countess!" The bracelets, the *sautoir* and the black fox worn by the Countess de Bellancombre were beyond Nadia's range of possibilities, or even dreams. But she made a mental note of the other accoutrements: the handbag, the stockings and the striking green gloves, which Nadia would have passed by in a store because she would have been afraid that her taste might be questioned. "But with all of it she still is an old woman and all the bracelets in the world will not help her!" she consoled herself.

Kangarov had made no attempt to seat the guests, smilingly suggesting instead that everyone take the nearest chair. But somehow, of its own accord it came about that the most distinguished guests, the Countess and Vermandois, sat on the host's right and left. They were the recipients of his sweetest smiles. On the other side of the Countess sat Wislicenus, then Doctor Mayer, the Count, and Nadia. Beyond Vermandois were the financier,

Cerisier and Tamarin. Thus only half of Nadia's wish had been fulfilled. On her right sat Tamarin, but on her left was a Frenchman and a Count to boot! Nadia had never in her life sat at a table with a Count. "What shall I talk to the old man about?" she wondered in a panic and looked at Tamarin with eyes pleading for help. But the old man turned out to be not in the least formidable. Politely he entertained her with simple questions: How long had she been in France? How did she like Paris? Now and then he addressed a few words to the German who was his neighbor on the left. Nor did he seem to mind an occasional silence of a few minutes' duration.

The waiter poured the sherry. Nadia drank her glass at one draught and only then realized that it was not the safe thing to do. Almost at once she felt carefree and gay. On several occasions in Moscow she had had as many as five or six glasses of brandy or vodka, but she had been tipsy only once. That was the day when Sasha Pavlovski had kissed her for the first time and had told her that when it came to drinking she could hold her own. With the fish course a white wine was served in beautiful, long, narrow bottles such as Nadia had never seen before. She wanted to taste it, but she did not know how to go about it. There were several glasses in front of her—which was the right one to use? Once again she felt embarrassed because she did not know the customs of bourgeois society and because she was self-conscious about it. "Why should I care about their genteel conventions? . . ." The waiter filled her glass and the wine proved to be very light, but slightly bitter—vodka had a much better taste. Out of the corner of her eye Nadia watched the Count handle the difficult fish; she followed his lead and everything went along smoothly. She no longer was afraid of the old man, on the contrary she in turn began to ask him polite questions. "The Count is just like any other man. The French are a funny people," Nadia whispered to Tamarin. The old men around the table spent much more time with their eyes fixed on her than they did looking at the Countess. It even seemed to Nadia that the Countess was conscious of the fact and annoyed by it. This pleased her immensely. "Serves the old witch right! . . ."

Tamarin was bored. He kept thinking how nice it would be to return to the comfortable coziness of his hotel room and to stretch out on the bed with a book. But as long as he had to be present at the dinner Tamarin was determined to get as much as he could out of it and he was prepared to do justice to the wines, especially the sherry. "I haven't tasted anything like it since the flood. . . ." During the early part of the evening he had tried to encourage Nadia to drink more. "How about another half a glass, Nadia?" "Well, if you insist—just to make you happy," Nadia had answered, becoming bolder and bolder under the influence of wine. "Here is to your papa . . . And here is to your mama . . ." Later, Tamarin began to think that Nadia had had too much and he no longer volunteered to refill her glass.

"Just think," Vermandois said, "that all true literature, religious and secular, creative and philosophical, everything that the wisest people have dwelt on for the last three thousand years, is nothing more than eschatology in the purest and most terrifying sense of the word. Take theological literature for example—it's indescribably vast and I am familiar with an infinitesimal portion of it. All the fathers of the church with the possible exception of Saint Irenaeus insisted that the world is old, that the world is debilitated, that the world is approaching its end, that the world is a body eaten away by incurable diseases and breathing its last on a deathbed, that the world is a structure about to collapse and parts of which have already fallen, that the eclipse of the world is at hand: '*in occasu saeculi summus.* . . .'"

"We can find examples of it even nearer to our own times," Doctor Siegfried Mayer remarked in his atrocious French, feeling that it was his turn to say something. "Friedrich Nietzsche said that the world is about to suffer its last convulsions and that he was the last philosopher. '*Den letzten Philosophen nenne ich mich, denn ich bin der letzte Mensch. . . . . . .*'"

"Here is a horrible thought: what if everything they say does not make any sense?" Nadia whispered to Tamarin. The general glanced at her and sighed.

"Nietzsche used such marvelous words!" the Countess said addressing the German. She wondered for a second whether she should or should not invite him to one of her Tuesdays? "He speaks such awful French. . . . Well, we'll see. . . ." The Countess was in the best of humors. The Soviet Ambassador's dinner was a success. There was something so poetic about the philosophical Romans, or Byzantines, or ancient wise men engaged in a clever and learned argument in some sort of a citadel, besieged by some sort of barbarians. The Countess was slightly hazy on the score of who the barbarians were, or who was besieging whom, but she was very pleased.

The important social position enjoyed by the Countess de Bellancombre was due primarily to her amazing capacity for becoming excited about political matters, and to her sustained ability to voice her excitement. There were other reasons for the brilliant position she occupied, but without that capacity none of them could have led her on the road to social success. By birth she was a South American. Vermandois, who was very much at home in her house and who because of that made sarcastic remarks to her face as well as behind her back, said that her biography should begin with the day on which she arrived in Paris. "Your entire youth should be omitted, just as Mommsen omits in his famous work the entire period of early Roman history, since because of its legendary nature it does not deserve the attention of a serious historian." The Countess pretended to be angry. According to her version she belonged to a noble Spanish family which for some reason or other had lost its titles and had migrated to South America. Before the fall of the monarchy she was entitled to a seat at the court in Madrid and her father had the right to wear a hat in the presence of the Spanish king. She had been educated in a Catholic convent in France and she was very religious. In some way her piety had been reconciled with her extremely Left convictions. Her marriage to the Count de Bellancombre had been arranged by her parents as a matter of business. She brought to her husband as dowry a sizable but not a tremendous fortune. In return her husband, who was much older than she, supplied her with a resounding but none too distinguished title. The marriage did not turn out happily. Their friends said that the Count was unfaithful to his wife "whenever and as often as possible." It was also rumored that the Count and Countess could not abide each other—a fact which they made no effort to conceal.

Prominent political figures who frequented Countess de Bellancombre's salon ascribed her social position to her family and her wealth; members of the nobility who still had money ascribed it to the brains and the education of the Countess. Some people referred to it as "the first political salon in Paris," which was indicative of its importance; others who shared the accepted point of view that salons were disappearing and were a thing of the past called it "the last political salon in Paris." Much the same things were said about dozens of other drawing-rooms. Her political salon was built around political personalities rather than political ideas, but no one person played in it the part which Clemenceau, Jules Lemaître, and Anatole France had played in similar surroundings. The general tone of the salon was radical, but it was popular with well-known conservatives as well. Count de Bellancombre belonged to the republican union, which meant that he was a monarchist. But no one expressed any interest in his opinions. Newspaper reporters, who constantly besieged the Countess for interviews and who, she said, made her life unbearable, never asked the Count any questions, unless it was something connected with bridge—a field in which he was a recognized authority. But inasmuch as the Countess called herself "seventy-five per cent bolshevik" and the Count sympathized with the monarchists, people who would not deign to speak to one another anywhere else, rubbed shoulders in her salon. It was said that only the Countess de Bellancombre could risk such combinations of guests. This was a peculiarity of her salon which attracted radicals and conservatives alike. Both were bored by their regular associates. Both found the society of political adversaries stimulating. As a rule enemies are more appreciative of nice things said to them than friends. It was at the house of the Countess de Bellancombre that the feud between two leading political rivals had been settled peacefully. This event did much to bolster the fame of her salon and to build its prestige.

Until recently the Countess had been ageless. Her specialty was youthfulness of the spirit. She firmly considered herself a member of the younger married set and there seemed no reason for her to be anything else. But of late young married women with whom she sold champagne at charity bazaars told her with such glowing affection: "You look younger than any of us!"—and beamed at her with such radiant smiles that the Countess became uneasy. Apparently, youthfulness of the spirit had its limitations. The Countess was very generous, frequently arranged various charity concerts, mailed tickets and solicited contributions. She gave money to the causes in which she was interested, but not much, because her chief contribution was a natural gift of initiative, advice and social energy. It was said that there were needy cases whom she helped secretly, and it was always added that both on economic and religious grounds this was the best way of doing it.

Countess de Bellancombre's salon had certain secondary characteristics. Dinner in her house was served at an unfashionable hour, half an hour earlier than anywhere else. Among the dishes served there were two or three which had been specially concocted for her by a well-known gourmet who was a frequent caller. Foreigners received invitations to her Tuesdays more readily than Frenchmen, on the same principle that makes it easier for a foreigner to receive the order of the Legion of Honor, than for a Frenchman. The salon never had the reputation of being too exclusive—individual talent was the key to admission. Any celebrity, or any man who gave promise of future fame, was likely to be invited by the Countess, provided he had reasonable

manners and did not transgress certain broad political limits.
These limits were never static and kept abreast of the general
trend of events. In 1920, for instance, it would have been futile
for any German celebrity to hope to receive an invitation from
the Countess, but by 1922 such were admitted. The bolsheviks
also had not won their admission immediately, and at first they
were invited only for tea but not for dinner. The Countess was one
of the five or six ladies who prided themselves on being the first
ones to receive the bolsheviks and on having the others follow
their example (just as the Versailles courtiers had vied with one
another in their eagerness to have their fistulas removed, after
Louis XIV had undergone this operation). In the case of Soviet
officials the prerequisite of fame was waived in favor of important
position within the party or of exceptional knowledge in the sphere
of world affairs. Of late, Soviet diplomats had become worth their
weight in gold. The Countess did not invite any French communists. Her communist sympathies were partly an outgrowth of
her radical convictions, and partly of her love for everything Russian. Vermandois suggested that she adopt as her perfume a mixture of "Amu Darya" and of "Cuir de Russie" and keep a volume
of Dostoyevsky on the occasional table in her drawing-room. "Not
one of the long novels, God forbid! But one of the shorter things
that are coming into their own, something like the 'Eternal
Husband'. . . ."

Vermandois intended this remark in a kind way because he
was fond of the Countess de Bellancombre; at least his feeling of
revulsion for her was not as great as it was for most people.
Besides, her comfortable, smoothly functioning household had
become a habit with him. Her particular brand of snobbery did
not interest him, he could read her like a book and was convinced
that there was little there to learn. The one thing that amazed
him about the Countess were her eyes; they were beautiful, black
and deep-set with dramatic circles around them—"and the circles
are not the kind that indicate weak kidneys." Even more amazing
was her appreciation of music, which was real, without any con-

cessions to fashion, and without any urge to discover new genius such as possessed Pauline Metternich when she "discovered Wagner." The Countess could listen with eager delight to the most difficult and intricate music for hours on end. Occasionally she held musicales in her salon which were always superb and which made such severe demands on the listeners that many of them could not meet them. One by one they disappeared, or else retreated to the billiard room. Sitting on a low stool in an awkward, lop-sided, far-from-graceful position, the Countess listened, with her right hand grasping her left shoulder, and with her eyes staring into another world. "Are they pseudo-spiritual eyes? Or did the good Lord forget something in creating the soul of this silly woman?" Vermandois wondered, watching her.

"I don't believe I remember ever coming across this passage from Nietzsche," Vermandois said to the German, whose face at once assumed an expression of gratification at being able to present the famous man with such a valuable gift. "But the very thing I want to say is that, along with religious literature, the same thoughts were expressed by a literature the probity of which is very questionable. One at least can place a conformist interpretation on religious literature, though even in that case the power of the nonconformist figures of speech is too great. But in the case of secular literature that sort of an interpretation is out of the question. All the greatest thinkers of the world had either a vague or a well-defined consciousness of the approaching end of the world. They consoled themselves as best they could."

"But don't you think that there is a certain incongruity there?" Cerisier asked in the same gay and ironical key. "According to you all the wise and learned men of all times thought that the world was approaching its end. But the world, thank God, somehow managed to continue to exist. Could it be possible that the stupid and ignorant men were right?"

"Your argument has a certain validity. Clement of Rome answered it thus; the fools said to him: 'we have heard these things in the days of our fathers, and now we have grown old and nothing like it has come to pass,' 'Look at a tree,' Clement answered the fools, 'first it loses its foliage, then . . .'"

"Let's leave Clement out of this for a moment. Allow me to repeat my humble and simple objection," Cerisier said, not too well pleased with the part he had taken in the dinner table discussion: after all, a famous lawyer was fully as important as a famous writer. "You claim that the world is going to the devil and that all the great thinkers of all times took that point of view. My answer is: first—so far the world has not gone to the devil; second—it is doubtful that all great thinkers took that point of view; third—great thinkers are likely to err in appraising the eras in which they live. Frequently they have denounced and damned the contemporary scene and foretold all sorts of horrors, but fifty or a hundred years later it was generally conceded that their particular eras had been outstanding, productive and beneficial and that they themselves had played a very important part in the progress of humanity toward a better future. It was true in the case of the English revolution, and it was even more so in the case of our own."

"That's correct!" Kangarov exclaimed with a great deal of force. He no longer smiled, realizing that the conversation was veering away from all the philosophical nonsense and turning toward political and therefore serious channels which in some way were concerned with bolshevism.

"Please notice, gentlemen, that as usual we have deviated from our original subject," Vermandois, who was in a benevolent mood, said with a smile. Early in the evening he had forgotten completely the promise he had made to himself not to discuss anything except the weather. He was conducting the discussion in a style to which he was accustomed, enlivening it with properly erudite quips of a kind that were customary in an exchange between the old and the newly elected members at the formal meetings of the French Academy. But making an allowance for the lower level of the audience Vermandois somewhat simplified the style—a fact that pleased him above everything else: he saw it in the light in which Mallarmé must have seen his contributions to

the *Petit Journal*. We were talking about the end of the world.
Now you are discussing the progress of humanity toward a better
future. Let us pose the question in this way: the world continues
to exist, developing along a firmly-established modern course.
With a deep and heartfelt sigh I ask: in view of that is its continued existence justified? Man has certain qualities, but unfortunately he is very stupid. And you bolsheviks have rendered the
invaluable service of being first in modern history to demonstrate
this fact with telling simplicity [Kangarov smiled uncertainly,
not being sure how to take the words of Vermandois]. I don't
deny his so-called mastery over nature. Airplanes are traveling at
a speed of four hundred miles an hour, very soon they will travel
at a speed of one thousand miles. But all these airplanes and the
people who fly them bore me. These wonders of progress are used
to carry mail from Australia at an unreasonable risk to the post-
man, or else to destroy cities like Paris, should the occasion ever
arise. But I receive very few letters from Australia and there is
nothing in them that cannot wait, and, perhaps as a matter of
habit, I am rather fond of Paris. . . ."

"The question of whether the continued existence of the world
is justified is hardly rational," the lawyer interrupted him. "The
world exists and, whether you like it or not, it will continue to
exist. In view of this the rational question is one of social and
spiritual progress. Nothing you have said so far convinces me of
the approaching collision between the earth and a comet, but
even if it were inevitable you and I are powerless to do anything
about it. The betterment of society is another matter."

"Wait and see! The way it will happen is that just as soon as
an ideal social order is created with due assistance from the French
socialist party and from you, my dear friend, the earth will collide
with a comet. I must confess that when the impact throws me out
of my grave I shall be very much amused," Vermandois said, once
again lowering the plane of the conversation. He always did this
at the right psychological moment, living up to his reputation as
a splendid 'causeur.'

"You will lie with a sarcastic smile on your face even in your grave," the Countess said. "'Dors-tu content, Voltaire, et ton hideux sourire—Voltige-t-il encor sur tes os décharnés? . . .' Do you like these divine lines? '. . . Eh bien, qu'il soit permis d'en baiser la poussière—Au moins crédule enfant de ce siècle sans foi —Et de pleurer, ô Christ! sur cette froide terre—Qui vivait de ta mort, et qui mourra sans toi!'" she recited in a quiet voice. "You see, I also can quote."

"But the quotations you use have such unpleasant words! 'Hideux sourire!' I never should have expected it from you!"

"Unpleasant words or not, a comparison to Voltaire is not uncomplimentary," the Count came to his wife's rescue. "Besides, as you know, I am not responsible for my wife's words, so don't bother sending your seconds to see me."

"Gentlemen, the duck!" Vermandois exclaimed. "There will be a short intermission in our discussion."

"Will you pour me a little more of that wine over there," Nadia asked Tamarin under her breath.

"Are you sure it will not be too much?"

"There is nothing for me to do except eat and drink!"

"Eat all you want, but too much wine is bad for you."

"I just want to taste it: I haven't tried it yet. . . ."

XIX

THAT EVENING the main road was deserted. A hum of gay voices emanated from the cafe on the square opposite the railroad station. The scarcity of pedestrians was almost disconcerting; it did not fit in with his expectations. "Anything unexpected is disconcerting. If I am wrong in my calculations on this point, I might find that I am wrong about something much more important." Alvera was calm and proud of being able to control his excitement; even

the attacks of yawning had left him. Only when he reached the
spot where the footpath branched away from the main road he
involuntarily caught his breath. Following his plan he first walked
past the crossing, merely glancing at the path out of the corner
of his eye. Up there, about half-way up the hill, there was a soft
spot of reflected light on the ground. The light came from a window in Monsieur Chartier's villa; there were no other houses
along the path. Alvera walked down the road for another hundred
paces (this also was part of the plan), then with a gesture of
irritation, as though he had forgotten something (though there
was no one to watch him), he turned back. "No one in sight!
Everything in order. . . ." Quickly he turned up the path and
started in the direction of the irregular, widening quadrangle of
soft light.

Suddenly Alvera stopped in his tracks as the sound of music reached his ears: nothing could have surprised him more.
"What is this? What kind of music is it? Where is it coming
from? . . ." At the same moment Alvera felt a surge of inexpres-
sible joy the cause of which he could not realize at once. "If he
has guests the whole thing is postponed; no, it is off for good and
not through any fault of mine! . . . But I don't remember ever
seeing any musical instrument there! . . ." he thought, and suddenly he understood: "A radio! . . . If it's a radio he may be
listening to it alone. . . . It all will be settled in a few minutes. . . ." When he was about fifteen feet away from the gate
Alvera stopped and with an awkward, theatrical gesture pressed
his hand against his side: his heart had almost stopped beating.
A man's voice was singing and he could distinguish clearly every
word. ". . . *Et puis, cher, ce qui me décide—A quitter le monde
galant* . . ." The singer was shouting the words, simulating a gay
abandonment. The radio puzzled Alvera. He could not make up
his mind whether it would work to his advantage, but somehow
felt that he would rather not have it there. "Probably he will turn
it off. . . ." He took several faltering steps forward and saw that
the window in Monsieur Chartier's study was open. "How did I

ever overlook such a possibility? . . . There is nothing surprising about an open window on a warm night! . . . But it is extremely important! . . . The sound of the shot will carry a long way. But there are no houses near, and no one uses this footpath. . . . The radio might come in handy after all. . . . It will drown out all other noises, and the shot is not too loud anyway. . . ." Alvera took off the glasses, blinked several times and put on his gloves. He glanced at his watch: he was two minutes behind schedule, but this was not fatal; he had time enough to spare. ". . . *C'est que ma bourse est vide, vide,—Vide que c'en est désolant . . .*" The voice was still singing. Once again he glanced over his shoulder at the empty darkness. With an almost mechanical move of his thumb he switched the safety catch on the gun. "I will say: 'I believe you have guests, Monsieur Chartier? Don't let me disturb you. Here is the manuscript and you can pay me next time. . . .' But there never will be a 'next time.' Why should he make another appointment with me at night? And, besides, how will I be able to stand another month, or even another week like this? . . ." ". . . *Or pour peu qu'on y refléchisse,—Quand on n'a pas le sou, vois-tu . . .*" With determination Alvera opened the gate, crossed the garden and rang the bell. Above the sound of music he could hear the shuffle of unhurried footsteps. "Who is it?" the old man asked from behind the door. "It is the copyist," Alvera answered (only his breathing was not quite as regular as usual). "Oh, it's you . . . I had forgotten about you," Monsieur Chartier said, opening the door. ". . . *Il est temps de lâcher le vice—Pour revenir à la vertu. . . .*"

"Good evening, young man. I forgot that you were coming tonight. Come in. . . ." There was only one hat on the coat-hanger. "Is it his, or is someone else here?"

"Am I disturbing you? I believe you have guests, Monsieur Chartier?" Alvera asked forcing a smile. "My voice is not steady, but I doubt that he noticed it, and my smile was natural. . . ."

"A man my age never has visitors after nine!" Monsieur Chartier said gaily, raising his voice in order to make himself heard above the din of music coming from the study. "No, I am all alone. It's my radio. I bought it so I would have something to do in my old age."

"Is that right? Hope you will enjoy it," Alvera said. For a second his breathing stopped completely. ("Well, I am glad. The end is now here.")

"It's a good machine. Seven tubes and a short-wave attachment . . . Come in."

"I feel badly about disturbing you. . . ."

"You are not disturbing me. On the contrary, I feel badly about bringing you out here at night. I was in a hurry to get the papers, but after all they could have been sent by mail. Didn't you say that you came here to get some fresh air? Come on in."

They entered the study. It was a large room conventionally and inexpensively furnished, with a carpeted floor and with a window opening on the garden. A new radio, its varnish bright and shiny, stood on the chest of drawers. Still enjoying the novelty of ownership, Monsieur Chartier led his guest directly toward it. "I must shoot when he pulls out his pocketbook," Alvera remembered. "But how about the open window? Should I try to close it while he is not looking? No, that's impossible."

"Have you brought everything? Thank you," the old man said and, without waiting for an answer, leaned over the radio. "Maybe this is a good time? . . . No, I will stick to my plan. . . . When he reaches for his pocketbook. . . ." Monsieur Chartier twisted the dial and looked up with a pleased expression. The sound was not as loud. "Anti-fading device, superheterodyne," he said, relishing the newly acquired vocabulary. "It's the last word!"

"Unfortunately I know very little about radio. . . But if you have a short-wave attachment you should be able to get America?"

"With seven tubes and a short-wave attachment I can get anything," Monsieur Chartier answered with a laugh. "America, the colonies, Moscow—anything you want. Let's have a look at the papers. Thirty-two pages. I owe you forty-eight francs. Would

you like the money now, or would you like it when you finish
the whole thing?"

"If you don't mind, I should like to have it now. I have to pay
rent on my apartment."

"Pay rent now?" the old man seemed surprised. "Why? This
is not October."

"I have a single room and I have to pay for it by the month."

"Why don't you lease an apartment by the year? You will find
it much less expensive."

"I should have to pay three months' rent in advance and make
a deposit besides. I never seem to have enough cash to do it."

"You haven't the cash?" Monsieur Chartier sounded as though
he doubted the words. Apparently it was difficult for him to conceive that there were people who were so hard pressed for money.
"You wouldn't need very much. What are you paying now?"

"Hundred and fifty a month. . . ." "What is all this about?
. . . Time is getting short," Alvera thought angrily, feeling that
he could not bring to an abrupt end this unexpected conversation
for which there was no allowance in his schedule. "A hundred
and fifty a month. . . ."

"You see! . . ." Monsieur Chartier said. "This means eighteen hundred a year. You could find an apartment with a kitchen
for around twelve hundred, or if you are lucky for as low as a
thousand. At this time of the year you should be able to find a
place where they would not ask you for a deposit. Do you mean
to tell me that you can't scrape up three hundred francs?"

"No," Alvera answered in a hollow voice and with a nervous
shudder dropped his hand in his pocket. Monsieur Chartier
seemed lost in his thoughts.

"Look here," he said (Alvera released the grip on the gun in
his pocket as though the "look here" left him no choice except to
continue the conversation). "I will have a great deal of work. I
believe that you are an exceptionally good typist. How would
you like an advance of two hundred francs? You can get a lease
on an apartment, and then you can pay me back in installments.

You are a very accommodating young man. You even bring the work to my home, which suits me perfectly. Later, I will reimburse you for your transportation. Don't think that I am forgetting it," he said carried away by an outburst of generosity and once again moved toward the radio. The loudspeaker sounded hoarse. "*Tur-lututu*," a chorus thundered. It was followed by a woman's voice:

"Hier à midi, la gantière
Vit arriver un Brésilien. . . ."

A man's voice answered:

"Il lui dit: Voulez-vous, gantière,
Vendre des gants au Brésilien?"

"Lovely!" Monsieur Chartier said and laughed. "Do you enjoy light opera, young man? This is one of Offenbach's best. . . ." He twisted a dial and the sound became louder. "There is no sense in renting a room by the month," the old man repeated with conviction, raising his voice again and at the same time listening eagerly to the song. ". . . *C'est mon état, dit la gantière,—Quelle couleur, beau Brésilien?*" he repeated after the singer, accompanying his words with a smile, a shrug of the shoulders and a light tapping with his right foot. "I can let you have a hundred and fifty or two hundred francs, and you can get the rest somewhere else. At least you will have a place you can call your own. '. . . *Sang de boeuf, charmante gantière,—Lui riposta le Brésilien. . . .*' I owe you forty-eight francs now? Give me two francs change." He reached inside his coat for the pocketbook. Suddenly the left side of his face became disfigured with a horrible convulsion, the muscles jumped once, and then with frightening speed again and again. Quickly Monsieur Chartier turned away. As though the convulsion resolved his last doubts, Alvera pulled out the gun and aiming at the back of the old man's head, fired. The explosion was loud, much louder than it had sounded in the open air. Monsieur Chartier emitted an animal grunt, turned around, the muscles of his face were still jumping and his eyes were bulging from their sockets. He opened his mouth, took a short step forward, lifted his hand and fell. With horror Alvera glanced in the direction of the window. On the carpet Monsieur Chartier with a convulsive movement twisted his body on one side, drew up his legs and became still. Death was almost instantaneous. The room was vibrating with the deafening sound of the chorus which with triumphant joy was repeating the words of the soloist:

". . . Et dans la main de la gantière
Tremblait la main du Brésilien. . . ."

Two policemen riding their bicycles along the Paris road heard the clear, distinct report; it was either a shot, or the backfire of a car. They slowed down and listened, but could hear nothing else to alarm them. "It sounded as though it came from the direction of father Chartier's villa. . . ." Only the strains of music reached their ears. "A few days ago he bought a new radio," one of the policemen said with envy; for some time he had been dreaming about a new radio and saving advertisements of radio manufacturers which he had been cutting out of the papers. "He paid twenty-two hundred for it. No installments—spot cash." "He made his money on the stock market selling short," the other one grumbled. "How about enjoying the music for a while? It sounds good. . . ." "We are not supposed to trespass on private property, but I don't think he will mind." They turned up the footpath and approached the villa. There was nothing there to arouse suspicion. Gay words and music reached them from the open window. "A wonderful machine! Dynamic speaker and a push-and-pull volume control," the first policeman said bitterly. "I wish I could afford one! Rich people can have anything they want." "They could not give it to me. It's worse than having a canary. . . ." Something strange was happening to the sound; the music dissolved into a wild howl. "The old fool! He buys an expensive machine and has no idea how to handle it! Monsieur Chartier! . . ." he called through the open window. "You are turning the wrong dial! . . ."

A shadow darted along the wall of the room and disappeared. "Monsieur Chartier! . . ." the policeman called again. This time the shadow fled in the opposite direction—it seemed to move much too fast for an old man. The policemen exchanged a puzzled glance. With a purposeful air the first one leaned his bicycle against a tree.

The first minute of horror produced by the unexpected force of the explosion was over. Alvera watched himself with a sense of inward triumph. He had passed the examination with flying colors. He had no feeling of fear, or of the remorse which people talked about. Only his breathing was slightly more labored than usual. Later it seemed to him that during that minute his act had not penetrated his consciousness, that he had had no time to comprehend what had happened. But he argued with himself that that was not so: everything had worked according to plan, he had rehearsed the sensations of a murderer a number of times before and he had discovered that his imagination had not deceived him.

Keeping a firm grip on himself Alvera dropped the gun in his pocket and leaned over the body: the old man was dead. "Not a pleasant sight, but it would have been just as unpleasant if I had killed him in a duel or in a war." It pleased him that from a technical point of view everything had gone off perfectly. One shot had done the work and it had been unnecessary to fire a second time. He had considered such a possibility—he would have had to shoot again, though this would have augmented the risk. He knew that his nerves were not strong enough for him to use a knife or a blackjack.

Alvera glanced at the watch: he was progressing on schedule. He had thirteen minutes to search for the money. Glancing around, cautiously (though there was very little blood) he picked up the pocketbook which the old man had dropped on the floor and with casual indifference peered inside. "Apparently a reasonable amount of cash. . . . Shall I count it now? No, I can do it later." He stuck it in his pocket and glancing around once again decided that he should begin the search with the middle drawer of the desk—the key was in the keyhole. "Everything is moving along fine," he repeated in his mind and took a deep breath. He looked at the old man, shuddered and quickly walked away, as though afraid that the body would lunge at him from the floor.

Tiptoeing (though there was no reason for it) toward the door, he looked into the dining-room. "What is there here of any value? Silver? . . . No, I will not fool with silver—it is too difficult to sell. I must examine the desk drawers first, and then I can search the bedroom which must be over there, beyond the dining-room. But how can I do all this in a quarter of an hour?" Only now he realized that there was an oversight in his schedule: it was impossible to make a thorough search of a house in fifteen minutes without knowing what was hidden there! "How could I have made such an obvious mistake?" he thought anxiously and for the first time his coolness deserted him. "Everything is moving along fine. . . ." Looking around again he tiptoed toward the body and stared at the old man's face. It still was disfigured by the last convulsion and for some reason the realization of this unnerved him. His hands were shaking.

The opened window preyed more and more on his mind. "It is too high for anyone standing on the path to see inside. Should I close it? That's too dangerous: someone might be passing by and see me. No one heard the shot—there isn't a house anywhere near. And, besides, the radio! . . ." He jumped: it was his first realization that the radio was still going full blast. The woman was singing: ". . . Partez, s'écria la gantière,—Partez, séduisant Brésilien. . . ." Suddenly quick nervous shivers ran down the full length of his frame. "How stupid!" Alvera thought in an effort to calm himself. "Everything is moving along fine. Delay? If worst comes to worst I can wait until the next train. It goes through Louvécienne half an hour later. Few passengers use it, but that is not vital. . . . If so, I will have forty-five minutes to search the house and that should be more than enough." But the idea of spending three-quarters of an hour longer enclosed in this house was so unpleasant he almost could not bear it. He felt the urge to do something at once—to act with energy and precision. "I will begin to search right now! Right this moment! If I find it in the next thirteen minutes—no, there are only twelve minutes left!— I will leave at once; if not—I will wait for the next train. . . . In that case, I must allow myself fully seven minutes to get to the station. Before leaving I must not forget to turn off the damned radio! . . . Or else it will keep on screeching all night, neighbors will hear it, and the entire plan will go by the board. Actually I could turn it off right now: if someone is passing it will seem only natural that an old man should cut off the music after nine. Yes, it's better to turn it off now," he thought with a vague sense of uneasiness growing within him. His hands were shaking more than ever. Alvera tiptoed toward the radio and stood listening. The ridiculous voice was singing: ". . . *Tu veux donc, cruelle gantière* . . ." "How strange that a light opera is being rendered somewhere, people are listening and laughing, and I am listening with them. . . . But they also can hear me! . . ." He cursed himself for his stupidity: how could anyone hear him over the radio! "I must be losing my mind. . . . The damned radio has to go off right now! . . ." Selecting one of the dials at random Alvera turned it to the right. To his great dismay, instead of stopping, the sound became louder than ever. Alvera jerked his hand away from the dial as though it had burned his fingers, then he grabbed it once again and began twisting it. As though to spite him the Brazilian's voice shrieked in a wild metallic pitch. Terror seized him. "How can I stop it?" he asked himself panting for breath. "People are certain to hear it. Shall I leave it this way and let it shriek? No, that's impossible. Someone is sure to come and inquire. . . ." He grabbed the dials with both hands, pulled them, and then tried to push them in. Tauntingly the Brazilian continued to scream: ". . . *Tu veux la mort du Brésilien* . . ." In a frenzy he hit the machine with his fist, pushing it back against the wall, and at the same instant he pressed his hand against his side, but this time there was nothing theatrical about the gesture. He felt that he could not get enough air into his lungs. And at that very moment a new voice assailed his ears—a voice which came not from the radio but from the direction of the window. There was nothing artificial or mechanical about it; it was alive, real and hoarse: "Monsieur Chartier . . ."

Alvera could not distinguish the rest. For one second he was paralyzed with fear. Then, doubling up, he darted across the room into a corner. Leaning against the wall he took the gun out of his pocket and stood gripping it tensely in his hand. "I have four more rounds . . ." He realized that the voice came from the path outside. His brain was working feverishly: "Should I call: 'leave me alone—I am going to bed'? . . . No, he would recognize the voice. Should I pretend that I have not heard him? Should I walk over to the window and be ready to shoot? No, it's better not to answer . . . He may try again and leave. If he rings the door-bell, I will not answer. What if he calls the police? Before he returns I will have time to escape. . . ." The inhuman voice of the Brazilian was shouting: ". . . *Et voilà comment la gantière . . .*" A grating noise reached him through the window, but this time it was nearer, somewhere in the garden below; it sounded as though someone were trying to reach the window sill. Alvera raised the gun. Just like a figure materializing gradually on a screen, first a cap, then a bearded face, and then a pair of blue shoulders appeared in the dark square of the window. "Police!" he thought, catching his breath. "But why are they here? . . ." Fear was written on the bearded face. There was a shot, an agonized scream, and the policeman jumped or fell down. Alvera rushed for the door. He was pursued by the ululating howl of the chorus:

"*. . . Et voilà comment la gantière*
Sauva les jours du Brésilien . . ."

Throwing open the door Alvera crossed the garden on the run. A dark figure at the gate jumped out of his way. He was racing down the footpath. Behind him a long shrill, penetrating whistle broke in on the howl of the radio. "A chase! I am lost!"

his mind warned him as he panted heavily down hill. He ran out on the main road and another figure leaped aside. "Good God! What's happening?" a woman's voice exclaimed in the darkness. Lights flashed on somewhere, and somewhere else a window was thrown open. There was a piercing scream: "*A l'assassin! . . .*" Alvera continued to run, knowing that there was nowhere he could hide, that now there was no escape from the guillotine. The shouts behind him grew in intensity. Most terrifying of all was the never-ending, angry sound of the whistle. The lights of the café flickered in the distance. From the left, in the direction of the track, came the deep wail of the engine blowing for the station. "That's my train! . . . I still can make it . . . I will pay the extra fare to the conductor. . . ." His brain was no longer functioning. From behind came the deafening roar of a gun. Without breaking his stride Alvera glanced over his shoulder: a policeman on a bicycle was only twenty feet away. Without taking aim Alvera fired at the policeman, threw his gun at him, and marshaling his remaining strength continued to run. A terrified figure on the side of the road pressed itself against the fence. Alvera remembered the third rail. "That's the only thing left . . . Sing Sing . . . If I can only make it! . . ." Behind him was a constant, swelling clamor of angry voices: "*A l'assassin! . . .*" A man with a bottle in his raised hand appeared in the door of the café. "If the policeman is not dead I still may escape the guillotine," was Alvera's last thought. He felt a blow, there was a sharp pain in his mouth and in his head, he lifted his hand to his chin, and fell to the ground covered with blood.

XX

". . . CUVIER'S BRAIN weighed eighteen-hundred grams and this fact was used as foundation for a hastily concocted hypothesis that a definite relation exists between a man's genius and the size of his brain. Later it was discovered that the brain of Cuvier's butler weighed two-hundred grams more. I am afraid that a similar fate will overtake your idea of the historical mission of the proletariat. Suddenly people will realize that some other social group is superior to the proletariat. Not much superior, but superior just the same. For instance, Hitler's storm troopers. . . ."

"I believe that you are oversimplifying the whole thing. I am inclined to think that the psycho-physiological theory you mention was based on more than just the weight of Cuvier's brain. And as far as the scientific theory of progress is concerned, it was based by Marx on a more than adequate number of established facts."

"A scientific theory of progress is an absurdity, my dear Monsieur Cerisier," Vermandois remonstrated. "It is an absurdity because the basic factor underlying all social phenomena is man, who is an incalculable, variable and paradoxical quantity. Your theory, on the other hand, insists on considering man as a calculable and, at least over considerable periods of time, an unvarying unit. True, your theory admits that during the stone age, or even five hundred years ago, man was not what he is now. But in considering the social problems of our day it uses a fictitious conception of man, arbitrarily dividing him into groups according to class characteristics and arbitrarily endowing him with certain universal, unvarying, human qualities. Your theory uses terms such as bourgeois, peasant and proletarian in the same way that chemistry uses the terms hydrogen and oxygen. But hydrogen and oxygen remain always the same; a thousand years from now they will still be what they are today. While man, whether he is a proletarian or a bourgeois, is endowed with only one invariable characteristic: his collective soul changes from day to day. Today he wants democracy, tomorrow he wants Hitler, day after tomorrow something else [Vermandois glanced out of the corner of his eye at Kangarov]. It is absurd to build a theory of progress on such shaky foundations. Your theory assumes that man knows what he wants, whereas in reality he has no idea of it. Your theory assumes that man is guided by selfishness, but in reality he is guided by only God knows what. Under identical conditions men belonging to the same social category—or shall we use the term social class, though in our day the boundaries between social classes are very different from what they were in the days of Marx—these men are just as likely to be drawn toward Hitler as they are toward Stalin," Vermandois said, unable to restrain himself.

"I know that at present it is fashionable to ridicule Marxism," Cerisier began, his tone indicating that he intended to make himself heard without any interruptions. "He has the voice of a radio announcer," Vermandois thought, with respectful attention written on his face. "Marxism never undertook to explain everything in this world . . ."

"On the contrary, that is the very thing it undertakes to do."

"Please, don't interrupt until I finish what I have to say," the lawyer said angrily. Everyone at the table looked up at him with surprise. "Granted that Marxists occasionally are carried away by their theories, but you must remember that all young scientists are likely to go to extremes. Let me ask you one question! What can you offer as an alternative?" Cerisier said. His manner and the tone he had assumed were so unpleasant that everyone in the room felt embarrassed. "An embittered man. He has been disappointed once again about the ministry," Vermandois made a mental note.

People who knew Cerisier cheerfully said that his disposition was getting progressively worse due to a succession of failures. Judging by outward appearances one could hardly call him a failure. Cerisier received a sizable income from his legal practice and he occupied an important position in the world of politics. By comparison with the majority of people he was a success, and he could be considered a failure only by comparing him with the man he should have been according to the hopes (or fears) of the men who had known him fifteen years ago. He was not ranked among the first ten men in his profession, but his merits justly placed him among the second ten. Recently, for the third time in his career, Cerisier had been a candidate for the office of president of the Paris bar association. He had polled a gratifying number of votes, but the total was so far short of the necessary majority that it gave his enemies an opportunity to say triumphantly: "This is the end! He never will be given another chance!" He had served as a minister of state, but in a department of secondary importance and without being able to accomplish anything brilliant. Besides, the cabinet of which he had been a member had been in power for so much shorter a time than usual, that though he enjoyed it very much, he found it somewhat embarrassing to be addressed in the drawing-rooms as "Monsieur le Ministre." Neither could Cerisier become the titular head of the socialist party. On the contrary, as the years went by his relations with the party became cooler and more distant; of late he seemed to be entirely away from the main current of party life. There were a number of reasons for this. Cerisier was too busy with his law practice, he did not have enough leisure to devote to party activities and his income was much too large for a prominent socialist. He had accepted the appointment in the ill-fated cabinet not contrary to the wishes of the party, but without its blessing. It was no longer clear whether officially he was considered a socialist or not. In party publications he was still referred to as "comrade," but it was evident that any day now his name might be expected to appear preceded by the fatal "Monsieur." The party had learned by experience that Cerisier was not important, or at least not indispensable to its welfare. Avoiding open breaks and public disputes, acting slowly and showing him every consideration at first, then changing to more effective and less polite tactics, younger and more persistent men shouldered him away from the pinnacle of a party career. Years ago he had done the same thing to his predecessor, but then circumstances had been different: it seemed to him that in his case it had been a clash of principles.

Most important of all, the worst thing that can happen to a man's career had happened to Cerisier: without any apparent reason, people in the know suddenly refused to take him seriously any longer. He handled important and famous cases, he received tremendous fees, he had acquired the right to be addressed as

"Monsieur le Ministre" until the end of his days, and he was firmly entrenched in the upper crust of French parliamentary life. But at the mere mention of his name smiles seemed to imply that something amusing was known about him; something that was no longer a surmise or a rumor, but a universally recognized fact. In reality there was no ground for such an attitude. Cerisier could not be charged with any specific misdeeds, he never had gone back on his political convictions, and in his legal practice he refused to take questionable cases (though he did handle certain cases which he would have refused if the fees offered had been smaller). His reputation could not be called bad, but—what was even worse—it was no longer serious. To top all his misfortunes he had gained weight to almost ridiculous proportions. No one had any more illusions that Cerisier would ever win for himself a place among the first ten men in his profession. In his more lucid moments he realized this himself. He had three ambitions in his life: to become president of the Paris bar association, to become titular head of the socialist party, and to become head of the government. Now he could see that none of the three would ever be realized.

Vermandois lifted his hands in protest.

"As far," he said, "as your new social theory is concerned—incidentally it is a little under a hundred years old—I hold nothing against it, but even if I did I should be careful to spare your feelings, as well as the feelings of our gracious host. All the other social religions have collapsed, and probably the same fate awaits the social religions which will replace it. The crucial factor underlying the collapse of every social teaching is that history is even more senseless than the most senseless social theory. . . . Do you enjoy moving-pictures, Countess?" he asked, using the old weapon of experienced monopolizers of conversation, who like to lend to their monologues an appearance of a fair exchange of ideas. "I never go to see them, I detest them!" she said. Without in any way acknowledging her answer Vermandois continued: "I enjoy them very much, but I seem to have difficulty in understanding them. In my entire life I have never smiled at Charlie Chaplin or at the animated cartoons, at the sight of which both the élite and the mob roar with laughter. The films I like best, and that mean most to me, are the ones in which men shoot guns, ride at a gallop, and bail out of airplanes. I admit that they are part of the gangster school, but they also are part of the energy school. I never go to see clever plays, but at least once a week I go to the movies. What then is the basic difference between my attitude and the attitude of my cook? My cook instantly unravels every plot, no matter whether it be love or mystery. She understands intuitively what is taking place and what the motives are which guide the leading characters: why the count wants to poison the impostor, and why the model accuses herself of a crime which she has not committed. I, on the other hand, have to have time to understand the plot; frequently I leave the moving-picture theatre without being able to fathom its mainsprings. The reason for it is that I cannot keep pace with the stupidity of the plot. I find it difficult to choose without hesitation from among all the impossible and stupid combinations the one that is most absurd, which usually happens to be the one chosen by the scenario writer. Historical events never fail to surprise me in the same way. I never expect anything good or intelligent from history. But invariably it chooses something so monstrous in its stupidity and repulsiveness that all I can do is say with despair: I never could have guessed it, I never could have foreseen it, I never could have imagined it!"

"Allow me to take the part of your cook and to disagree with you," Cerisier said with an angry chuckle. "Unless you intend to write your own brand of world history. In that case, here are a few chapter headings I would suggest: 'Authorities crush the uprising of July 14, 1789. With a few well-placed shots Commandant de Launay disperses the unruly mob . . .' Or this: 'German army enters Paris, November 11, 1918. Wilhelm II is crowned ruler of the world in Versailles. . . .'"

"And here is my suggestion for the final chapter," the Countess said. "'Carrying out the sentence of the resurrected inquisition court the books of Louis-Etienne Vermandois are burned in a bonfire. Later, after having his tongue cut out, he, too, is destroyed in the same manner.'"

"To burn him in a bonfire is not such a bad idea," the financier remarked with a benevolent smile. "But why cut out his tongue? He says so many entertaining things."

"Perhaps it would be better to follow the precedent set in the case of Galileo, and make him renounce his convictions. Let him acknowledge under torture that history represents the triumph of reason."

"I can promise you a resounding *'e pur si muove . . .'* I wonder if you could fix the pineapple according to my special recipe?" Vermandois asked the Maître d'hôtel. "Two teaspoonfuls of cherry brandy, sugar, maraschino and a drop of armagnac. Just a drop."

"I second your suggestion. Your recipe sounds much better than your philosophy of history, my dear Monsieur Vermandois," Cerisier said, considerably mollified by the success of his argument. "It appears that your aim in life is to deprive people of their hopes."

"For instance, my one hope in life is to see socialism triumph over capitalistic society and he is trying to deprive me of the one thing I live for!" the financier remarked. Everyone laughed.

"But in Germany they actually are burning books in bonfires," Doctor Siegfried Mayer said, searching for the French words with apparent difficulty. "They even may be burning your books!" he remarked to Vermandois.

"You don't say? What excellent advertising for his publishers!"

"I am afraid that so far I have not earned such a distinction," Vermandois answered indifferently. He was not too well pleased with the familiar tone the conversation was assuming. Not only the financier, but even the other guests, whom he knew only casually, were referring to him in his presence in the third person. "I am glad you mentioned it, Monsieur . . ." he said to the

German, whose name he could not remember. "You will have to admit that if ten years ago someone had told you that Germany would be ruled by Hitler, you would not have believed him?"

"On the contrary, I should not have been surprised in the least," Mayer instantly warmed to the subject. "Knowing Germany, knowing the quasi-republicans who were at the helm, I always believed that . . ."

"In that case, you are a man of far greater perception than most. I know I never imagined it. But then, as I sit through a moving-picture, I never imagine that the countess has covered herself with tattoo and jumped into the ocean, in order to direct the suspicions of her husband to the machinations of the seductive adventuress."

"And still, though there are setbacks and deviations, history is moving toward a socialist society, no matter how much you ridicule it, my dear friend," Cerisier said. "What is past is past. Even the Austrian house-painter who is firmly seated on the throne of the Hohenzollerns and who does not seem averse to the idea of consolidating with it the throne of the Hapsburgs, has taken no steps to restore monarchy, has not been openly over-indulgent with the capitalists, and has not gone back to the precepts of the Manchester school. By degrees social injustice is disappearing everywhere."

"Everything being equal, your social injustice will rest in an historical tomb, until, worm-eaten and considerably the worse for wear, it is resurrected by popular acclaim. All you need is time for one generation to forget and for another to grow up. In contrast to real ones, historical tombs are built with an eye to resurrection. This charming young lady may witness the resurrection of capitalism in her homeland. But, I am afraid, the new brand of capitalism will do without manufacturers who fancy themselves as humanitarians and without the worker's freedom to strike."

"Capitalism will never be restored in Russia!" Nadia said emphatically, managing her French without difficulty.

"I hope you heard her, you incorrigible misanthrope," Kangarov said with an anxious note in his voice, scanning the faces of the people around the table.

"No one can say what will tempt the romantic side of man after socialist society becomes an established fact. I believe the issue that probably will tempt men's souls most will be the restoration of social inequality, either through a violent upheaval, or through gradual evolution. Revolutionary and evolutionary capitalists will appear on the scene, and each of the two groups will develop its own theory of social progress. How can one prevent them from holding an opinion as to what constitutes progress? . . . But no matter what happens, one can be certain that the world will not be any worse than it is today."

"Cassandra, don't dance on the ruins before Troy has fallen! No matter how you argue, what is past is past."

Vermandois glanced at the Countess and gave her a gentle smile.

"I know I am boring you. Why should we dwell on unpleasant things, so long as good books, beautiful women and the earth still exist? You say, what is past is past? I am inclined to regret it. I am disappointed that due to some oversight I appeared on this planet in the nineteenth century. I should have been born three hundred years ago. Then I would have been a lover of Ninon de Lenclos, I would have admired knights wearing armor, I would have seen Popes with long beards, and instead of tricky publishers Louis XIV would have provided me with a living."

"There is a chance that you would not have thought them all quite so charming if you had been their contemporary."

"Very likely, but it is only human to seek variety. Goethe said that humanity twists and turns like a person on a sick bed, trying to find a comfortable position. And Luther expressed the same thought even more clearly by saying that the world is like a drunken peasant astride a jackass; if you support him on the right, he will slide off on the left; if you support him on the left, he will slide off on the right . . ."

"You really are much too generous with your quotations, my dear friend."

"That's my worst vice. . . . It would not surprise me in the least if in Germany Hitler should be succeeded by a German Stalin. . . ."

"Amen!" Kangarov said fervently.

". . . And in Russia Stalin will be succeeded by a Russian Hitler," Vermandois was interrupted by the financier, who saw no further reason to spare the ambassador's feelings: the deal, which they had been negotiating, was definitely closed.

"That's the incorrigible bourgeois speaking in you."

"What would you suggest, cher maître? Cherry brandy, maraschino or armagnac?" Kangarov asked quickly, casting an uneasy glance at Wislicenus.

XXI

As soon as coffee was served the guests began to move about the room. Kangarov left his place at the head of the table and, carrying his chair with him, visited first with one guest, then with another. He spent a little time with the Countess, then with Cerisier and finally, achieving the real purpose of his maneuvering, wedged himself between Nadia and Tamarin. The dinner was a success. The guests had received everything they could have expected, beginning with the brilliant conversation of Vermandois and ending with sherry and champagne. The host now could have a few minutes to himself, especially as long as the general conversation showed no signs of dying down. Only Wislicenus took no part in it. "He might at least be polite and say a few words, but to hell with him!" Kangarov thought, the feeling of contentment taking the edge off his rancor.

"It wasn't a bad dinner? Was it, my dear commander?" he asked, placing his chair between Tamarin and Nadia. "At last we can relax and talk Russian. No one will mind it now."

"A wonderful dinner! They know how to serve food," Tamarin answered, and, to be on the safe side, added: "At least by comparison with the places where I usually eat." It was more discreet not to give the impression that he frequented expensive restaurants when he was on his own. Actually, Tamarin had not visited this particular place for twenty-five years. At the beginning of the dinner he had tried to remember under what circumstances he had been there last, when and with whom. Recollections of the world before the deluge seemed dimly strange. The thing he found most disconcerting tonight was the peculiar assortment of guests. His entire life had been spent in a homogeneous society, first among guard officers and later among Soviet bureaucrats. Though Nadia was in no way a part of the society to which he was accustomed, it was natural for him to cling to her, just as Christians on a sightseeing visit to a synagogue or to a mosque cling together instinctively, no matter how interested, or how much carried away they are by the beauty of the ritual.

"So that's how the people's money is spent?" Nadia said, or rather her lips formed the words without any exercise of will on her part. They seemed to take the line of least resistance and repeat a familiar combination of sounds. If it were not for the wine, despite Kangarov's fatherly attitude, she would never have permitted herself to say a thing like that, even as a joke. But the ambassador showed no indication of being annoyed.

"And what would you think if I were to box your ears for using such language?" he asked tenderly. "If you look at it in that way, you are right, but when in Rome do as the Romans do. . . . And they do know how to cook," he added with a sigh to show that only the thought of spending the people's money would not allow him to enjoy the dinner to the fullest extent. "The day will come when everybody will eat like that all of the time. Though some people frown on it, I make no attempt to conceal the fact that food is one of the real joys of my life. What did you think of the duck stuffed with oranges?"

"It's a tasty dish, but I don't see any reason for stuffing a duck with oranges, and as far as the duck is concerned, we have fatter ducks in Moscow."

"Fatter ducks!" Kangarov imitated her voice, thinking at the same time that her smile and her impudently shining eyes were dearer and more important to him than anything else in the world. "Fatter ducks!" Someone touched his shoulder and he looked up with displeasure. Doctor Siegfried Mayer was standing with the air of a conspirator behind his chair.

"*Moment,*" he said. "*Ein moment.*" Reluctantly Kangarov arose and walked to the window with him.

"What is it?"

"I hope you haven't forgotten?" the German said mysteriously, indicating Wislicenus with his eyes.

"Haven't forgotten what? Oh, yes! You wanted to have a talk with him. That's why I put you two together at the table," Kangarov lied.

"I would like to talk to him privately. . . . Two is company and three is not," Mayer insisted with an ingratiating smile.

"Go out into the corridor," the ambassador suggested irritably. The idea that an important matter was being kept secret from him infuriated him. "I believe he speaks German, and the waiters will not understand you. . . . Or, better still, step into that little room. No one will overhear you there," he added, pointing at the curtained door. Mayer nodded approvingly. "I will tell him."

When Wislicenus with a somber look on his face followed Mayer behind the curtain, Kangarov took a seat next to the Countess, talked with her for a few minutes and involved her in a general conversation about Spain. Only then he returned once again to Nadia. "Now if I could only get rid of them," he thought and turned to Tamarin:

"These gentlemen can't wait to hear what you think about Badajos. I already have heard you express your opinion, my dear commander, but maybe you would not mind repeating it for their benefit?"

"Show them what a Soviet general is like!" Nadia urged, surprised at her own lack of restraint.

"Give them a sample of our military education! You are one of the shining examples. Give them something to talk about!"

"Military education means little in this kind of a war!" Tamarin argued, feeling both flattered and embarrassed. He found it difficult to shine before strangers, especially with the additional handicap of having to shine in French. But he obediently took the chair vacated by Wislicenus and joined in the conversation, which absorbed him completely within a few minutes in spite of his firm conviction that civilians were not fit to discuss military matters. Tamarin deeply regretted the horrors of the Spanish war —"though how can a war be fought without horrors?"—but the progress of the war exhilarated him. He watched the newspapers for every bit of information, as a chess player who, unable to take part in an international tournament, watches every move to see whether his theories are borne out by the experience of other players.

"I have wished Badajos on them, and now we can have a half-hour to ourselves!" Kangarov whispered, leaning toward Nadia. For some reason he had great hopes for this evening. Uneasy and happy at the same time, he felt that he was about to lose control of himself. "But what difference will that make? Nothing else matters! It is now, or never! . . ." "I hope you are not too anxious to hear about Badajos?"

"No, not at all, but don't you want to listen?"

"I am only interested in you, and you know it, you bad girl!" he said, no longer concealing the meaning of his words behind sweet smiles. With a puzzled, naïve expression she half-opened her mouth. "Her lips are driving me crazy! . . ." Hypnotized, he pushed his face even nearer to her.

"Would you like another benedictine, my child? . . . That's my favorite liqueur."

"Thank you."

"Here it is. . . . You don't know how to drink it, you little fool! I want to drink it with you. . . . And then I want to tell you something . . ."

"You better not—I don't want to listen. . . . Why are you pouring it in my glass? . . . Your glass is over there . . ."

"I want to know all your secrets! Would you like to know mine?" Kangarov was speaking under his breath. With a professional eye Vermandois was watching them from across the room. "Is she already his mistress, or is that still in the future?" he wondered enviously. "He looks at her like a Fragonard cupid who is about to unveil a beauty."

Wislicenus had remained silent all through dinner despite the repeated efforts of the Countess to make him join in the conversation. A black mood had taken hold of him almost as soon as he arrived at the restaurant. He saw Nadia while he was still standing in the doorway and he was frightened by the intensity of his delight. "She is becoming beautiful! . . ." He waved at her, spoke to the host, was introduced to the guests, who made a polite effort to conceal their surprise at his appearance, and walked over to Nadia. But it seemed to him that she was not in the least glad to see him. This was not so. On the contrary, in her initial embarrassment Nadia found a familiar face very reassuring. But bearing her etiquette in mind she made a special effort not to show her feelings.

"I am so glad to see you!" Wislicenus said, warmly shaking her hand.

"I am also very glad," she answered with restraint, thinking: "He has aged a great deal. He looks like an old man. . . . I wonder if he is ill? . . ." "Have you been here long?"

"No, not very long. . . . Only a few days," Wislicenus said, feeling that he was being put in his place.

"Are you planning to remain in Paris?"

"Yes. . . . You are growing prettier than ever," Wislicenus

was surprised to find himself saying such things. "Will you be in Paris for a long time?" he asked her in turn. "How are you? . . . How are you getting along?"

"I can't complain," Nadia answered, trying to impress him with her social graces. At that moment they were joined by Tamarin, who in this strangely assorted crowd felt more at ease with the Russians. He gave Wislicenus a warm welcome and, lowering his voice immediately engaged him in a Russian conversation on some remote subject. At intervals Nadia managed to put in a word or two. Then the old French writer arrived and everyone moved toward the table. Wislicenus hesitated a second too long, and the seats on both sides of Nadia were taken.

He chose the first empty chair, which happened to be next to the Countess de Bellancombre. The Countess took one look at him and at his brown suit and guessed at once that he was a real revolutionary—"a bolshevik fanatic!" She had met a number of bolsheviks before, but never a real fanatic, and she went out of her way to be polite. Kangarov, who had begun by watching them with misgivings, soon was reassured. "Dinner jackets and full dresses are nothing new to her. Very likely she will find something charming about his brown shoes and his soft collar."

During dinner Wislicenus ate very little, but he drank everything the waiter poured into the row of glasses before him: sherry, Rhine wine, claret, champagne and liqueurs. When he was a young man he had alternated months of total abstinence with periodic sprees. During the early days in Moscow he drank heavily, then he stopped, and in recent years he had not had anything to drink. But he still retained some of his old capacity for absorbing alcohol. Wislicenus was not intoxicated and he did not feel any gayer, but his face was whiter than usual and his heart was pounding. He answered the Countess with abrupt monosyllables and he mumbled something unintelligible in response to his neighbor on the right, who expounded in German his belief in the not far distant and inevitable downfall of Hitler.

As soon as sherry was served there was no further necessity for the guests to talk. Vermandois took possession of the floor and gave no one else a chance to utter a word. Wislicenus thought: "No one can wrestle the initiative away from him. . . . But why should Nadia's attitude disappoint me so much? Did I expect her to greet me with open arms? As far as she is concerned I am a complete stranger, and I must be losing my mind to even think about it. . . . Offended? . . . The lives of most people consist of a series of affronts, humiliations and insults. One more or one less does not make any difference. . . ." Wislicenus tried not to look at Nadia, but whenever he raised his eyes he saw the reflection of her face in the mirror on the opposite wall. "When a man has one foot in the grave and is contented about it, he should be able to forget that sort of thing. . . ." At intervals he forced himself to listen to Vermandois, but it only aggravated him more because there was a certain similarity in their ideas.

"It's not what he says, it's the way he says it!" Wislicenus thought, watching Vermandois with a jaundiced eye. "His coy smile alone is enough to damn him! He, a great writer and a genius, loves moving-pictures! He goes to see them like any other mortal, but there is something different in the way he does it! The end of the world, the end of civilization—why not have a good time talking about it? Just as glibly he could take the opposite side and prove that the world will never come to an end, and that civilization is at its highest. He is the best argument I know in favor of doing away with civilization. His most serious thoughts congeal as soon as he puts them into words, just as blood congeals when it leaves the human body. These drawing-room jesters babble about inquisitions with the greatest faith in their own moral superiority. But just as the real bolsheviks were slandered, so were the first inquisitors. Despite anything people think about them they at least had faith in what they were doing and saying. We also did not become inquisitors overnight. The real monsters are those who spill human blood for profit, indifferently, as a matter of course. . . ." With malicious satisfaction

Wislicenus remembered the news he had read in the evening papers. "They may not spill as much blood, but they are dirtier about it. And even about blood they are not any more humane. They may not have Chekas, but the war for which they are preparing will kill twenty or thirty million. And even if partly deliberately and partly out of stupidity, ignorance and inefficiency, we did starve a million peasants the blood balance may still be in our favor," his mind was conditioned to think in terms of balances, debits and credits. "But what if this drawing-room jester is right and civilization is coming to an end? What difference will it make to a person like me who soon will be pushing daisies? . . ."

Once or twice in the course of the dinner Tamarin, from across the table, asked him a question, and once Nadia said: "How are you getting along?" "I shouldn't be surprised if she has forgotten my name," he thought and wanted to say: "Fine, I believe I shall be pushing daisies very soon. . . ." Instead he answered: "Very well, thank you. And you?" But she already was talking to the old Frenchman. Later, when the dinner was over, Kangarov moved his chair next to her, and for some reason Wislicenus was revolted by the sight. He turned away, his face became darker than a storm cloud, and he had several more drinks. "How absurd! . . . Like all coarse natures he is inclined toward platonic friendships. This odor of food, wine and cigarette smoke is nauseating. . . . Everything is nauseating! . . ." Suddenly he felt a dizziness, a sharp pain shot through his chest and up his arm, and his heart began to pound more furiously than it ever had pounded before. "If I kick the bucket now this bastard will find himself in an awkward position," he thought. "But the others at home will be relieved to hear about it. . . ."

As in the café that afternoon, Wislicenus again was assailed by thoughts of the men who had been executed in Moscow, of his old comrades who now were rotting in unmarked graves. "I don't believe I loved any of them. But regardless of what they were like, they had spent their lives in the service of a revolutionary ideal, and they died disgraced and bespattered with mud."

Sitting in an expensive restaurant, at a table lined with bottles, the vision of those men who had perished in dark cells was fantastic and terrifying. His heart pounded faster and faster. Wislicenus glanced at the mirror and above the bald head of the financier saw his own reflection. "People look better lying in a coffin, in a box. . . ." Suddenly a wooden box appeared in the mirror. Not a coffin, but an ugly, unfinished packing case, the kind that filled with excelsior stands in a dark corner. He was seized with panic. "I really must be losing my mind. This is the second hallucination in one day! . . ."

"Comrade Wislicenus, the Teutonic gentleman wishes to have private words with you," a disagreeable voice said behind his back. "Is anything wrong? Are you ill?"

"No, there's nothing wrong. Probably I have had more to drink than is good for me. I shall be glad to talk to him. Where is he?"

"In that room over there, if it suits you. No one will disturb you there. I doubt that the grand dukes and the ladies used that divan for political discussions. But the grand dukes have had their day, and now you and I have ours. . . . Go right ahead. If you don't stay too long, no one will notice your absence."

While Kangarov was arranging the meeting between Mayer and Wislicenus, Nadia was being entertained by the cordial Count de Bellancombre. In contrast to the other old men, her proximity did not seem to excite or particularly please him. With a slight trace of irritation Nadia instantly became conscious of his lack of interest. "I suppose a woman, unless she is a countess or a princess, does not exist for him! . . ." "Well, he can have his countess! . . ." But there was no evidence that his interest in the Countess was any greater. He very seldom looked in her direction, and when he did there was nothing tender about his expression. The Count ate very little, drank mineral water only, and made no pretense about listening to what was being said. "Probably he is annoyed to find himself in such company," Nadia thought, realizing angrily that without increasing her respect for him and in spite of her convictions, the old man's title undoubtedly heightened her interest in him.

Nadia was mistaken. True, the Count considered that everyone present, including his wife, belonged to a questionable layer of society. But this did not disturb him in the least, because he was accustomed to being surrounded constantly by such people at the meetings of the various boards of which he was a member, and in the clubs where he played bridge with bankers, merchants and self-designated, or even real aristocrats who, from his grandfather's point of view, were no better than bolsheviks or socialists. The Count was not interested in what was being said. Twice a week he listened to conversations more or less brilliant in his wife's salon. He knew that Vermandois could speak as cleverly and entertainingly on any subject, using just as many quotations and aphorisms to support his arguments. For some years now women excited the Count on very rare occasions and only in theory. He assumed toward them a tenderly ironical tone, somewhat modified by pleasant recollections and by the fact that most of them played an erratic game of bridge (they did not seem to realize that they had no conception of the game). Ever since the doctors had forbidden him anything alcoholic, had put him on a strict diet, and had told him to confine himself in the evenings to fruit and vegetables, all dinners bored him whether the guests were dukes or bolsheviks.

The question uppermost in the Count's mind was: how soon would the evening be over? If the guests should leave by eleven he still would have time to stop in at the club and play several rubbers of bridge. The Count was one of the leading bridge experts in France, a system of bidding was named after him, and playing with him was considered a special honor in all the clubs. Jokingly he referred to it as a form of masochism: pivoting and having him for a partner every third rubber a person had one chance in five to win, and none if he played a fixed game against him. The Count always played calmly, without arguments (no one dared to argue with him), without accusations and without asides. No matter how difficult the hand, he did not pause or waste any time, and he played it in such a masterful fashion that for days afterward it served as a subject for respectful discussion among club members.

The chances were slight, the Count felt, that the Soviet ambassador's evening would be over by eleven. It would be hours before someone, most likely Vermandois, would drop a casual hint that it was time to think about getting home. The conversation after dinner would have to last a couple of hours to show proper appreciation to the host. The Count knew that the first mention of the late hour would be firmly dismissed without a single word, by the silent expression of horror, pain and despair on the host's face. Twenty minutes later a second attempt would be in order, but it, too, would be dismissed by the host, though with less firmness. Then, in another ten minutes, the guests would begin to take their leave. By that time it would be past midnight, and his wife would insist that he accompany her home. Apparently there would be no bridge tonight. The Count ate his salad, drank his Vichy water, occasionally saying a few words to his neighbors, and made a half-hearted pretense of listening to the brilliant conversation. If it were not for his wife and this damned invitation, he thought, he could be enjoying himself at the club, hopefully dealing a new hand, or trying to make a difficult bid surrounded by the watchful attention of his fellow members. Whenever he was playing, a small crowd assembled behind his chair. He accepted this as his due and he did not become impatient even when people who invariably brought him bad luck were among the watchers. "It is amazing that human beings lack the courage to do away with stupid pretenses and to show, once and for all, their preference for real, simple and natural pleasures."

When his eyes accidentally met the eyes of Tamarin, who had been thinking about his bed and the volume of Clausewitz, the Count instinctively sensed an ally and smiled. He knew that at every formal dinner there was a party in power consisting of peo-

ple who were enjoying themselves, and an opposition party which
was composed of people who, depending on their temperament,
ridiculed the others or damned everything in sight. Here, he felt,
the opposition consisted of himself, the old general, and the
strange man sitting next to his wife.

The Count was aware that his wife showed signs of special
interest in her dinner partner. "Probably he will be invited shortly
to our salon." He sighed and quietly asked his neighbor on the
left who the man was. Learning that he was a member of the
Communist International and a famous revolutionary who at
present was using the name of Wislicenus, the Count nodded his
approval, at the same time lifting his eyebrows as an indication
that he had heard, understood and appreciated every word. Now
he was certain that the man in the brown suit would be a guest
in his house. "But what on earth is she after? . . . When she was
chasing Lord Balfour I could at least understand her. . . ."

Struggling to overcome the sharp pain which now seemed to
center around the shoulderblade, Wislicenus listened to the German. He disliked all liberals, radicals and moderate socialists in
general. But he had a special aversion to German democrats,
since they had surrendered the power to Hitler without firing a
single shot and without any serious attempt at resistance. He considered Doctor Mayer a typical case in point. Wislicenus had seen
him a few times when he had been at the height of his social and
political glory. In those days Mayer, who was a minister of state
(this was a chapter in his life which even now brightened his
existence), entertained everyone in Berlin. Later, the very people
who recently had considered it an honor and a sign of social success to be invited to Siegfried Mayer's house refused to recognize
him on the street. He escaped to Czechoslovakia, migrated to
Switzerland and moved to France.

After talking for several minutes on general subjects Mayer
came to the point. He was in possession of important documents
which were of paramount interest to the Soviet Government or to
the Communist International. "Or to both," he added with a know-

ing smile. "So that's it," Wislicenus was relieved. This was a type of transaction with which he was familiar. Such purchases came directly under his department. This had been especially true in the old days, and people who had something to offer learned about him by word of mouth. Having briefly described the contents of the papers, Mayer explained that they were actually in the hands of a third person who was willing to part with them on certain terms. Wislicenus nodded impatiently: expressions like "third person" and "willing to part with them" were part of the routine in such negotiations.

The offer was an interesting one: the documents sounded as though they could prove embarrassing to the German government. Wislicenus answered with the formula he always used on such occasions. There was no reason why the offer should not be considered, but he would have to examine the papers because it was bad business to buy a cat in a sack—he knew of no foreign expression which was an equivalent of this Russian saying, and he translated it word for word. Usually the people with whom he was dealing immediately understood what he meant, though some of them considered it their duty to appear insulted. On this occasion Doctor Siegfried Mayer's face showed that he was hurt by this lack of confidence.

"I am willing to vouch for the authenticity and the exceptionally interesting character of the documents," Mayer said, emphasizing the "I" and pausing for effect. A deep-seated timidity flickered in his eyes: the timidity of a man who has tumbled down the social ladder, and who momentarily expects to be insulted. The dismal thought occurred to him that he had enough money to last only three more months. Wislicenus remained silent, refusing to indicate his reaction to the German's words. "Without an assurance that they will be bought, I doubt whether the man would be willing to show the papers. . . ."

"Well, if he doesn't want to show them, so much the better," Wislicenus answered, assuming the indifferent air of a horse trader. "The papers are not very important anyway. There is nothing timely about them; their chief value is historical."

"Those gentlemen haven't changed their ways, and this will give you the account of an eyewitness, who was a participant in the events. . . ."

Mayer supplied several other details, and to his surprise Wislicenus became convinced that a "third person" actually existed. Apparently the doctor was receiving merely a commission on the sale. There was nothing improper about it; he had been in reduced circumstances ever since his property had been confiscated. Neither was there any reason to doubt the authenticity of the documents (forgeries appeared on the underground market only under very special circumstances, and they were always offered as a bargain). After a few more minutes it was decided that they should meet again in the presence of the "third person."

"For my part I make only one condition. These papers must be published as soon as they are bought. The interests of world democracy demand it!" Doctor Mayer said emphatically and blushed. The contempt written on Wislicenus' face left no room for doubt that he was in no position to make demands, or to defend world democracy. They exchanged telephone numbers and returned to the dining-room, carrying with them mutually unpleasant impressions.

In the meantime Nadia unobtrusively slipped out into the hall, stopped in front of a mirror, took the small enameled box out of her bag, looked at it admiringly, and powdered her nose, forehead, and the dimple in her chin. Eagerly she inhaled the novel, exotic scent of the expensive powder. She patted her hair, touched up her eyebrows with the pencil, and used the new lipstick. She knew that everything was in order and there was no real reason for all this. Her head was whirling and she felt gay— gayer than she had felt for a long time. "Why should I be so happy? Must be the dinner, the wine, and the liqueurs. . . . Too bad they are old men. The ambassador seems a little too susceptible tonight. . . . Why are the mirrors placed like that: one here, and one in the dining-room? You can see everything that is going on, even in that little room. . . . I should think that during an orgy they would find it very embarrassing. . . ."

Just then the mirror reflected the figure of Kangarov, who had entered the hall. For no good reason Nadia pretended not to see him; when he came nearer she acted as though she had just noticed him and was startled and annoyed by the interruption.

"It's you!" she spoke without moving her lips. The new lipstick she was using at that moment made her voice sound funny and unnatural.

"It's you!" Kangarov imitated her, pushing his face closer. He exuded a strong aroma of wine, but Nadia did not find it unpleasant, just as she did not resent his proximity, or the expression of his eyes. "No one can see us here, and even if they can, I don't give a damn!" he thought, feeling more reckless than ever. "If they want to gossip, nothing can stop them! . . ."

"You are a fine host, leaving your guests like that!" Nadia said, slipping her vanity-case into her bag.

"They can get along without me. How did you like it, my dear? Did you have a good time?" he asked her quietly, suddenly hesitating between a playful and a fatherly tone.

"Yes, certainly I enjoyed myself! I am terribly grateful to you for asking me. . . ."

"Well, if you are grateful, you can at least show it," he whispered, and kissed the back of her neck close to the roots of her hair. This time Nadia did not have to affect surprise. Nothing like that had ever happened to them before. She tried to be angry with him, but her effort was in vain. "He is forgetting himself!" she thought, and was about to say so aloud, but it was too late. Kangarov was no longer in the room. Happy and excited he glided —glided like a skater—back to rejoin the guests. At the same moment Nadia's eyes met in the mirror the eyes of Wislicenus, who was entering the dining-room from the opposite direction. It seemed to her that he stopped dead in his tracks. "Could he possibly have seen us? . . ."

Wislicenus had not seen the kiss, and neither did he stop dead in his tracks. But he saw Kangarov leave the hall where he and Nadia had been alone, and he noticed their flushed, embarrassed faces. The feeling of disgust which had taken hold of him during the dinner and which had continued to grow during his conversation with the German now became unbearable. For several minutes Wislicenus sat talking after a fashion with Tamarin—among those present the general was the only person who did not irritate or disgust him—then, without taking leave, he went into the corridor and handed his coat check to the boy, who jumped up from a chair on which he had been sitting. Almost immediately Kangarov followed him.

"Anything wrong, my dear comrade? Are you leaving à l'Anglaise?" the ambassador asked, putting on an air of jovial indignation. "Why so early? I cannot let you go!"

"I hope you will excuse me. I am very tired."

"But it is still so early! I hope you had enough time to talk to Mayer?"

"Yes."

"I am glad that this silly dinner at least was useful to that extent," Kangarov said, shaking his head with a smile which meant to imply: "It's terribly wearing! You can appreciate how unpleasant it is to have to spend my time in this way. . . ." He was silent for a full minute, waiting for Wislicenus to deny it and to say the expected: "Oh, not at all! It was a most charming evening!" But Wislicenus did not utter a word. He took his worn grey hat with a faded ribbon from the boy, who handed it to him with a puzzled expression, and gave the boy a one-franc tip. "Everything he does is a disgrace!" Kangarov thought and in a disappointed voice said:

"Must you really go? Are you traveling by subway? The station is just a few steps down the street. . . . Do you have to travel a long way?"

"Yes."

"It is still early. Even if you have to change trains, you have plenty of time before the last one. I wish you could stay. You haven't seen Nadia for ages. If you are not too bored, why don't you change your mind?" Kangarov persisted. He was so happy that he actually would have been glad if his unpleasant guest had decided to stay. Suddenly all the anger inside Wislicenus exploded.

"I am not bored, but I am disgusted! Damned disgusted!" he barked and walking out of the door, added: "Goodbye!" Kangarov was taken aback. "What's the matter with him? Has he gone completely insane?" the ambassador wondered, his first reaction being one of amazement. He wanted to call Wislicenus back, but the door already had closed behind him. Only gradually the ambassador's surprise changed to a cold fury. "What a lout! What a bastard!"

"Is Monsieur looking for his hat and coat?" the boy who was disappointed in his tip asked with casual insolence. Kangarov gazed at the door with unseeing eyes. His happy mood had vanished completely. "What an ignorant lout! What did he mean? What happened to him? No, I will not let him get away with it!" he thought savagely. "Is Monsieur looking for his things?" the boy repeated.

"Don't you Monsieur me! See that you address me as Your Excellency!" Kangarov shouted at him, and turning sharply on his heels returned to the dining-room. There he saw Nadia silhouetted against the curtained door. "What if he is in love with her? Whatever the explanation, this Trotskyist shall not get away with it! I will show him a thing or two!" he said to himself.

"Why isn't anyone drinking, gentlemen?" the ambassador asked in a flat voice, making an instinctive effort to assume once again the playful rôle of host. "That's simply unheard of, gentlemen! How about ordering another bottle of brandy? No one contrary minded? The motion is carried."

"I believe we have demonstrated that we appreciate the masterpieces belonging to the era of the great emperor!"

"What touching credulity. Do you really believe that there is a single bottle of Napoleon brandy left anywhere in this world? The human race certainly should have sense enough to consume it within one hundred years!"

"Did you hear him? Our dear Vermandois is now banking on human reason!"

"He does not believe in socialism and he does not believe in Napoleon brandy."

"The brandy is excellent, but the sherry was perfection!"

"What do you mean 'was'? I am still sipping it instead of a liqueur."

XXII

THE GUESTS began to leave earlier than the Count had expected. At a quarter of eleven Vermandois paused and said: "It is getting late, gentlemen. I hate to bring this delightful evening to an end, but isn't it time for us to be going home? . . ." Kangarov's face immediately assumed an expression, as if to say: "If you have made up your mind to ruin my evening, there is nothing I can do. . . ." But there was something about it that rekindled the Count's hopes for a few rubbers of bridge. "No, no, cher Maître! We will not let you go! You cannot deprive us of your brilliant conversation," Kangarov exclaimed. Without a murmur Vermandois submitted to the wishes of his host, thinking angrily that he would have to pay night rates for the taxi. The Countess became involved in a last political argument with the ambassador. Everyone listened indifferently: they had heard too many arguments in the course of the evening. "Yes, that's true! In many ways you are right. I will go even further than that and admit that you are right most of the time," the Countess was saying softly. "But nothing you can say will convince me that in Soviet Russia you have freedom of the press. Those of us who are your friends feel hurt when we see you use fascist tactics in certain matters. . . . Don't be angry with me. . . . I confess that perhaps I don't know enough about your wonderful country. . . ." "She looks like a moving-picture spy who is willing to change her allegiance because she fell in love with a counter-espionage agent," Vermandois thought. "It would be nice if the old fool would drive me home in her car."

Half an hour after Vermandois' false start had paved the way for him, the Count made a desperate attempt to break away. Unexpectedly he received support from the other guests: "Yes, it is late. . . . Time to go home. . . ." After arguing with them as a matter of form, Kangarov made a secret sign to the maître d'hôtel and they retreated to the far corner of the room. The guests at once became engaged in an animated conversation. The ambassador picked up the bill on the tray and paid it, inwardly horrified at the amount. Though he invariably drew on his expense account for entertainment, whenever he was paying a bill he looked as though he were being robbed of his last penny.

With a pleasant smile the host soon was back among the guests. "Must you really go? Why are you leaving so early?" He knew that if he insisted long enough he could detain the guests for another twenty minutes. But the incident with Wislicenus had ruined his festive mood. "What do you call late? I am always in bed by eleven," the financier protested. "You will find me regularly in bed with a book by ten," Cerisier chimed in. It seemed in some inexplicable way that all these socialites, who never spent an evening at home, were never up after ten, or eleven at the latest. "It has been an exceptionally pleasant evening. We hope to see you very soon," the Countess said meaningfully, but without making her invitation more specific. She was not quite sure about inviting Kangarov for dinner, and, besides, she could not say anything in the presence of Cerisier whom she had no intention of inviting at all. The famous lawyer quickly turned away and began talking to the financier. "Without fail. . . . Soon, very soon," Vermandois was saying warmly, but keeping it also on an indefinite footing so he would not be under any obligation. He said something else amusing, but without any real effort to be brilliant because of the lateness of the hour. Sticking his fingers in his vest pocket he tried to find three one-franc notes which he thought were there, but not finding them he angrily tipped the boy five francs. Outside, on the sidewalk, everything proceeded according to the usual custom. Politely, but with their voices expressing a firm faith in his refusal, both the financier and the Count said: "Can't we drop you on the way, cher Maître?" And just as politely he answered: "Don't even think of it! You are going in the opposite direction."

When at last he was settled in a taxi, Vermandois leaned back against the cushions, stretched his legs, and gave a shameless, cynical yawn. "Thank God, that's over! . . . Now for a hot bath and bed. . . ." He rode halfway home in a state of blissful anticipation, thinking that the dinner had been excellent, that he should not have had quite so much wine, and that the girl, known as the ambassador's secretary, was charming. "I think it's unfair that she belongs to a man like that! . . ." Whenever the taxi passed under a street light Vermandois cast a sullen glance at the meter, but in the semi-darkness he could not distinguish the figures. "The fare will be somewhere around fifteen or twenty francs, depending on whether the taxi-driver is an honest man, and whether he lets his conscience choose the route. . . ." With lazy amazement he remembered that in the old days he had been fond of the two-hour dinners with seven main courses, with the deadly mixture of drinks, and the never-ending conversations which he had to conduct in a brilliant fashion because of his reputation. Not without satisfaction he decided that considering the audience, he had shone creditably that evening. "The people were definitely so-so. But in our crowd [he meant the literary world] one always has to be on guard. We never expect anything except sly digs, or unpleasant and outright rude remarks. We exist in an atmosphere of disrespect, animosity and hatred for one another. At least there was no trace of that here. Some listened with admiration, others indifferently, still others did not listen at all and among them was the girl with whom I did not get a chance to say a dozen words. But there was no animosity in the air, and no reason to expect anything unpleasant. Is the difference due to their intellectual level? In our circle we spend most of the time gossiping about publishers and royalties. It would never occur to me to talk with Émile about socialism or about the end of civilization. If I ever should try, he would be carried away with delight, because then and there he would decide that I finally had lost my mind completely! . . ."

Vermandois found the reclining position and the night air refreshing. His thoughts went back to his novel. "Tomorrow I shall settle to work early in the morning. I only hope I get a good night's rest. . . ." He knew that wine was not conducive to more than three or four hours of sleep. "Should I take some veronal? If I do I shall feel groggy in the morning." He was so absorbed in his work since it had taken a new turn that he wanted the night to pass quickly. The taxi stopped at last; the meter showed eighteen francs; apparently the taxi-driver had a mediocre conscience.

Letting himself in with a key, Vermandois entered the hall with an eerie feeling which always clung to him when he returned home at night. The emptiness of his sizable apartment oppressed him. The arrangement of the rooms was not inviting and rather inconvenient. The door from the hall led into the drawing-room—a wasted space which he disliked. He had furnished it some time ago, when he happened to have some extra money. The furniture was, for the most part, "antique." A Vanloo of uncertain parentage hung on the wall: it had been bought as a Charles André, but experts insisted that it was by Jean Baptiste, or even by Jules-César. The other remarkable piece in the room was a peculiar and absolutely useless little table designed in a style which in the eighteenth century was known as 'Athenian': gilded bronze with a marble top. The word 'Athenian' probably was the thing that had made him buy it. The more responsive guests to whom Vermandois showed his collection of antiques smiled with appreciative understanding: where did an eighteenth-century Athenian table belong if not in the apartment of Louis-Etienne Vermandois?

He crossed the drawing-room, moving cautiously through the darkness; even the switches in the apartment were not convenient; the drawing-room lights could not be turned on anywhere except by the door leading into the study. In spite of long years of practice, Vermandois bumped into something, slipped on the rug and cursed. Feeling along the wall he found the button and switched on the lights. The Athenian table by the door was empty. Feeling that she should get something out of an otherwise futile piece of furniture, the old woman, as a rule, used this particular table for depositing letters which had come in the last mail. Vermandois remembered that he had left the apartment after the last mail was in. He put the lights on in the study and turned them off in the drawing-room. "The kingdom of lies and the kingdom of truth! In the drawing-room everything is false and pretentious. In the study nothing pretends to be what it is not. A plain, cozy red carpet, shelves, book rack, roll-top desk—all useful, straightforward and unassuming junk." The study was the honest room of the apartment.

With a sense of luxurious freedom Vermandois took off the tight collar and the dinner-jacket, put on soft slippers, unbuttoned his pants and vest, and almost fell against the dark yellow cushion of the low leather armchair standing by his desk. The rest was a prelude to sleep. "The greatest joys in life are very simple: after five hours of suffering, to take off the idiotic stiff collar, the only purpose of which is to chafe a man's neck. . . . Or, on a hot day, to drink at one gulp a glass of cold water. . . ." In considering the simple joys in life he remembered the ambassador's secretary and heaved a deep sigh. "What was I thinking about? Perhaps I should jot it down? Oh, yes! . . . The study is an honest room. In here I am in my rightful and natural surroundings, just as much as an animal is in the forest, or a Pope in the Sistine Chapel. . . . Though there are times when a Pope must feel self-conscious in the Sistine Chapel. . . ."

Relaxing without a collar, with his chin resting on his chest, was sheer joy. Lazily Vermandois thought that he should move to the bedroom—the bed would feel even better. "Perhaps I should try to work for a while? I would find it difficult at first, but before long I would forget about being tired. . . ." Uncertainly he glanced at the desk, one end of which was occupied by a thick cardboard file with the manuscript. "No, there is no sense in settling to work at once in the morning, but at least I can have a look at what I wrote before dinner. . . ."

Bracing himself heavily against the arm rests, Vermandois rose to his feet, considered for a second the effort it had taken him to move, pulled a chair over to the desk, put on his glasses, and reached for the file. Suddenly he realized that wine was not alone responsible for his convivial mood during dinner and his irrepressible desire to talk. He had carried with him an unconscious reserve of happiness due to the new turn in his novel after Lysander's meeting in Corinth and to the new possibilities it offered. Despite his contempt for literature, in the final analysis Vermandois' spirits were determined by the progress of his work. "Yes, that was a wonderful idea!" he decided gaily, extracting from the file a stack of sheets covered with lines sprawling in every direction.

Vermandois began to read. His face fell. "What's the matter with it? . . ." The new version of the chapter was even worse than the old one! His heart dropped. He skipped the main narrative and began to decipher the corrections, abbreviated notes and reminders which he had jotted down in the margins, and up and down, or diagonally across the pages. None of it was any good. His head teemed with one reason after another why Lysander's meeting in Corinth did not ring true, why it was not only improbable, but downright impossible. "That's terrible! . . . Why didn't I notice it before? . . . I must have been blind, absolutely blind! . . ."

With something approaching despair Vermandois stuffed the sheets back into the file. "Good Lord, what shall I do now? . . ." Once again he told himself that he must give up forever this disgusting, shameful profession of story-telling, and once again he answered himself that he could not give it up. His only reason for living was his writing, his only joy—the mixture of false and honest impulses known as inspiration.

"If I look at it again tomorrow, perhaps it will look differently to me. . . . After all, I was not a complete idiot five hours ago! . . . Right now I will go to bed, and tomorrow I will begin work with a fresh head. . . ." But inwardly he knew that after this shock sleep was out of the question.

With a heavy sigh Vermandois pushed the file with the manuscript aside and went into the bathroom. On the way he stared with disgust at the pretentious drawing-room. "Yes, undoubtedly it is one of the younger Vanloos, and a bad one at that! And even if it is a Charles-André, what consolation is there in that? The Athenian table is also a piece of junk, and those cabinetmakers who created the eighteenth-century furniture known as the triumph of French taste were foreigners. Most of them were Germans: Riesner, Weissweiler, Schwerdfeger . . . I should sell all of it as soon as I can, while people still are stupid enough to pay good prices for it! . . ."

In the bathroom Vermandois perched on an uncomfortable, straight-backed chair, and gazed absent-mindedly at the water rushing out of the spigot. His mind was crowded with many things, but chiefly with thoughts about his inexcusable, artificial life. He could not stand it any longer, and he could see no reason why he should make the effort; his nerves were all on the surface, the least unpleasantness assumed the proportions of a disaster, and anything more serious became a catastrophe. "Why should I be so upset today? What if the meeting in Corinth was not a good idea? . . . Yesterday I had not thought about it, and I was perfectly happy. . . ." But this form of reasoning did not satisfy him. Everything seemed offensive, especially the people, and above all himself. "Sticking my nose in the air at that idiotic dinner, and strutting like a peacock! . . . Discussing the end of the world with that fool of a countess, with Cerisier, and with that nonentity of an ambassador! . . . 'Brilliant paradoxes' are

as much my specialty as stuffed duck is at La Tour d'Argent.
Quoting a hundred thousand people—was there anyone I did not
quote? Never, never again! I swear by everything that is
holy! . . ." With a feeling of shame and in all sincerity he promised himself once more.

Despite the assurances made by the landlord the water in the
hot spigot was barely warm. There was no relaxing in the tub
without driving away the last vestiges of sleep. Vermandois was
irritated more than ever. "I shall make it a point to write to him
about it tomorrow. I better tell Alvera to type the letter, or else
the son of a bitch will sell my autograph! . . . After a heavy dinner I might suffer a stroke in cold water. . . ." He knew that he
would not have a stroke tonight—his blood-pressure was down to
normal—but he imagined with great clarity how he would wheeze
in the bathtub until morning when the old woman would find
him. "She will run after the janitress, and the two of them will
try to lift me and carry me to my bed. . . ." He was struck and
absorbed by the tragic obscenity of such a scene. "Half an hour
later the doctor will arrive. He will satisfy himself that I am dead,
and then, with an important air, he will call the right people:
'Louis-Etienne Vermandois has passed away!' Later, reporters will
rush in, a book (or maybe loose sheets bordered in black) will
appear from nowhere, and friends will come and sign their names.
The young psychopathic case who has been my secretary will
supply the reporters with human interest details of my life. He
will be torn between grief and joy: he will have no more salary,
but he will have the realization that while I have rejoined my
forefathers, he still has another fifty years to go! While my closest
friend the Countess, struggling to control her sobs, receives
the representatives sent by the President of the Republic and the
Ministry of Education. 'Only yesterday we were together, and
he was more brilliant than ever. . . .' There will be great excitement at the Academy: an unexpected vacancy on which no one
has counted. . . . Émile will come with a long face and signing
his name with a flourish, will say: 'what a loss!' The reporters

immediately will put down in their notebooks: 'what a loss—
he exclaimed.'"

Charged as they were with irony, his thoughts stirred Vermandois. He even had a sensation of actually suffering some kind
of an attack, though deep down in his heart he knew that it was
mere imagination; there was nothing wrong with him, and his
blood pressure was normal. "Well, if it does not happen tonight,
it will happen in another year, especially if I become excited
about everything without any good reason. No, I simply must
leave Paris! I will get rid of the Vanloo and of all the porcelain
and wooden junk. As long as it has the special appeal of coming
'from the collection of Louis-Etienne Vermandois' I may be able
to realize something from it. Then I can go away and leave a clear
field to my friend Émile to write novels until his untimely de-
mise! . . ." As usual, the knowledge that Émile's style was becoming worse and worse with every book gave Vermandois a certain
satisfaction. "If I were to die tonight I would have the consolation of knowing that I never should see Émile again. . . ." He
undressed and, with a feeling of revulsion for his old body, settled
into the water.

While Vermandois was sitting in the tub his mood became
darker than ever. His sense of irony forsook him entirely. The
attack he was suffering was no longer imaginary; it was an attack
of devastating, all-embracing despair. He did not see a ray of
hope anywhere: everything his memory could recall was trite,
sickening and unsavory, every recollection increased his feeling
of shame. By comparison with the intensity of his personal despondency, the fact that the world was poised on the brink of
disaster seemed secondary in importance, or perhaps the two
were so closely interwoven that he could not tell where one ended
and the other began. His teeth began to chatter from sitting in
the cool water. Exercising his will to the utmost Vermandois
climbed out of the tub, brushed his teeth, went into the bedroom,
and stretched out on the bed. He turned out the light and for a
quarter of an hour lay in the darkness waiting for sleep to come.

When he realized that it was hopeless he gave up struggling with his thoughts. He turned on the light once again and picked up a book from the table.

It was a French translation of the conversations between Goethe and Chancellor Müller. A perfectly respectable *livre de chevet*, one that could be mentioned in an off-the-record interview without any misgivings. Only last week he had told a reporter, who was in search of a human interest story, that he much preferred this book to Eckermann. "Eckermann's portrait of Goethe is drawn by a none too brilliant, not to say stupid, young man. Müller shows us a moody and relaxed Goethe engaged in an argument with an intelligent, mature and civilized man." Later he was ashamed that he had described Eckermann as a none too brilliant young man—it was a cliché. In another three days, filled with abhorrence and dismay he saw in the paper the interview, adorned with his portrait and headlined: *"cet immense bonhomme de Johann-Wolfgang vu par Louis-Etienne Vermandois."* He could not decide whether this was usual newspaper technique, or whether it was sarcasm under a cloak of respect. The reporter had had clever eyes.

Vermandois turned over several pages, looking at every word with preconceived disfavor. "This is the only way to read great writers unless you want to be enslaved by them. . . ." "The life of Baroness Krüdener is like a pile of wood shavings: one can expect from it at best a few ashes that can be used in the making of soap. . . ." A metaphor good enough for a conversation or for a rough draft, but one that never should find place in a final manuscript by Goethe. Besides, why can't it be applied to any human life? . . . "The Germans should be scattered over the face of the earth like the Jews: only then could they demonstrate the measure of their abilities. . . ." This, too, was a "brilliant paradox," and a practical politician like Chancellor Müller must have listened to it with resigned boredom. There was no way for him to prevent a great man, who had reached the venerable age of eighty, from giving voice to any absurdity that came into his head. . . . "Censorship is useful because it teaches one how to disguise thoughts and express them in a fine and witty fashion. Usually the direct expression of a thought is ponderous. . . ." Perhaps . . . But this was obvious rationalizing, intended to justify censorship in Weimar. Goethe could reconcile beliefs in the freedom of conscience and in the benefits of censorship, in the accomplishments of the French Revolution and in the greatness of the house of Rothschild; he ridiculed the immortality of the soul, but he feared that the world would come to an end if an Ober-Hofmarschall and a Jewess were joined in holy wedlock. . . . Undoubtedly he said many things to annoy the person whom he was addressing. Probably Müller's intelligent features vexed him even more than Eckermann's naïvely-adoring face: "I must not miss a single brilliant thought of His Excellency. . . ." The amazing thing was that these everyday random conversations, conducted over a period of years under absurd circumstances, should result in such absorbingly interesting and valuable books.

Even during the rare moments of professional self-glorification, to which as a rule Vermandois was not given, it never entered his head to compare himself with Goethe. But he found a degree of pleasure in discovering that this man, who had won eternal and universal fame, had lived under similar circumstances, that he too had been bored by people, that he too could not live without them, that he too had suffered insults and had been forced to conform to existing customs. "His Mephistopheles is a conformist and a very human devil. No wonder that the German youth of each succeeding generation admires him so much! . . . And that is the reason why compared with the poem he loses so little in the opera! . . ."

"He demanded for himself the right not to believe in anything, and in moments of frankness made no effort to conceal that he held no beliefs. He ridiculed the stupidity of kings, the atrocities of the revolution, the truth of the revelations, faith and his own lack of it. He envied most simple people, whether they were tailors or artists. Asked why there was so much joy in his oratorios, Haydn had answered: 'When I give thanks to my Maker, I am overcome with indescribable joy.' When these words were repeated to the aged Goethe, he wept."

In desperation Vermandois closed the book. "Well, you who were so wise, you who thought and knew so much about life, about so many things, about everything, what can you teach me? What real truths, which do not need the help of paradoxes, poetry and resounding words, can you teach another old man who has not much longer to live? Do I dare guess your advice, without looking inside your books, by recreating your personality in my mind and by trying to penetrate your real wisdom, rather than your printed words?

"If your work in life has or can be endowed with a single grain of reason, do it as well as you can. The tailor should sew and the writer should write, putting his soul into his work. . . . Don't pretend that you are working for the sake of work alone. Like others, Goethe hoped for tremendous audiences, and he said that a man should not write unless he had hopes of reaching millions of readers. . . . Do not attack the beliefs of others, or at least be considerate when you do so. . . . Do not tilt with windmills and itinerant knights, unless this happens to be your profession, the profession of a political Don Quixote, which is as much a profession as shoemaking and healing. . . . Don't play to the gallery and don't defy it: think as little as you can about it, and nurture no hopes of reforming it. In proportion to the strength which has been allotted to you, help the simple and indisputable principles of good to win in this world. A famous doctor in his old age was known to say that he had retained faith in the beneficial qualities of only five or six proven drugs, such as quinine. Indisputable principles of good are just as few in number. . . . Some, though not many, men can go a little further. 'Cool detachment' has its value. Thoughts, as well as life, can rise higher, when spiritual fire is held down. Most successful men fairly burn with life, but the heart of Napoleon beat at the rate of only sixty a minute.

"Just as precious as blood, which, having given its nourishing substances, returns through the veins to the heart, are the truths returning to the heart, even though they no longer nourish anyone. Cherish and preserve them against the day when you will have nothing ahead of you, except a properly worded obituary. Live calmly, knowing that the world is steeped in evil. Accept eternal evil as the general rule, but rejoice in the occasional good."

Vermandois opened the book again. Not a word of this was in its pages.

Book Two

I

THE HOME of the famous doctor had no elevator. Wislicenus labored slowly up the steps. He had observed that the pains (he persistently refused to call them attacks) appeared most frequently when he ascended stairs. "I am in fine shape," he thought in an ironical mood, which he had begun to cultivate toward himself recently. "It all fits together nicely: an invalid and a hypochondriac rolled into one. . . ."

A plain-looking girl, wearing a black dress and with a face which bore a permanently frightened expression, was sitting at the head of the stairs on the second floor. Having asked his name, she nervously consulted a leather-bound notebook and with evident relief said: "You have an appointment at three-thirty, but I am afraid you will have to wait. Someone is with the Professor now, and another patient is in the waiting-room. It is impossible to say exactly when the Professor will be free. . . ." She used the word "Professor" without bothering to add the last name and pronounced it in a way which implied that no other professors existed. Unconsciously imitating her subdued, sick-room voice, Wislicenus asked her almost in a whisper where he could wait. "First door on your left," she answered with a note of surprise, as though such questions were superfluous.

"She is not here," Wislicenus thought with disappointment as he glanced quickly around the waiting-room which looked more like a library. The walls were lined with books. The center of the room was taken up by a table adorned with a single issue of an illustrated magazine; several straight chairs and armchairs were grouped around it, giving the effect of a stage setting in a modern production. An old man, holding a pair of light gloves in his

217

hand, was sitting by the fireplace. Wislicenus bowed instinctively
and was irritated when he received a puzzled stare in response.
"There are more and more people in this world who do not believe in good manners," he thought and turning away, took a
chair by the window. "It faces the street. I can have a good look
at the grey coat. . . . Yes, there he is." The individual who had
shadowed him from the moment he had left home was a short,
nondescript man in a grey coat. He was pacing the sidewalk on
the opposite side of the street. It was impossible by looking at him
to guess his nationality.

"What a fool!" Wislicenus thought and smiled wryly. The
detective's juvenile technique irritated him. "This dick uses the
same crude and elementary methods in trailing an old revolutionary that he would in following some amateur who is not dry
behind the ears." He felt a wave of nostalgia as he thought about
his early revolutionary career and about the detectives who had
followed him in the days of the old regime. Suddenly he remembered his exile: the Yenisei, the thermometer reading forty below,
Mary, the stifling hot room and the old couch with broken springs,
steaming tea with strawberry jam, and the books bound in red
oil-cloth. The fragments blended into a single vision and overwhelmed him with despondency, as though the exile had been
the happiest part of his life.

"Maybe they were indeed my happiest days . . .

"But who is this very real detective of today? I keep persuad-
ing myself that I noticed him at once. Probably I am right—
after all, thank God, I have had enough experience. But my
reasoning is not conclusive: I know when I noticed him, but he
may have been trailing me long before that. Who is he: Gestapo
or Gay-Pay-Oo?" he asked himself again, trying to consider the
question impersonally. The first time he had become aware that
he was being followed he had experienced an acute depression, a
sharp pain in the region of his heart, and a shortness of breath—
those very symptoms which he refused to call an attack. "Why
are you so excited, young fellow? By now you should be accus-

tomed to things like that. You have been under police observation
in every corner of the earth. In the old days you would have felt
unnatural unless someone was on your trail, but apparently of
late you have lost the habit. In recent years you have spent too
much time having other people shadowed. . . . There is something absurd about changing from subversive, underground activities to police work, and then back again to the underground.
That is a new phenomenon. Such transformations, at least on
such a scale, would have been impossible in the old days. But to
hell with it all!"

Walking over to the table Wislicenus picked up the illustrated magazine and returned to his chair. The old man, waiting
for his turn, looked up at him with curiosity. "If they did things
as they do them in mystery stories, this old man, who arrived here
ahead of me, would be the detective. Technically speaking, it
would not have been difficult. . . ." Out of boredom he tried to
find an answer to this problem: how to place a detective in a
doctor's waiting-room so that he could watch a man who had an
appointment with the doctor. "All important police chiefs are
exceptionally fond of mystery stories, and their imaginations
thrive on them. I enjoyed them, too; both when I was the hunter
and when I was the game. Yes, there is something ridiculous about
these transformations! Probably it is better for me when I am
being hunted, at least it is more in keeping with my face and
with my entire life," he thought, and immediately answered: "No,
that's not so, it is not better, it is worse, much worse! They could
not have known that I was planning to consult the "greatest
specialist in the world." Not unless Nadia is working for them,"
he dismissed this possibility with a smile.

His eyes lazily scanned the advertisements: the warriors in
football uniforms, the beauties smiling dazzlingly out of car windows, the famous people singing paeans of praise to mineral
waters, tooth powders and safety razors. Wislicenus found perverse pleasure in this superfluous, unimportant, but entertaining
evidence of the triteness and cupidity of the bourgeois world.

*"Ne pas connaître Unic c'est aller nu-pieds . . ." "Le Burberry
est chaud. Le Burberry est frais,"* he read. When he became tired
of them, he glanced at the articles on world events. Japanese
generals with feminine names were winning victories in the Far
East. Without being completely in sympathy with them, the
magazine gave their due to the brilliant generals who with the aid
of airplanes were destroying thousands of defenseless people
every day. Somewhat similar events were taking place in Spain.
Someone was making energetic representations to someone, and
someone was lodging a firm protest.

Wislicenus, letting the magazine drop in his lap, became lost
in thought. "Everything, no matter whether it is political or personal, everything is disgusting and nauseating! . . . my asthma,
—I am lucky if it is asthma,—being under surveillance, the events
in Spain and Japan, and the triumph of evil in the world."
Lumped with everything else was the fact that Nadia should
have been here, but this did not seem so important any more.

Nadia had telephoned him three days ago. He was delighted
when he recognized her voice, but not as delighted as he would
have been the year before. She said that she was in Paris for a
brief stay ("undoubtedly with him," he made a mental note) and
was anxious to see him. "I hear that you haven't been well? What's
the matter? What is wrong with your health?" "It's not too good."
"Who is your doctor?" "No one." "Don't be ridiculous: that's
impossible!" "Well, it happens to be true. The last doctor I saw
in Moscow told me it was asthma, and that there was no cure for
it." "In Moscow? You are joking? How long has it been since you
left Moscow? You must see a doctor right away, and be sure that
he is a leading specialist in his field!" "Sounds like mollycoddling!"
"It's not mollycoddling, it's common sense! I will arrange it for
you, and there is no point in making dates until then. I will give
you a ring tomorrow. So long." She hung up. Next morning she
called him again. "Everything is arranged. You have an appointment with Fouquot day after tomorrow at three-thirty." "What
Fouquot? What nonsense is this?" "It's not nonsense. You better do

as I tell you, or I never want to see you again. It will cost you three hundred francs, but you shouldn't try to economize on things like that. You can pay him later, or if you haven't the money now, I will gladly lend it to you." "What three hundred francs are you talking about? Is he a doctor?" "He is a famous professor. Haven't you heard of Fouquot? He is considered the leading heart specialist in the world. His usual fee is six hundred francs, but he will not charge you more than three hundred." "But why should I go to see him? There is nothing wrong with me." "In that case he will tell you that there is nothing to worry about, and it will put my mind at rest. I need you even more than the party needs you. Besides, I already have made the appointment. If you don't go I shall have to pay the three hundred francs out of my own pocket, without doing anyone any good. All joking aside, please go for the sake of my peace of mind!" "Why should you pretend to worry about me? Have you ever dropped me a single line while you were away?" "I am not much of a letter writer. I write other things." "What for instance?" "Never mind; besides, you haven't written to me either! Are you going?" "If you insist." "I insist! I most certainly insist! Thank you, my dear! [He was touched when she called him "my dear," though actually she simply had forgotten for the moment his first name]. Don't forget: day after tomorrow at half past three." "And why is Fouquot giving me a special rate?" "That's a long story . . . I am here with the ambassador," he thought he detected an angry note in her voice. "I suppose you have heard about it?" "No, I haven't heard about it. But what has that to do with me?" "Fouquot happens to be treating the ambassador. Though he is as strong as a bull, Kangarov has lost his mind on the subject of health. I am so tired of him! I can't begin to tell you how tired I am! Well, for obvious reasons the ambassador pays the regular fee of six hundred francs for every visit, and on the strength of that I managed to get from our doctor a special rate for you." "That was unnecessary. I have no desire to be a free adjunct to your ambassador." "In the first place it is not free. In the second place, he is not my ambassador.

. . . If you only knew how he sticks in my craw! And he is not the only one! They all are impossible! But there is no sense in talking about it over the telephone. As far as fees are concerned, Fouquot always makes a special rate for two patients," she lied: actually, the Professor had said that the matter of money was not important. "What? Just remember: if you don't keep the appointment, I never want to see you again!" "Don't be angry! . . . You really have been very sweet about it. . . . Do you think it will be possible to see you?" "Not only possible, but absolutely necessary! I will give you a ring, and we can make a date. Better make a note of Fouquot's address, though you always can find it in the telephone directory. . . ."

Wislicenus hung up with a smile: it was thoughtful of her. A year ago her thoughtfulness would have touched and excited him a great deal more. Since their last meeting a trace of something unpleasant had crept into her manner of speech. Her choice of words and certain expressions she used belonged to a Soviet foreign-service jargon which was never heard in Russia. She spoke like many of the young Soviet officials who, after spending a year in France, feel confident that they have mastered the secrets of Western civilization and, more particularly, have absorbed the very essence of Paris. "But that is not the thing that grates. . . . Could it possibly be true? . . ." About two months ago, in the course of a conversation, one of his colleagues had mentioned that Kangarov was living with his secretary. "That's just idle gossip. They may have slipped a time or two," another one had answered. "Just a taste, not a steady diet! . . ." Wislicenus had not uttered a word. It would have been hopelessly quixotic to create a scene. He refused to believe it, but more than once his mind returned to that conversation with acute physical revulsion.

The idea of proper medical care had occurred to Wislicenus before. During the last two months the sharp pains continued to grow in intensity. An acquaintance, who was not a doctor, but who was interested in medicine, had said casually that the symptoms seemed to indicate pericarditis, rather than asthma. "Maybe it's cancer of the lung?" Wislicenus had made a lame attempt at being flippant. "Maybe, but I doubt it," the man answered indifferently. "In any event, these days either disease can be treated." Now Wislicenus was almost happy that things had arranged themselves of their own accord. "Three hundred francs is a lot of money, but my finances are too uncertain at present to worry about them. If they stop my salary, three hundred francs will not make any difference. . . ."

"Perhaps my letter was too impetuous . . ." Once again Wislicenus checked the dates. "The letter reached Moscow thirteen days ago. I noticed the detective day before yesterday. Eleven days should give them ample time to make a decision and take proper steps. Too fast? He does everything in a hurry. The fact that I am one of Lenin's old comrades will carry no weight. If anything it makes the possibility greater. . . ." He felt a sharp pain in his chest. "No, no! It's the Gestapo!" he tried to reassure himself, shaking his head. There were reasons that made the Gestapo theory plausible. "I did buy the papers from Siegfried Mayer. They must have been tailing him, saw us meet, and, to be on the safe side, put a tail on me. That's possible. Even probable . . ." Indifferently he considered the likelihood that Mayer was an agent of the German secret police. During his lifetime Wislicenus had known so many agent-provocateurs and other people leading double lives that he accepted them as natural phenomena. They did not arouse his curiosity in the least, because he had observed that most of them were uninteresting, simple-minded men with a few distinguishing characteristics. In his early revolutionary activities, whenever he met new party members, as a safety measure, he assumed that they were police agents. He had no feeling of special contempt for them, but, for that matter, he could not see on what grounds one man could have sincere contempt for another. "No, it's not very likely that Mayer is an agent of the Gestapo. Probably they have ferreted out the fact that he has sold the papers. They are interested in them; public opinion does not bother them, the documents are not too important, but they still are interested. Why shouldn't they watch me? If I bought these papers, the chances are that I will buy others; they want to know who is offering them for sale. That is important. As far as they are concerned that is very important. . . ."

The other patient in the waiting-room continued to watch him with interest. Wislicenus glared at him in return with hatred and disgust (the patient immediately looked away). He rose to his feet, crossed the room, and stopped in front of the book shelves. "How queer!" The shelves were filled with treatises on witchcraft ,and black magic, and with transcripts of medieval trials for sorcery. These occupied only one section; beyond them were volumes on medicine and natural science, and further on bound magazines and books on cardiac diseases. "If I have heart trouble, why should I worry about who is trailing me? Infirmity gives me certain prerogatives." But, as he returned to his chair, he could not resist glancing once again out of the window. The detective was still walking up and down the sidewalk. "What amazing technique! Is this department also going to pieces? At one time we had created a very adequate organization. He does not look like a German, but that does not prove anything. In any case, I must be prepared to tender my resignation. . . . But if I leave the party, leave the Comintern, leave everything, where will I go? Join Trotsky?" He detested Trotsky, and, besides, he knew that the Fourth International had virtually no organization, that it was a product of police imagination. A thought about the Second International occurred to him only in passing. "I would rather join anything and anyone than have any dealing with those slobbering humanists who for fifty years hurled accusations at everyone, only to prove their own incompetence in the end. They never have won a single battle. But what about us? . . ."

Once again Wislicenus was assailed by the familiar, almost habitual, depressing thoughts that everything had been in vain, that his entire life was a mistake, that no one had retained any part of their old faith. His doubts had become especially persistent after his negotiations with Mayer. "What is the difference?

They have a stable of Aryan thoroughbreds, and we have a communist zoo, which produces specimens like Kangarov, and which even is directed by creatures like him. The future? What possible good can evolve from the present? We have created the largest and finest school for producing scoundrels—why should we fool ourselves with thoughts about the future? 'Planned economy?' 'Proper food?' 'Cheap housing?' The Germans have solved all this better than we have: their food is better, their houses cleaner, their plan more practical, and their 'talents' are given more opportunities to assert themselves. In the end they probably will gobble us up. This will mean that Lenin has sacrificed his life to create another Aryan stable. Moral and political bankrupts of all ages have always raised the cry that their experiments have failed through no fault of their own, that the future belongs to them, that coming generations would vindicate them, and that history would render judgment in their favor. Those of us who remain alive will offer the same excuses. But what can be done in the meantime? What is the solution? As far as I am concerned it is all over. Along with many others I have been checkmated by life! . . ."

The sound of voices and of some inner door being opened came from the direction of the professor's study. Wislicenus instantly was on the alert. "So there is no danger?" "Not the least, Mademoiselle; as I have told you before, there is no trace of anything," a slightly bored, contentious old voice was saying. "The ambassador is an exceptionally healthy man." Nadia appeared on the threshold, followed by Kangarov and by the old professor, who bowed to the men in the waiting-room and glanced at them inquiringly, as if to ask: who is next? The patient by the fireplace arose with a determined air to preclude any possibility of anyone depriving him of his turn. *"Au revoir, Mademoiselle . . . Au revoir, Monsieur l'Ambassadeur . . .* You have nothing to worry about," the Professor said, stepping aside to allow the new patient to enter. The door closed behind them.

At the sight of Wislicenus, Nadia barely controlled an ex-

clamation: "Good Lord, how he has changed! . . . He looks fifteen years older! . . ." Kangarov was obviously embarrassed.
There was no doubt that the meeting had taken him completely
by surprise. At first he even stepped aside, leaving Nadia and
Wislicenus facing one another, so that they found themselves in
the position of two billiard balls at the beginning of a game of
carambole. "We have seen each other since the incident at his
dinner," Wislicenus, as he greeted Nadia, noticed and was
puzzled by the ambassador's embarrassment. They had met on
Kangarov's previous visit to Paris and had exchanged a few distant
words. Wislicenus guessed—he also had been told—that he had
made a deadly enemy of Kangarov. "He can do as he pleases: if
he wants to speak to me, I have no objection; if he doesn't—so
much the better. . . ." Kangarov took two halting steps forward,
shook hands, and immediately retreated to his original position of
the third billiard ball in the game. It was apparent that the meeting had upset him. Nadia, on the contrary, tried to talk about
several things at once: about the health of Wislicenus—"you
really don't look at all badly"; about Paris—"what a wonderful
city! even though it is not Moscow, I always am delighted to get
here!" about the professor—"he is a remarkable man; he understands everything and sees right through you!"

"Sees right through you? Well, that's a tall order. I came only
because you insisted: I have little faith in doctors, and I don't
like to be mollycoddled."

"There are doctors and doctors. This one is a world celebrity.
He is so considerate! Talked to us for half an hour! You will be
grateful to me!"

"What seems to be wrong with you?" Kangarov asked drily,
glancing impatiently around.

"Someone said that the symptoms indicate angina pectoris.
The doctor in Moscow said it was asthma."

"As far as I know, the two are very different?"

"Well, at Nadia's request, I thought I would come and find
out, though I can't say that I fancy one more than I do the
other."

"Here is hoping you receive reassuring news . . . We must hurry, my child. . . ."

"Yes, I know. Are you doing anything tomorrow evening?" Nadia asked Wislicenus.

"Aren't you forgetting that we are going out of town tomorrow?"

"To see that old fool? I forgot all about her. Then we better make it day after tomorrow. I will give you a ring at nine in the morning, if that is not too early? Fine, you will hear from me day after tomorrow at nine. But how will I find out what Fouquot tells you?"

"I will report to you when you call me."

"Day after tomorrow? No, I would like to hear the news sooner. But today we will be running around, and I don't know when I shall get to a telephone. I suppose I shall have to wait a day. . . . I am sure that there is nothing wrong with you except that you look tired and overworked. I suppose . . ."

"Nadia, I am in a hurry . . ."

"If you are in so much of a hurry, why don't you run along?" turning to Kangarov Nadia asked angrily. "I don't believe you will need the services of an interpreter again today?" She stressed the word "interpreter." "But I will be ready to follow you without a murmur in a second. You know, one has to allow for the whims of a temperamental superior," she remarked to Wislicenus with a forced laugh. "Tell me just one more thing: are you on good terms with Commander Tamarin?"

"I never see him."

"But you would not mind if I should ask him the same evening?"

"I shall be delighted."

"Aye-aye, as one of our colleagues always says. I will ask both of you . . . Though I am not sure yet. It seems as though we will stay longer in France than we had expected. Aye-aye!"

With a radiant smile Nadia gave him both her hands. Wislicenus looked at her sadly: his feeling for her was fading. "Not a hundred per cent, but at least a seventy-five per cent cure. If

I only could get rid of my asthma as easily! Either she has changed, or I have, or we both have," his eyes followed them out of the door. Kangarov unquestionably was running away from him. "He must have learned something already. Now he will get after her. But she also is none too anxious to see me. 'I will ask both of you,' means 'I will kill two old birds with one stone.'" He crossed the room to the window and, seeing the detective, thought with a smile that if the nondescript man was from the Gay-Pay-Oo, Kangarov's name was certain to appear in his report. "They will jump at conclusions, and decide that we held a secret meeting over here." The possibility pleased him. Nadia and Kangarov stepped out of the door. They were walking in silence. "I suppose they had a family row on the staircase. Even her 'if you are in so much of a hurry' had the sound of a family squabble, though she seemed anxious to prove that he was nothing more than a superior. Well, if she feels like proving things, she can prove anything she wants. It makes very little difference to me. . . ."

II

PROFESSOR ALBERT FOUQUOT, an old childless widower, who outwardly resembled Clemenceau, and since 1918 had unconsciously underlined this resemblance worked in his study early in the morning. Usually, before going to the hospital, he read magazines and research reports in various fields of medicine, but especially in that branch in which his authority was supreme. In writing on that subject other people frequently mentioned his name, and almost always the references were very flattering. The article he had come across that morning also mentioned his work in a flattering way, but, though it was worded in polite and respectful terms, it outspokenly criticized his fundamental theories. In some way the writer had struck one of Fouquot's sensitive spots.

As a matter of habit, while reading it the professor angrily grumbled: "What a jackass!" "What an ignoramus! . . ."—but he recognized it as an important piece of work, which deserved a serious answer.

Precisely at eight-thirty the butler timorously knocked on the door and announced that the car was waiting. On the way to the hospital Fouquot went over the lecture in his mind. He had not planned to touch on the question mentioned in the article. But now, on the spur of the moment, he decided to speak about it, and, though he had only a vague notion of what he was going to say, he anticipated the pleasure of answering his critic.

The arrival of Professor Fouquot at the hospital produced, as usual, a state somewhat akin to panic: interns, doctors, nurses, attendants, and even patients instantly were on their mettle. Fouquot moved from one bed to another, looking at the patients with cold, penetrating, all-observing eyes, asked curt questions, examined new patients, and pronounced his diagnoses, without paying virtually any attention to the respectful remarks of the doctor who meekly followed in his wake. In spite of the fear and lack of affection which he generated in the people with whom he worked (doctors and medical students always referred to him as "l'animal"), they hung on his words in awe, and at times in enthusiastic admiration. He knew everything, he could see right through people, and in a few minutes he noticed things which others had failed to see during months of watching a patient. In the hospital and in the medical world in general he was surrounded by an atmosphere of servility, fear, envy and adulation. Most doctors, specializing in his branch of medicine, depended on him for their theses, their degrees, their positions, and their practice, and, besides, he was universally recognized as an adornment to French science, a genius as a diagnostician, and the leading heart specialist in the world.

But, in spite of all this, the lecture Fouquot delivered that morning produced after his departure a strange reaction among the more able listeners, who did not accept his words in blind faith; there were sighs, a shaking of heads, and a general feeling of embarrassment. Fouquot spoke well, and in defending the theory which bore his name, he displayed his usual clarity of thought and brilliant reasoning. The arguments the old professor used were forceful, and they were strengthened still further by his tremendous prestige. But the best doctors even in his own hospital considered the Fouquot theory obsolete, faulty, and repudiated by the latest findings of French, Austrian and American scientists. His closest pupil—the one who according to tacit universal assent would ultimately take over the hospital and the Professor's chair—thought sadly as he listened that the great diagnostician in his old age was becoming more and more a menace to clear thinking and an obstruction to the progress of medicine. It was no secret that recently the career of a young and exceptionally gifted doctor, who had had the temerity to criticize the Fouquot theory, had been smashed relentlessly.

The morning at the hospital proved to be a quiet one: there was no occasion for reprimands or vituperative outbursts. From the hospital Fouquot drove to make two calls on patients in their homes. Both of these calls irritated him. The first patient was a healthy man who apparently believed that his wealth entitled him to monopolize Fouquot's time. The second patient, on the contrary, was dying. In his case the old professor had been called, as so frequently happened, at the very last moment: if he could not help, no one else could. The old man merely shrugged his shoulders, and, as soon as he was closeted for the consultation with the family doctor, without the usual polite preliminary of asking his colleague's opinion, he angrily said that calling him had been absolutely pointless. "Nothing ever pleases this animal!" the puzzled doctor thought. "He spent ten minutes of his time and received a tremendous fee, which no one else would dare to ask. One would think that he would at least be grateful. . . ."

Returning home, Fouquot ate a heavy lunch. At his age it was advisable to eat lightly, but he did not intend to deprive himself of his last pleasures. He was annoyed to notice that eating occupied more and more of a place in his life. As a concession to medicine, or rather to chemistry (he had greater faith in chemistry than he had in medicine) he ate food rich in vitamin content —he had come to believe in vitamins, though he had not believed in them at first. After lunch he went to bed for a quarter of an hour. The butler had strict orders to wake him in exactly fifteen minutes. He fell asleep at once, and the short sleep refreshed him. After that he sat at his desk and read. The hour remaining until the arrival of patients was given to the reading of books which had no connection with medicine. For the most part his reading consisted of works devoted to the history of human ignorance and to the writings of universally recognized thinkers who had stood the test of time. At the moment he was reading Spinoza, for whom he had a special liking: he placed his own interpretation on what he read, and in reading Spinoza he detected between the lines a world conception closely akin to his own.

"Divine power is manifested through usual and unusual channels," Fouquot read that day. "His usual powers are manifested in the way He maintains a definite, established order in the universe. He uses His unusual powers when He wants to transcend the laws of nature, and performs miracles such as endowing a she-ass with human speech, or permitting the apparition of angels, or other things of that kind. But there are good reasons for doubting this latter form of Divine power manifestation, because the miracle is even greater when He governs the universe in accordance with established and immutable laws, instead of changing the laws He has designed so wonderfully of His own volition to suit the limited understanding of human beings. . . ." "Sacré Juif," Fouquot murmured with a smile. He was pleased to find another proof of his accord with Spinoza, and he made a mental note to call the attention of the philosophers among his friends to this passage. He did not have to copy it because his prodigious memory served him as well and as accurately now when he was approaching his eightieth year, as it had thirty years ago. It occurred to him that his life also followed firmly established, immutable laws. If anything were to disarrange his tremendous, planned-to-the-minute labors, everything would be disrupted: "the she-ass would begin to speak in a human voice. . . ."

Fouquot wanted to go on with his reading, but the visiting hours in his office began promptly at two-thirty. The frightened secretary brought him the list of appointments. He glanced at it moodily: "there are too many rich fools in this world. . . ." The professor had a huge income—it was said that he had saved between twenty-five and thirty millions—and he spent not more than a fourth of what he earned, an unusual proportion even in France. Money as such did not interest Fouquot, especially since his heirs were remote nephews and grandnieces (he had willed most of his estate to the Pasteur Institute). His usual fee for consultation in his office was six hundred francs; occasionally he wondered why he had set it at six hundred—it was an odd figure. But he made frequent exceptions to the rule, especially if he found the case interesting. Very often he sent some of his richest patients to his pupils, and in their place took charity cases who could not afford to pay a cent. Not many of the people, who called him *"l'animal"* because of his stern and disconcerting manner, knew that he donated considerable sums to charitable causes and to individuals, without ever mentioning it to anyone. He did not need the advertising. He was a member of many academies and scientific societies, he had been decorated with the Grand Cross of the Legion of Honor, and he had been the recipient of many foreign, and for the most part exotic decorations. More than once he had been called abroad or to the colonies to make a diagnosis in the cases of kings, shahs, maharajahs, or private individuals who had more money than they knew what to do with.

The Soviet ambassador, his first patient that afternoon, had been to see him once before and had returned in spite of a reassuring diagnosis. "This gentleman does not have to be treated for anything, except for his hopeless hypochondria and his stupidity which is just as hopeless. . . ." People as individuals did not

interest Fouquot, but in order to get at their afflictions and whenever possible (this happened comparatively seldom) cure them,
he had to understand the mental and spiritual inner workings of
every patient. The Professor had uncanny powers of perception.
In the case of Kangarov, as soon as he had examined him for the
first time, he not only committed to memory forever all the rather
uninteresting, in a medical sense, peculiarities of his organism, but
he also correctly diagnosed the character of the patient. He wondered who the nice and good-looking girl who accompanied him
was, and chiefly on her account he did not answer with a blunt
refusal when the ambassador with a happy smile had asked:
"Perhaps, my dear Professor, you will allow me to come back with
an analysis and with an electrodiagram?" "I shall be glad to see
you, though there is no need for it," he had answered drily. This
was the reason why he had to waste a half-hour of his time, which
he could have spent more pleasantly over Spinoza.

The second patient was a little more interesting. His was a
common, classic case of angina pectoris, without any complications, not too far advanced and lacking any unusual features.
Professor Fouquot advised him to rest, observe a light diet, abstain
from tobacco and alcohol, and gave him a prescription for tri-
nitrate in case of an acute attack. While he was writing it occurred
to him that any greenhorn just out of school could have made the
same diagnosis without the aid of X-rays and electro-cardiograms,
and would have charged the patient only thirty francs. "The diagnosis is not unfavorable, but try to avoid excitement of any
kind. . . . Don't forget your gloves. . . . There is no reason for
you to consult me again," he repeated to the patient, as he opened
the door, and with a nod of the head invited Wislicenus to
enter.

"We'll see now what the leading specialists in the world are
like," Wislicenus thought as he entered the study. "One can tell
by looking at him that he belongs to all the philanthropic and
soul-saving societies. Though he has an intelligent face . . . I
believe most doctors of his generation wore beards." He tried to

keep himself in an ironic frame of mind, but actually he was nervous and ashamed of himself. "At last I shall know what to expect. . . . His waiting-room looks like a library, and his study —like a physical laboratory. That's an X-ray machine, but what is that thing over there?" There was no desk in the room. In one corner stood two armchairs and a low, round table with nothing on it. A small bunch of colored crayons was lying on the mantel, near the X-ray machine.

"Won't you sit down?" the Professor said, indicating an armchair by the table. "The weather is none too pleasant, is it?" Having ascertained that his patient spoke French, Fouquot asked him how long he had been in Paris, what he thought of France, and what conditions were like in Russia. Without paying much attention to the answers (which were very brief) the Professor studied the patient intently. Even before examining him, before asking him a single medical question, without any proof, but simply as a matter of intuition, he knew that this was a sick man, who had led a hard life, and whose organism was hopelessly run down. He was willing to go a step further and make an intuitive guess: angina pectoris, but a much more advanced and dangerous case than the one that preceded it. "What is the population of Moscow now?" he asked, getting a card out of a drawer. "Three and a half million? I never should have guessed it. . . . How do you spell your name? Is it 'ts,' or just a 'c'? There was a famous chemist by that name. . . . So Moscow gradually is catching up with Paris? . . ." Continuing the conversation he casually asked some pertinent questions and wrote out the answers with a fountain-pen: age, nationality, address. "Are you married? . . . Have you ever been married? . . . You say before the war the population was a million and a half? That's interesting, extremely interesting . . . What is your profession?"

"I am a revolutionary," Wislicenus answered and immediately knew that he was being childish. "But what else can I call my profession?" he thought angrily and added aloud: "I am an employee of the Soviets." Fouquot put the card on the table and

studied the patient. It was the first time in forty-five years of
practice that he had received such an answer.

"That's very interesting," he said with a straight face and
retaining the same expression with which he had discussed the
present population of Moscow. "Obviously, it is as much a profession as any other. Just as here in France we have forgotten to
look at it that way, I thought, perhaps, that you, too, were beginning to forget? Would you say that your profession is more wearing than most?" He looked at the patient inquiringly, but Wislicenus remained silent. "That charming young lady said that you
were complaining about your heart? . . . Incidentally, is she
related to your ambassador?"

"No, she is his interpreter and secretary," Wislicenus answered curtly. The Professor studied him again.

"She is very charming and very good-looking. . . . So she is
his interpreter and secretary . . ." the Professor repeated indifferently, still studying the patient. "You are complaining about
your heart . . . Do you have pains?"

Fouquot proceeded to ask medical questions. He worded them
briefly and seemed to know the answers as soon as he heard the
first few words. At times he prompted the patient, cutting him short
whenever he attempted explanations, and translating his hesitant
descriptions into precise medical terms. Apparently he knew all
the aches and pains better than the patient. *"Douleur precardiale
avec sensation de constriction thoracique . . . Irradiations bra-
chiales . . . Sensation d'angoisse allant jusqu'à l'impression de
mort imminente,"* he said with evident relish and approval, as
though he were enumerating good omens which were greatly to
the patient's credit. "Your explanations are unnecessary," the
Professor said coldly when the patient ventured to express an
opinion. Wislicenus was taken aback. "Have you ever had syphilis?" Fouquot asked in a business-like tone, as though it was something that was taken for granted. "You have never had syphilis?"
he repeated, and it was difficult to say whether he was surprised or
disappointed. "You are sure you haven't? But you have always

been afraid of it? Have you ever had gout? Just a touch of it. . . .
Fine! Step over here to the X-ray machine."

Taking a crayon from the mantel, Fouquot switched on the
motor and began to draw. With a sense of satisfaction he saw that
his intuitive, preliminary diagnosis was absolutely correct: angina
pectoris with injuries to the aorta and with other complications.
"He has three or four months of life at most," he thought with a
certain pride at the exactness of his prediction. He had lost his
capacity for pity a long time ago. No normal man could have
retained it and witnessed as much sorrow, suffering and as many
deaths as he had seen in his lifetime. "Fine, fine," he repeated
several times.

Wislicenus watched him hopefully. He did not want to reveal
his anxiety by asking whether there was any immediate danger. "I
have waited a long time, and I can wait another five minutes! He
can have his fill of black magic. . . ." But he was worried and
unpleasantly surprised by the old man's silence, which seemed to
put his courage and self-restraint to a test. The Professor turned
on the lights. The bored expression had left his face and he was
looking at Wislicenus with a mixture of tenderness, gratitude and
affection. Due to a number of complications this was a very
interesting case. "Fine, very fine," he repeated.

"Well, Professor, is it dangerous?" Wislicenus asked, unable to
contain himself any longer.

"I will tell you in a second. I can't quite make up my mind.
Will you step over here, to the electro-cardiograph?"

Fouquot led the patient to a peculiar contraption which stood
in the middle of the room. He made him lie on a couch, asked
him to roll up a trouser leg, covered him with material made of
cork, put something moist on his leg, switched on the motor, and
continued with his witchcraft. "These are electrodes . . . What
was it they taught us about them in school: electrodes, electrons?
. . . I shall have to allow for his effort to spare my feelings,"
Wislicenus was tired. "If he says: 'there is no immediate danger'
—it will mean that it's dangerous. If he says: 'it's quite serious'—
it will mean death. But when? In a year? In two years? . . ." It

occurred to him that the people who had put a detective on his trail were probably wasting their time. The Professor stopped the motor. As far as he was concerned everything was settled: he knew definitely how and when the patient was going to die. This remarkable and valuable case fitted in nicely with the Fouquot theory.

"There is no immediate danger," he said with finality. "You have angina pectoris . . . Put on your clothes."

Seating the patient in an armchair, the Professor briefly and concisely outlined the necessary regimen. Alcohol was out of the question, except in very small doses. Smoking was definitely forbidden. He could eat anything he wanted, but not to excess. "Rest is the most important thing; try not to worry and to avoid excitement," the professor said, wondering at the psychological absurdity of his own advice. "Do you live alone?"

"Yes."

"Perhaps there is someone to whom I could describe the necessary regimen in greater detail? They could call me, or come to see me. Maybe that young lady would do it? No? She is a stranger? Well . . . It's not very important. The regimen is very simple. Could you go to the country? That would do you a world of good. Fresh air is important for the heart."

"I am afraid that's impossible."

"You can stay here. The city has its advantages [*"Le Burberry est chaud. Le Burberry est frais,"* Wislicenus thought]. I will give you a prescription in case you have an attack.

"Should I be under the care of a doctor?"

"That would not do any harm. Your doctor is an experienced man," Fouquot said. He considered the embassy doctor an ignoramus and a nonentity, but he held the same opinion of most doctors. He could not discern in any of them the qualities of a true diagnostician, and neither could he see about them any trace of real scientific culture. Most of them had only a vague idea of chemistry and bacteriology. Some, because of their arrogance, their ignorance and their lack of understanding, should have been put in prison years ago—they had more murders on their conscience than the most hardened criminals. "I should like to see you again in six months," he said, knowing well that in six months this man would be in his grave. He made a mental note to ask the embassy doctor about the date of death so he could complete his record. The Professor changed the subject of conversation back to politics. "He is much cleverer and much more of a person than the ambassador," Fouquot deduced not from the patient's curt and uninteresting answers, but from his general appearance and the expression of his face. "Too bad they cannot exchange places." He had no use for communists, but he had a weakness for intelligent people. Without interrupting the conversation the Professor wrote something on a piece of paper. "Here are all the instructions." He rose to his feet.

"Thank you very much," Wislicenus said, also rising and placing three hundred francs on the table. "I was told, Professor, that you have made a special rate in my case. . . . I am . . ."

"That is completely immaterial," Fouquot interrupted him. "If you happen to be in financial difficulties, I will not charge you at all."

"No, no," Wislicenus exclaimed, his face turning red. "I am very grateful." The Professor saw him off to the door. There were two new patients in the waiting-room. "I was very happy to see you. If you ever need anything, please call on me. I am always at your service. . . . Come in," he addressed the new patient, with a nod of his head.

III

"This looks like the end," Wislicenus thought as with slow, tired movements he descended the stairs. "I knew it as soon as he asked whether there was someone he could talk with. . . . Well, I was expecting it, and I am not frightened. . . ." He was so upset that in walking out of the building he forgot to look around for the detective; he remembered him only when he turned into a side street. "Seems to have disappeared . . . To hell with him! What difference does it make now, anyway?"

The street lights were on, and the wind was blowing. "It's cold . . . Orders or no orders, I believe I will stop in a café and have a drink. . . . Maybe a glass of Pernod? . . ." He liked this drink because its taste reminded him of absinth, and that brought memories of his young years and of the pre-war days. "There was a saying: *l'heure sainte de l'absinthe* . . . If the greatest specialist in the world says so, there cannot be any room for doubt. . . . Angina pectoris has such an unappetizing sound!"

With a sense of revulsion Wislicenus pressed a hand against his chest as though expecting to feel the angina through his ribs. A yellow leaf floated down from a tree and fell on the sidewalk. "And that is the poetic symbol, which has been used more than once, I believe. . . ." Suddenly he felt a pain—an instant, madly onrushing, choking pain, accompanied by despair and by a horrible sensation of approaching death. "An attack . . . This is the end! . . . Oh, God, not just yet! . . . Just a little longer! . . . Just a few days! . . ."

Wislicenus stopped and, gasping for breath, leaned against the wall. A pedestrian glanced at him uneasily and hurried on his way. The pain continued to grow unbearably—another second and his heart would burst! With dull, unseeing eyes he stared at the yellow leaf and at the metal grillwork around the base of the tree. "Will it come right here? . . . Right now? . . . No, no, that's impossible! . . ." The thought struck him that if he were to die that moment it would be as a direct result of his visit to the doctor and of the excitement caused by it. And just as suddenly, with indescribable relief he felt the pain begin to ease away. "It is passing . . ."

He pushed himself away from the wall and stood swaying from side to side. "I did not fall . . . There is a bench over there, and I must reach it . . . The pain is definitely better! . . ." Utterly exhausted, Wislicenus sank on the bench facing the window of a shoe store. In the rapidly vanishing light of the fading day he could see in the glass, among the rows of neatly lined shoes, the reflection of his convulsed face. He could breathe easier now, but his mind still was not functioning. His entire body was covered with cold sweat. "I have never had an attack like this before . . . Perhaps the end would have been more merciful . . ." A huge dark shadow quickly crossed the bright patch of light reflected from the window on the wet sidewalk. The figure of a tall red-haired man, moving swiftly in the street behind the bench, glided across the reflecting surface of the window glass. "I think I know him," Wislicenus thought with a sensation of weird horror. "Where could I have seen him? . . ." Gathering the last ounce of his strength he turned. The tall man was disappearing around the corner. "How ridiculous . . . That's the *'impression de mort imminente'* . . . I feel better—the pain is leaving . . . It is still there, but it is going away . . . In another minute it will be gone. . . ." He tried to get to his feet, fell heavily on the bench, rose with determination for a second time, and reeling like a drunken man started to walk.

IV

CERISIER'S CAR came to a stop at the prison gate. Despite his many years of law practice he always entered the prison with a disagreeable sensation, approaching physical nausea. Today's conference with his client on the eve of the trial was more than usually unpleasant. He disliked cases of this kind as a rule. Arguments, dialectics, and a careful analysis of the evidence would have little bearing on the outcome; the chances for a favorable verdict were nil. True, because of the very hopelessness of the case, a conviction would not in any way reflect on the defense counsel. But even allowing for that, and for the publicity resulting from the sensational nature of the case, Cerisier sincerely regretted that he had undertaken to represent Alvera.

On the morning following the murder the police, making a routine investigation, called on Vermandois. He was completely dumfounded and for a long time unable to recover from his amazement and horror. While he was listening to what they said his eyes bulged, and he emitted continually exclamations of surprise. In response to the diffident questions of the people conducting the investigation, he gave ambiguous and embarrassed answers, apparently feeling that indirect accusations were being leveled against him and that at least a part of the guilt, disgrace and responsibility rested on his shoulders. After the police left he was besieged by reporters. The murder was a sensation in its own right (it so happened that there was no other sensational news that day), but much of the interest in the case was due to the fact that the murderer was the secretary of a famous literary figure. Vermandois completely lost his presence of mind. In his distraught state he gave interviews to the first two reporters, then, burying his head in his hands, gave the old woman strict orders not to admit anyone else to the apartment, and took the telephone receiver off the hook.

Shutting himself in his study Vermandois took a long time to recover. "What is this? What kind of a man is he? . . . Why didn't I notice anything? I always considered him a psychopathic case, but this does not make any sense at all! . . . I try to understand the mind of the imaginary Lysander, while a real murderer talks to me, spends days with me, and I can't see anything unusual about him! . . ." The thought struck him that he could have been chosen the victim. He shuddered. "The only thing my career lacks is a lurid finale like that! . . ."

The old woman brought him the papers. With small variations every paper carried huge headlines: "Double murder in Louvécienne." Though Vermandois had been interviewed by only two reporters, his statement appeared in six of seven different papers. Some of them carried his picture next to the picture of the hand-

cuffed murderer. One of the stories hinted that he intended to
provide a defense for Alvera. "I must talk to someone about
it! . . " He remembered Cerisier, who had been one of the guests
at Kangarov's dinner the night before. "There are other lawyers
who are much better in criminal cases, but he will do! They are all
alike! . . . At least, because I happen to know him, he will not
charge me as much. . . ."

In the course of the very first telephone conversation Cerisier
made it clear that he would not take any money. He did not make
it a practice to take free cases. The lack of a fee lessened the
pleasure he experienced in planning the defense, but he followed
certain principles without deviation. "Money is out of the question, my dear friend." "But why?" "Because there is no reason why
you should pay for the sins of this promising young man. Why
should I accept your money? But, to be frank with you, I am not
too well pleased with his case. You realize I am not a specialist in
matters of this kind, though, obviously, I have had occasion to
appear in criminal cases. . . ." "Your addresses before juries are
masterpieces of logic and style!" Vermandois protested. "I read
them in the newspapers faithfully." "You are a liar! You are delighted because I have refused to take your money," Cerisier
thought, but like others he was susceptible to flattery. "Thank
you very much, but I still think you had better go to a specialist."
"I have faith in you and in you only!" "Then let me think it over.
So far I have only glanced at the papers. In any event, should I
undertake the defense, I shall do so only out of my admiration for
you and out of my professional sense of duty." "We will discuss that
later!" Vermandois assumed a jocularly threatening tone, knowing very well that in the end he would not have to pay. As accustomed as he was to the idea that in his person French culture
was being honored, he was touched. "If he paid me a thousand
francs, he would bother me every day, and besides, he would tell
everybody that I had robbed him," Cerisier thought with a contented smile. "I will read the details of the newspaper accounts,
and I will stop in to see you." "Wouldn't you rather have me

come to your office? I shall be delighted." "No, no! Besides, I have
a call to make today in your part of town."

Cerisier carefully studied the papers. The afternoon editions
carried the story that the wounded Louvécienne policeman had
died in terrible pain. "What possible hope can we have?" he
thought with a sigh. But it was too late to back out. He went to
see Vermandois and listened to him in amazement.

"I am simply horrified! I could not have been more dumfounded if someone had told me that you or I had committed
a murder."

"So he had certain peculiarities? Do you think he is insane?"

"I don't think anything. I simply am unable to understand."

"What is the matter with the youth of today?" Cerisier exclaimed, and proceeded to expound his opinions about the
younger generation, the excessive interest in sports, and the demoralizing influence of newspapers and moving-pictures. "Just
think! This promising young man could have killed you."

"I never have given this a thought! But why do you imagine
he went all the way to Lucienne (instead of Louvécienne, Vermandois said distinctly Lucienne, using the old pronunciation,
and Cerisier immediately made a mental note of it for future
use). He always could have counted on finding such a beggarly
sum in my apartment. Do you believe there is any chance of
saving his life?"

"Less than none, especially since the death of the policeman.
What possible mitigating circumstances can we suggest? Probably
I shall have to prove that he is insane. But, to be honest with you,
pleas of insanity have little effect today on Paris juries. His
case very likely will be tried in the Versailles court, but that is
virtually the same thing. Has he at least a mother?"

"I don't know. It seems to me that I heard him say that he has
no relatives."

"You see! We cannot produce even the tears of an aged
mother. But that, too, is an obsolete method these days, like the
mention of the 'unfortunate young man who never knew the lov-

ing caress of a mother.' In any event I will do everything in my power for your Raskolnikov. And you should write a novel about it," Cerisier concluded with a laugh.

"That is an idea! Paul Bourget most certainly would have written it, and he would have made the young man an illegitimate son of a duke, led astray by a sinister member of the masonic order. Too bad Paul Bourget is dead. As far as Raskolnikov is concerned, you must make it a point to reread that masterpiece. In a large city, in the capital of a country, everyone knows everyone else and keeps meeting them almost fortuitously. This Svi . . . Svi . . . —whatever his name is?—happens to live next door to the angelic prostitute, and it is only natural that he overhears the noble murderer when he makes his confession to her. Certainly I am not a Dostoyevsky, but I should hesitate before relying on so many coincidences, which play into the hand of a novelist. After all, there were more than two furnished rooms in Petersburg? And he was so proud of his awful French, which he persisted in using by constantly inserting French sentences in his novels! Our translators faithfully preserved them as relics! But this did not prevent him from hating and despising us, just as he hated and despised all people. After two weeks in Paris he was convinced that he understood France, the French people, and all the mysteries and peculiarities of our national character. He understood everything! . . . But I am getting away from my subject: I hate that man, though I admire him as a great writer. His murder scene is perfectly magnificent. . . . You must, you absolutely must re-read *Crime and Punishment* before the trial. I believe this is the third generation of lawyers to use Raskolnikov's name in the courts? . . . By the way, or rather to change the subject: I insist that you allow me to reimburse you, my friend."

"I repeat that that is out of the question. But you can render a real service to your charming secretary. I assume that you are prepared to appear as the chief witness for the defense."

"Good Lord! Do I have to appear in court?"

"What else can we do? Your very presence in the court room will help him in the eyes of the jury."

"Please, be reasonable! Can't we get along without that?"

"Impossible."

"Good Lord! I did not expect this."

"How could you have failed to expect it, my friend? It is elementary."

"It may be elementary, but it is very disagreeable. What if I am not in Paris at the time? I very frequently go out of town."

"In that case you will make it a point to return. You will be cast in the role of the jury's conscience," the lawyer said with evident delight.

Though he had not expected to meet anyone pleasant, Cerisier's first impression of his client was most unfavorable. In addition to a repulsive exterior, he was overbearing in his manner and quite evidently in love with himself. He was so uncommunicative that it was impossible to judge the level of his mentality. He answered questions in monosyllables; all attempts at a heart-to-heart talk with him produced no results: the young man's face wore only an expression of hatred. "Perhaps you did not have enough food?" Cerisier suggested. "I had lunch and dinner every day." "Perhaps love for some woman whom you tried to help drove you on a path of crime?" Alvera laughed. He explained that he killed Chartier because he intended to rob him. His philosophy of anarchism was not clear, and it was impossible to say in what way he differed from any ordinary criminal. During the conversation he yawned continually, either because he was exhausted, or as a gesture of defiance. It was apparent that the young criminal placed no value on his own defense and would not be in the least disappointed if he were not represented by a lawyer. "He is simply a degenerate," Cerisier decided.

Those were the words Cerisier used in talking to Vermandois when he called him on the telephone the same evening. "Did he actually do the work of a secretary?" "I can give you my word that he performed his duties in a most competent manner. He has a college degree, he graduated from a lyceum with honors, and he has read a great deal." "I don't know what to think of it. He seemed to me a dull and vicious degenerate. Perhaps practically it can be explained by the beating they gave him when they arrested him—he is a horrible sight. As hard as I tried, I could not learn anything that would tip the scales in his favor. At the preliminary hearing he volunteered information of the most damaging nature." "The poor fellow! Can't anything be done for him?" "I will plead that his first statement was made when his mind was not functioning, and that it is not admissible as evidence. For instance, without any argument he conceded premeditation." "How terrible!" "We will see what the experts say, but I repeat that his case seems hopeless." "Do everything you can, my friend. I depend on you entirely!"

After his first visit Cerisier saw his client a few more times. Either Alvera did not understand his cautious hints, or he had no desire to defend himself. No new hope appeared when the medical experts pronounced the murderer a sane man. When Cerisier read their opinion he merely shrugged his shoulders.

Now, on the·eve of the trial, Cerisier, as a conscientious officer of the law, felt that it was necessary for him to have one more conversation with the accused. He had laid plans for the defense, but he could not fail to realize that his arguments were very vacuous: a youth who is almost a child, unhealthy daily surroundings, lack of a family life, inherited weaknesses, bad books, absurd ideas which frequently are confused with socialism, persistent thoughts of revenge against society, purely abstract theorizing on the subject of murder, and then a sudden mental aberration at the crucial moment. . . . Cerisier had little faith in all this. Besides, he knew that, as luck would have it, the prosecutor was an able man who would annihilate his arguments without much effort: there was no question of real poverty, inherited weaknesses are difficult to prove, the criminal is a young man, but a long way from being a child. Cerisier could not conceive any other line of defense. The fact that one of the victims was a policeman made Alvera's position still more vulnerable; it almost excluded any possibility that the head of the state would commute his sentence. In addition the murderer had a foreign-sounding name, though he had no accent which would tend to antagonize the jury. No matter what one said about anarchism (the value of mentioning it was also questionable), the immediate purpose of the crime was revolting in its simplicity. If Cerisier were on the jury, he doubted that he would give the accused the benefit of the doubt. "The chance of saving his life is one in a thousand," the lawyer thought, as he entered the sinister-looking building. In his imagination he already saw all the usual corollaries to such cases: waiting for the verdict, brief words of consolation, excited hand-shakes, maybe a fainting spell ("Give him some water! Quick!"), the call on the president of the republic equally uncomfortable for both sides, and then the final scene at which it was customary for the defense lawyer to be present. Considering his high-strung nervous system and his natural softness of heart, all this was very hard on him.

Wrinkling his nose at the disagreeable odor of the prison cor-ridors, Cerisier proceeded to the visitor's room. He sat at a table and with a heavy feeling tried to think of a way to impress his client with the necessity of stressing a certain type of evidence. "I went to see Chartier without intending to do anything—then suddenly something happened to me!" Putting words into the mouth of a criminal was not permissible. Many lawyers used such methods, but though Cerisier did not like them, he could not see any other way out. Any infinitesimal hope that remained of sav-ing Alvera's life hinged on this point of sudden mental aberra-tion. But a young degenerate like Alvera could be counted on to do the most unexpected: he was likely to make a speech extolling anarchism and proclaiming his hatred for the bourgeois world, or he might declare that he was proud of what he had done, or he was just as likely to collapse, losing the last vestige of courage and producing a feeling of disgust in the jury. Not having seen his client recently, Cerisier was afraid that he would find him in a tearful mood. He knew that prison life had a tendency to break a man's spirit. If the boy were to burst into tears in the court-room at the right moment, and in the right way, it might conceivably help his case. But here, in the visitor's room, tears were absolutely useless.

V

ALVERA HAD been in prison for more than a year. His life there was very different from what he had imagined it would be: in certain ways it was better, in others worse. He had expected to spend nights and days thinking about his fate: in reality he thought about it very seldom, and, it seemed to him, with indifference. He suffered in prison chiefly from bad living conditions, from boredom, and from a lack of something to do.

Alvera had changed a great deal. The change was not so much a result of his crime and of waiting for the punishment, but rather of the terrific blow with a bottle which he had suffered at the time of his arrest. During the first days horrible pains obscured all other sensations; in the beginning he testified without any notion of what he was saying. The prison doctor expressed an opinion that the prisoner probably would show indications of concussion of the brain, and in that case would have to be transferred to the hospital. But Alvera developed no other symptoms, and remained in his cell.

The dentist extracted the roots of the broken and crushed teeth, blood mixed with saliva stopped oozing from the corners of his mouth, the pain gradually disappeared, and the swelling on his face went down—at least as far as he could judge by feeling it with his fingers, or by the occasional glimpse he caught of himself in some shiny surface (there were no such surfaces in the cell, but there were one or two in the magistrate's office). And still the blow had left a definite mark on him. In rare moments of his old introspection, which came to him at night, it seemed to him that his mind was degenerating into a state of idiocy. "Maybe the shock brought out the cretinism which was latent in me," he mused with a smile. But having invented this explanation himself, he had no faith in it.

His own position Alvera appraised soberly, and he nurtured no illusions about his fate, especially after he learned that the wounded policeman had died. This fact in itself made little impression on him, but he knew that it was the end. Not a chance remained of saving his life: a robber, a killer of two people, one of whom happened to be a policeman, and a foreigner (*sale étranger*). The only possibility out of a thousand was that the majority on the jury would be enemies of the existing order: communists, anarchists, and left-wing socialists. This seemed too far-fetched. "Six or seven men out of twelve! They pack the juries with their own kind of people. . . ."

More than once the thought of committing suicide occurred to Alvera. There was only one way to do it: to smash his head against the wall. He frequently stared at the wall, which was painted to the height of about six feet from the floor with black paint that smelled of disinfectant. What would happen if he were to put his hands behind his back, take a sprint, and hit it with his head? Eight feet were hardly enough for a real sprint, he would not have much strength behind the blow, probably he would not die, instead he would inflict on himself a permanent injury and turn into a complete idiot. It was not worth it: that kind of death was worse than the guillotine. To hang oneself was extremely difficult: the authorities had taken effective measures to prevent it. Slash his wrists? That, too, was almost impossible. The barber who visited the cells once a week, did not let the razor out of his hand. Alvera refused to be shaved because of a feeling of repugnance: the idea of prison shaving-things nauseated him. He grew a beard, which served the useful purpose of concealing the scars from the blow. For the first few days he nervously fingered the stubbly growth, but as time went on he became used to it. Having considered all the possibilities, he discarded the thought of suicide.

Strange as it seemed, his crime occupied only a small place in his thoughts. The very first night, when he still was delirious, he remembered the study in the Chartier house and began to shake. Later, in order to regain his strength, he barred such thoughts from his mind. When recollections forced themselves on him, Alvera tensed his muscles, shook his head and literally drove them away—an accomplishment which he considered greatly to his credit. On the whole he behaved just as he had intended to behave if he were caught. Long ago he had decided to assume an attitude of proud disdain, and now he was trying to live up to this mental picture. All famous anarchists had behaved like that in prison. At times he wondered whether the anarchists had a better justification for their attitude: perhaps he should not have chosen a miserable old man of modest means for his victim? But this made little difference. Whenever Alvera was assailed by doubts he hid from them behind his proud disdain. Several times he rehearsed his final plea in court: he intended to tell them the whole truth.

There were no newspapers in prison and Alvera had no conception how much of a sensation his crime had made. But when he was being led to the magistrate's office people in the corridors stared at him with horror and curiosity, heads appeared from behind doors, and cameras clicked. As a result he sensed that his case was in the public eye. Another indication was the vaguely respectful manner in which he was treated by his fellow prisoners. This attention pleased him. When a photographer for the first time trained his camera on him, Alvera made no futile gesture of trying to cover his face with manacled hands; instead he posed with a smile, as if to say: "if you want to take a picture of me— here I am!"

On the very first day word reached Alvera by grapevine that two lawyers were anxious to take his case. This also was proof that he was in the limelight. Even in his condition he realized that they were probably young lawyers who wanted to build their reputations on his fame. On the same day Cerisier appeared from nowhere. Alvera knew his name from the newspaper accounts of the parliamentary debates, but he was not sure that the fat lawyer was the same man: perhaps he is only a namesake? Alvera felt that it would be awkward to ask him: a question of this kind would smack of the drawing-room and would not be in keeping with his position. Later, while he was exercising in the yard, he learned from another prisoner that this was the right Cerisier. *"T'as de la veine, c'est un as! Un ancien ministre!"* the prisoner said simulating envy. No one really envied him, because everyone in prison knew that his goose was cooked. Alvera smiled mysteriously, but he was pleased—it flattered his vanity. He could not help wondering whether the lawyer had received any money from Vermandois, and if so how much. But this was another awkward question he could not ask.

His first conversation with the lawyer lasted only fifteen minutes. Alvera could not even remember the details of what was said. He had a dim recollection that Cerisier tried to probe into his soul, and that he was annoyed when he met with no success. The lawyer said that everything would depend on the type of jury they would draw: until then everything was guesswork.

"No case is hopeless, my friend," he announced in a brisk and spirited voice, dropping a gentle hint that he would build his defense around a plea of temporary insanity.

"Temporary?" Alvera asked and stopped short. Before taking his leave Cerisier expressed the hope that he would not become discouraged and warned him that he would be in prison for a long time (this was his way of letting him know that, in any event, the execution was a long way off).

"In the meantime my assistant will come to see you. She is a very competent and business-like young lady, and she will supply me with all the details. You can rest assured that I will do my best to look after your interests. When the time comes I will see you again. . . ."

"You are aware that I am unable to pay you anything," Alvera said with a bitter smile. "I did have a few hundred francs, but that will not be enough for you, and, besides, I don't know where they are now. The money they found on me belonged to Chartier. I assume that I have no right to spend it, and I imagine that you would not want any part of it."

"Let's forget that part of it," the lawyer said drily ("he certainly is an impudent bastard, or else he has no conscience whatever," he thought) "I am not representing you because of a fee. . . . Any time you want to tell me anything, you can send word to me by Mademoiselle Mortier."

As he was leaving Cerisier ostentatiously shook hands, with the air of a man forcing himself to do something out of higher considerations.

Next day a young, good-looking girl appeared in the prison to see Alvera. She had just been admitted to the bar, and she was happy because through her connections she was able to become associated with Cerisier (the famous lawyer was always surrounded by women). When the prisoner was brought into the visitor's room, Mademoiselle Mortier rose abruptly to her feet and greeted him nervously. At the sight of his bruised, swollen and scarred face, her eyes reflected a fleeting horror. Alvera had a feeling that she was afraid of him: she followed the retreating guards with an uneasy glance. She began to talk rapidly with exaggerated casualness as though they were discussing the most commonplace things. Mademoiselle Mortier was in love with her work, with the bar association, with Cerisier, with the code of laws, and, more than anything else, with her robe, which she already had had four occasions to wear in court (not counting the number of times she had tried it on at home). From memory, but with minute precision (she had passed the examinations only recently and before leaving the office she had glanced hurriedly at the criminal code) she explained to Alvera that in accordance with the meaning and letter of article 295, and of subsequent articles, causing the death of another human being constituted homicide—"*homicide*"; if it were committed intentionally "*homicide*" became "*meurtre*"; and if it were proven that the act was premeditated, then "*meutre*" became "*assassinat*." In addition,

special forms of murder were recognized, such as parricide, infanticide, and poisoning. A further distinction was made in cases when
the accused had been lying in wait for his victim—this was known
as "*guet-apens.*" But inasmuch as parricide implied the murder of
one's father or mother, and infanticide the murder of an infant,
articles 299 and 300 were not applicable in his case—she explained
in a cheerful and encouraging voice. Article 298 in regard to
lying in wait also could not be used against him because its exact
wording was: "*le guet-apens consiste à attendre plus ou moins de
temps, dans un ou divers lieux, un individu soit pour lui donner
la mort, soit pour exercer sur lui des actes de violence.*" No such
accusation could be made in his case. They could try him under
article 295 for "*meurtre*" if they could not prove premeditation,
or they could try him under article 302 for "*assassinat*" if they
undertook to prove that his action was premeditated.

"What difference will it make as far as I am concerned?"
Alvera asked gloomily. He was self-conscious because his face
was bruised and because he spoke indistinctly, lisping on account
of the missing teeth and the blood oozing from his gums.

"In accordance with the letter and meaning of article 302,
'*assassinat*' is punishable by death," Mademoiselle Mortier said
apologetically, gracefully dropping her eyelids and indicating
that she did not approve of this article.

"And what about '*meurtre*'?"

"'*Meurtre*' is punishable by a life sentence to hard labor. You
can see readily how important for us is the question of premeditation." She explained in great detail how the courts interpreted
premeditation, and in what way "*préméditation*" differed from
"*volonté criminelle.*" These distinctions, which she only recently
had mastered, gave her a great deal of satisfaction. Alvera listened
to her absent-mindedly, thinking that in the case of the policeman premeditation could not be established. The young woman
slipped away like a visiting angel.

An examination by the medical experts followed. Alvera was
asked various stupid questions. He was convinced that he would

have been adjudged sane if he were to lose his mind completely, that the doctors were defending an existing order and believed that all criminals simulated insanity, and that the whole procedure was ridiculous.

The simple, monotonous, tiresome prison life dragged on. At five-thirty they were awakened by a bell, at six they were given a mug of black coffee and the daily ration of bread, at nine—soup with floating pieces of meat, at four—more soup. There was enough food to keep one from starving, but Alvera was permanently hungry. After he had been there a week he was advised that Vermandois had placed two hundred francs at his disposal and that he could order against that amount various things from the prison commissary. When on the following morning the door opened and he was handed a sausage and a chocolate bar from the delivery wagon, he devoured them with such greed that he felt that from now on he was an old-timer and that he had entered the spirit of prison life.

Food became his chief interest. Alvera learned what soups were served on what days of the week, and what were the cheapest and best things at the prison commissary. With a sense of shame, he anxiously wondered what would happen when the two hundred francs were exhausted and whether Vermandois would provide any more. After a lapse of one day, another hundred francs arrived, and from time to time he received additional sums.

Besides insufficient rations and the poor quality of the food, the thing from which Alvera suffered most was boredom. He could take books out of the prison library, but they were exchanged only once a week. The evenings and nights were worst of all. Lights went out early. There were three reasons why he could not sleep: the odor of disinfectant (his head ached continuously), coarse linens, and bedbugs. Battling the bedbugs was one of the main occupations of the prisoners and the chief topic of their conversation during the exercise periods. They walked in a circular yard subdivided by stone walls radiating from the center. This arrangement made it possible for a guard standing in the center to watch simultaneously all sectors of the yard. Two or three prisoners walked in each sector. The attention of the prison was focused on Alvera because he was the only one there under the shadow of certain death. His unique position won for him special consideration from his fellow inmates, as well as from the guards. He was treated politely, but for that matter so were the others. Some of the prisoners tried to ask him questions about his case. But he persistently refused to discuss it, changing the subject of conversation to the bedbugs or to the soup.

Alvera felt that little was left of his proud disdain. How could he retain it when he spent his time fighting bedbugs, thinking about sausage, and wondering whether that bastard Vermandois would charitably throw a few more francs his way? Gradually Alvera reached the conclusion that now there was no longer any sense in worrying about it: the famous anarchists in history must have reached the same conclusion. The best thing to do was to accept life piecemeal, from day to day. Was he becoming a different person? What if he were—he already had expressed his thoughts to the world and had demonstrated his courage. In order not to deviate from his plan, he still covered himself with proud disdain when he was being questioned, or when he had a visit from his lawyer, but he spent less and less time rehearsing the court-room speech he had intended to make in his own defense. He continued to bar thoughts about the murder from his mind. But occasionally—though more and more seldom—in the small hours of the night he suffered horrible hours of wakefulness.

VI

AN EYE appeared at the peep-hole and almost immediately the door was opened. A guard entered and told Alvera that his lawyer was waiting to see him in the visitor's room. "Very good, very good," Alvera answered indifferently, but inwardly he was glad to hear the news; the visit offered a diversion, and it indicated that people had not forgotten him. He was disappointed not to find any photographers or curiosity seekers staring at him in the corridors. "If there has to be a trial, a sensational case is better than something third-rate. . . . But there is no way for photographers to get inside the prison. . . ."

With a disdainful smile Alvera entered the visitor's room, casually bowed to the lawyer and looked at him with inquiring eyes. Cerisier rose to meet him and making an effort to lend a cordial sound to his words said: "Good day, my friend." The guard left the room and they sat down at the table.

"How are you?" the lawyer asked.

"Reasonably well, thank you," Alvera answered. He wanted to add: "and you?"—but he was conscious that such levity would be out of place.

"I am glad that you are in good spirits. The trial begins tomorrow. . . ."

"Yes."

"I wanted to discuss a few points with you before the opening of the trial. First of all, let's consider our main problem." Cerisier paused and continued with much greater feeling. "I will be absolutely frank with you. You are an . . . educated [he caught himself wanting to say "reasonable"] young man. I am sure you realize that this is a difficult, a very difficult case. . . ."

"Yes, I know."

"You must be prepared for anything."

"I am."

"This does not by any means imply that I consider your case hopeless."

"I do."

"You shouldn't. There is always hope. Obviously our only hope lies in finding mitigating circumstances."

"That would mean a life sentence at hard labor?"

"Possibly not even life, but, say, a twenty-year sentence," Cerisier said drily, annoyed by his client's tone. ("He certainly cannot expect to be decorated for this little affair!")

"I prefer the guillotine."

"Yes, yes, I know! People say things like that very frequently, but they never mean them. You are young. You can be away for twenty years and still return in the prime of your life. Conditions in the penal colonies now are much better than they were thirty years ago. Finally, all sorts of unforeseen circumstances might arise: a general amnesty, or a universal commutation of sentences."

"For instance if a son is born to the president?"

"No, the president's son has nothing to do with it," the lawyer said angrily, but he immediately got his temper under control, realizing that he was talking to a doomed man. "Imagine another Eleventh of November. A war can flare up at any moment. It is very possible that lots of innocent Parisians will die much sooner than most of the convicts in Cayenne. You will at least be safe from air raids over there," he added with a smile. "Besides, my friend, you knew what to expect when in a moment of sudden aberration [he stressed the last two words] you committed this terrible crime. . . ."

"I am afraid that is not quite logical, sir," Alvera interrupted with a crooked smile. "If I knew what to expect, there could not be a moment of sudden aberration; if there was a moment of sudden aberration, I could not know what to expect."

"Which was it?" Cerisier asked with a puzzled expression and immediately regretted his question. In cases of this kind it was best not to encourage a client to be too frank—it only would embarrass his lawyers.

"I was sane then, just as I am perfectly sane now."

"Entendons-nous," Cerisier said significantly (such a statement could be interpreted in several ways). "I am not trying to say that you are insane. But I refuse to accept from you statements that are prompted by your youthful pride." Alvera shrugged his shoulders. "You are not qualified to sit in judgment on your own case. Probably I can understand your state of mind at that crucial moment better than you can. As a matter of fact I am certain that you have no conception of it whatever. I am convinced that

you went to Louvécienne with absolutely peaceful intentions,"
Cerisier continued, stressing every word. "I know, I know. . . .
You had those persistent thoughts about murder, revenge, anarchism . . . I know. . . . There are many cases like that known to
criminal psychopathology." Alvera gave another shrug of the
shoulders. "But if it were not for the sudden aberration, you never
would have killed Chartier. You would have given him his papers,
and you would have returned home peacefully. . . . My friend,
I am convinced, absolutely convinced, that that is so. . . . My
only problem is to make the jury share my conviction. You can
smile all you please, but I have evidence, a great deal of evidence,
to support me. For instance the fact that those copies you made
for the old man were perfect. If you were planning to commit
murder that night, why would you have bothered to make them
at all? How could anyone in a state of mind like that copy thirty
pages without a single mistake? You would have brought with you
any old parcel, and you would have shot Chartier before he had
a chance to unwrap it. And this strange business with the radio!"
Alvera's face began to twitch. Cerisier paused for a second, looked
at him and continued: "I ask you whether any normal man would
have twisted the dials on the radio, taking the chance of assem-
bling the entire population of Louvécienne under the windows?
A normal person would have left the radio alone, or else he would
have pulled out the plug. Any child knows that when the current
is cut off the radio stops working. . . . You see, the mere mention
of this makes your face twitch and turn white. . . . But the fact
that this recollection makes you lose control of your facial muscles
is likely to influence the jury in your favor ["I hope he understands what I am trying to impress on him," Cerisier thought].
In any event, my friend, there is one thing you must remember,"
the lawyer said emphatically. "Your only hope to save your life
lies in convincing the jury, just as you have convinced me, that
you acted in a moment of sudden aberration. And you must not
bear me any childish grudges if in the course of the trial I have to
go beyond my present description of your mental and emotional

state. Suppose that, since you are hot-headed and obstinate, you announce in court that you consider yourself perfectly sane, though I refuse to believe that you would do such a thing. That alone would be irrefutable proof that you are insane. But the jury and the judges refuse to take into consideration such fine points, especially when expert opinion is unfavorable, as it is in this case. Keep that in mind! But if I can prove to the jury that you are not in a normal state and that you are experiencing sincere repentance, I have great hopes that they will find other mitigating circumstances. What evidence can there be that your action was premeditated?" he continued, thinking aloud. "The gun? But maybe you always carried a gun? Maybe that is one of your peculiarities? . . ."

"That, as a matter of fact, is so. . . . I carried the gun with me constantly for three months."

"Is that right? Why didn't you tell me that before? That is very important! . . . Has anyone seen you with the gun? Can anyone testify that you carried the gun with you? That is extremely important! . . ."

"No, I didn't show the gun to anyone."

"Why did you buy it? Perhaps because of your political convictions? Maybe you believe that an anarchist should always be armed? Or perhaps it was simply a boyish love of guns? A childhood recollection of the novels of Gustave Aimard?"

"I bought the gun to kill Chartier."

Cerisier looked at him with exasperation.

"Naturally you know the answer better than anybody else. But if you intend to make my task of defending you in court more complicated than it is, I wish you would tell me so now! I can withdraw from the case, and you can get along without a lawyer, or else you can get someone else to represent you. . . . As it is, you have prejudiced the case by your statements during the preliminary hearing."

"I am very grateful for everything you have done, sir," Alvera said hurriedly.

"If you are, please try to understand what I am saying. I repeat once again: your only hope is that the jury will not be convinced that your action was premeditated. If in their minds they concede that the murder was premeditated, there is no hope for you: you will be executed," Cerisier said angrily, though he knew that this was not the way to talk to a client. "When you return to your cell, give this matter some thought. . . . Now I have a few minor questions to ask you. . . ."

Cerisier began to discuss additional testimony which had been submitted by the experts. But this was only a subterfuge: he did not want to admit even to himself that he had been rehearsing testimony with a client. In another ten minutes Cerisier arose and was ready to leave. Alvera made an awkward gesture as if to stop him. The lawyer felt a sudden surge of pity. "The miserable fellow must spend horrible nights!" he thought and said in a brisk voice: "Don't give up hope, my friend. I am counting on many mitigating circumstances. A case tried before a jury is like a lottery ticket, but there are good reasons to believe that the jury will take into consideration your sincere repentance and your youth. . . . Incidentally, why don't you get a shave? . . . The prosecuting attorney will find it difficult to establish premeditation, unless you help him. . . . Until tomorrow, my friend!" With a feeling of relief he hurriedly left the room. "Thank God! At least we managed to avoid any tearful scenes. . . ."

"Yes, he is right. Any child would have known it!" Alvera thought as he returned to his cell. "Everything is lost because my presence of mind deserted me for one minute. But how could I have foreseen the radio? Every detail of the plan, except one which no one in the world could have foreseen, had been considered systematically. Obviously if I had not touched the radio, the neighbors would not have noticed it for another two hours, or probably not even until next morning. If I had pulled the plug no one would have known anything about it until the arrival of the charwoman. In either case I would have been safe. They never would have found me in Paris. But, at that, I would not have been rich—that was another mistake. . . ." In the course of the questioning he had learned that Monsieur Chartier's pocketbook which the police had found on him contained only fifteen hundred francs. The first time he had heard it, he had been struck with amazement: another error in his calculations! . . . "Apparently I was wrong, and the result is that I am caught like a fool, like any child! . . . Now I will have to pay my 'debt to society.' I wonder how many times they will repeat this expression in court, and in the newspaper accounts: *'Il paya sa dette à la société'?"* A crooked smile played on his face. "My debt to society! A fine way to exact payment of debts! . . ."

To Alvera's surprise the guard entered the cell earlier than usual and let down the bed, which during the day was secured against the wall. "They are making allowances for me already!" He was flattered. As soon as the guard left, Alvera took off his clothes and stretched out. A chill hung over the cell. He felt warmer under the blanket, and he was pleased when he remembered his belief that life consisted of disconnected episodes. "Yes, I was right. I feel grateful for this particular episode, for my last night. . . . But it can't be my last night—they hardly can finish the case in one day. And there will be other days and nights, after the sentence. Nothing will be changed, because there is no doubt in my mind now what the sentence will be. . . . The lawyer will make a pathetic statement that he intends to appeal the case—or whatever the proper expression is? I will pretend to be polite—though why should I?—and try to dissuade him, but in the end I will give in. This will take another month." More than once he had intended to ask Cerisier how much time usually elapsed between the verdict and the unfavorable decision of the upper court, but he was ashamed to reveal his fears, and had remained silent. "Is it really worth while to appeal the case? The logical answer is: no! A few miserable weeks of life like this are not worth foregoing that beautiful formula: 'he refused to appeal his case.' On the other hand, this is no time for beautiful formulas, and it makes little difference what will be said about me in the newspapers, which I shall never have a chance to read anyway. I believe I should give this a little more thought. . . ." Inwardly he was certain that he would let the lawyer file an appeal. "Why shouldn't I consent? It will give me another month of episodes! Others don't get even that much. If there really is a war millions of innocent Frenchmen will die a much more horrible death. They will be torn to pieces, burned and gassed. It does not bother me so long as millions of Germans die the same kind of death, or maybe God will provide something more horrible for them! They can destroy one another all they please. They deserve it, and so does their 'society' to which I shall pay my debt so soon. . . ."

Alvera's thoughts dwelt on this problem for a long time: when did he incur this debt—seemingly even before he was born? Those papers indicated clearly that his father had contracted the disease a year before his birth. With a bitter smile Alvera remembered how much misery and horror those papers, letters, prescriptions and records of blood tests had caused him. The whole thing had descended on him out of the blue sky. "That was the beginning. That is when I incurred my debt to society." Such thoughts no longer frightened or disgusted him. "A congenital syphilitic is a natural candidate for idiocy, or for a lunatic asylum. . . . *Kératite interstitielle, convulsions épileptiformes.* . . . What other road is open to him? No, as far as a philosophy of life is concerned, I have made no mistake. Life is the product of quantity multiplied by tension. . . . $A = U + T \frac{dA}{dT}$," he remembered, and was pleased that his memory was so clear. "I wonder where my notebook is now? . . . The whole purpose of life is to increase the degree of tension, in order to live excitingly and dangerously, no matter what the cost! That is what I have done. It is not my fault that an incalculable, stupid mistake spoiled everything." Suddenly he remembered that after the appeal had been refused one could petition the president of the republic for a pardon. "That would mean another week! Another week of life!" Joy took possession of him, as though the extra week of life was an unexpected present. "Will it be childish? Ridiculous! The lawyer will file the petition against my wishes. . . ." Another week of episodes, of pleasant moments like this one: he was warm, he was not bothered by bedbugs, what more could he want?

The light went out. Almost at once Alvera went to sleep. He had a strange dream,—the same dream he had had a long time ago—the dream of the shepherd who had quarreled with the sun. The sun was breathing revenge on the shepherd, while he was playing some musical instrument—maybe it was a flute? He was playing something awful. Alvera could not get the tune or the words. The charming Mademoiselle Mortier was singing: "*Courage, du courage!*" He was dragging her somewhere and with a sense of exaltation, thinking that it was wonderful, that he was drunk with love and passion. . . . "*Défense de déposer et faire des Ordures,*" a stern voice reached him from the path behind the fence,—from that familiar path. Two girls were walking hand-in-hand across a black and yellow triangle. A car whisked by and tooted its horn. The sound of the horn began to grow in strength, it grew to horrible proportions and blended with the sound of the flute, until Alvera was able to distinguish a melody. He ran in blind panic, but the car was at his heels, shrieking at a horrible pitch: ". . . *Tu veux donc, cruelle gantière,—Tu veux la mort du Brésilien! . . .*"

Alvera woke up with a scream, and gasping for breath, sat up in bed. He heard the clanking of keys against the steel doors. At night, every two hours, the guards made the rounds of the prison, opening and closing the doors. The noise reverberated through the entire building. "They are coming after me!" he thought, shaking with fear. At the same moment in the darkness below him he saw the face of Monsieur Chartier with its convulsing muscles and its bulging eyes. "Young man, I will give you two hundred francs, you can rent an apartment, you are an accommodating young man," Monsieur Chartier was saying, and the muscles of his face jumped faster and faster. There was a clanking of keys in the distance. Alvera threw back his head, hit it against the wall with all his might, and lost consciousness.

VII

THE FAT, ROUND, amazingly vigorous-looking man was singing a song praising the gypsy heart. The assortment of hors d'oeuvre was excellent. "Not as good as at Donon's of blessed memory, but better than in most French restaurants," the pleasantly surprised Tamarin said to Nadia. "Listen to me, and you will never go wrong," Nadia answered. "He even is singing our songs. Strange that they have not forgotten them. . . . I am enjoying the evening immensely! How about you?" "I haven't enjoyed myself so much for a long, long time," the General's voice rang with sincerity.

Quite unexpectedly Kangarov had made up his mind to spend his entire leave in a quiet sanatorium near Paris. With deep sighs of self-pity he told everyone that he was following strict orders given to him by the doctors. "There is nothing I can do about it, comrades; Albert Fouquot himself gave me the strictest orders; my heart seems to be acting up. . . ." Actually, in answer to Kangarov's question whether he should take a rest cure in a sanatorium, the Professor had answered that he had no objections. "Which one would you suggest?" "Anyone you prefer."

In recent months Kangarov had developed a regular case of hypochondria. Nadia said frankly that he was suffering with a persecution mania, and inwardly blamed it on the Moscow trials. The events undoubtedly had affected his physical condition: he was afraid of everything and everybody; he avoided people, and he tried to write as few letters as possible; when he opened Soviet newspapers his face lost its color, and he appeared to read them in a state of mortal fear. At first Nadia believed that he pretended to be a very sick man so he would have an excuse not to take a long journey if he were recalled to Moscow. But as time went on she became convinced that he was serious about his illness. Occasionally he had fits of unbridled temper. Nadia talked back, but without overstepping bounds: officially she accepted the myth built around the notoriously short temper of a sick person. Most of the time, instead of speaking, Kangarov growled; he rapidly was becoming one of those people who under the pretext of being truthful constantly say unpleasant things.

Association with him became more and more unbearable. Nadia was not Kangarov's mistress—the very idea was revolting to her. But using his fatherly affection as an excuse, and later not even bothering about excuses, he permitted himself to do things when they were alone, which could not be treated as jokes. At first it would have been a simple matter to stop him. "If I had told him where to go, he never would have tried again!" Nadia thought angrily and wondered why she had not obeyed her impulse. "Maybe I am an immoral person at heart?" More than once, looking at her with glistening eyes Kangarov had told her that devils always concealed themselves behind virtue. It became more and more of a problem to keep him within reasonable bounds. "To call him down now would seem stupid!" Later, there had been a stormy scene with Helen Kangarov. For two days after it Nadia cried from anger and resentment. She discovered that all her fellow workers believed that she was Kangarov's mistress. She was amazed: "What fools! It is simply ridiculous!" She made a firm resolve not to pay any attention to their gossip, but she found that the whole affair was extremely disagreeable as well as ridiculous.

Without any warning Nadia received a substantial raise. Her duties as a typist and stenographer were combined with the duties of an interpreter and private secretary, the two classifications were merged, and her salary doubled. In the face of all the gossip her promotion carried with it unpleasant implications. Nadia could not and had no desire to refuse a doubled salary which at last gave her a chance to buy the clothes she had always wanted. Besides, she felt that she was blameless, or at least not as guilty as other people seemed to think, and actually she did perform the duties of a typist, stenographer, interpreter and private secretary. "I would be silly to refuse a raise because nonentities with dirty minds happen to gossip behind my back!" But involuntary thoughts about her awkward position of late became a nightmare in Nadia's life. She often cried at night and promised herself that she would ask for a transfer to Moscow, but she never could summon enough courage to take the necessary steps, and besides she did not quite know how to go about it: was it better to act through Kangarov, or should she make her request directly?

On one occasion Nadia dropped a cautious hint about her return to Russia. Kangarov's face immediately turned purple and his eyes became yellow. "Have you lost your mind? What is biting you? Moscow? Why Moscow? What will you do there? Who will give you a job if you leave me after all the things I have done for you? I suppose you are plotting my undoing! I will not let you go, and you may as well forget about it right now!" There was a mixture of conviction, love, despair and threat in his voice. Nadia felt sorry for him, and at the same time she was amused and a little frightened. She did not believe that he would persecute her if she left him—she was sure that he would not stoop that low—but she could not fail to realize that without him she would not have an easy time finding a job in Moscow. Besides, Nadia was not too anxious to go back, or rather the desire came and went spasmodically. The news from Russia was not very cheerful. Even if three-fourths of what she read were lies appearing in the mercenary capitalistic press, still the remaining fourth was true. . . . And she found Kangarov's love for her, while it amused her, also a little touching. "After all, the man has lost his mind about me!"

That same evening Kangarov came to see her and with tears in his voice explained to her at great length that as a matter of principle he had firmly decided to divorce his wife, but that he could not do it right away, because circumstances beyond his control made it necessary for him to wait. He spoke ambiguously, but with a great deal of fervor. Nadia understood that at present he was afraid to do anything that could be interpreted as a lack of self-discipline. He said something vague about the common accusation of being contaminated by the morals of class enemies, and while he spoke he looked at her significantly. There was no doubt in Nadia's mind that he intended to marry her after his divorce. This amused, repelled, and touched her. "What if he really is a sick man and will die if I tell him to go to the devil?" she wondered. Everything continued as before. Only Nadia became much more sensitive and conscious of every smile and hint dropped by her fellow workers.

Nadia received the news about the sanatorium with ill-disguised exasperation. Kangarov had persuaded her to go on leave with him by saying: "We can spend a week or so in Paris, then we can go to Nice, or even better to Italy, where there are not so many White Russians. . . ." The thought of a long journey in his company did not arouse any enthusiasm in her, but she could resign herself to it for the sake of seeing Nice and Italy. Spending a rainy autumn in the suburbs of Paris in some god-forsaken sanatorium was a very different matter!

Later Nadia decided that perhaps it was all for the best. "I will go to Paris every day and spend most of my time there. . . ." Officially she accompanied the ambassador as his private secretary. Actually there had been little work for her to do, since Kangarov had begun to avoid people and letters. "He cannot keep me chained. As long as he is in a sanatorium he must obey certain rules, and he does not need a secretary to look after him. Whatever work there is, I will do in the mornings while he is still asleep. If he gets temperamental about it, I will tell him frankly that I am fed up and that I am leaving. I will go back to Moscow if it kills me! . . ."

Nadia had one other thing to console her. During the year and a half she had spent abroad she had tried her hand at many different things—after all, she had no intention of spending the rest of her life as a typist and a stenographer. She had tried water colors, she had worked designs in burned wood, and she even became interested in adult education. Nothing came of it. From sheer desperation she began to keep a diary in which she recorded everything that happened during the day. At first she made only brief notes, but soon she began to describe things in greater detail with many introspective passages. Still later she began to feel that some of the pages were rather charming, almost as good as passages by well-known writers who used the diary form. "Maybe I should try writing a story and send it to Gene in the editorial office? . . ." That evening and part of the night she spent dreaming about a literary career and next morning she settled to work. A quiet autumn spent in the suburbs of Paris would give her time to finish her story. Most writers,—Pushkin, Tolstoy,—liked to work in the country. She remembered reading in a magazine that some famous writer did his best work in the autumn.

It was to this sanatorium that Nadia invited Wislicenus. Because of her invitation, immediately after their meeting in the Professor's waiting room, Kangarov made a terrific scene which began while they were still descending the stairs. As soon as he learned that she had asked Wislicenus to their retreat in the country, the ambassador seemed to lose his self-control entirely. "You can do as you please, but I will not permit that impudent Trotskyist to cross my threshold," he shouted, his eyes burning with a yellow light and his face disfigured by hatred. "He has no intention of crossing your threshold; he will cross mine." "That does not make any difference! You persist in consorting with my enemies. It looks like a conspiracy!" "What conspiracy? Be yourself! A man is coming out for tea, and you keep talking about conspiracies." "It's a conspiracy against my peace of mind. I am a sick man and I need rest! I don't want you to drink tea with that bastard! I don't want to have anything to do with him, and I don't intend to see him!" "I repeat that he is not coming to call on you. If you can't bear looking at him, you don't have to come out, or else you can spend the day in Paris. He is coming Wednesday at six o'clock." "That is the very thing I shall do, if you persist in treating me that way!" "Very good. You see what a simple solution there is for everything, provided we don't lose our heads." Nadia said with deliberate calmness, inwardly delighted to discover that besides everything else, Kangarov obviously was jealous of Wislicenus. "As long as you take my friendships so much to heart, and to avoid any misunderstandings, may I inquire whether you mind if I invite the general?" "What damned general are you talking about?" "Our General—Tamarin." "You can invite that silly old man any time you feel like it." "Very good. At least that much is settled."

But in spite of Kangarov's official permission Nadia did not invite Tamarin to the sanatorium. She would have liked to discharge her obligation to both old men in one evening, but from the inflection of Wislicenus' voice she knew that they had to be asked separately. Besides, Nadia was not pressed for time and she knew no young people in Paris. She found the company of Wislicenus rather difficult. Tamarin bored her at times, but he never was difficult. "The General is a wonderful person, even if in very large doses he becomes unbearable. . . ." She decided to spend an entire evening with Tamarin, and so that she might not be burdened with too much conversation she suggested that they go to a theatre.

Tamarin was very glad to hear from Nadia. "To the theatre? With you? Delighted! . . . What play would you like to see?" "Does it make any difference to you? No? Well, let's go to the . . ." and she named the theatre. "Isn't that the place where they have horror plays?" "Yes, but it is not all horror. They say it is very entertaining. I have been to all the Paris theatres except that one. Don't you want to go there?" "Anywhere you say." "Well, then I will meet you tomorrow night at a quarter to nine in front of the ticket office." "Right." "So long." "Not so long— *au revoir!*" She laughed. "I recognize the master's touch. Do you remember how you tried to improve my manners while the ambassador was in Amsterdam? I always forget that you are a contemporary of Pushkin."

They were so pleased to see each other again that they embraced and kissed to the delight and embarrassment of the general and somewhat to the amazement of the people standing around the ticket office (someone in the crowd could not resist making a personal remark). They spent the first few minutes together in a gay, disjointed conversation. "How have you been?" "And you?" "Reasonably well." "Why only reasonably?" "Oh, I don't know. . . ." Then they bought the tickets. "I am paying for the tickets tonight. I invited you! . . ." "Don't be silly! . . ." "Why do you have to argue about it? Why can't I invite you?" "Sorry, it just isn't done." "Let's make a solemn agreement like two sovereign powers, *sur un pied d'égalité absolue*: I will buy the tickets and after the show you can take me to supper. I will be honest with you, I haven't had time to eat dinner. All I had was a sandwich in some café." Tamarin laughed. "How fortunate! I also haven't had any dinner, but in my case it was done deliberately because I was hoping that you would do me the honor of having supper with me." "Is that true? You are the nicest general I know, but then you are the only general I have ever met. . . . In any case that gives me the right to buy the tickets." "Not on your life! You are an out-of-town visitor, and you are my guest. . . ." The argument was finally settled: Nadia paid for her own ticket and made a mental note to choose a less expensive restaurant than she had intended.

Tamarin's spirits drooped noticeably as soon as he saw the stage setting: a domed ceiling of oak beams, queer statues of angels, and narrow doors shaped like wooden crosses. "Are they caricaturing a chapel?" he asked with a frown. "I detest that sort of thing!" As the show progressed he was shocked even more to see a ferocious, medieval executioner who took pleasure in torturing his enemies, a fully equipped torture chamber, and people stripped to their waists with blood streaming down their chests. "What kind of a place is this? You certainly have chosen a nice theatre!" he said. "It's a very good show! I find it very entertaining," Nadia protested. "Where have you ever seen an inquisitor like this? He should have been buried along with the Dark Ages—

why bring him back to life?" When the curtain rose again on a scene from the Boxer Rebellion in which revolting soldiers were putting out the eyes of their prisoners, Tamarin could not restrain himself any longer. "Nadia, my dear, how can you watch this? Don't tell me you find it entertaining?" "Why, certainly I find it interesting, and I never would consent to leave, but I must confess I am terribly hungry!" "That's better! Let's go, my dear! Devil take all these queer people!"

"The evening is not progressing according to schedule," the general said when they were in the street. "We intended to have supper, but it looks as though we are just in time for dinner. It's not ten yet. . . . Where shall we go? Do you like oysters?"

"Oysters?" Nadia asked and considered it for a minute. "No, what I want is shashlik! And I want some vodka: not eau-de-vie, but real vodka! And I want some real hors d'oeuvre: not the French snails, cabbage and potatoes with olive oil, but smoked salmon, caviar and herring! And I want . . ."

"My dear! . . ." Tamarin interrupted her with a laugh. "Though many years apart, we seem to have been born under the same star. I also love that kind of food, but you are forgetting that we are in Paris and not in Moscow."

"You are the one who is forgetting that there are Russian restaurants in Paris. There is one near here, and they have everything my soul desires. That's where we are going!"

"But that is an *émigré* place! . . ."

"What difference does it make whether it is *émigré* or Soviet shashlik, or whether it is white or revolutionary vodka? All our people go there, why can't we?"

"It might be awkward!"

"Nothing awkward about it! I tell you all our people go there frequently."

"Are you sure?"

"I know. I wouldn't take the ambassador there because of his position, but you and I can go: no one will pay any attention to us."

"What if they recognize me?"

"Recognize you? Don't be silly! After twenty-five years? You told me yourself that you had sideburns in the old days! And even if they do recognize you, what of it? Are you afraid?"

"I am not afraid, but there is no sense in looking for trouble."

"No one will recognize you, and there will be no trouble, I promise you! Just think about the shashlik!"

"Did you say shashlik? Shashlik is a great institution, there are no two ways about it."

Ten minutes later they were entering the restaurant. Tamarin felt very self-conscious. "Shall I talk to them in French?" But Nadia, keeping her voice low, was already speaking Russian. They were shown to a corner with a small table covered with a checkered cloth and with checkered napkins folded in stiff triangles standing on the plates. Nadia also was not quite herself. "They must all be white guards," the thought both interested and frightened her.

The waiter handed them a sheet of paper with words written in ink between the lines of print. Tamarin glanced up at him: "No, thank God, he is not an officer!" He buried his nose in the menu which listed in French all the usual Russian dishes: kilkis, pirojoks, bitkis and pelmenis. "Shall we begin with some hors d'oeuvre, Nadia?" "Yes," she refrained from calling him by his name. "How about a little vodka?" "No meal is complete without it! What kind have you?" "Zubrovka, Polish, White Head?" "You mean you have some real White Head?" "Yes, sir." "That's what we want." "Yes, sir. What would you like in the way of hors d'oeuvre: herring, mushrooms, smoked salmon?" "That will be fine," the general said; he was puzzled: "just like the old days, except that he does not call me 'Your Excellency.'" "Would you care for some fresh caviar, sir?" "How about caviar, Nadia?" "No, I am not too fond of it," Nadia said, not wanting to spend too much of Tamarin's money: she guessed that on this occasion he would not let her pay her share. "In that case we will get along without it," the general said with some relief. "You were right about the shashlik. . . . There it is: *chachliks caucasiens*. Why do they always use the plural on the menu?" "The shashlik is very good, sir. Would you like two orders?" "Certainly! You didn't expect us to divide one order between us?" The waiter smiled respectfully and walked away.

Tamarin breathed more freely. "It really is very cozy. . . ." He glanced around and saw that the walls were decorated with portraits of generals in the old pre-revolutionary uniforms. They were all men whom he had known in the old days; some of them he had known well, certainly much better than the restaurant proprietor had known them. He found the thought disagreeable. "How about wine?" Nadia asked. "Certainly," he said absent-mindedly and rattled a knife against the glass. The waiter was standing only a few feet away, but even if he was not a former officer, Tamarin could not bear to shout: "waiter!"—at him across the room. "Give us the wine card, please!" "Yes, sir. . . ." "There is something pleasant and decent about this place, even if it does look like a second-rate night club. Probably it's the atmosphere of broken lives. . . . The same thing happened to all of us," Tamarin mused, but he would not voice a thought like that even to Nadia. "You mean to tell me you have real Caucasian wines?" he said happily. "Kardanach?" "Yes, sir. . . . We are the only ones in Paris who have it." "Better bring us a bottle. . . . In the old days this was my favorite wine," he explained with animation to Nadia.

After the vodka, which was excellent, after the first glass of Kardanach which was real, and after listening to a few numbers on the entertainment program which was good, their spirits began to rise. They argued about the play they had seen; the general insisted that it had been terrible. "I am in my sixties and I never have witnessed horrors like that!" "Perhaps you have something to look forward to?" "No, no! You will have to admit that your choice of a theatre was not so good." "But I made up for it with the restaurant. You have no more regrets that you came here?" "On the contrary, I am grateful. It's very cozy, and the food is good. Even the decorations . . ." He paused. "What about the decorations? Don't try to fool me! I know you are a gold-striper at heart." "I am surprised that you should say things like that to me, Nadia."

In another ten minutes their tongues loosened and they became more frank. Tamarin confessed to Nadia that one of the gold-stripers whose portrait was hanging on the wall had been a class-mate of his at the army staff school, and another had been his commanding general through most of the war. "What kind of people were they?" "They may have been wrong in some ways, my dear, but . . ." "What do you mean 'they may have been wrong'?" "They were wrong," the general corrected himself with a chuckle (without the vodka and wine he would never have spoken so lightly about such a dangerous matter, even if he was alone with Nadia). "They were wrong in some ways, and they made mis-takes, but they were decent men and they loved their country! . . ." Being frank in her turn, Nadia made it known to him how much she disliked Kangarov and how difficult she found their associ-ation.

"Do you imagine that I don't know what is being said about me?" she asked, blushing suddenly. "You know what I mean . . ."

"No, my dear, I haven't the slightest idea . . ."

"Probably you know and will not admit it, because you are a gentleman, while they. . . . In so many words they say that I live with Kangarov . . ."

"My dear!"

"I thought someone had told you [Tamarin actually had heard the gossip, and the first time it was repeated in his presence he had been very upset]. They all talk about it, and it's a lie and a slander! I swear to you that it is not so!" Resting her hand on Tam-arin's sleeve, Nadia continued vehemently as though he had rea-son to doubt her word. She drank a glass of wine at one gulp. The general watched her with uneasy eyes. "The truth is that he has been annoying me and he is annoying me now. He is in love with me! I suppose if I wanted I could make him divorce his horse-face and marry me. But I don't want to think about it. He is . . . [she wanted to say "an old man," but caught herself in time]. I don't love him. And I don't care for him as a human being. Is it my fault that he will not let me go? I am his secretary, and if he does not worry about my reputation I have to travel with him when he insists. Do you blame me?"

"Not in the least."

"You don't blame me, because you are a gentleman, because you were brought up that way. But they. . . . How do we treat each other? We hate, we are always ready to think the worst, we try to trip one another. . . . No, I will leave it all and go back to Russia! I have already asked for a transfer, but he will not let me go!" There were tears in her eyes. "I can't go on like this any longer!"

"What makes you think it will be any better in Russia?"

"It may not be any better, but it will be different. . . . There is some backbiting there, but there are other things, too. The atmosphere is different. . . . Everyone works much harder than we do. And there are lots of young people. I hope you will not be angry with me for saying things like that. I like you very, very much, but here I am surrounded by elderly people. The youngest one is forty years old. . . . But let's not talk about it. Let's listen to the singer. He is singing about the heart again! 'Go to sleep, my poor heart—What has passed will not return. . . .' Everyone sings about the heart, but very few know what it means."

"You shouldn't look at life in such a dark light, Nadia," Tamarin said tenderly. He was sincerely moved, and he sympathized with the things she said about Kangarov. "You are young . . ."

"Youth goes quickly. 'What has passed will not return,'" she repeated the words of the song. "I shall go back to Moscow and settle down. . . . Everyone has a place for which he is intended: I have one, you have another, Wislicenus has a third. . . . By the way, did you know that he is very ill?"

"No, I hadn't heard about it. What's the matter with him?"

"I made him go to Professor Fouquot. You know, the greatest heart specialist in the world? The ambassador consults him about his imaginary illnesses. But there is nothing imaginary about Wislicenus' condition. . . . I thought of asking him to join us tonight, but I decided against it, not knowing how you felt about him."

"Sorry you didn't. . . . I have nothing against him."

"Haven't you heard? They say he has fallen into disfavor."

"In Moscow? No, I haven't heard about it."

"The ambassador was furious at me because I worried about Wislicenus' condition. And just to spite him I decided to show my independence: I invited him to the sanatorium to see us, and I made it a point to ask him while we were in the embassy and everybody was listening. He is coming Wednesday for tea. The ambassador raised hell about it: one—I should not invite Wislicenus at all; two—I shouldn't invite him to the ambassador's residence; three—if I have to invite him, I should do it on the quiet. I told him where to go. . . . What are we—slaves? Why don't you join us Wednesday? It's a lovely spot! Away from everything, nice, quiet, lovely. . . . Why don't you come out?"

"No, I am afraid I better not. . . . You will have to excuse me this time."

"Suit yourself. . . ." She glanced at him and smiled. "Let's have some more wine! . . ."

"Certainly! . . . But there is none left. You and I have finished a whole bottle."

"I feel I should make a correction: you drank three-fourths of it. Let's order another bottle! . . . We may as well enjoy ourselves. . . ."

With a warm sense of intimacy they talked for a long time about many different things. Nadia recovered her calm: there was something reassuring about Tamarin's presence, she was pleased that he had not heard any gossip about her ("he looks as if he was telling the truth—he does not know how to lie"). He had immediately dismissed the whole subject ("ridiculous! No use worrying about it!"). On the spur of the moment Nadia told Tamarin that she was writing. At first he did not understand her.

"What do you mean: writing,—my dear?" "I am writing a story, or maybe a whole novel." "What for?" "What do you mean: what for? . . . Why do people write books?" Nadia asked with a puzzled expression. "Is that so? That's interesting, very interesting. . . . Perhaps, some time you will read it to me?" "Not on your life!" "Too bad," the general had a suspicion that if he were to insist Nadia could be persuaded. "Too bad. . . . What is the setting of your story?" "I won't tell you a thing about it!" "Why? So you want to become a writer?" "Why shouldn't I? Funnier things have happened. . . ."

Nadia told him about her newest plans. ". . . Sooner or later, in some way or other, I will get a transfer to Moscow. Europe fatigues me! . . ." "Don't say: 'fatigues'. . . . You want to be a writer and in that profession the choice of words, and that sort of thing, counts for everything. . . ." "You are right. They all talk like that in the foreign service—it's like a contagious disease. That's another reason why I should go back to Russia. But don't interrupt me. So I am going back. I have saved enough money to live for a few months. Then one of two things will happen. If I haven't talent, there is nothing I can do. I will get back into harness, but at least I shall be home in Moscow. I will have two years of experience and three foreign languages. That's not so bad, is it?" "No, that certainly is not," Tamarin agreed. "Or if I have a talent—nothing very spectacular, just a trace of an aptitude—they will accept my story. Then I can quit work and be a free person. Maybe my dream will come true, and I shall become a real writer!" "I am sure you will!" In passing, Nadia mentioned that a young man in Moscow had written her a wonderful letter. "I am so glad to hear it. Is he nice?" "Very. He has just graduated from an engineering school. But don't go imagining things! There is nothing to it. Besides, I received the letter three months ago, and not a word since." "I wasn't imagining anything. I merely asked whether he was nice?" Nadia laughed. "Very. And so are you. And what's more you are about the only person to whom I would consider showing my story!" "It would make me very happy." "I may be wrong, but I think it is pretty good. Anyway I like it! Only the plot does not seem to work out. . . ." "The plot against whom?" "The plot of the story! . . . I can't make it work. . . . But let's not talk any more about me. You haven't told me anything about yourself." "What is there to tell about an old man?"

Without much urging Tamarin told her that his work was progressing, that one chapter—the one about the tactical use of motorized troops in Spain—already had appeared in print and had received a great deal of attention: it had been mentioned twice in foreign publications. "That's why about two weeks ago I sent a report to Moscow asking them to extend my foreign assignment: when all is said and done I am doing original and useful work. In Spain all the new weapons of war have been tested, and very few people at home know enough about it. They haven't taken sufficient cognizance of the Spanish experience. You may say: what sort of motorized troops did they have to use! Let me tell you: on the Estremadura front . . ." "You mean you want to remain abroad?" "Certainly!" he answered with some warmth, but immediately checked himself and explained: "It would be a shame to leave this work unfinished, and in Paris I am close to the sources. . . ." In her turn Nadia listened patiently to his opinions about the Spanish war—the points it had proved in regard to the tactical use of motorized equipment.

It was well past eleven when Tamarin asked for the bill. No matter how hard he tried to press down the upper half of the folded sheet of paper, as though it contained something extremely indecent, Nadia caught a glimpse of the amount and exclaimed: "I have ruined you! . . ." "On the contrary! The whole thing is very reasonable, and, besides, I have enjoyed myself immensely. . . ." "What about me? I haven't had an evening like this for ages. . . . But let's keep to ourselves everything that has been said, especially my secret sin—writing. . . ." "You don't have to warn me!" "I mentioned it only because I never have met another gentleman like you. . . . If only the others were like that! . . ." Her eyes

again were filled with tears, but this time it was unquestionably
the effect of the wine.

Tamarin took a parting, self-conscious glance at the portraits
on the wall. With every sign of respect he and Nadia were ushered
to the door. "An excellent supper," the general said to the proprietor, feeling much more expansive and giving a generous tip to
the coat check. "Shall I call a taxi?" the man asked. "Yes, I
think so. I better drive you out, my dear," Tamarin said. "Don't
be silly! The subways are running, and I have only one
change. . . ." He saw her off to the nearest subway station.
Another line was more convenient for him and, besides, he felt
like a walk. In parting, Nadia embraced and kissed him again.
"You are very nice and a perfect gentleman!" she said, apparently
delighted with an expression which she had few occasions to
use. "So long. . . . I beg your pardon: *au revoir!* Sorry you will
not come out and have tea with Wislicenus. You, too!" she said
playfully and ran down the stairs.

VIII

"A VERY NICE GIRL," Tamarin thought, not in the least offended
by Nadia's parting remark. "A charming girl! Spoiled by their
ugly way of life, but charming by nature." The pleasant evening,
the wine and the kiss left their mark on the general. He walked
more briskly than usual and his bearing was such that even a
blind man could see that he was an old officer. "Hard to believe
that there are people who don't enjoy life! The evening was simply
marvelous!" As a rule he was careful with his money, and he had
forgotten his old extravagant habits, but on this occasion he almost
had no regrets about the hundred and forty francs he had spent.
"Why should I worry about money? I never spend my salary, and
as far as my position is concerned I don't believe I have anything
to fear. . . ."

Only Nadia's very last words did not sit well with him. "She teases me because I am afraid of this . . . whatever his name is?" Tamarin shrugged his shoulders. "I would be stupid to risk everything for the sake of meeting a half-cracked individual who happens to have the misfortune of being in disfavor with other half-cracked people. Anyway, courage is a relative conception." He knew that he was a brave man. He had spent much of the time during the war in the front line trenches, and more than once he had set an example of calm courage to the soldiers. But he also knew that he detested rows of any sort, and that he would go to any length to avoid them, just as he would do anything to avert losing his position, which enabled him to serve Russia and the Russian army. "I don't see anything to be ashamed about. And she didn't mean it that way! . . ."

In the best of spirits Tamarin crossed a square brightly illuminated by advertising signs and bearing the name of a famous sculptor whose memory was honored by rows of bawdy houses. "What a queer spot," thought Tamarin, who very seldom visited this part of town. "Every building is of a different size, color and style, as though every period wanted to leave its imprint behind it. And the imprints are none too attractive. . . ." Along the boulevard the lights were not so bright. Dark, mysterious, sinister, deserted streets and alleys branched off in every direction. An occasional lonely figure like a danger sign lurked in the shadows. An endless number of cars were parked along the curb of the boulevard, but the chauffeurs were nowhere in sight. Tamarin wondered where the chauffeurs were—like that fairy-tale in which three hundred and thirty-three ships were tied at the docks with not a soul on them. He walked along the boulevard registering benevolent surprise at everything he saw: the crowded sidewalk, the people, the signs, the wildly illuminated bars with questionable names, the night club with an entrance designed in the shape of human jaws, the night club decorated outside with funereal black cloth, the stores open for business at night. "I can understand keeping food stores open," he thought, looking at the sausages and the raw meat with the disgust of a man who had eaten too much. "I can understand the drugstores. Those Blenyl and Santal Bleu are very appropriate here. . . . But what man in his right mind would go to buy books at midnight, or take his fountain pen to be repaired, or make a reservation for a transatlantic passage? . . ." The streets were alive with strangely dressed young men, some of them without topcoats, but all of them strolling with a cocky air; they invariably walked with their hands stuck in their pockets and with scarfs wrapped around their necks: "Every one of them has a cigarette drooping out of the corner of his mouth. There is no way to judge them by their appearance: they may be perfectly respectable young men, and they may be cut-throats who have just murdered some old woman and who now are going to one of those places where they are taught how an old woman should be murdered—the moving pictures!" A villainous-looking mulatto was shown on a poster in front of a theatre, and a villainous-looking mulatto just like him was walking along the street arm in arm with a woman whose face reflected a mixture of submissiveness and rapture: "I will follow my man through hell and high water!" "C'est fantastique, je te dis, chéri, que c'est fantastique! . . ." the woman was saying. A married couple, who apparently lived in the block, strolled by peacefully with a small boy clinging to his father's hand. An old man in a peaked white hat, who had been selling chestnuts at the same stand for the last fifty years, and who had known every murderer taken from this street to the guillotine, was watching the family with a benevolent expression. "Yes, c'est fantastique how everything is mixed here. Degradation, vice and crime are only on the surface; underneath, honest, workaday provincial life goes on, just as it goes on everywhere else in France. I don't believe such a contrast between day and night life exists anywhere else in the world. . . ."

Once again Tamarin's thoughts wandered back to Nadia. It made him happy to think that she was not living with Kangarov. "I would almost be willing to bet my life that it is a malicious lie!" he thought and instantly was ashamed of the qualifying "almost." "She kissed me twice." It occurred to him that perhaps he was not so old after all. "I am becoming maudlin. . . ." The blissful smile did not leave his face all the time he was traveling in the subway. To round out the illusion of a rich and carefree life he bought a first-class ticket.

The hotel proprietor was still behind the desk—Tamarin never could understand when the man slept. They greeted each other in a friendly manner. The general was considered one of the best, quietest and most desirable guests by the hotel management. He paid his bills on the day they were presented. *"On vous a fait parvenir un paquet,"* the proprietor said, the intonation of his voice implying that it was very important. He explained that he had signed for it ten minutes after Tamarin had left for the evening. Instead of sticking it in the cash register the proprietor had put the large envelope in the drawer of his desk. "I wonder what it is?" Tamarin thought anxiously. He thanked the proprietor and began to unseal the envelope while he was still in the elevator. There was a second envelope inside. "That's it—the answer from Moscow!" Tamarin mechanically crumpled the outside envelope and stuck it in his coat pocket. His hands were shaking. He wanted to make a bet with himself as to whether his assignment had been extended, but he was too superstitious to take a chance. "I hope to God they have extended it!" The elevator stopped. With hands that refused to obey him Tamarin opened the door of his room, turned on the light, then without waiting to sit down or to take off his coat tore open the second envelope, and went completely numb. His orders were to proceed immediately to Spain.

IX

THE OPENING of the trial was set for the most inconvenient hour of the day—one in the afternoon: how could one eat a leisurely meal and be in Versailles on time? Vermandois decided to have lunch in a small Versailles restaurant. The proprietor of the place was a man with a conscience, who fried excellent lamb chops and whose prices suited the pocketbook of an impecunious celebrity. The advance against the novel with a Greek setting was entirely exhausted, though where the money had gone was a mystery. Eating alone, a good lunch with half a bottle of Bordeaux (he could not afford any more), was about the only real pleasure left him.

A slight pain in his side spoiled the festive mood with which Vermandois always started for the suburbs in the morning, and which this time had nothing to do with the reason for his journey. The day before, the Countess de Bellancombre had called him on the telephone and suggested that they drive down in her car. "Oh, God!" he thought in a panic, frantically searching his mind for some excuse. "I would be very happy! . . . But why are you going to the trial?" "I am terribly interested. You have to admit that this case has an immense social and psychological significance. It is Raskolnikov all over! Most important of all, I want to hear you!" "My friend, you sound as if I were going to sing the part of Siegfried! After all, I am not a tenor—I am a witness." "But you are an unusual witness. Can you come with us?" "I am in a terrible quandary. . . . When are you planning to start?" "At eleven, sharp." "That's awful! I have a business appointment at noon." "I am very sorry!" the Countess said. "Cerisier is driving down with us—he secured tickets for us for the trial. He is a very charming person. My opinion of him was absolutely unjustified." "He is a delightful person. I only wish he would not call himself a socialist." "Don't be so sardonic! Why don't you change your mind? Can't you cancel your appointment? We could have lunch at the Trianon?" "I am simply desperate, but I don't see how it can be done: this appointment is with the most boring person in the world and it was made a long time ago." "In that case we will plan to have dinner or supper together, depending on when this terrible affair may be over. . . . Or, perhaps, the reason you are not coming is because you dislike Cerisier?" "I am very fond of him!" ("The leader of the proletariat has crashed the salon of the Countess," Vermandois said to himself and realized that probably the same thing was being said about him). "Until tomorrow then. You cannot imagine how this case and this miserable young man have upset me. I have not been able to sleep a wink for two nights." "I know how your angelic heart goes out to all unfortunates!" "Don't joke about it—it's so horrible! What is the matter with the younger generation? Until tomorrow." "Until tomorrow, my dear," he said with a feeling of relief.

There were reasons for and against accepting the invitation. If he were to refuse he would not have to talk for three solid hours with the old fool, with her idiotic husband, and with the leader of the proletariat. If he were to accept he would not have to pay the taxi bill out of his own pocket. On the other hand, the time had come for him to show some "politeness" to the old fool. Vermandois was on such a friendly footing with the Countess that he very seldom bought her any flowers—only once in a great while something very inexpensive, more in the nature of a *charmante pensée*. "My friend, I saw the first violets today, and they made me think of you." He applied this principle of *charmante pensée* to all the ladies in whose houses he dined (but, for all that, he accepted dinner invitations only when a hostess was exceptionally persistent). In other seasons other flowers replaced the violets. "My friend, the first lilies of the valley have appeared today—I only hope you haven't seen them yet. . . ." But there were limits beyond which even the most economical friendship could not be stretched, and the time had come when the necessity for reciprocating was imperative. "If I were to go down in their car and accept their invitation for lunch at the Trianon, it would be the last drop. After that, the least I could do would be to invite them for dinner! . . ." The expenses connected with a dinner did not frighten him unduly; but in the last year Vermandois had become more and more convinced that when life was drawing to an end it was absurd and stupid to waste his time on people who bored him. "This way, I can wait a little longer before inviting them: so far we have reached the stage of the next to the last drop. The 'for' is more than outweighed by this additional 'against.' . . ."

On the way to Versailles Vermandois contemplated sadly the

disproportionate place occupied in his life by trivial thoughts and considerations—such as might occupy the mind of any marquis or shopkeeper. Louis Etienne Vermandois had changed a great deal; he had grown noticeably nervous and irritable. "Can't you see that he has gone through a spiritual break? It is a veritable crisis in his life!" the Countess said with a pleasant and frightened air, as if she were discussing a serious illness which luckily had taken a turn for the better.

His health, too, was said to have changed for the worse. During his last periodic visit to the doctor he was flabbergasted to learn (Vermandois had no idea that anything was wrong!) that his kidney, his liver, and some other organ were not behaving, and that his blood pressure had suddenly risen and needed to be brought down at once. "But the last time I saw you everything seemed to be in order?" Vermandois said in a querulous and hurt voice, as though he resented being misled in such a fashion. The doctor, who felt that he was not to blame, merely shrugged his shoulders. "The surprising thing is that everything has functioned so perfectly until now. You must not forget that you are past seventy. . . ." His statement was indisputable, but Vermandois resented it: people were so tactless; "'Un septuagénaire!' —the word has such an unpleasant sound!" "There is nothing for you to worry about," the doctor continued. "There is no danger. At seventy the organs of the human body cannot be expected to perform as though they were twenty. A man of your age lives not on the income from capital, but on the principal. In your case the principal of your health is large, and if you are careful it will last you a long time." The doctor enjoyed using picturesque language. He placed more things on the forbidden list, and wrote a new prescription to which the blood pressure responded almost immediately. But whenever in reading the papers Vermandois came across the words "septuagénaire" or "vieillard" (the most disgusting expression he saw was "un septuagénaire robuste") he frowned with a disagreeable feeling. "How unexpectedly old age has crept up on me! Why did I ever permit it to happen! . . ."

The doctor must have had an evil eye, because shortly after the

visit a slight pain occurred in his side. Besides his physical condition, the course of world events embittered Vermandois and increased his contempt for the human race. He realized that this
feeling was the only immutable quantity in his mental and spiritual equation: everything else about him changed constantly with
a speed that surprised and worried him. His financial position also
was not very strong: until he completed the Greek novel he could
not ask for another advance. It was difficult to say what cause was
chiefly responsible for his condition: the pain in his side, the
baffling and elusive threat of blood pressure, the lack of money,
or world events. Very likely it was a combination of all four.
Vermandois' friends noticed that one of the most pronounced
changes was in the general tone of his conversation, which until
lately always had been benevolently satirical to a tiresome degree.
He became abrupt in the way he said things, he lost his zest for
small talk, and on occasion (though not very often) he remained
silent for an entire evening, especially when his hosts offered him
as a delicacy to the assembled company, just as old brandy is
offered to connoisseurs. "My presence should be enough for them!"

His former political companions also complained about Vermandois: communists and their fellow travelers noted a growing
indifference about him which they attributed to his age. Largely
because he was absent-minded he left unanswered two invitations to be present at important meetings. He continued to sign
appeals and protests but without putting his heart into them. Siegfried Mayer, the German emigrant, was the last one to come to
see him on a party matter, and loosed a veritable torrent of awful-
sounding French. Vermandois was supposed to listen with warm
sympathy, and in parting to shake his hand with a special show
of understanding. He managed somehow to go through with it,
but inwardly the German emigrant infuriated him. "I had to
hold myself constantly in check so I would not shout at him:
'Heil Hitler!' But, if some reactionary had come to see me, I should
have had an irresistible urge to send in his presence a telegram of
greeting to Stalin." Recently Vermandois had received an invita-

tion to visit Moscow, with the understanding that the State Publishing House would publish on the most favorable terms the Russian translation of his book describing his Soviet impressions. He needed the money badly, but he gave them a politely evasive answer. "Human beings are weak and during dangerous moments in their lives they should be confronted by horrible, visual symbols, such as the signs picturing a skull and bones that serve as warnings to drivers on sharp curves. . . ." In everyday affairs, on the other hand, his communist sympathies asserted themselves more and more. He believed that he was the only national figure in France who had no money, and at times he spent long hours wondering what he would do if he were to win millions in the National Lottery (though he never bought tickets unless they were forced on him). Vermandois hated the rich with greater violence than ever.

In Saint Cloud his car was overtaken by a huge, shiny automobile, the back seat of which was occupied by a man and a woman. Vermandois had no idea who they were, but he was overwhelmed by a sudden surge of hatred for them. Except for books which had the sensational flavor of moving pictures, and night clubs, literature no longer had any value. Writing was a luxury which belonged to another age, otherwise an old writer could afford an expensive car, like these speculators. His liver and his imagination told him everything about them: a vigorous, ignorant, sharp, rich stock broker who had just made millions on the market and who was taking his mistress for an outing. Or perhaps they were running away to America? The threat of war was very real. They were the people who instead of being imprisoned were enjoying the benefits offered by the laws and the social system. They were the ones who gave receptions for ministers of state and writers, who contributed money to charitable causes, and who received decorations; they were the socially prominent who passed judgment on literature. "I bet he has the latest novel by Émile in his bag (I hope it is not mine). I can understand Alvera," Vermandois was becoming bloodthirsty. "Why should it be a crime to kill a person like that? When the time comes every one of them will dangle from a lamp post, and it will be a good riddance! Too bad that some of them will die a natural death before. . . ."

The pain in his side eased and his thoughts became less violent. With a smile Vermandois decided that even if he was riding in a taxi instead of a private car, he truthfully could not count himself among the victims of social injustice. "All this did not begin yesterday, many clever people have tried to find a solution for it, and no one could think of anything better than hanging them from lamp posts. To hell with it all! . . ." A wholehearted "to hell with it" always relieved his feelings.

The autumn morning was beautiful—"worth paragraphs and paragraphs of description that Emile uses on every tenth page to fill out his manufactured novels." Squinting his eyes (his eyesight also was becoming weak) Vermandois read the names of the streets,—Sèvres, Viroflay, Versailles,—and felt that there was something charming and entrancing about them that all other place names lacked. In the past this road had been the main thoroughfare of the world. Now ugly, grey, monotonous life clung to every stone, every ruin, every three-hundred-year-old hovel along the Avenue de Versailles and Avenue de Paris, and the few modern monuments it had created were just as flat, grey and uninteresting. "The fate of Europe was decided between the Tuileries and Versailles. Was it poorly managed? At that, it was managed better than it is now! . . ." The car slowed up to let by a load pulled by a brown Percheron. The huge, heavy, slow-moving, exceptionally comfortable-looking horse had something reassuring about it that proved irrefutably the advantage the old had over the new.

When they reached Versailles Vermandois ordered the chauffeur to pull up in front of the palace, realizing with acerbity that he had no desire to go to the restaurant: he was not in the least hungry. An hour still remained until the time set for the opening of the trial. He strolled through the town, obeying an old habit, stopped in front of a bookstore window, and saw a display of Émile's new book. There was a paper band on each copy with an inscription: *"Vient de paraître. Enfin le livre qu'on attendait."* Vermandois cursed under his breath. "He writes a new novel every six months. It's fortunate that he is past seventy-five!" In his mind he always added three or four years to Émile's age, and felt gratified that he was that much younger by comparison. He walked through the garden and it occurred to him that this might very well be his last visit there. "I should bid farewell to the place. . . ." He enjoyed bidding goodbye to various historic sites, but it sounded more natural when he was in Seville or Venice. Deep in his heart he could not make himself believe that he was parting with Versailles forever. It was too much an integral part of him. Vermandois paused on the stairs and once again admiringly surveyed the most amazing view in the world.

"Versailles. . . . What does Versailles stand for?" Vermandois asked himself. "Order? The French mind? French harmony? French common sense? Certainly it had not prevented the dragonades, the revocation of the Edict of Nantes, or the series of senseless wars. And with all of that the order maintained under Louis XIV gains stature by comparison with present-day chaos. Racine had no fear of being poisoned by gas in the middle of a peaceful night. He knew very well that under no circumstances would the revolting street mob try to hang him. Racine lived in his own house, and he had his garden, his horses, and his dogs. Granted that his contemporary world should not be judged from the point of view of Racine alone. But even the average French peasant led a calmer life than he does now—provided always that he was a Catholic. Why should he have bothered to become a Protestant? . . . He understood as little of Bossuet as he did of Luther. . . . For that matter, as a writer Bossuet stands inestimably higher than Luther, though as thinkers they were equals. . . ."

Vermandois strolled back, staring with disgust at the groups of tourists who were standing opposite the palace entrance. "They came here by rail to admire the palace, but probably in the near future they will fly here to burn it. . . ." His eyes took in a crowd of Germans (or at least of people who he thought were Germans), and he again experienced an attack of mounting anger. "I believe there is a logical reason for my hatred—it is difficult to love people who tomorrow will be destroying my treasures. But the logical reason is not everything. What can I do if I hate them instinctively, just as dogs hate cats? The esthetic feeling will never become reconciled to the idea of world domination by Germany at any time, and especially of present-day Germany. However, the esthetic feeling is an unreliable standard of measure. . . . It is most annoying that through some mistake Goethe and Schopenhauer were born in Germany! I should be perfectly willing to leave Schiller and Kant to them with my compliments. . . ."

Vermandois found a table in the café on the terrace. He still was not hungry,—"probably in addition to everything else I shall soon lose the capacity to enjoy food,"—but he ordered a sandwich and cup of coffee which tasted surprisingly good. Suddenly a familiar voice called his name. Glancing with annoyance over his shoulder Vermandois saw the Countess de Bellancombre. She was accompanied by her husband, who wore an expectant smile as if he were prepared to hear something clever and amusing. "What? You here? What became of your business appointment?" "My dear Countess, I just this minute arrived." "Now I understand! You simply are trying to avoid us," the Countess said with a laugh which clearly indicated that such a supposition could not be entertained by anyone in his right mind. Vermandois smiled a silent assent: "People make such outrageous suppositions!" "Your hat is extremely becoming!" he said as a matter of course though he barely noticed what the Countess was wearing. "Don't tell me you have already had lunch at the Trianon?" "Certainly, we had a most pleasant lunch. Your friend Cerisier is a very nice person. We decided to take a walk because it is still so early. First we saw Cerisier to the court. Everyone seems to treat him with tremendous respect: all the lawyers and clerks came up to him as if he were holding a formal reception! . . ." "It is the same principle that gives every American citizen the right to shake hands with the President." The Countess laughed. Her laughter and her smile were remarkably youthful. "I am so delighted that you are in a good humor again. . . . I consider our meeting a veritable stroke of luck, my dear friend! I always have wanted to visit our Versailles with you as a guide!" "The 'our' is most flattering. . . ." Count de Bellancombre thought irritably that his exotic wife and the over-educated grandson of a shopkeeper had an equal right to refer to Versailles as 'our'. "Really, my dear, you know as much about this place as I." "I have read many things about it, but not nearly as many as you have. My only regret is that fifteen minutes is all that remains before the miserable fellow goes to trial." "My dear Countess, you sound as if you were providing a theme for a leftist writer, or for a reporter from a socialist newspaper. 'The revolting spectacle of women dressed like fashion plates, who came to enjoy a glimpse of the doomed man. . .' The thing I never can understand is why the socialist papers carry verbatim accounts of these trials if they find the spectacle so revolting." "You are changing the subject. Please tell us everything you know about Versailles. Regardless of your political opinions you are a man who belongs to the eighteenth century. When I am listening to you, I always expect you to take a pinch of snuff out of a beautifully enameled box. Why don't you wear a long blue coat and shoes with red heels? . . ."

The Count thought with satisfaction that from now on the conversation would not require any effort on his part: the talking machines were set to grind out their usual light and serious tunes. As they walked leisurely toward the court house Vermandois in the same conversational tone related a number of stories about Versailles without trying to think of anything unusual: he knew that his listeners were so illiterate that the most generally known facts would be news to them. ". . . This is the spot from which Montgolfier sent up his balloon." "I had no idea that this took place in Versailles." "Yes, this is the historic site of a fatal event that ultimately will destroy civilization, which rapidly is approaching a natural death anyway." "What will destroy it? Balloons?" "No, probably airplanes" . . .

They strolled leisurely while Vermandois continued to speak. He knew something entertaining about every inch of ground in Versailles, and he found it easier to do the talking than to exchange ideas with the Countess who, in turn, was determined not to permit the initiative to pass into the hands of her adversary. ". . . You will have to admit that all this would have been impossible without Louis XIV! He set the general style of Versailles." "Certainly. I never would attempt to deny it. Incidentally, do you know how this style of architecture originated: the mixture of stone and brick? In order to keep the courtiers in their proper place Louis forbade them to build houses entirely of stone. He intended to show them that there was no sense in trying to keep up with him! To circumvent his orders our architects conceived this charming invention: a mixture of brick and stone. And that is the way in which seventeenth-century architecture came into being." "And the gardens?" "The man who created the gardens was Lenôtre and not the king." "But the king rewarded him with the rank of nobility," the Count interrupted drily. "That is correct. In return, Lenôtre asked that a sickle and a shovel be included in his coat of arms. He was a man of great natural dignity." "My dear denouncer of tyrants, no matter what you say, I am eternally grateful to the sun-king for his marvelous vision which has given us so much joy: the vision of Versailles." "I agree wholeheartedly. And the reason the sun-king had this marvelous vision was because the windows of Saint-Germain overlooked the royal tombs in Saint-Denis: he had no desire to have his future resting place constantly before his eyes. In the realm of arts the whims of despots at times bear the most unexpected and fruitful results. For example, the Count is not very fond of Stalin, but it is possible that at this very moment some unknown Soviet poet is composing in honor of the dictator

an ode which will be considered a masterpiece in years to come."
"What a paradox! A bolshevik dictator and Louis XIV! You
certainly cannot deny that under the sun-king there was no such
irresponsibility or peculation as are common in the world
today. For appropriating money that belonged to the state Nicolas
Fouquet spent nineteen years in a fortress, and died there. Is such
a situation conceivable today? Then there was one man who did
not need anything and who was above suspicion. Who is there
to take his place now?" "Louis XIV had no earthly reason to rob
private individuals, as long as he could openly and freely rob the
state," Vermandois answered immediately, forgetting his recent
trend of thought.

At the doors policemen were examining the tickets. Several
telephone booths had been improvised in the gallery. The
photographers recognized Vermandois. Immediately there were
several flashes. The Countess froze with a charming smile: when
through sheer accident one found oneself in the company of a
celebrity, things like that had to be expected. "Witnesses will
please come this way. This way please, sir," a police officer said
respectfully, giving every indication that he knew whom he was
addressing. Assuming the appropriate expression, Vermandois
proceeded to the seats reserved for witnesses. The stimulation
which the cup of strong coffee had produced deserted him. It
struck him that nothing was more disagreeable than entering a
hospital, a police station, or a court room.

X

THERE WAS a stir in the court room. Guarded by policemen
Alvera entered the cagelike enclosure reserved for prisoners. This
was not the usual procedure: the presiding judge had given
permission to bring in the accused before the court convened, for

the benefit of the photographers. Perching wherever they could find room,—in the aisles by the lawyers' bench, behind the judge's table, on the railing of the jury box,—the photographers blew their flash bulbs and clicked their cameras.

With his head bowed Alvera stood in the box. The first glimpse of him made a generally unfavorable impression on the audience. Experienced court room reporters at once put him down as a faker. "Just watch him! He will pretend to be an idiot," some- one close to the defense table whispered. Mademoiselle Mortier, looking very smart in her new robe, turned around and glanced indignantly at the person who said it. Cerisier was nowhere to be seen. The witnesses were in their seats. "Thank God! there are only four of them. We should be through by dinner time," a reporter from an evening paper said in a loud voice. "That re- mains to be seen. Figure it out: the prosecutor will take an hour, the defense an hour and a half . . ." "He will not talk for an hour and a half when there is nothing in it for him." "He will find someone who will foot the bill! In cases where capital punish- ment is involved they feel that it is their duty to talk as long as they can. . . ."

Vermandois stared with horror and amazement at his former secretary. "I never would have recognized him—he looks like a different person! How did I ever fail to notice that he has the face of a degenerate? And that blank, idiotic stare! . . ." Their eyes met, and Alvera quickly turned away with a startled expression. Forcing a friendly and encouraging smile, Vermandois several times nodded demonstratively in his direction. The public, which had filled to overflowing the main floor and the gallery, obviously was disappointed in the prisoner. "Just as at a bullfight, where uninteresting bulls are greeted with whistles. . . ." Uncertain how they should behave and feeling conspicuous, the jurors were speaking to one another in whispers.

There were two loud knocks, the sound of a bell, and every- one rose. The judges entered the room. The presiding judge, a grey-haired, very good-natured old man wearing glasses, settled

in his armchair, took in at a glance the public, the lawyers and
the reporters, shrugged his shoulders at the sight of the photographers who were now taking pictures of the judges' table, and,
waiting for the disorder to subside, began to whisper to his
neighbor. His expression showed clearly that he resented such a
lack of decorum, but that he was helpless. The presiding judge
could not understand the interest which the public displayed in
criminal cases in general, and in this case in particular. Obviously he, the prosecutor, the defense attorney and the jury would
have to go through the motions that were expected of them, but
there would not be a single moment when the outcome would be
in doubt. The presiding judge knew by heart what the prosecutor and the defense attorney would say. There could be several
variations in the testimony of the accused (though the limits were
well defined), but that, too, would have no effect. Finishing the
conversation with his neighbor, the judge gave a perfunctory
smile to Cerisier and to several other people whom he recognized
in the room, dispassionately scrutinized the prisoner, and also
decided that he would try to fake insanity or idiocy. This was a
variation which seldom benefited the accused, and in this case, in
view of the unanimity of the medical experts, it would be a
forlorn attempt. At least the case was not a difficult one, and
would not be a strain on the presiding judge. This consideration
was not due to laziness,—he was accustomed to work industriously
all day,—but he was a kind man, and he detested stern and merci-
less questionings, which frequently it was his duty to conduct. He
preferred to maintain a benevolent, almost fatherly atmosphere in
his court, though during murder trials it was somewhat out of
place. The presiding judge waited for everyone to get settled,
glanced reprovingly at the photographers, and assuming an expression which seemed to say "lie all you want, but do not delay
us too long,"—addressed Alvera.

"*Accusé, voulez-vous donner vos nom et prénoms?*"

Barely able to distinguish the answer, he asked the second
question.

"Entendez-vous bien quand je vous parle?"

"Oui, Monsieur le Président," Alvera answered in a louder voice. Everyone was straining eagerly to hear him. The judge looked at him over the rims of his glasses: "yes, he intends to fake insanity." Having asked him when and where he was born, he said: "Sit down!"

"Messieurs, les Jurés, voulez-vous vous lever."

The jury rose. Slowly, distinctly, and impressively the presiding judge repeated from memory:

"La Cour va recevoir votre serment. Vous jurez et promettez devant Dieu et devant les hommes d'examiner avec l'attention la plus scrupuleuse les charges qui seront portées contre l'accusé Alvera Ramon Gregorio Gonzalo [his shoulders moved just a trifle], *de ne trahir ni les intérêts de l'accusé, ni ceux de la société qui l'accuse; de ne communiquer avec personne jusqu'après votre déclaration; de n'écouter ni la haine ou la mèchanceté, ni la crainte ou l'affection; de vous décider d'après les charges et les moyens de défense, suivant votre conscience et votre intime conviction, avec l'impartialité et la fermeté qui conviennent à un homme probe et libre. . . ."* (he paused for a few seconds and looked inquiringly at the jury). *"A l'appel de son nom, chacun des jurés répondra en levant la main: 'Je le jure.'"*

After each juror in response to the roll call had said: *"Je le jure,"*—the presiding judge instructed the accused to listen attentively to everything that was said, and ordered the indictment to be read.

Alvera could not hear a word. His head was aching miserably. Though there was no outward sign of it, except for a huge lump which was concealed by his hair, the injury he had inflicted on himself the night before was severe. The guard had noticed in the morning that the prisoner was not himself, but this was to be expected on the first day of the trial. "And there is always a chance that he is faking. . . ." Learning that he was suffering with a headache the guard had brought him an aspirin tablet from the dispensary. He had no reason to call the doctor, and time was getting short. Without any help Alvera had dressed in his own clothes, instead of in the prison uniform he had been wearing. He had a vague idea of where he was going, but he saw everything through a fog which seemed to become thicker every minute. He had no appetite, and he barely touched the food, which was better than usual. Before being taken to the court house through an inside passage (the two buildings adjoined) the prisoner was given a cup of coffee, and for a short while he was aware of his surroundings.

While the strangely dressed man read the indictment in a weary monotone, Alvera stared at the public. Among them Vermandois was the only person who interested him. He wondered whether he should bow to him and, deciding against it, turned away pretending that he had not seen him. Much later he remembered his former employer again, but by then he could not find him in the sea of faces; for no apparent reason he spent his remaining energy trying to recollect whether the witnesses had been ushered out of the room before or after he had testified, or before the indictment had been read.

Alvera knew no one else in the room with the exception of his lawyer and Mademoiselle Mortier. He noticed that everything in the court room looked shabby and cheap. The walls were painted yellow with a dark brown border,—he thought that the brown and yellow clashed: "what color should they have used? Black? Blue?" Across the room from where he sat was a high door, also painted a dark brown: "where does it lead? What's behind it?" He noticed that out of the six lights suspended from the ceiling four were burning, and the two at the other end of the room from the judges were out. "Why? Are they economizing? Have they burned out? I wonder how they change bulbs in them? No one standing on a chair could reach them. They must use a ladder. If there is enough light with only four of them burning, they must use powerful bulbs. . . ." The light switch was on the wall behind the armchair of the presiding judge: "could it possibly be his duty to put out the lights? . . ." A typewritten notice was hanging on the wall behind the judges' table and beyond the light switch, but he could not read it from where he was sitting. There were large cardboard signs on all the walls: "*Défense absolue de fumer et de cracher.*" One of the signs was hanging next to a shelf which housed the marble bust of a woman with flowing hair. Alvera guessed that this was Themis, the goddess of justice; he tried to think whose daughter she was: "Jupiter? No, not Jupiter . . ." He remembered that she usually was pictured blindfolded, holding scales in one hand and a sword in the other,—at least that was the way she appeared in the lyceum textbook. "This one has no scales and no sword." It made him uneasy. "If she is not Themis, who is she? . . ." Then he studied the men in black and red robes sitting behind the table,—the men who would have to pronounce the sentence of death on him. He was not impressed. "Too bad they are not wearing wigs; most of them are bald-headed and they would look much handsomer with powdered hair. . . ." The table also looked shabby; the green cloth barely covered the edges as though there had not been enough money to buy a larger piece, and the table lamps and decorations were cheap and ugly. "They could not have cost more than thirty francs each," Alvera guessed. "Mine cost nineteen ninety." His heart missed a beat: he remembered his room and its furnishings which he had collected so lovingly, examining them carefully in the stores and trying to find the best he could afford. But he at once dismissed these recollections and absent-mindedly began to study the faces of the people who were crowding the room. Many were standing downstairs behind the railing, others stood in the gallery. "Why haven't they provided them with chairs, or with benches? Strange . . . Will they stand there packed like that until evening?" Certainly he would have to watch the proceedings until the court adjourned around six or seven. . . . "I doubt that they will be finished with me today. . . ." He tried to make himself comfortable on the wooden bench, as if boredom and discomfort were his only concerns. Leaning to one side he rested his head, which ached more and more, on his left hand. The public was some distance away from his seat and with his nearsighted eyes he could not distinguish their expressions. He made an effort to listen to the strangely dressed man who still was reading, but he found the words disagreeable and difficult to understand. When his name was mentioned for the first time in the indictment he gave an involuntary start, just as he always had in school when he was called unexpectedly to the board. From that moment his consciousness began to fade. When at last the reading came to an end he no longer knew what was taking place. An overwhelming drowsiness took hold of him.

Cerisier half-rose from his seat and asked his client some unimportant question. Mademoiselle Mortier, who was sitting next to her chief and who was transported with happiness, also came to life. Her name infallibly appeared in all the newspaper accounts of the case, and judging by the direction of the cameras she also would appear in all the pictures. Mademoiselle Mortier leaned toward Alvera with an expression so tense that anyone watching her would have imagined that the outcome of the entire case depended on his answer to Cerisier's question. Alvera stared at them blankly, made an effort to speak, but remained silent. "What is the matter with him today?" Cerisier was puzzled and uneasy (he knew nothing of what had happened the night before). Alvera's rambling answers to the questions of the presiding judge had surprised the lawyer. "Evidently he has decided to play the part of a lunatic, but he is overdoing it! He has not the ghost of a chance no matter what he does . . ." Cerisier thought. Not receiving an answer to his question, he made a slight gesture with his hand as if to say: "we will go into that later,"—and settled heavily on the bench.

In the court room were many Versailles lawyers who had come to hear their famous Parisian colleague. A robed, mannish-looking woman, her head a mass of rumpled hair, and her eyes flashing from behind gold-rimmed glasses, stared maliciously at Mademoiselle Mortier and in a whisper which could be heard a long way explained to her neighbor that Cerisier was the wrong man for this case. "They should have gone to . . ." she mentioned the name of a well-known lawyer. "Cerisier is definitely second-rate." "Do you imagine Vermandois is paying a large fee?" "Probably. Cerisier never would have taken the case without it." "That's very decent of him." "Very decent of Vermandois? To a man with his income five or even ten thousand francs means nothing at all." "He has such an intellectual face!" "Who? Alvera? Don't be ridiculous: it's the face of an idiot! . . ." "I was talking about Vermandois." "Oh, Vermandois? Yes . . . Though I can't see anything extraordinary about him. His fame as a writer is out of all proportion to his accomplishment. . . ." "I can't agree with you. He has written some remarkable books." "What, for instance?" "Take, for instance . . . I don't seem to be able to think of a single title right now, but they are very interesting books." "There is not one good book among them. Not a single one! He has written himself out a long time ago."

XI

IN THE room where they waited to be called the other witnesses respectfully offered Vermandois the best seat under the light. He thanked them and to show that he was a true democrat exchanged a few words with them. They were all plain people: the policeman who had arrested Alvera, the baker who had hit him on the head with a bottle, and the janitress from the house in which Alvera had roomed. Having discharged his democratic duty Vermandois unfolded the noon paper, but he did not feel like reading. He frowned at the unpleasant memory of Alvera's face. ". . . C'est malheureux quand même! Quelle figure qu'il a!" the janitress said, lowering her voice.

Soon the first witness was called, and five minutes later the second one. "Thank God! they are not questioning them very long. The trial is moving rapidly. . . ." At last with a polite bow the police officer invited Vermandois to follow. With hurried, uncertain steps he approached the designated spot. An excited murmur ran through the audience, accompanied by more flashes and the clicking of cameras. The presiding judge waited patiently, sighed and with a becoming show of respect addressed the witness. Without asking Vermandois his name or occupation,—the judge supplied this information as a matter of course,—he swore him in.

"What can you tell us about this case?"

"I should prefer to answer questions."

"The accused was your secretary until the day he committed the crime? You knew him. What impression had you formed of his character?"

"A very good one. I always had a most excellent impression of him. He was very efficient and conscientious about his work, never left anything unfinished, and was always pleasant and polite ["I am already perjuring myself," Vermandois thought]. I don't believe I ever have had a more satisfactory or capable secretary."

"Would counsel like to ask the witness any questions?" the judge asked, stifling a yawn.

"Have you ever noticed anything abnormal about Alvera?" the prosecutor asked.

"Never. He was a most pleasant, educated and intelligent young man," Vermandois answered and immediately checked himself. Cerisier instantly came to his rescue.

"In other words, his inner qualities always made a most favorable impression on you?"

"Yes."

"You are a famous writer [Vermandois made a deprecating gesture with his hand and inclined his head to one side]. You are one of the leading authorities on the workings of the human heart, and you understand what motivates people. How can you explain this crime?"

"I can only say that I was completely amazed! I actually could not recover from my amazement. This terrible crime seems to have nothing in common with the pleasant young man I know so well. . . . I can explain it only as a sudden mental aberration."

"Gentlemen of the jury, I should like to impress these words particularly on your minds because of the perception of the man who spoke them," Cerisier enunciated each word impressively.

"I should like to ask another question," the prosecutor said. "Was Alvera in need of money?"

"I cannot answer this question. He never has asked me for an advance, though I certainly never would have refused him."

"He never has asked for an advance though he could have had the money for the asking? This would seem to indicate that the accused was not in need of money."

"I cannot answer this question," Vermandois was embarrassed: again his testimony had helped the prosecution. Cerisier's face wore an annoyed expression.

"May I ask what salary he was receiving from you?" the prosecutor asked in a gentle voice.

"As a witness you may refuse to answer this question if you so desire," the presiding judge interposed. They both felt slightly self-conscious. The jury became noticeably more attentive. They wanted to hear the answer, but they realized that the right of a citizen to withhold personal information of this kind was one of the foundations in an orderly state.

"He received from me five hundred francs a month. In these times this is a very insignificant sum. But my secretary worked only two hours a day. I intended to give him a raise of my own accord,—he had not asked for it—but before I had time . . ." ("The great writer is not extravagant about the salaries he pays," Cerisier thought).

"Had he any other employment?"

"I don't know. I believe he did some typing, or something of that sort."

"I can understand very well that you could not pay more for such short hours," the prosecutor said even more gently. He was particularly well pleased to be able to strengthen his case with the testimony of a defense witness. "Once and for all, I should like to put an end to the impression that this young man was in need of money. He received five hundred francs a month from you. Gentlemen of the jury, that is not such a trifling sum! We all know honest working people whose income is less. The witness has testified that in addition Alvera had other sources of income. . . ."

"That is incorrect," Cerisier interrupted. "The witness offered no such testimony. He said that he did not know whether the accused had any other employment."

"I beg to differ! The witness testified that Alvera had other sources of income: typing or something of that sort. All of which, incidentally, we already know. It was Alvera's work as a typist that opened for him the house of the unfortunate Chartier, whom the able counsel for the defense would do well not to forget . . ."

"I am not forgetting about him!" Cerisier was on his feet and raising his voice (everyone realized that a court room incident was in the making). "I am not forgetting a single thing! The memory of the dead is just as sacred to us as it is to the representatives of the state, and we will not permit anyone to imply anything to the contrary [Half-rising from her seat, Mademoiselle Mortier also stared indignantly at the prosecutor as if to stress the words: "we will not permit! . . ."] But as my learned colleague well knows, all this has little to do with the case! Alvera's incidental earnings were a mere pittance. Most of the time the unfortunate man lacked even the proper food—a fact which I intend to prove. And I very decidedly object to any attempt to read into the testimony of a witness a meaning which it did not and could not possibly have!"

"And I very decidedly object to any attempts on the part of the defense to ascribe dishonorable intentions to the prosecutor who represents the interests of society!" jumping to his feet, the prosecutor said, also raising his voice. "I am not in the habit of distorting the testimony of witnesses, Monsieur Cerisier!"

"I did not say you were!"

"That is exactly what you said! Everyone here heard you!"

Both men began to shout at each other. The reporter from the evening paper gleefully put down the word "incident" in the middle of a line, underscored it twice, and began to write at the rate of a hundred words a minute: "*Brusque sursaut de flammes. L'avocat général acère ses griffes, mais il a affaire à forte partie. M. Cerisier bondit. La voix, si riche d'accents, du célèbre avocat, gronde. Dans un superbe mouvement d'éloquence il conjure son éminent adversaire . . .*" The prosecutor and the lawyer were facing each other, screaming at the top of their voices, with Cerisier's booming tones drowning out the words of his opponent. "*Il ne me plaît pas que . . .*" "*Maître, je ne suis ici ni pour vous plaire ni pour vous déplaire! . . .*" "*. . . Tant qu'il s'agira de parler pour l'infortune, il sortira de mon coeur des accents . . .*" "*Maître, vos accents ne m'ôteront pas le courage de mon devoir!*" "*. . . Monsieur l'avocat général, je représente ici les intérêts sacrés! Je m'appelle la Défense! . . .*" Everyone in the room listened tensely with the exception of the presiding judge, who displayed no interest in the exchange, listening with apparent indifference. He knew that heated arguments could not be avoided, especially in a case of this kind: both the prosecutor and the attorney for the defense wanted to liven the proceedings and to clear their throats. After they had been shouting for two or three minutes—a length of time they considered justified by the circumstances—the judge suggested that they calm themselves. For just a second he also was tempted to go through the motions of becoming exasperated, but he decided against it.

"Alvera!" The judge addressed the accused. "Perhaps you will tell us what your monthly earnings were?" ("Stand up!" the policeman sitting next to the accused whispered.) Alvera rose and fixed a blank stare on the judge, who repeated the question.

"I . . . I earned good money," Alvera said dully and sat

down. Excited whispers ran through the audience. "Not very convincing," a reporter said to his neighbor. The prosecutor looked triumphantly at the jury and at the press box.

"Gentlemen of the jury!" He was stressing his cool logic. "My eloquent opponent promised that we would consider later the finances of the accused. But there are certain facts I ask you to bear in mind. Alvera received from the witness a fixed, assured income of five hundred francs a month. In addition he did some copying for which he was paid at the rate of a franc and a half for a typewritten page. At the preliminary hearing the accused testified that on the day of the murder he was delivering some papers he had copied, for which he was to receive forty-eight francs from the man who was brutally murdered and who had provided the accused with part of his livelihood. This was the last instalment of a larger order. All told, Chartier had paid the murderer about two hundred francs. Let us assume that orders of this size were not common. . . . Though there is plenty of work for typists in Paris: individuals and entire organizations make a business of it. . . . Let us assume that copying gave the accused five hundred, or four hundred, or even three hundred francs a month. In that case, his total income was in the neighborhood of eight hundred francs a month, which is not inadequate for a single man. Naturally, I have no way of knowing what one of the most famous lawyers in France considers a 'mere pittance,' but, gentlemen of the jury, not every French citizen has millions at his beck and call!" There was a biting quality in the prosecutor's voice. Cerisier's face registered indignation, but inwardly he was quite pleased by the implication of his opponent's words. "Probably not all of you are millionaires. And certainly you and I can think of a number of our acquaintances, who are honest people, who work all day long, who live on eight hundred francs a month or even on less, and who never contemplate murder or robbery, in contrast to this young foreigner who chose these strange means of repaying our hospitality."

The prosecutor resumed his seat. An almost imperceptible

ripple of approval ran through the jury. Cerisier sensed that on this point he had suffered a decisive defeat which in the end might prove fatal, but from the very beginning he had had little hope of saving the life of his client.

"For the time being let us forget this question and all the fine hair-splitting," he said with impressive self-control (his face and his voice showed clearly that he controlled his indignation with difficulty). "Gentlemen of the jury, you will not and you cannot be influenced by the consideration that this man is a foreigner. In France, as my learned colleague well knows, we have behind us a thousand-year-old tradition of justice [these words might easily have led to another warm exchange, but both opponents were satisfied and had no desire to become involved in a second argument]. And, besides, why should we call Alvera a foreigner? Gentlemen of the jury, you have heard him speak—he speaks French, even as you and I. . . . Returning to our distinguished witness, I should appreciate it if he would describe in greater detail his opinion of the character of the accused."

Vermandois sighed and began to speak. Afraid of giving the wrong impression, he was more cautious,—he had no desire to assist either side in distorting the truth. Briefly he mentioned the terrible circumstances of Alvera's childhood and the psychology which had arisen since the war. "I am sure you will understand me," he said, trying to make his words sound clear, natural and convincing. "During those four horrible years people became inured to the idea that killing is a simple matter" (resentment was written on many faces in the audience: some other writer probably might have expressed the same thought without creating any ill-feeling, but Vermandois' communistic leanings were too well known. The prosecutor shrugged his shoulders). "I am sure you realize that I have no intention of comparing the profession of a soldier with that of a murderer. I merely am calling your attention to the atmosphere in which his unfortunate generation was reared. . . ." Then he touched on the demoralizing influence which was exercised by the moving pictures (he did not mention the newspapers: there were many reporters present and it seemed silly to antagonize the press). He spoke about the temptations offered by a large city, especially to a young man without money, who could not afford anything except the bare necessities. Then he described Alvera's temperament. "He always gave me the impression that he was a decent person [the prosecutor shrugged his shoulders again], but a person who was not well balanced, and who was over-sensitive to social injustices and contrasts." Vermandois elaborated on this subject for five minutes, and, though he still was self-conscious, he spoke well. The audience listened attentively, but with an undercurrent of hostility. Among those present only two people paid no attention to what he said: Alvera, who still sat leaning to one side with his head resting on his hand, and the presiding judge, who had heard all of this hundreds of times, knew it by heart, and was not in the least interested. Listening in silence was just as much a part of his duties as making the witnesses swear to tell the truth and nothing but the truth.

"Thank you very much," Cerisier said with deep feeling when Vermandois had finished. "We shall never forget that these brilliant words so full of humanity, kindness and wisdom, were spoken to us by a writer who is one of the jewels in the crown of France, and who enjoys a world-wide reputation as one of the greatest authorities on human emotions. Gentlemen of the jury, you will agree with me that the psychological observations of Louis-Etienne Vermandois are worth much more than the combined opinions of three mediocre physicians, especially if you take into consideration the fact that the doctors talked to the unfortunate Alvera for ten minutes, while the great writer knows him intimately. I have no more questions," the lawyer said and returned to his seat with an air which made it obvious that after such testimony any verdict, except one of not guilty, would be ridiculous.

The judge asked the prosecutor whether he had any other questions, thanked the witness, and informed him that after he had testified he might remain in the court room if he so desired. Vermandois bowed, chose a chair close to an exit, and in a few minutes edged his way out.

In the street Vermandois breathed more freely, but he was disgusted and depressed. As soon as he found a café he went inside, walked to the darkest corner, and, disregarding the doctor's orders and his high blood pressure, ordered a glass of armagnac.

XII

To THE delight of the reporters the trial was progressing more rapidly than they had expected. The witnesses were few, the experts testified briefly, and the prosecutor spoke for only half an hour. The consensus was that he had made a strong case. "He will travel a long way! A splendid speaker," the reporter from the evening paper said with a show of respect, though during his long career he had become tired of all eloquent prosecutors and defense attorneys. He already had furnished his paper with an account of the first part of the trial (the city desk had put it through without any cuts, which made the "incident" worth sixty francs). "The morning papers will get all the breaks," he cheerfully said to his neighbor. "With any luck we should have the verdict by seven." "I don't think so. Whenever capital punishment is involved, juries feel they must take plenty of time: they will pretend to weigh carefully every scrap of evidence." "What is there to weigh?" "Not a thing! The prosecutor could have said: 'I demand his head,'—and that would have been enough." "Cerisier seems to be in good form." "I can't tell you how tired I am of that fellow. They refuse to listen to him in the chamber of deputies and in party councils, so he does his talking in court rooms where people have no choice." "There is

Vermandois. I thought he had gone home, but apparently he decided to come back." "After all, he has to show that he has some conscience. . . ."

The section reserved for the public was not as crowded as it had been at the opening of the trial. Standing was tiresome, the criminal was a disappointment, and the case itself was not particularly interesting: everyday murder and robbery somehow tinged with anarchistic ideas which the accused so far refused to avow. His answers had been dull: if he was faking idiocy he was not making it convincing. Count de Bellancombre left in a bad humor. He had not quarreled with his wife, but they parted very coldly: she had insisted upon staying. "If your mind is made up I will send the car after you. I am tired, and I am going home." "Suit yourself." "If you will be ready to leave after you listen to the speech of . . . —whatever his name is?—your friend, I will wait for you." "I want to stay until the end—until they bring in the verdict."

The presiding judge asked whether the defense was ready to address the jury. Another murmur ran through the room, as Cerisier arose, adjusted the sleeves of his robe with a professional gesture, and let his eyes wander over the faces before him. In comparison with his political speeches his court room addresses produced no reverberations in the press. But he was nervous, chiefly because of his natural kindness: a human life was at stake. As an experienced lawyer he knew that only a miracle could save Alvera. But this knowledge did not in any way dampen his humane and professional zeal: he had to do everything, everything possible, to save his client. He had planned his address and developments at the trial had introduced no new elements. The thing that worried him most was that he was not certain about the best way to approach the jury, though he had been watching them intently all through the trial. Cerisier took his customary position opposite the other actors in the drama: the prosecutor, the jury, the reporters, and the public—waited until silence had settled over the room, and in a quiet voice began:

"*Messieurs de la Cour, messieurs les Jurés . . .*" He always opened his addresses in court with this old-fashioned formula. He was silent for a second, and then he began to speak slowly, pausing after every two or three words. "*Très brèves . . . très sincères, très simples . . . seront les observations que j'ai à vous présenter. . . .*" "This means at least an hour and a half," the presiding judge decided resignedly.

Vermandois sat for a long time in the café. Forgetting his high blood pressure, as soon as he had finished his drink, he ordered a second glass of armagnac, and at once began to feel less dejected. "There is no reason why I should be ashamed of my testimony," he thought. "Even if I said a few things which would have remained better unsaid, I corrected myself immediately. I spoke sensibly, without becoming involved, and without hemming and hawing. I said everything that I possibly could say, and that wagging tongue [he meant Cerisier] will make the most of my testimony. If the papers are not satisfied, as God is my witness, it makes no difference to me" (he checked himself on this point, and decided that it was almost true). "Then what is the matter with me, and why should I have the feeling that I have taken part in something dishonorable? The laws? The right to punish? 'Judge not that ye be not judged'? All this does not apply to me. I never have denied the authority of the state and of the courts."

Vermandois took a newspaper out of his pocket. The crucial hours in the siege of Gijon . . . Franco's planes have sunk another British ship. . . . According to information released in Tokio, since the beginning of the peaceful Japanese penetration into China the Chinese have lost a hundred thousand men killed. . . . Adolf Reinte and Robert Stamm were executed in Berlin for attempting to revive the communist party. . . . Fourteen Soviet employees confessed that they had mixed ground glass with flour intended for the Red Army, and were sentenced to die. . . . The last news item Vermandois found particularly distasteful—it could not be classified as a fascist atrocity. But even with due allowance for that, such a show of concentrated evil in a single issue of a newspaper amazed him, though he had thought himself immune after following the events of the last few years. "Satan is doing everything in his power to achieve world domination. . . ."

A boy selling evening papers entered the café. In some miraculous fashion the paper already carried an account of the trial. The exchange between the attorneys was described very effectively under a special heading—Vermandois was not aware that he had witnessed anything so spectacular. They had used an old picture of him. "Taken from the morgue . . . It's a bad picture. I must remember to send them a new one. The pictures taken in the court room probably will appear in the next edition. Or maybe the photographers were from the morning papers?" The reporter's version of his testimony was friendly. Though the paper had conservative sympathies, Vermandois was on good terms with the editor, who even had published one of his stories. The impression gained from the newspaper was that the famous writer had put forth noble and exalted ideas typical of his broad humanity, but that still the culprit deserved to be convicted. They referred to Vermandois as *"le célèbre écrivain"*. This annoyed him; he would have preferred *"l'illustre écrivain. . . ."*

Vermandois paid the check and returned to the court house. No one asked to see his ticket, and he was admitted with every show of respect. Once again Vermandois was gripped by an uneasy feeling such as is experienced by a healthy man when he enters a hospital with its medicinal odors and its immaculate cleanliness: the farther away from it the better. As he tiptoed into the court room Cerisier was beginning his address. Vermandois took a seat near the exit. "At the right moment I can leave without being intercepted. . . ." He felt that he could not leave at once because of the Countess, and because he had to show his appreciation to the lawyer who had undertaken the defense without a fee.

Cerisier was talking about the pitiful, depressing life of the unfortunate youth, about the horrible atmosphere in which the new generation of the poor was coming into manhood, about the contrast between the lives of the people who enjoyed luxuries as a result of the fortunes they had amassed in the war and the privations of the lower classes. "He is saying all this for the benefit of the socialist press," Vermandois thought glumly. "It's all very nice, but how will the jury take it? To be honest, when I was testifying I said pretty much the same things, because there is nothing else to say. . . ."

Vermandois studied the jury. "They seem to be listening with attention, but their faces make me think that his words will have an adverse effect on them. Particularly on that man over there, who looks like Torquemada." Vermandois shifted his eyes to the judges' table. "They, including the presiding judge, are not paying any attention to what he is saying. They must have heard all this hundreds of times. As far back as the eighteenth century these ideas had become trite, and by now every lawyer has memorized hundreds of these clichés. They keep on call not only the ideas but even the exact wording. Their favorite passages are polished and balanced, as perfect as false teeth. It cannot be a question of plagiarism, for word-for-word repetition is almost a necessity. Thousands of crimes are committed in the world, thousands of lawyers have to defend their clients, and in most of the cases all they can say in behalf of the criminals is what Cerisier is saying now. They could simplify matters by using talking machines and records, instead of prosecutors and defense attorneys. . . . Everything here was a certainty before the trial began: the verdict, the sentence, the execution. The whole thing is an inhuman machine which carefully and inexpertly conceals its lack of soul, and pretends to be very humane. That is why the workings, perfected through the ages, of this majestic, outwardly beautiful, but inwardly hideous machine leave me with the impression of a superfluous and malicious comedy. . . ."

He was startled when he heard his name mentioned. In a respectful and ingratiating tone Cerisier was saying: ". . . *Monsieur Louis-Etienne Vermandois, avec son intelligence supérieure de grand écrivain, avec sa lucidité de psychologue connaissant les abîmes de l'âme humaine, Monsieur Vermandois, gloire des lettres françaises, n'est-il pas venu vous demander miséricorde pour le pauvre désequilibré. . . . Ah, Messieurs les Jurés, Dieu sait s'il y a des heures poignantes dans le ministère que je tâche de remplir* [he raised his voice]. *C'est une noble mission que la nôtre, Messieurs les Jurés! Quand un homme, un malheureux, est abandonné par ses amis, traqué par les pouvoirs publics, maudit par tout le monde, c'est une noble mission, vous dis-je, que le défendre contre tous! C'est ainsi, Messieurs les Jurés, qu'un prêtre se dresse devant le condamné, s'attache à lui et l'accompagne jusqu'au lieu de l'exécution à travers les clameurs et les hurlements de la foule qui ne veut pas comprendre. . . .*"

A murmur of admiration ran through the audience. "I must admit that he speaks exceptionally well. I never could hope to equal him. . . . What took me a few minutes to say, he will stretch into a speech that will last an hour, and if necessary—three hours. And no matter how long it may last, his speech will be a thing of beauty; there will be no errors of logic or grammar; he will not violate a single rule of the precise oratorical code; his voice will modulate in a range of keys that I would not attempt under penalty of death. But why does he irritate me so? He is working conscientiously on the case, he is doing everything he can, he is spending his time, and he refuses to take a fee. True, he is doing it out of consideration for me, and he would not have taken the case of just anybody's secretary. True, if invited to assist in the prosecution, with just as much ease he would take the other side of the argument. They ask for a complete vindication or for capital punishment, depending upon who invited them first. . . . But why should I worry about it at this stage of the game? . . . That good-looking girl who is his assistant is apparently in love with him—my readers never look at me with such adoring eyes. . . . The prosecutor is making notes—probably he also has prepared a classic on the same subject: they remind me of Corneille and Racine, who wrote 'Bérénice' to spite each other.

But the prosecutor is confident of his victory. Cerisier himself told me that he had no hope of finding any extenuating circumstances. . . . Everything about the case is predetermined and therefore everything about it is low comedy. Anyway, any semblance of justice existed only before the appearance of state banditry. Now that 'lawfully constituted governments' commit monstrously shameless crimes, the criminal courts have become the height of duplicity. But that is the very point a lawyer never will admit. . . ." Vermandois listened. Cerisier was beginning to sift the evidence. Having finished the part of his speech devoted to a general social philosophy, he proceeded to prove that in this case there could be no question of premeditation, and that Alvera's confession should have no bearing on the verdict:

". . . Avoué, Monsieur l'avocat général? Oui, Monsieur l'avocat général, Alvera a tout avoué! La volonté criminelle? Il l'a reconnue. La préméditation? Il l'a reconnue aussi. Il a tout reconnu, il a tout reconnu, la tête fracassée par un terrible coup de bouteille, il a tout reconnu après un interrogatoire dont je n'ai pas été témoin, après un interrogatoire de quelques heures dans lequel il ne fut pas soutenu par son défenseur . . . [the prosecutor indignantly shrugged his shoulders]. Ah, Monsieur l'avocat général, si la torture existait aujourd'hui, si un homme se présentait dans cette enceinte, dégagé de ses fers, mais la figure ensanglantée et les os brisès, lui diriez-vous en voyant couler son sang, lui diriez-vous: tu n'a rien à dire; tu as avoué! . . ."

Boiling with indignation the prosecutor jumped to his feet. Even the presiding judge began to take notice of the proceedings. The reporters made notes with incredible speed, and the murmur in the audience grew in volume. But there was no explosion. Cerisier took up new positions, covering his retreat with rear guard actions. He conceded that force had not been used in questioning Alvera, but he called the attention of the jury to the terrific mental pressure to which the unbalanced young man had been subjected at a time when his mind was dimmed by a terrific blow he had suffered during the arrest. Clearly, logically, rationally, he considered the questions of the neatly copied papers, of the gun, and of the amount of money involved, and proved that premeditation was out of the question. His reasoning was clever and convincing. Forsaking dramatics, Cerisier spoke very simply, as a disciple of the new school of Henri Robert. Having dealt with premeditation he proceeded to consider the medical evidence and to deal with the experts. After paying them a few back-handed compliments tinged with sarcasm, he artfully showed to the jury that these experts were bureaucrats rather than scientists, that they had little standing in the medical world, and that they discharged their duties in a perfunctory fashion. He pointed out that they had spent fifteen minutes on Alvera's examination—"the time of these 'princes of science' is too valuable even when a human life is at stake! . . ." From a book by a widely known scientist, the famous Professor Fouquot, he read a quotation which discussed the inadequacy of expert testimony accepted by the courts and gave several apt illustrations. Cerisier always used this quotation when he found it necessary to counteract the impression made by medical experts; he had a different quotation from the work of another famous man which he used when he wanted the expert opinion strengthened. Slowly, deliberately, in a determined voice he reminded the jury that they had the right to reject expert opinion: that was one of the cardinal principles underlying the French jury system. Momentarily falling back on civil law, with which he was more familiar, Cerisier read article 323 which prescribed that the jury should disregard any expert opinion if it ran contrary to the opinion of the jurors. ". . . *Quant au code d'Instruction Criminelle, il n'avait même pas à affirmer cette règle qui est le corollaire indiscutable du régime des preuves morales . . .*" With the exception of the presiding judge everyone was absorbed in his speech. Obviously his address to the jury was a tremendous success. "He is a genius! What a marvelous speech! The jury is certain to find mitigating circumstances!" the Countess de Bellancombre whispered ecstatically to a stranger who sat next to her.

"Without him it would have been much worse," Vermandois thought, becoming reconciled to Cerisier's manner. "And his mention of torture is justified. Our legal procedure is inestimably higher than the procedure which existed before the revolution, or which exists now in countries under fascist dictatorship [he again remembered with distaste the unprecedented case of the fourteen men who had been executed for mixing ground glass with the flour intended for the Red Army]. No matter how stupid men are, the jury system is better than any other [he glanced dubiously at Torquemada]. But our own indifference has made of it a mere inhuman machine. And that can be said of all our free institutions. With all their imperfections, with all their short-comings, they are still the best in the world. The tragedy, the great tragedy is that they have lost their spirit of humanity which was the source of their strength, that we no longer have any civic pride, that we no longer can mention the rights of man without a smirk, though they were written in blood. The tragedy is that our free institutions are being eaten away by indifference, selfishness and cupidity, and that we have deprived them of their spiritual essence by making of them an absurd and senseless pantomime. The men who conceived free institutions had not foreseen the spirit in which they would be administered by a generation which is not interested in anything except money and which is eternally seeking something new and thrilling. Frequently it is said that this 'new' is 'not in keeping with the French national character.' If due to a combination of tragic circumstances a large band of well-armed bandits were to find themselves in the midst of a disarmed people, they would not pay any attention to our national character, or else they would take drastic steps to change it. . . ."

Suddenly Vermandois realized that in the course of one day he had turned from communist ideas to monarchism, and from monarchism to a democratic philosophy of a special kind. "I really should take a cure. . . ." But he immediately answered himself that nothing could cure him. "Probably I shall never change my label, but my inner opinions will continue to change frequently, on occasions such as today measuring themselves in terms of hours. . . ." Unexpectedly his eyes met the eyes of the Countess de Bellancombre, who smiled at him enthusiastically and made a gesture as if she were about to applaud. But it was not clear what had kindled her enthusiasm: his testimony or the lawyer's speech? The Countess signaled that she was worn out with excitement and that they must get together as soon as possible. Vermandois nodded to indicate that he understood her: "Just as soon as possible. He is about to finish. . . ." Cerisier's voice rose again. One of the peculiarities of his talent consisted of his ability to change instantly from a cold and logical analysis to a tone charged with drama. Everyone sensed that his speech was nearing the end.

". . . L'heure est venue pour vous, Messieurs les Jurés, de tendre une main secourable à un pauvre dément. Si vous trouvez que l'action qui vous est dénoncée est dûe à un coeur endurci et sanguinaire . . . si vous trouvez que cet enfant de vingt ans n'a pas été assez malheureux, alors condamnez-le sans pitié. . . . Mais une erreur de jugement est vite commise, Messieurs, et les morts ne reviennent pas. Le couperet de la guillotine tombe dans un sens unique, l'échafaud est, hélas, irréparable. Je vous abandonne une âme malade et tourmentée, je vous livre Gonzalo Alvera, triste victime d'une triste fatalité! Serez-vous inflexibles? Ah, puisse-je vous épargner un repentir! Au milieu des incertitudes morales, mettez la main sur votre conscience et prononcez. J'ai rempli mon devoir . . . Messieurs les Jurés, allez remplir le vôtre . . . Nous attendons de vous la vie ou la mort. . . ."

Cerisier spoke the last words in a breathless whisper, and happy and exhausted settled heavily on the bench. The court room was not the proper place for applause, but he could sense from the expressions on the faces and from the current of enthusiasm with which the atmosphere was charged that he had spoken exceptionally well, that he had made a deep impression, and that he had done everything in his power to save the unfortunate client. Mademoiselle Mortier gave him both her hands in silence—no words could express what she felt. Wiping his forehead with a handkerchief Cerisier turned to Alvera with a few words of encouragement, but the accused again answered with a blank stare.

As confident of victory as ever, the prosecutor was satisfied with a few brief remarks: he protested against the insinuations regarding the police authorities, and he answered the defense contentions on premeditation. Cerisier replied with not more than a dozen words, realizing that he could not add anything to his speech. Though the prosecutor mentioned the *"insinuations qui ne sauraient atteindre la justice française,"* and Cerisier exclaimed: *"Pourquoi cette affirmation inexacte, indigne de vous et de nous, Monsieur l'avocat général?"*—both men were punctiliously polite, and in glowing terms complimented the opposing counsel.

Vermandois watched the jury. "Torquemada looks gloomy. Nothing will ever move him. . . ." He tiptoed to the dimly illuminated gallery and found the Countess de Bellancombre, who was begging the policeman on duty to let her through to the defense table. The Countess was in a state of excitement unusual even for her. As soon as she saw Vermandois she rushed to him and grasped his hands. "It is simply marvelous! I never have heard such a speech in my life! I simply am shaken! Aren't you?" "I also am shaken, my dear." "No, no, you don't feel about it the way I do! He has surpassed himself. And I am not the only one: all around me people who I know are not socialists were carried away with enthusiasm." "Yes, there cannot be any question about it. It was a very good speech." "'A very good speech!' It was not very good, it was marvelous!" the Countess exclaimed and placing her own interpretation on Vermandois' coolness, added: "Your testimony, too, was exceptional! Too bad you spoke for only four minutes: I timed you. You took the part of the jury's conscience, and I am certain that your testimony and Cerisier's speech will save his life! I am absolutely certain!" "Don't be too sanguine, my friend. I believe that there is not more than one chance in a thousand." "You are mistaken! I am sure that you are mistaken! . . . I think you missed some of the arguments?" "Yes, at first they kept me locked in with the other witnesses, and later I went out for a breath of fresh air. I am dying to know what happened in my absence. It is just like watching the disconnected and exciting scenes in a moving picture theatre, when they are advertising the coming attraction. . . . Where is the Count?" "He left. He promised to send the car after me, but I am afraid that I will not be able to wait for it. I hope that in that case you can give me a lift?" ("That's just my luck!" Vermandois thought. "I will have to listen to her for an hour, and then pay for the car"). "I shall be very happy . . ." Suddenly she made a dash for the door through which Cerisier had entered that moment. "Should I take this opportunity to escape? No, that's impossible, I have no legitimate excuse." He walked over to the lawyer and congratulated him effusively.

". . . It was one of the best speeches I have ever heard."

"You overwhelm me."

"Do you believe there is any hope?"

"None whatever."

"That's impossible! I don't believe you!" the Countess said. "You will see that they will find mitigating circumstances! I simply have to be present when the verdict is brought in. How long do you think it will take them?"

"I would hate to make a guess."

"Do you believe they will take an hour?"

"At least that long. They ordered their dinners brought to the jury room."

"Maybe while they are eating the three of us can have dinner?"

"Unfortunately that's impossible. I cannot leave the court house. There is no telling what may happen."

"Then you and I can have dinner alone, my dear friend?"

"I shall be delighted," Vermandois answered without enthusiasm: that would mean paying for the dinner as well as for the car: "At least this will cancel all my obligations!"

"Shall we go now? We ate lunch very early . . . Just one second," she turned to the lawyer. "How about that wretched fellow? Will he have dinner?"

"Certainly."

"Can't we get something extra for him: some wine or something sweet? Please! . . ." She took a hundred-franc note out of her bag. "You can do anything here—they all take orders from you. . . . I watched them. Can you give him this money?"

"I cannot give it to him, but I can deposit it with the prison authorities. They have a commissary for prisoners, and someone has been depositing money regularly to Alvera's account," Cerisier explained, giving the Countess to understand that that "someone" was Vermandois. "I also helped once or twice . . . I will see that he knows about it."

"Thank you so much! I hope he can have something tonight: some wine, or perhaps some cognac? I am so grateful to you, my dear friend! ["He, too, has become a 'dear friend.' That's very rapid promotion," Vermandois thought]. Let's go . . . But I warn you I refuse to swallow my food whole. Perhaps we better not try to go all the way to the Trianon—we can find some little place nearby. All I want is some cold meat and a glass of champagne. . . . My nerves are in a terrible state! . . . And this awful lighting. . . ." "I have no objection to cold meat, but why should I feed her champagne?" Vermandois thought, but he was good-natured about it: he also wanted something to eat and drink. "You know, I haven't been in a court room for ages, and I expected it to be like Tolstoy's *Resurrection*. Do you remember?"

"How could anyone forget? But I regret to say Tolstoy followed the line of least resistance, using a judicial error as basis for the entire novel. After all, judicial errors are not the general rule in our institutions. Finally, even when Tolstoy uses them, humanitarian clichés always depress me," Vermandois said and immediately regretted his words: the clichés he and Cerisier had used that day were far worse than anything Tolstoy had ever used.

"I have the impression that you take an ironic view of the courts. That's unfortunate," Cerisier remonstrated, concealing his irritation behind a smile: he did not like Vermandois' tone. "If you will pardon me, it is very easy to be ironic, and everything under the sun has its ridiculous side. You don't approve of humanitarian clichés, but neither do you approve of punishment. What would you suggest as a substitute? Humanity has its limitations. Sceptics and overzealous humanitarians who deny society's right to judge and to punish have not so far been able to suggest anything better than the existing institutions with their jury system and criminal code. Until they suggest something better we have every reason to discount their mocking enmity toward the courts and the bar. As a matter of principle I am opposed to capital punishment, but neither do I believe that murderers should be given their freedom, or that they should be pampered in hospitals, unless they are actually insane."

"In God's name, let's not talk about it!" the Countess exclaimed. "We are about to go to a restaurant where we will enjoy champagne, but that wretched fellow will be taken to his cell where he will sit for several months waiting to be killed. . . . No, no, I can't believe it! I simply refuse to believe it after your speech and your testimony!" she half-closed her eyes and pressed her hands against her temples. Suddenly her eyes were filled with tears. She tried to say something and began to sob. Vermandois looked at her in amazement. "She really is a very kind person, and I should not make fun of her. . . ." "Excuse me, I am such a fool!" the Countess said with difficulty. "I react to everything as a musician, and there is a horrible overtone here. . . . I am sure you understand me? . . . These lights are so dim . . . And the lights in Alvera's cell must be just as dim. . . ."

Puzzled and uneasy, Cerisier walked toward the door. The reactions of a musician were incomprehensible to him, but he felt an indefinable fear. His satisfaction with the brilliant speech vanished. He wondered what Alvera was thinking at that moment. "I should go to him, and say something heartening. . . . But what can I say? . . . This waiting for the verdict is the worst part of all. . . ." He found it difficult to talk to a man whom only a short while ago he had publicly described as feeble-minded ("even if I explained that I had said this for the jury's benefit"). But it would make it even more difficult if the words of encouragement were to strike a false note, and he had no hope of saving the man's life. Cerisier had no doubt that Alvera was trying to fake insanity. "Only yesterday he spoke to me like a reasonable person. . . ." The idea that a man might be transformed overnight never occurred to the lawyer. He forced a bright smile and walked briskly toward his client.

XIII

WISLICENUS WAS in excellent humor. Probably because he had stopped smoking, his health seemed much better. At first he had intended to give up cigarettes altogether, but finally he decided to make the change gradually: five cigarettes a day, then three, then two. Now Wislicenus was down to one cigarette which he smoked between five and six in the afternoon, and for which he waited impatiently from early in the morning. He had had no heart attacks for some time. "What more can I ask," he thought, remembering the horrible, ever-increasing, unbearable pain and the *"sensation de mort imminente."* "Happiness is a simple and elementary state: absence of need and disease are synonymous with practical liberty which, no matter what people say about it, is much more valuable than the right to play a part in the comedy of elections, or the right to read worthless books and newspapers."

Though he was ashamed to admit it even to himself, Wis-

licenus realized that the disappearance of the detective who had
been trailing him also contributed to his peace of mind. He no
longer noticed in the streets the nondescript man of uncertain
nationality. Being shadowed had not frightened him, but it had
created a state of mental unrest, especially inasmuch as he never
was able to settle the question: "Gestapo or Gay-Pay-Oo?" "Any-
how they were right to do away with this unnecessary expense:
the beast is old and no longer dangerous, and he is not contemplating any forays. As a matter of fact the old beast sees a new
freedom in discarding the ferocious demeanor of so many
years. . . ."

"Freedom . . ." Wislicenus thought. "Only a month ago I
was thinking about suicide. People who are afraid of death say
that suicide is the weakling's escape. That's ridiculous. I knew
many people who have committed suicide, and there was not a
single coward among them, while the people who accused them
of being weaklings could not always be counted among the brave.
In principle even now I have nothing against suicide: situations
in life can and do arise in which no other solution is possible.
Seeking death is not necessarily a weakness—it may be the only
honorable way out. But why should I think about suicide? Out
of fear of death? That's absurd on the face of it. Because of my
mental state? I seem to have found a solution for myself, and I
see nothing shameful about it. I have not gone back on my convictions, and I don't even consider my life a mistake. At least it
was not a mistake as long as I had a sincere or an almost sincere
desire to follow other sincere or almost sincere idealists and to
become merged with the mass of humanity, retaining at the same
time a grip on the torch, or beacon, or whatever it was. Everything else was a logical sequence worked out by the various
Engelses of whose second-rate mentality I was not aware at the
time. Perhaps even that desire to merge with the mass was not so
overwhelming. . . . Lenin was a great political chess player,
and he loved the people no more and no less than Lasker loves
his pawns when he is playing a tournament game. In addition to

his brilliant mind, his strength was dependent on his hatred for
everything in the opposite camp—a hatred which I shared and
which I unfortunately am losing, or which now I feel as much
toward our own camp. But there were no divided loyalties for us
—the pawns—then. The only period when we knew that we were
not sincere came after the death of Ilyich, after we had exhausted
our personal fund of decency, faith and conviction in the first
bloody years, but still continued to talk about the torch, the
bright future, the revolutionary wave, the world conflagration,
and so on. Trotsky retained his faith in all this until now, or at
least he pretends that he has, for the benefit of his biographers.
Actually, one by one we came to realize that, though we had
defeated the enemy, the result was a muddle. The habit of looking
at the world with the eyes of political pamphleteers remained
with us, just as the habit of dunking bread in coffee remains
with an upstart who has made his mark in the world. The other
thing that stayed with us was the peculiar Marxist slang which
in its way is just as technical as sport slang: one tennis player has
beaten another tennis player, or the powerful red mare had her
revenge for last year's race—things like that cannot be taken
literally. . . . We did away with bourgeois morality—that was
a good thing—but the revolutionary morality evaporated along
with it. . . ."

Lazily Wislicenus picked up a book: he was tired of these
thoughts which were so out of tune with his plans. "No, I still
am not in condition to think things through. . . . I am not a
'penitent bolshevik.' Any man who reaches my age should be
entitled to keep his rank and to be retired on a pension. I am
not to be blamed that by mere coincidence when I reached my
retirement age I became for the first time aware of simple, elementary life and of simple, elementary happiness, which until now
had been concealed from me. I am putting away for good my
revolutionary uniform, and for the few remaining years of my
life I need only a modest pension: bread, soup, cheap wine, and
a little sun. Probably there is nothing new about it, and in my

newly found freedom I must be in accord with scores of other revolutionists who lived and died a long time ago. Happiness? What is happiness? It is possible that the young Aryan stallions find happiness in their German stables. Stable philosophy may make some people happy, but I have no desire for any part of it. There is no reason why I should have any philosophy. Let vermin destroy other vermin. That does not make it necessary for me in my dying years to fall on my knees before non-vermin. . . ."

It occurred to Wislicenus that the call he intended to make on Nadia also was unnecessary. "There was pain in her eyes, the kind of pain that is intended to express atonement. Maybe the pain is a result of being Kangarov's mistress? Or, maybe it is simply a very urgent desire to get married? She was uncomfortable with me, and she wore an expression such as a man wears when he steps out of a public toilet and meets face-to-face some lady he knows. . . . I am not in love with her any more, or I would not think about her in such cynical terms. Probably I never loved her—actually, I doubt whether I have ever been in love with anyone. Unless it was Mary, when I was in exile? But that was partly boredom, and the physiology also was overshadowed by figures of speech, so that I cannot tell whether I was in love with a woman or with a party comrade, or whether I was in love at all or merely seeking a loyal partner in my work. At the time we deceived ourselves successfully. For a long time I was convinced that a revolutionary has no time for a personal life: fighters are the hermits of the revolution. Probably I have missed life, or the best things in life. And when finally I fell in love it was stupid and disgusting. Even poets—and they are the most accomplished liars! —have never succeeded in making the love of an old man poetic. That is the tragedy of old age, but then there are many ridiculous tragedies in this world. Young people—and they are the real masters of this situation—always have laughed at it. Though many poets have written remarkable things in their old age, in literature an old man in love always cuts a ridiculous figure and becomes a sensualist (an old lecher!) The distinction between the two is very slight. Every cricket should know his blade of grass. What can an old man do? Well, there are philosophy, cards, politics, fishing, thoughts about the immortality of the soul, collecting postage stamps. . . . There are all sorts of things, and, besides, who was it said that a man can always find a solution?" he asked himself. "Nadia most certainly laughed behind my back, and she was right. What is the sense of fooling oneself into thinking that if Nadia lived with me instead of living with Kangarov that in itself would make it better, purer, and more ennobling. Country solitude is the only answer—there is nothing else left. With the exception of the local French sheet, I shall not look at the newspapers. If my money gives out I will manage somehow. Sooner or later the angina pectoris will come into its own—probably sooner. At least I shall not have the feeling which I have had until now: the feeling of a man who is stuck between floors in an elevator. . . ."

After rendering his final accounting to Moscow, Wislicenus found that he had saved eight thousand francs out of his salary—a much larger sum than he had expected. Having delivered the money that belonged to the government he took his money to the bank—the novel idea that he had a checking account in his own name seemed absurd. It was funny that the detractors and enemies of bourgeois civilization were constantly forced to utilize the advantages it offered. On the way home from the bank he stopped on the quay. With their rods in their hands the shabby Parisian fishermen were sitting over the water—this picture always amused him: fishing in the Seine! He remembered the river Yenissei, and suddenly thoughts about his new freedom, which until then had been vague, became crystallized. "That's what still lies ahead for me!" Wislicenus thought, feeling a sudden surge of joy. "Why should I stay in Paris where the eight thousand francs will disappear in six months? I can go to the country where living is a hundred times more restful and costs a third of what it costs here. Man was made to enjoy nature and the sun." For some reason he remembered Castellan, a tiny hamlet in Provence, through which he had traveled before the war. His only recollection was a lovely old square flooded with southern sunlight so bright that it hurt the eyes. He could not remember anything else. "Perhaps there is no river there, or if there is there may not be a single fish in it? Anyway, there is sure to be a river and good fishing nearby in some village which will be just as charming, just as sunny, and just as comfortable. I will go there, look around, and settle for the remainder of my days. I shall live where no one knows me, where I can get up with the sun and go to bed with the sun. Can I spend all my time fishing, as I did on the Yenissei? There Mary was with me, and I had shelves full of volumes by various Engelses, but the Engelses don't appeal to me now. I cannot expect to find a Yenissei in Provence, but the catch is of minor importance. During the days of my idyllic exile I also went shooting, but with angina pectoris shooting is out of the question, and, besides, it is an expensive sport. Fishing costs very little and is not tiring—on the contrary. If I find that I am bored, I can always write my memoirs," he thought with a smile. "American publishers are a new version of the rich uncle, for retired politicians. The money I have will last for more than a year. In a village I should be able to live on five hundred francs a month. What will my living expenses be? I can rent a shack—they almost give them away now in France. The less meat I eat the better. I shall have plenty of fish, some bread and potatoes, and some cheap local wine, which frequently is better than any of the expensive vintages one buys. A few francs for newspapers, stationery, fishing equipment, and an alcohol burner. This will not be the first time that I have had to count pennies. Before the revolution all my life I lived on twenty-five roubles a month. . . . Why haven't I thought of it before? Because I had no notion that I had eight thousand francs. I shall live in a place where there is not a single Russian, no Gay-Pay-Oo, no Gestapo, no Nadia, and no Kangarov. I can live there quietly for a year, and after that we shall see. Probably I will die, and the mayor will have to issue orders to bury me at the town's expense. That will

be the end of the stormy career of a man who was known as
Ney, Chatski, Ooralov, Kirdjali, Dacocci, Wislicenus, and devil
knows what else. . . . The proper thing to do is to die in
someone's arms [that also is an idiotic expression: no one ever
died in anyone's arms!], but one can die nicely without that,
without urns, without speeches, without lies, without mentioning
the fight for freedom. . . ." He was happier than he had been
for a long time.

Next day Wislicenus visited several stores which sold fishing
tackle: for a long time he stood gazing at the windows, entered,
inquired about prices, and carried away a catalog. For three hundred francs he bought everything he needed and could not stop
admiring his new acquisitions. "I cannot decide which is the
cause and which the effect: am I retiring to the symbolic Castellan
because of my politico-pathological state, or is the politico-pathological condition the result of my urge to retire? Probably it is not
a question of cause and effect—everything happened simultaneously. All I know is that I refuse to be one of them any longer.
I stood the cruelty, the rottenness, the spilling of blood as long as
I believed that we were building a new life. But when it becomes
apparent that we are heading for a hopeless muddle to everyone's
sincere and malicious delight, there is nothing else I can do. Join
the enemy camp? Write sensational disclosures about our affairs
and our people for the capitalistic press? Not on your life!" he
thought with disgust.

Wislicenus glanced at his watch: it was time for his appointment with Nadia. "I can spend a half-hour there. We will chat
about all sorts of trifles, she will say that I look well, that I am
on my way to recovery, that angina pectoris is not uncommon,
and that I will live for a long time, provided I follow strictly the
instructions of Professor Fouquot. I doubt that I shall see Kangarov: he thinks that it is better to avoid courtiers who have fallen
into disfavor. As long as I have promised her, I had better be on
my way. Probably she will enjoy my visit even less than I, but our
time is not that valuable. I will stay until six, then I will return

to Paris, have dinner, and go to a moving picture theatre, or else
I can go home and finish reading Gogol. I am sorry the weather
is bad. . . ." He was annoyed when he remembered that in the
evening he had an appointment with Siegfried Mayer. "What in
the devil is he after? I told him that I was going out of town today,
to the sanatorium, that I would return late, and that I would
leave the day after tomorrow. No, he insisted upon seeing me!
Probably some gossip. . . . He is a curious fellow—he wants to
know everything: where, when, why . . . I ought to call him,
and tell him that I cannot keep the appointment. . . ."

Lazily (the very thought of his new freedom made him lazy)
Wislicenus rose from the couch and began to dress: he had been
lying on the couch in his shirtsleeves, like a character out of Gogol.
He examined his coat with distaste: there were spots on it, and
one of the buttons hung by a single thread. Wislicenus reached
into the cupboard for his other, more presentable suit. Absent-
mindedly he stuffed some change, the bus tokens, his pocketbook
and his fountain pen into the pockets. Buttoning the collar he
noticed that its tips were frayed, but he did not care ("a year ago
I would not have gone to see her looking like this"). He consulted his notebook for the best way to get there. Over the telephone Nadia had explained everything in detail. . . . "If you
come by train, it will be quicker, and the railroad station is nearer
the sanatorium. But the buses run on a regular schedule, and I
would advise you to take a bus—it's only a fifty-minute ride, and
a pleasant walk at this end. Get off the bus when you see a small
tavern with the peculiar name of '*Taverne du Puits sans vin.*'. . . .
The conductor will tell you. . . . They know the place because
most people, with the exception of capitalists who have their
own cars, come out by bus. It's about a ten-minute walk from the
bus stop. I hope that does not frighten you?"

Wislicenus stepped out of the hotel door and looked around:
his shadow was nowhere in sight. With a feeling of relief he
strolled toward the subway station, and walking down the stairs,
found difficulty in breathing. "That's not my heart. The subway

is hard, even on people who have nothing wrong with them. It's a breeding ground for microbes—the sun never penetrates down here. . . ." He remembered that the hour for his daily cigarette was near, and was annoyed to discover that he had forgotten his cigarette case. He had emptied the vest and coat pockets of his other suit, but he had overlooked the pants, and he always carried cigarettes and matches in his pants pocket. "I will buy some on the way, and then I will have enough for my trip to Provence. If I have no heart attacks for a month, I may increase my daily allowance. . . ."

XIV

"This is your stop, Monsieur," said the unusually talkative conductor who had been chattering throughout the trip. "Take this road up the hill, turn right at the second corner, and walk toward the grove of trees. Hidden behind them is the sanatorium—it's a large, three-story building. A blind man may miss it, but a cross-eyed one will run right into it." "Is it about a ten-minute walk?" "That depends on how fast you walk. A track man could make it in five minutes, but an average person, if everything goes well, should be able to make it in a quarter of an hour. There is no pleasure in being outdoors in weather like this—sitting at home is much better." A passenger in a black coat stepped off the bus, looked around, and turned up his collar. "If you intend to live in this sanatorium you should buy a car—then it's a very convenient place. . . ." "This road, up the hill?" "Yes, second turn to your right. If you are not in a hurry you might want to sit down in that tavern over there and have a glass of wine. That's where the other passenger is going. . . ." "Professional buffoons who have a local reputation as wits are always unbearable," Wislicenus thought, irritated by this form of democratic familiarity. He thanked the conductor and stepped into the street. "Happy cure, Monsieur," the conductor called and pulled the bell rope with more than the usual vigor. "Maybe I should wait until this shower is over. I may be a few minutes late, but I will not be soaking wet. There is the '*Taverne du Puits sans vin.*'. . ." It was a miserable-looking place in an ancient, dilapidated, single-story building. "The house must be three hundred years old. You find places like this only in France."

The man in the black coat, who apparently was not sufficiently tempted to go in, stepped out of the doorway to let Wislicenus enter. In the grim semi-darkness of the room a woman who had a figure like a crinoline was standing at the bar talking to a man in a denim blouse and a pair of blue, tattered pants. Two other men were sitting at a table in a far corner. There was no one else in the place. "A glass of hot wine," Wislicenus ordered, taking a table by the window. "Shall I have my smoke now? No, I will wait until later. Then I can have all these pleasures at once: a cigarette, Nadia, and tea. . . . I am beginning to sound like that conductor on the bus."

Wislicenus pulled aside the window curtain. The sky was hopelessly and depressingly grey, he was struck by the ominously dismal appearance of the country; all he could see was sickly, wet trees and a monotonous road leading uphill toward a grove. "Why should anyone build a tavern on this spot? Can they possibly depend on these bus passengers? But there are thousands of taverns like this all over France which exist no one knows how or why. The proprietor ekes out a bare living, and that's all. '*Taverne du Puits sans vin*'? A hundred or two hundred years ago something must have happened in this house. People have long since forgotten what it was, but though it has changed hands at least fifty times, the tavern still retains its old name."

The woman who looked like a crinoline brought the wine, complained about the weather, and to show her appreciation to a new customer turned on a light. The glare of the bulb disclosed endless rows of full and empty bottles, standing or lying on the shelves along the wall. *"Vous vous ruinez, patronne,"* the fellow in a blouse said with a laugh. Wislicenus took a sip of the wine, and his thoughts ran on to his future life in sunny Provence. "About this time of day I shall be housekeeping in my shack: making soup, or cooking something else." The picture made him smile. "I wonder whether I have forgotten how to make fish soup since the days on the Yenissei? A table set with fresh bread, wonderful country butter, a bottle of wine and tea. What else can a man need to make him happy? . . ." Suddenly he felt gay. "Perhaps the fresh air will help me? I might squeeze through another ten years—who knows? What else can happen? Maybe Nadia will come down for a visit? Kangarov also is a sick man. It would be most appropriate if they were to bury him in the Red Square to the tune of 'You have fallen a victim.' . . . How amazing that every one of us has someone he hopes to see die. . . ."

Wislicenus drank the wine and gazed out of the window—the rain had changed to a drizzle. "I can't wait any longer. It will turn dark, and I shall lose my way. . . ." *"Quel sale temps,"* the woman said again as she took the money. "Yes, that's our hard luck that we have to live in this *'sale temps,'* " he thought gaily. "In the twenty-first century the world will be a better place. But even the twentieth century is not bad if you are under the southern sun, and away from people. . . ." Wislicenus walked out of the door and with relish inhaled the moist country air. He directed his steps toward the side road and up the steep incline. "I hope that I won't have an attack as a result of this climbing. . . . That is the only thing lacking to make the afternoon a success. . . ."

Beyond the wall of the inn ran a high fence covered with ugly, battered posters, and farther on was a row of crooked, leafless bushes which seemed to grow at extraordinary angles. A cyclist riding in the opposite direction, toward the inn, glided past. A house with a lighted window appeared for a second from behind the foliage of a tree. After that there was nothing but barren ground. The day was drawing to a close, but darkness had not

yet settled. Somewhere in the distance a train blew for a crossing—there was something unexpected about the long, angry sound.
"Where is the railroad? Nadia told me that I could come out to
the sanatorium by train. The station must be on the other side of
the hill. . . ." Because of the rain Wislicenus was walking faster
than usual. "By the time I get there I shall be wet, and my shoes
will be covered with mud," he thought. "I hope that the tea is
boiling hot. . . ." With glee he remembered that he still had his
cigarette to look forward to. "And what about Nadia? It will be
nice to see her. . . . This is the first crossing. The second crossing must be up there, where the road is lighted. For some reason
a mixture of twilight and artificial light is always unpleasant...."

A man emerged from the shadows, looked over his shoulder,
and started to walk in the same direction ahead of him. "What
looks so strange about him?" Wislicenus asked himself uneasily.
A long way up the hill a straight line of tiny lights appeared.
"That must be the sanatorium. Another ten minutes at least. I
haven't reached the half-way mark. . . . Why, that's the man
who came down on the bus with me!" he suddenly was electrified by an uncomfortable realization. "Where was he while
I was drinking the wine? . . ." Wislicenus stopped and saw not
more than fifty feet away two men approaching him from behind.
His heart missed several beats: they were the men who had been
sitting silently at the corner table in the tavern. "Certainly! . . .
That's who they are! . . ." Even in the failing light there was
no mistaking them. "What is this? Can this possibly be it? . . ."
He quickly reached for the back pocket of his pants and with a
chill remembered that along with the cigarettes he had forgotten
his gun. With a nervous jerk he resumed the climb. "How was it
arranged? . . . Mayer? . . . I told him where I was going. Could
it have been anyone besides Mayer? . . ." The bobbing, reddish
light at the second crossing became brighter. "It's a car. . . ."
Rapidly increasing his pace Wislicenus glanced back: the men
also had increased their pace and were keeping up with him.
"There cannot be any doubt! . . ." Panting, almost on the run,

he approached the corner. Along the side road from the right, quite close to him, a large automobile with low red lights was slowly approaching the crossing. "Is that also part of it?" Wislicenus asked himself in a whisper and stopped. His heart was beginning to pound. Suddenly he felt a pain—a cutting, dizzily growing pain. "A heart attack! That's the end! Is it the Gestapo or the Gay-Pay-Oo? If it's the Gay-Pay-Oo, it's Nadia! . . ." A red-haired man with a brutal face sat next to the driver. "That's the man! But where have I seen him before?" strangling with an unbearable pain Wislicenus had time to ask himself. His hand shot up to his heart. A yellow wooden packing box flashed before his eyes.

XV

"I AM LOSING my mind!" Nadia sighed and deposited the beautiful, transparent, modern fountain pen on the writing-desk. It was a present she had received from Kangarov on her birthday. "This Parker has just about ruined me," he had said, kissing her and presenting her with the package (it was a perfunctory, fatherly kiss, warranted by the occasion). "The price of a present is not supposed to be revealed, but I will tell you a secret: it cost me three hundred and fifty francs. . . ." Nadia glanced at her watch: quarter past five. Wislicenus had promised to come at five, but it was difficult to time a bus trip from Paris to the minute: the buses frequently ran considerably behind schedule. "Perhaps the rain detained him? . . . He will not stay more than an hour and a half. This will give me a little more time for work before dinner, and after dinner I can work as long as I please! . . ." Proudly Nadia remembered that when she worked in the evening, she found it difficult to fall asleep: all writers, even the great ones, had this trouble. "Nothing can be done about it. . . ." She re-

signed herself to a sleepless night—or rather to a sleepless evening
—though usually she was ready for bed after about thirty minutes
of strenuous mental effort.

Waiting for a guest interfered with her creative mood. "As
soon as I begin to write, he will arrive, and I shall have to ask
him about his health and pretend that I am terribly interested.
Why did I ever invite him?" Nadia asked herself angrily. She
had no time to waste. Exerting her will power she picked up her
pen and resumed work on the end of the chapter: "Everything
was ablaze with orange, autumnal flames. The puddles splashed
heavily under one's feet. Eugene Gorsky entered the machine
shop. 'Yeremeich, we shall finish the sixty-first one today!' he said
happily. 'Let's go to it, old fellow. We are working for defense—
the defense of our Soviet land!' 'We will make it, Eugene,'
Yeremeich answered. 'We understand things now. . . . We have
not fought the civil war in vain. . . .' 'So you haven't forgotten
that battle on the Volga, old comrade?' 'It was not the kind of
thing one forgets in a hurry. . . .' An angry light flashed in the
steely eyes of Kartalinsky, who was working on the motor."

The plot she had built around Kartalinsky was worrying
Nadia. A man who sold the secrets of aviation production in the
U.S.S.R. to foreign fascists and White guards deserved no consideration, and could not expect any mercy. There could be only
one end: the firing squad. But Nadia had no desire to execute
him. In the first place, there was no sense in describing a firing
squad: the story never would be published. Besides, Nadia was
not at all certain how and where firing squads operated; she
had heard sinister stories, repeated in whispers, about the "Ship
of Death" and about the "Black Raven," but she was afraid that
these stories were dated. Anyway, an execution was not a pleasant
theme, even if the criminal was a saboteur and a wrecker. "Shall
I let him off with ten years? No, that would make the punishment
disproportionately light. . . ." Most important of all, deep in her
heart Nadia found the man with the steely eyes not sufficiently
repulsive for such a fate: she felt sorry for Kartalinsky.

Nadia had compromised with her conscience: she had chosen the subject with an eye to the market. Gene, who worked on one of the Moscow magazines, had suggested that she send two stories to the editors, so they would have something to choose from. "We will publish the better one of the two." (Nadia knew very well that in this instance the editorial "we" should have been "they.") He offered her other advice. At least one of the stories should be about wrecking activities. "If the story is about wreckers and saboteurs we cannot very well afford to turn it down. You understand. Period." Nadia was annoyed. Her first was a simple story about love, and about the adventures of a young and very beautiful Soviet girl who worked in one of the embassies abroad. But saboteurs and wreckers were out of place in that story.

The second story presented an entirely different problem. In a way it was also about a young and very beautiful Soviet girl, and it also was a love story, but the background was sabotage and wrecking activities. The action took place in an airplane factory. Nadia never had been near an airplane factory, but Basil, the young engineer who had written her the charming letter from Moscow—"not exactly a love letter, but something of that sort" —was working in one. In the story he was portrayed photographically as Eugene (Eugene was Nadia's favorite name). The only difference was that she changed the color of his eyes to black so that readers should not recognize him—if he himself guessed it, she would not mind. Eugene was an engineer-flyer. Nadia was doubtful on this technical point. Was there such a thing as an engineer-flyer? Maybe the engineers never flew planes? But the plot of the story left her no choice: it was while Eugene Gorsky was piloting the plane that horrible suspicions first assailed him.

"What has happened to Wislicenus?" Nadia wondered. Instead of ordering tea at the sanatorium, she had prepared everything herself. "My dear child, they will soak you twenty francs a head for five-o'clock tea!" Kangarov had told Nadia in a voice which indicated admiration for people who could charge such prices. "Ten francs for a glass of awful port!" She made a mental note

of the information. She did not want this particular bill for entertainment charged on their joint account, though Kangarov had
given her a free hand. "Order anything you want, my dear! Ask for
birds' milk if you want it!" he had said in a tender, fatherly voice.
The sanatorium was not in a position to supply birds' milk, and
their tea was not very good: buttered toast—"you can hear people
chew it a mile away"—lemon, milk, and a limited quantity of
cookies. Nadia paid for everything with her own money, and
without going to any great expense. Early in the morning she went
to Paris and bought some common pâté instead of Strassburg pie,
some red instead of black caviar, and some Banyuls instead of
port—"I will tell him that it is port; after all, he is not a connois-
seur of wines." The round table was loaded with a decanter, a
cake, and three kinds of sandwiches (the third kind was Nadia's
specialty: something vague and involved, topped with a slice of
tomato). At the sanatorium she had won the right to make her
own tea, using the excuse that she had to have Russian tea. "The
manager definitely disapproves: he keeps looking at our teapot
out of the corner of his eye," Nadia had said the first time she
made tea. "I hope that thief and robber keeps looking out of the
corner of his eye until he is cross-eyed!" Kangarov had answered
indignantly.

"'Don't try to be too clever!' Olga said in a calm majestic tone.
Kartalinsky blushed. 'You will regret this!' he said in a horrisonant
voice. 'I doubt it. You will have more reason for regret than I.
People like you are not wanted in the Soviet Union.' At that
moment, squeaking in a minor key, the door of the machine shop
opened, and they heard the strained hum of an airplane motor. . . ."

Nadia was very pleased with this passage and felt that it could
not be improved. She was proud of the "horrisonant voice," even
though she was afraid that the typesetters would be tempted to
spell it "horizontal." Only one thing annoyed her: she remembered that the door squeaking in a minor key already had been
used by another Soviet author. "But that was years ago, and, be-

sides, I am sure that he used 'major key.' Not all doors make the same noise, and not all writers have a perfect ear," she reassured herself coyly. The details were of secondary importance, and the finest writers could not have done any better. The important thing was the plot: what should be done with Kartalinsky?

For a minute Nadia let herself daydream. The story would be accepted for immediate publication. It would be a success—nothing extraordinary or sensational, but still a success—she would be paid for it and asked to contribute regularly; invitations would arrive from other magazines. "From then on I will be able to write a story a week. Very soon I shall have enough of them for a book. . . ." She imagined a small volume in a dark blue binding with the title in silver letters, or a grey binding with letters in two colors: red and black. There would be a charming colophon in the middle, and in the bottom right-hand corner the price: "4.50." In her mind she even saw the last page: "Editor . . . Technical editor . . . Proofreader . . . Chief typesetter . . . First printing: 40,000. . . ." "Why shouldn't it be forty thousand?" There also would be a blanket invitation: "Reader! Tell us how you liked the style and contents of this book, indicating your age and occupation." Nadia could see hundreds of letters from people of every conceivable age and occupation, which would be forwarded to her abroad. "I will try to answer most of them. Every writer has had to do it. . . . But what about Kartalinsky? What should I do with him?"

She pushed aside the notebook. "I will work some more this evening, and I will finish it tomorrow. I will make a copy for myself and send the original to Gene. Perhaps I better make two copies: if one magazine should refuse it, I can send it somewhere else. Those robbers say openly that they will not be bothered returning manuscripts. . . . Apparently Wislicenus is not coming? . . . He may be ill, or else he is terribly rude! If he arrives after six he runs the chance of having to face the ambassador. . . ." Nadia laughed at the very thought of such a meeting. "And there was a day when the ambassador referred to him as 'my dear comintern' . . ." Her fingers idly picked a piece of candied fruit off the cake. Though she resented Wislicenus' failure to keep the appointment, Nadia was in high spirits. "If Gene were here we could get some music, and dance. . . ." Nadia walked over to the radio and with one turn of the dial loosed the magic. The measured, rich voice of the announcer was reporting the latest news: ". . . *Le duc et la duchesse de Windsor ont terminé leur voyage à travers l'Allemagne, après avoir eu l'occasion de visiter en détail, sous la conduite du docteur Ley, chef du front du travail, la plupart des organisations du parti national-socialiste. . . .*" "*On parle beaucoup ces temps-ci d'entente cordiale, de solidarité des democraties française et britannique. Il convient de signaler le rôle patriotique considérable que jouent les 'Fines gueules,' cette élite gastronomique française, qui rend aujourd'hui visite à nos amis d'outre-Manche. Les marchands de vin de la Cité, aux traditions et privilèges séculaires, ont organisé en leur honneur une brillante réception dans une charmante hostellerie des bords de la Tamise, dont le propriétaire, un vieil ami de la France, a amassé quelques poudreuses bouteilles. . . .*" "*Maître Dominique Cerisier fera signer demain son pourvoi en cassation à Gonzalo Alvera condamné à mort, pour un double assassinat, par la Cour d'assises de Versailles. . . .*" "*Le célèbre orchestre de Cuban Boys nous est revenu après une tournée triomphale à l'étranger. Il nous apporte le Chévéré, un lamento nègre d'une rare beauté. Jamais encore l'âme noire, sauvage et sentimentale à la fois, ne s'est exprimée aussi fidèlement et avec une telle puissance. . . .*"

XVI

DURING HIS last days in Paris before leaving for Spain, Tamarin was kept busy every minute. The first opportunity to pack his things came two hours before train time. He hated to rush, and he was anxious not to forget anything. In the morning he had pulled out of the cupboard his suitcase which he had bought in

England before the war. Now he stuffed it with his shoes, books, underclothes, suits, and some food. The result was not impressive, and the general sighed, remembering his old orderly. When he was not rushed he could do better than that even without an orderly. His shoes, wrapped in a newspaper, were packed next to the sausage and the tea, the books were crushing the collars, and the sleeves of his new coat were not folded properly. Closing the suitcase required a tremendous effort; Tamarin found it necessary to rest and catch his breath: "I must be getting old. . . ." When finally the straps had been tightened he discovered something white—could it be a handkerchief?—sticking out at one end. Angrily the general forced back with his finger the offending white piece of cloth, glanced at his watch, cursed, hurriedly threw his toilet things into an overnight bag, and sent for a taxi. The typewriter was in the black case; the clamps held it in the right position, and he had no difficulty in adjusting the top. At the last moment he saw the Spanish pocket dictionary on the night table (though he had been very busy he had made an effort to learn a few Spanish words during the last two or three days). "Maybe it is better not to have it in the suitcase: I may have occasion to use it on the way. . . ." He stuck the dictionary in his pocket. "Have I forgotten anything else? Passport, papers, money, key. . . ." Tamarin took leave of the proprietor—"I shall rest for a month in the South and be back"—and accepted the proffered good wishes for a pleasant journey and good weather. He shook hands with the porter and found the procedure distasteful, as though the handshake was intended as a reward for services rendered or as evidence of a political creed. He had included the usual ten per cent for tips when he paid the bill in the morning. "Shall I give him something extra?" Tamarin pressed a twenty-franc note into the porter's hand, counted the pieces of baggage, and sighed with relief.

After all the rushing around the general arrived at the station a full half-hour before train time. There, too, he experienced some difficulty: he forgot to ask the station porter his number.

"Where in the hell is the damned fool? Only ten minutes left, and he is nowhere in sight! Has he run away with the baggage? . . ." But the porter appeared on the platform on time. Very much relieved the general gave him an extravagant tip, asked him as well as the conductor whether it was correct that the train made a direct connection to his destination, once again counted his baggage—"suitcase, overnight bag, and typewriter"—hung his overcoat on a hanger—"I must not forget that there are four pieces now"—and relaxed. He was ashamed of himself for acting like a country yokel. But his fellow second-class passengers at once recognized in him a man who by comparison with them belonged to the upper strata. His appearance as usual was that of an old-school gentleman.

The seat which the general had reserved three days ago was a good one: in the corner of the car and facing the engine. Tamarin had decided against traveling in a sleeper: probably they were watching him at the station, and would consider it an unnecessary extravagance. For a while he read the paper—he had not had time to look at it in the morning, so he had not bothered to buy the evening edition. Around ten o'clock his neighbors turned out the lights. As usual there was an awkward hesitancy: is it time to turn out the lights, or does someone wish to continue reading? Silently everyone agreed that it was time.

Tamarin rested uneasily: he had forgotten how to travel, and once again he thought sadly that his age was making itself felt in little things. "Before, I never would have started on a railroad journey without a traveling cap and gloves. I also forgot to buy some toilet water. . . ." He could not find a comfortable position in the corner: either his head was bumping against something hard, or his legs were going to sleep. After shifting his position he thought for a minute or two that he was comfortable at last, but very soon he found that there was no improvement. More than anything else an anxiety about his ill-fated Spanish assignment interfered with his rest.

Actually there was nothing alarming about the instructions he had received from his superiors: he was ordered to familiarize himself with the situation on the Madrid front, and to make a report to Moscow. "The mission is of a purely military nature and has no connection with the Gay-Pay-Oo, or with anything of that sort . . ." The assignment could be considered an honor which showed the confidence the government had in him. Besides, it was interesting, it gave him a chance to study a modern war at first hand—not much of a war, but still a war—and it provided him with an opportunity to verify his theories about the use of motorized troops. But even taking all this into consideration Tamarin would have given a great deal to be relieved of the assignment. His life in Paris had been so pleasant and so calm. "If they are sending me to Spain, they are just as likely to recall me to Moscow. . . ."

In a small French town near the border he was met at the station and conducted to the right place. A good, wholesome breakfast was waiting for him. At the door stood a large new Buick. Tamarin's first impression was excellent—everything was well planned. He took a stiff drink of brandy for good luck, saw that his suitcase, overnight bag and typewriter were deposited safely in the car, and started on his way. The morning was fresh and sunny. Tired after a night on the train, Tamarin closed his eyes and awoke only when they reached the border.

The place looked like a station, but there was no evidence of a railroad. Trucks and passenger cars were everywhere. The walls were plastered with flags, notices and posters. "A market day in a country town!" Tamarin thought and with eager eyes tried to read the signs while the car slowly made its way through the traffic. "*Partido Socialista Unificado . . .*" "*Confederación Nacional del Trabajo. . . .*" "*Federación Anarquista Iberica . . .*" The car stopped in front of a large building. From inside came a strong harsh voice of a kind that is not used in private conversation, but is reserved for public speaking. "What is going on in there? Are they holding a political meeting?"

A grey-haired man wearing a semi-military uniform, a black and red beret, and a black and red scarf, approached the Buick. The driver said something to him in a whisper. The man gave a clenched fist salute. Not knowing how to respond, Tamarin looked at him in silent amazement: "Do they really take things like that seriously? . . ." Taking the general's papers the grey-haired man introduced himself in French as an anarchist and as chief of the local "Investigación" (Tamarin guessed that this was another name for police). "Your papers will be ready in a few minutes. Would you like to eat something while you are waiting?" he inquired politely, giving Tamarin a firm handshake. "Thank you. . . . I believe you are holding a meeting?" "Yes, the Republic has received a gift of several ambulances from the British Labor Party," the anarchist explained coldly. "And something else has arrived from Moscow. . . . The Moscow shipment is not a gift. It has been paid for in gold," he added unexpectedly, apparently unable to restrain himself. "We are very grateful. A fellow-countryman of yours is about to speak. Would you like to hear him?" "My God! Did I have to travel all the way to Spain to attend political meetings?" Tamarin wondered. The anarchist glanced at him, and evidently reading his thoughts, smiled crookedly. "Perhaps it would be better if you were to eat something after your journey. You will have to excuse us: the food leaves much to be desired."

He led the guest to a buffet, said something to the waiter, bowed and left. The waiter also greeted the visitor with a clenched fist salute. The selection displayed on the counter was very small: two bottles, some sausage, and some dry bread. "I can make some hot chocolate for you," the waiter said in halting French. Tamarin hastily declined. "I believe I would enjoy a glass of wine."

There was no one else in the room. "They all must be at the meeting. . . . The wine is not bad. . . . But I better not try any sausage. . . . I am glad I had a good breakfast before crossing the border. . . . I hope they will not be offended. . . ." Tamarin wanted to be careful of their feelings. "I wonder if they will accept French money? . . ." He wanted to call the waiter, but he was not sure how to go about it—"it would be rude to bang the glass on the counter!" He held up a coin and said something indefinite. The waiter walked over, smiled and refused to take the money. "*Ami. . . . Ami russo,*" he said, and of his own accord offered to change the francs into pesetas. "Yes, please, if you don't mind!" Tamarin said. "That's where he will hook me! . . ." But to his amazement the waiter mentioned the same rate that had been quoted to him in Paris. "Official rate of exchange? He has not charged me anything extra. . . . What nice people!" "You still are using the old money?" he asked, noticing a picture of Alfonso XIII on the bill. The waiter laughed. From behind the wall came a burst of applause. The same voice shouted something loud and gay in Spanish. The applause grew in volume, was followed by a silence, and suddenly Tamarin heard an unusually high voice say in Russian the familiar: "Comrades and citizens! . . ." "One of our professionals! . . ."

For a minute or two Tamarin stood listening. The unnaturally high shouts alternated with Spanish sentences which also were spoken in a high voice though not quite as high. Evidently the interpreter was trying to speak in the same key. "You will never make it! That other fool began with a high *do,*" the general thought, examining the unfamiliar coins on the counter and trying to memorize their values. The waiter was saying something in an obvious effort to be polite and hospitable. Tamarin nodded obligingly in response.

The general found everything he saw strange and entertaining: the people who greeted one another with clenched fists, the way they said "*Salud!*", the newspaper called "*Solidaridad Obrera*" lying on the table, all the words ending in "*os*"—"*Mineros Asturios*"—the black and red poster floating opposite the window with huge letters: ". . . Miguel Bakunin." "The waiter has so much natural dignity, he looks more like a *caballero* than a waiter. The policeman, too, is very pleasant. He has an intelligent face and looks as though he has been through the mill. That's one thing I cannot understand: how can an anarchist have charge of the police?" Tamarin had a high opinion of the police as an arm of the state, but he also had a gentleman's inborn repugnance for policemen.

"Here are your papers. This is called 'hoja de ruta,'" the chief of "Investigación" said. "What does 'hoja de ruta' mean? 'Ruta' must mean 'route'? It must be a road pass," Tamarin tried to think quickly as he nodded pleasantly. "They may ask you the password." "Yes?" The anarchist leaned forward and, lowering his voice, said: "Durruti. Todos para uno." "Durruti. Todos para uno?" Tamarin repeated self-consciously, feeling like a child reciting a lesson. As they were walking out of the door, the waiter wished him good luck and firmly shook his hand. ". . . The fascist butchers of the Spanish people!" behind the wall the voice was shrieking wildly. The applause which lasted for almost three minutes sounded like a roll of thunder. There was an announcement in Spanish, followed again by a round of applause which this time was more restrained. The next voice spoke in English; it was not a professional, but rather a human, unassuming voice. "Like talking to a few intimate friends after visiting the circus."

The chief of police suggested that he leave the road pass with the driver, shook hands, and wished Tamarin good luck. "Salud," the general answered, feeling more at ease. "I must admit that their police are extremely polite. Well, I passed the first test with flying colors. God willing, I shall not have any trouble. . . ." Several more signs flashed by, they drove under a huge red, yellow and purple flag, under another that had broad yellow and red stripes, and then they were on the open road. At first Tamarin looked at everything with curious eyes. "So far, it is difficult to realize that this country is torn by a civil war. True, the front is a long way from here. . . . I must not forget the password. 'Durruti. Todos para uno . . .' 'Durruti. Todos para uno. . . .'" He could not think of a suitable mnemonic sentence.

The roads were as good as they were on the French side of the border. A row of snow-capped mountains could be seen in the distance. Mountains always exhausted Tamarin; their beauty seemed to him exaggerated. "After the French countryside this country seems poor. . . ." Occasionally they passed bearded pedestrians with sacks and heavy sticks over their shoulders. Going in the opposite direction they met a mule pulling a strange-looking vehicle which must have been built a hundred years ago. A young boy held the reins and behind him, sitting in a majestic pose, was a handsome old man with a grey beard, a red vest, a tremendous hat, and a dagger. Indifferently, without the least trace of curiosity, he glanced at the Buick. Actually it was not a glance: the car crossed his line of vision, and he merely refrained from averting his eyes. "A beautiful sight! A regular Spanish grandee, even if he is a peasant!" Tamarin thought with admiration, his spirits rising with the fresh air, the wine, and the brilliant sunlight. He liked the Spaniards better and better.

The general settled more comfortably, and made an effort to plan the balance of his day. The next stop was scheduled in a town where he was to receive travel information from a Russian official. Tamarin did not look forward to this meeting. "No, he cannot possibly be a representative of the Gay-Pay-Oo! . . ." The general looked at his watch—there was plenty of time. He stretched out his legs and once again closed his eyes; at intervals he opened them and stared with amazement at the road, the fields and the people.

It was some time before they reached their destination. "A nice-looking town. . . . Pleasant women, but there is nothing particularly Spanish about them. . . . Where are the mantillas?" Tamarin hummed lazily as the car made its way to the official's house. He was not quite certain about the position occupied by this official. "He is not an ambassador, he is not a consul, and he certainly is not a Gay-Pay-Oo man. Besides, what difference will it make even if he works for the Gay-Pay-Oo? He will tell me the best road to take and where to stop, and all I need say is 'thank you, comrade,'" the general tried to reassure himself though he knew very well that there was a difference.

The official received him in a nice office which must have

belonged to some private concern. A young, pleasant-looking man rose from behind a desk piled with papers, and warmly greeted the general. "No, he has no connection with the Gay-Pay-Oo. And he looks like a real Russian," Tamarin thought with relief.

". . . Paris notified me that you were coming. Unfortunately I only heard from them yesterday. But I am very glad that you are here. It's high time!"

From the very beginning the official was extremely complimentary. His words indicated that he knew with whom he was dealing, that he considered the visitor an important man, and that he attached great significance to his arrival: from now on everything would be different. As a rule Tamarin was not susceptible to flattery, but he found the official's attitude pleasing. At the same time he was somewhat embarrassed: apparently his arrival was linked with exaggerated and unjustified expectations. He wanted to clear up such a misunderstanding at once, and to say that he was sent merely as an observer, but he checked himself. "How can I tell with whom I can be frank? If that is what he has been told, why should I correct his impression?" During his stay in Paris Tamarin had forgotten many of the Soviet ways, but he firmly remembered that it was better not to say too much. "He certainly is not with the Gay-Pay-Oo. He is a civilized man, very much like the Russian officials before the war. This is the new school, which has nothing in common with Kangarov!" Smilingly the official discussed the civil war in an amused tone which seemed to imply: "They are a curious, a very curious people, and their war is curious, and if it were not for us the whole thing would collapse."

". . . If we are to discuss this subject at any length we may as well do it in a systematic way," he said. "When are you planning to leave for Madrid, General?"

"You even know my old rank? That's remarkable!"

"What is so remarkable about it? Everybody knows you."

"Thank you. . . . When am I planning to leave? Any time. . . . Right now. . . ."

"Please! You sound like Souvorov, but even Souvorov must

have bivouacked somewhere every night! Besides, you have to have some food. Let's do it this way: have dinner and spend the night with me. I have an extra room and an extra bed. Tomorrow you can start at dawn, and you will be in Madrid by nightfall. How about it?"

"I really don't know," Tamarin hesitated. He wanted to accept the invitation, but he was not sure whether it was the politic thing to do. Nothing about his assignment was pressing, but his instructions contained the words "proceed with all possible speed." "This can mean anything. . . ." "I really don't know," Tamarin repeated, hoping unconsciously to shift the responsibility for his decision on the official's arguments.

"Naturally, you must do what you think best," the official said as if guessing the thoughts which were running through the general's mind. "But how will you travel tonight? I can get a very good car for you. . . . Your car? Didn't they tell you that your car has to return to France? That's one of their rules," the official explained. For a second the word "their" seemed to bring them closer together, but they instinctively recoiled from each other almost immediately. "I will get an excellent Buick for you—there will be no trouble on that score. But it will be more difficult to find an interpreter."

"What interpreter?"

"Do you speak Spanish? Then you need an interpreter. For some reason we always get girls for that kind of work. They manage very well, and they are not afraid, though some of them are very young—the younger generation is very promising. Unfortunately, both of my girls are away. If only they had given me a few days' warning," the official expostulated. "So let's do it this way. We already have a very good chauffeur for you. He is a German from the International Brigade. He was wounded on the Madrid front, and now he works as a driver. You don't have to worry about him: he knows the roads, he drives carefully, and he takes good care of the car. But he cannot speak Spanish. He may know a word or two, but not enough to get along. As a bodyguard I can give you a real Spaniard who speaks French. You speak

French? That's fine! He is a very nice young man and a party member."

"Why do I need a bodyguard?"

"That's the usual procedure."

"Aren't the roads safe?"

"That depends. . . . Ever so often their planes go on a rampage. They drop bombs and strafe the roads. In some of the cities we now have anti-aircraft guns, but the open roads are not protected."

"But what could a bodyguard do against a plane?"

"All sorts of things have happened," the official answered evasively. "Anyway, that's the usual procedure. And he can serve as your interpreter as well. . . . How long are you planning to stay in Madrid?" he asked quickly. "Two or three weeks? Good! In that case he can stay with you, and you may return him to me on your way back. Does that suit you?"

"I am very grateful."

"Happy to be of service, Your Excellency!" the official said breezily. ("At times he sounds like Kangarov.") "If you will excuse me for a few minutes, I will make the necessary arrangements, and then we can enjoy our dinner." He started for the door, but suddenly remembering something stopped, came back, absent-mindedly pushed back the ash-tray, and just as absent-mindedly closed the roll-top desk. "No, he definitely is not one of the old school!" Tamarín decided without being offended, but with a certain bitterness, as though the action of the official characterized the essence of the difference between old and new Russia. "I only hope they will not recall me!"

"Everything has been arranged," the official announced as he re-entered the room a few minutes later. "The driver has his orders. The bodyguard has been told what to do. Incidentally, he is delighted to know that he is to accompany you. Your room is ready. If the dinner is not yet ready, it will be ready in a minute. Let's move to the dining-room. No one else is coming—just you and I."

They entered another room (apparently the official was not

cramped for space). A table covered with a passably clean white tablecloth was waiting for them. With satisfaction Tamarin noticed a couple of bottles and an assortment of hors d'oeuvre, including some caviar.

"Fortunately I am in a position to offer you some real food. I have just received a package from Moscow. Some vodka, some caviar—I am afraid they are spoiling me," the official said in an effort to justify such luxury, but noticing his guest's eyes fixed caressingly on the bottle, he relaxed. "Who else deserves to be spoiled? We lead a dog's life! . . . Do you ever take a drink? Allow me! . . ." By now Tamarin had had time to become convinced that the official was not one of the old school, but vodka and old-fashioned hospitality, which has overcome obstacles since time immemorial, created an intimate atmosphere. They both felt gay and carefree.

"How about another one? . . . That's good! I insist that you try the caviar—it left Moscow only a week ago. So you want to hear my opinion? I shall be glad to tell you all I know."

At great length the official expressed his views on the Spanish situation. He spoke with ease, with so much ease that Tamarin was surprised. "He is a competent bastard. All the young ones are competent: they have gone through a different school of life." The general listened attentively to every word. Much of what the official said seemed absurd to him, but the young man spoke with such confidence, and with such force, that Tamarin found himself unable to withstand the pressure, though the vigor of the words depended not so much on the speaker's conviction and logic, as on his emotion and the structure of his throat and vocal cords. The implied if not the literal meaning of the official's words was that the Spaniards had no conception of how to conduct a civil war, that they should not be allowed to plan military operations, and that the command should be left in Russian hands. "Whose hands in particular? Is he prepared to take over the command?" Tamarin wondered, though after the third vodka he was inclined to be benevolent.

"How about equipment?" he asked cautiously, taking advan-

tage of an interruption while the official was busy with a drink.
"How are the two sides matched in that respect?"

"Their air force is stronger. We estimate that they have about
seven hundred planes, a hundred of which they received from the
Germans, and the rest from the Italians. When it comes to infantry
we have the advantage, and most important of all, the people are
with us. In a civil war that's a very important factor."

"What about tanks? Artillery? Officers?"

"They have the edge in tanks and in artillery. But their officers
are no good."

"You mean there is not a single outstanding man among
them?" Tamarin sounded doubtful (inwardly he was prepared to
share this opinion: he had heard of no one with an orthodox
military education). He mentioned several names he had seen in
the papers. After each name the official said "blunderer," or "old
blunderer," or even something stronger.

"I never should have guessed it. . . . How about your officers?" Tamarin asked and instantly regretted his carelessness: he
should have said "our."

"To be honest, our officers are not much better. There are
some good ones in the International Brigade—some Frenchmen
and some Germans. They can command a battalion, or even a
regiment. Not to mention such people as Modesto and Lister,"
the host said playfully, his tone implying that they could be
included without any reservations. "They are fine fellows, but I
doubt that they can meet the situation."

"How about Miaja?"

"Miaja? . . . But what can he do? The entire situation depends on the rest of Europe. And on that particular point I should
like to hear your opinion. . . ."

Just then the main course was served and their conversation
was interrupted for several minutes. Later, Tamarin was not
given another opportunity to express his opinion on the European
political situation. The official took the floor and spoke inces-
santly with the same extraordinary and devastating forcefulness.
He mispronounced the names of all European statesmen: he

said "Daladier" as though it were spelled "Daladieu" (the first time he heard him say it Tamarin was startled), and in saying "Hore-Belisha" he managed to accent the "e." He passed judgment on the European statesmen with great self-assurance as though their souls were an open book to him, and he ascribed their every action to perfidious motives. Tamarin was no expert on international affairs, but it was obvious to him that the young man knew next to nothing about them. He was just as ignorant about military matters, though he never hesitated to venture an opinion or to use technical terms. "Why doesn't the damned fool shut up for a while? His opinions on international affairs are bad enough, but when he begins to apply his Marxist theories to military matters they are simply grotesque!" Tamarin thought. He listened patiently and politely. But when his host launched into a long discourse about the conflicting interests of the British capitalists and British middle class, the general felt that he was growing numb with boredom. With difficulty he swallowed a yawn, and though his lips remained firmly compressed he became frightened: what if he noticed the stiffened jaw and neck muscles?

"Yes, yes, the Paris and London policies are not too clear," Tamarin hurriedly agreed.

"Not too clear? They are very clear! Those capitalist hirelings hate the Spanish revolution, and their only desire is to strangle it. All as a result of their hatred for us!"

"That's possible. . . . It certainly is true of the attitude of Germany and Italy."

"I am not even mentioning those bastards! With the Germans we have a life-and-death struggle! It's either they or we!" the official said with finality, and poured himself another glass of wine.

"And what do you think will be the outcome here in Spain?"

The official set the glass on the table and glanced suspiciously at his guest.

"The outcome? Victory will be ours!"

"I hope so. . . . I merely wanted to know on what you base your hopes?"

"It is not a hope—it is a hundred per cent certainty! First of all it is based on the fact that the people are with us. Our soldiers fight like possessed men. The Fifth Regiment alone is worth an army! That's the party regiment—they are real fighters! In the second place the other side is staffed with blunderers. And third, and most important of all, we will win because Comrade Stalin told us to win!"

"Certainly!" Tamarin agreed hastily again. "This is an excellent roast. . . . Apparently you have no reason to complain of a food shortage?"

"It is very difficult to generalize," the official answered evasively. "Let me give you another piece. . . . How about another glass of wine? . . ."

"Thank you. . . . Are you here by yourself? Are you married?"

"I am married, but my wife and child are in Moscow," the official said with a sigh. "Probably they are being held as hostages," Tamarin thought and also sighed with compassion. The host looked at him out of the corner of his eye. They drank their wine in silence.

"With your permission I will leave you immediately after dinner. I am afraid I shall have to work most of the night. And if you will take my advice, you will go to bed early: it's a long journey to Madrid. I will tell them to wake you at six."

"Better make it five," Tamarin said, feeling that an early start somehow would repay for the pleasant night.

"Anything you say. You can be up with the sun, even if you have to use a Buick instead of Souvorov's old carriage. . . . Souvorov was a genius. . . . Western Europe never produced a general like him. . . . They cannot keep up with us, anyway! Why did we admire the West so much in the old days? If the truth were known, they are not good enough to serve as a doormat for us. . . . How about finishing the bottle? The wine is not bad, though personally I prefer Crimean wines."

"Just half a glass. . . . I never was particularly fond of Crimean wines. Give me Caucasian wines every time—they go to your head and your feet at the same time," Tamarin said sadly. "But this wine is very nice. I certainly appreciate your hospitality. There are several practical questions I wanted to ask you. . . ."

"Anything at all. You will have enough gasoline—the driver has the necessary requisitions. I also will see that he has the 'hoja de ruta.' You must memorize the new password. As far as Madrid you can use: 'Lenin dos dos.'"

"'Lenin dos dos?' That's easy. I almost forgot the old one: 'Durruti. Todos para uno. . . .' But no one ever asked for it. I certainly am indebted to you for all the trouble you have taken. Where would you suggest that I stop in Madrid?"

"I can make a reservation for you in a hotel without any difficulty. But my advice is that you stop where I usually stop. It's quieter and much more comfortable. . . ." He mentioned an address. "It is better not to write it down. Both the driver and the bodyguard know the place. They have been there a number of times, and I will tell them where to take you."

"I am very grateful. Just one more question. . . . It is just a minor detail, but I should like to have your opinion. . . . I brought a uniform with me, but I don't know whether I should wear it, or whether I should continue to wear civilian clothes? . . . In a way civilian clothes seem to be advisable, on the other hand if I visit the front a uniform seems more appropriate. Unfortunately, I forgot to ask them about it in Paris."

The official became lost in thought.

"As a general rule our people wear civilian clothes. But they have worn uniforms at the front. After all, there is no longer any secret about it. I would advise a uniform."

"You really would?"

"You will be shown the proper respect. At present the country is ours for the asking. The prestige of the Soviet Union was never higher than it is at this moment."

"Undoubtedly," Tamarin agreed dejectedly.

XVII

TAMARIN had difficulty in going to sleep in the Soviet official's house. For a long time he tried to systematize his first impressions of Spain. He wondered whether he had forgotten anything important, or whether he had said anything superfluous. "No, I believe there is nothing to worry about. . . . What impressions can I possibly have after one day of traveling in a car? At first glance the country and the people are delightful. It would seem that they should be able to get along without killing one another. God only knows why they are involved in this civil war? Perhaps they have no idea themselves. . . . Or, perhaps they know, and we cannot understand it. How much did Western Europe know about our revolution? Or what do we know about what is happening in China? After reading the papers for several years I remember only two names: Sun Yat-sen and Chiang Kai-shek. But that does not concern me: clearly, my job is to study the local situation, and to make a report to Moscow. Without knowledge of Spanish it will not be easy. I must admit that the talkative comrade said some interesting things. . . . No, I don't believe I told him anything I shouldn't," Tamarin thought lying on his back. "There are no two ways about it, this war is absurd. People united by ties of blood, language and faith, kill one another over ideas which are not even mildly interesting to nine-tenths of them. And now our Machiavellis are involved in it" (he remembered the voice in the border town saying: "Comrades and citizens! . . ."). "They simply cannot stay out. And I am working for them. . . . It seems to be awfully cold in Spain. . . . I wonder if I am catching cold? The comrade has excellent vodka. . . ." Tamarin remembered the last dinner with Nadia in Paris and sighed. "I wonder what she is doing now? I didn't have time to see her before I left. When I am in Madrid I will send her a postcard. My mission is supposed to be secret, but, after all, Nadia will not write General Franco about it. . . ."

He was dropping off when he was startled by a wild shriek in the street. *"Sereno!"* someone was yelling gleefully. "What in the hell is that? What does it mean? *'Sereno'* means 'quiet.' That's a wonderful way of settling everyone for the night," Tamarin thought with a smile. "Wonderful, that's wonderful! Just like a scene out of 'Carmen.' . . ." The shouting of the watchman gradually retreated into the distance. As though in answer to his cordial invitation the noise in the streets grew in volume. Trucks rattled along the pavement. Tamarin fell asleep with a broad smile on his face.

Though five was the hour agreed upon, the general was called at six-fifteen. Trying not to make any noise he washed his face and took his uniform out of the suitcase. It was slightly wrinkled and had an odor of mothballs. Tamarin was annoyed: after all, he was an official representative of the Russian Army. He took out the English razors, picked out the best one marked "Tuesday," and shaved very thoroughly. The process of pulling on his high boots seemed more difficult than it had been in Russia: he had lost the knack.

Despite the early hour, breakfast was waiting for Tamarin. It was brought on a tray by an elderly Spaniard who had waited on the table the night before. There also was a basket of food packed for his journey. "No, he really is a very nice and considerate person," Tamarin thought about the official, and was slightly nonplussed by his own "no." "He is a nice and considerate person. Too bad old Russia makes no effort to understand new Russians. . . ." The problem of tipping, which worried Tamarin more than usual, was solved very simply: after hesitating whether he should tip a Spanish comrade and if so how much, the general shook hands and while doing it slipped him a folded bill, just as he would to a doctor. The Spaniard responded with a warm handshake, stuck the money in his pocket, and thanked him with great simplicity and dignity. "Wonderful! A real *hidalgo*! . . ." Tamarin thought with admiration as he descended the stairs. "Strange that the comrade should have a Spanish servant: very unusual . . ."

The general walked straighter than usual—on parade grounds in the old days his bearing never had been more military. Even the wrinkled coat looked well on him. A large, new, shiny Buick was waiting for him at the door. Two men jumped up and saluted him with clenched fists, one of them freezing at attention. The other was a very young man. "That must be the Spanish bodyguard," Tamarin guessed, holding back a smile. Never in his life had he seen such a walking arsenal: the young man had a rifle, several hand grenades on his belt, a sword, two guns, and a dagger. The general's experienced eye immediately recognized the Russian, eight-round, regulation guns; the rifle was of a make with which he was not familiar, and the hand grenades were small and probably made in Poland or Czechoslovakia. "How can one make head or tail of all this: they are radicals, and they are helped by democrats, by fascists, and even by us. True, they pay for the help they are receiving. And they are not getting much help at that: 'here is two cents' worth of ammunition, and don't bother us again!'" Tamarin philosophized as he answered the salute: he raised his hand and, instead of clenching it into a fist, compromised by bending his fingers together. The young man was watching him with admiring eyes. Despite the number of weapons he was carrying, there was nothing military about the appearance of the young Spaniard. But the driver, an unusually blond man of about thirty, with a red stripe on his sleeve, was a real soldier. Even his clenched fist salute seemed military. Tamarin looked with appreciation at his motionless figure. "He is a German!" he remembered. "As a military salute the clenched fist may not be so bad. . . ."

"Were there any orders?" Tamarin asked the bodyguard, addressing him in French. "Let's get under way. Are you ready?"

"Oh, yes!" the Spaniard answered eagerly. The German also said something in French. His words were difficult to distinguish, but they sounded like: "Yes, Your Excellency. . . ." This was music for Tamarin's ears: for twenty years now he almost had forgotten their sound. "I cannot very well say: 'God be with us, boys!' I don't know how to say it in French, and it would be out of place. They are not boys, and they have no use for God." He muttered his approval, and climbed in the back seat. The bodyguard proudly removed the cover from the machine-gun mounted on the car, and to Tamarin's relief settled next to the driver. "Thank God, I shall not have to talk to him!" At the suggestion of the bodyguard Tamarin handed him the road pass.

Several street loiterers gathered around the car: the general's uniform seemed to arouse their curiosity. A wagon drawn by a donkey rolled slowly by. An unbelievably ugly old woman sang out: *"Agua! Quien quiere agua!"* Tamarin followed her with a fascinated and approving gaze: this woman leading a donkey and selling water fitted nicely into his conception of Spain. The bodyguard ran over to the wagon, politely raised his cap, and bought a bottle of water. *"Agua, agua! Mas fresca que la nieve,"* the old woman began to shout again. The German angrily pushed the bottle further down the seat, muttered something under his nose, and waiting for the final order fixed his bulging eyes on the general. "Go ahead," Tamarin said in German. The driver's face brightened, and once again he repeated the same unintelligible phrase. Gradually gaining speed the car rolled through the empty streets. They stopped at the city limits. With a flourish the bodyguard mysteriously gave the new password: *"Lenin dos dos"*—instead of the old: *"Todos para uno,"* and showed the road pass. The officer of the guard glanced at it quickly, handed it back, and saluted. Before them was an open road.

By contrast with the road which Tamarin had traveled the day before from the French border, there was evidence of war on every side. The military control was more strict. Patrols stopped the car at every bridge and crossing. At one post the loyalist officer stared suspiciously at the driver and evidently recognizing a German demanded to see his papers. The driver took out of his pocket a neatly folded booklet in a leather cover with blue stamps pasted on it. Leaning forward, Tamarin saw the words: *"República Española . . ." "Brigades internacionales . . ." "Grado Sargento . . ."* The officer exchanged a few words with the bodyguard (Tamarin could not understand what was said), and nodded. The soldiers saluted and let the Buick pass. "I am glad to see that they take such precautions. More power to them!" the general thought approvingly, but the outward appearance of the loyalist soldiers did not inspire him with confidence. They passed several marching columns. Tamarin studied the men from head to foot. He was unpleasantly struck by their ill-assorted uniforms: colorful coats of the old royal army marched side by side with blue and khaki blouses, leather jackets, African robes, and awkwardly worn frivolous-looking cloaks. There was just as little uniformity about their weapons. The soldiers made no effort to hold ranks: the general and the driver watched them with disapproval. "That in itself is not fatal. Some of the best armies— for instance the Japanese—are not much on parade grounds," the general tried to be open-minded: he disliked unmilitary-looking armies, and it was difficult for him to judge the fighting qualities of troops who showed lack of proper drill. "I don't give a damn what anyone says: the old Russian and Prussian Guards were the best troops in the world! But the Spaniards have excellent human material. Their infantry was always famous. . . . Too bad they have no organization."

The lack of organization was very apparent. By studying the tired, angry faces of the soldiers Tamarin guessed that they had been marching for a long time without proper nourishment. On a siding where the road crossed the railroad stood a long line of empty freight cars and of cars filled with soldiers. Judging by certain signs, imperceptible to the eye of a civilian, Tamarin knew that this was not the first day, or maybe not even the first week that the freight cars had been standing there. Around large storage oil tanks there was no evidence of interceptor planes or of antiaircraft artillery. "What would prevent them from blowing them up? Why do they leave them undisturbed? In a civil war espionage is always an easy matter. They must have many sympathizers over here, and these must have many of them over there. If they haven't located these oil tanks they are incompetent, and if they have and are not doing anything about them, they are worse."

Tamarin wondered about his report. "To find out which side

has greater chances of victory! How can I find out? Suppose that I can learn a great deal about the resources of the loyalists in Madrid. As usual they will exaggerate them and I shall have to make certain allowances. I will visit as many sectors of the front as they will show me. But what can I learn about the enemy? Let's assume that they have reports, estimates, and information gathered by secret agents. Usually that kind of material is not reliable. And even if the information is exact today, it may be worthless tomorrow. The Germans and Italians can deliver any amount of ammunition, planes or even men, to Spain. What can France and England do? They are handicapped: they are democracies!" Though a liberal in his sympathies, Tamarin had a poor opinion of democratic military efficiency. "That is another factor I have no way of judging. It is an equation with several unknown quantities," he fell back on the usual formula. "From a strictly military point of view neither side can count on a victory: one is weaker than the other. The most important unknown quantity is the fighting spirit. And what earthly way have I of judging that? They have saddled me with a great responsibility: I may predict one thing, and something entirely different may happen. . . ."

Tamarin stirred uneasily as he remembered his unfulfilled predictions about the Abyssinian war. "Then I was not the only one wrong. The greatest military authorities in the world shared my views. There was one who was worse than all the others, but, though he is an old man, if there is another European war probably he will command the French Army. No one will dare remind him of his predictions. It is different in our case—they are likely to put us against the wall, without a war. Wrong about Amba-Aladji, wrong about Spain, and that's that! Am I afraid? No, but it is not very pleasant. . . ." Tamarin remembered his thoughts about personal bravery. He had no doubt about his own physical courage. "But what they so glibly call moral courage is a complex matter."

The Spanish scenery was not inviting. Everything was bare, bleak and seared by the sun—the only color was grey. The sky was of the same shade: a muddy, greyish white, like water colored with several drops of milk, and when occasionally the sun broke through the clouds it turned a yellow-grey. Tamarin felt that the landscape seemed more African than Spanish, except for the temperature which was much too cold for Africa. "I suppose it can be said that there is a *'couleur locale'* but it is not very Spanish," Tamarin thought, trying to piece together everything he had ever known about Spain. He could visualize only a few things: "Carmen," castanets, mantillas, duennas, rope ladders, and a monument to Christopher Columbus. "The sun should be bright in this part of the world. This kind of weather is contrary to all regulations. In Spain there has to be lots of sun." Even with his coat buttoned all the way up, he was chilly. He was not hungry, but he wanted something to drink that would warm him. Impatiently Tamarin stared at the basket. of food. "I wonder what they have packed in there? I doubt that there is any vodka. . . . Who knows? Maybe my luck is holding, and they have not forgotten it. . . ."

Around eleven they reached a place that was either a large village, or a small town. The driver stopped at a garage, produced another neatly folded paper, and demanded gasoline. His request seemed to irritate the attendant, who complied sullenly. While the gasoline tank was being filled, Tamarin strolled around restoring the circulation in his legs and trying to get warm. In the town square stood a padlocked church. "Looks like a fine, old piece of architecture," he thought uncertainly: architectural styles were an unknown quantity as far as he was concerned. "Cervantes may have worshiped here, or some Lope de Vega. . . . There was a man like that, but I have no idea what he wrote: too bad I never have read him." Several street urchins gathered around the general: his uniform seemed to make an impression, though he was not sure whether it was favorable. In a small house a woman angrily slammed a second-story window and shouted something at him that sounded abusive. Tamarin hurried on. In the window of a food store he noticed some unappetizing looking sausage, some unwashed vegetables, and several empty bottles. The window glass was badly cracked. Sighing at the sight of the bottles Tamarin looked at his watch. "Time to eat lunch."

When he returned to the car the bodyguard, looking embarrassed, asked Tamarin whether he would allow them to stop and have something to eat. "Certainly! They have packed some food for us," the general reassured him hurriedly. "There is the basket. . . . Shall we eat here, in the car?" The young man blushed, stammered and explained that the basket was not intended for all of them: that they had their own food. He added that there was a café around the corner, and that while it was doubtful that they had any food, there always was a chance. "Good! Let's go there!" The bodyguard rushed to the driver and excitedly told him the news. Apparently the German also was pleased, but Tamarin had the uncomfortable feeling that he had slipped a notch in his estimation.

Tamarin made a motion to lift the basket. The face of the bodyguard registered horror, as if the weight of the basket was about to crush the Russian general, and with an air of determination he grabbed the basket handle. The driver carefully locked the car, his face indicating that hereabouts no one could be trusted. The café was only a short distance away. On the corner the bodyguard pointed out a building that had been bombed. On one side the wall was gone and two stories looked like open closet shelves. The moving-picture theatre next door also had been hit. On the remains of a crumbled wall hung a torn, but freshly printed poster, singed at the edges, which seemed dimly familiar to Tamarin. "If I am not mistaken there is something Russian about it. . . ." The poster showed a long-haired Hercules in a red shirt and with a sword in his hand, another man with empty bleeding eye sockets, and a brilliant gathering in a ballroom of fabulous dimensions.

"We seem to be quite the fashion!" Tamarin thought with mixed feelings. The young man explained excitedly that the last

time he was here he had seen a Russian film, and that on the
following night the town had been bombed, and many women
and children had been killed. "Everyone always kills women and
children!" Tamarin thought sceptically, assuming the artificially
solicitous expression customary when the death of strangers is
mentioned in the course of a conversation. They both felt that
in order to show proper respect for the subject they had to continue walking in silence. Strangely enough, most of the people
they met were women and children. But on the corner, in front
of a two-story stone house, they saw a crowd of men, most of
whom were armed, dressed in military and semi-military attire,
and wearing peculiar red-lined cloaks with slits for the arms.
For a second, Tamarin's memory went back to the regulation red
lining of his old general's uniform, and he sighed without knowing why. "They certainly are picturesque! And at least this
crowd looks Spanish. . . ."

Curious eyes followed their progress. Some of the soldiers
saluted the general, but many deliberately looked the other way.
There was a terrific noise inside the house. "This may be a house
like any other house, and then again it may well be the place
where Lope de Vega lived in his day!" From above came the
rasping, hoarse shouting of a loudspeaker which cut through the
roar and laughter of voices in the street. The noise became louder
as the crowd rushed inside the house. "This is the local republican
club," the bodyguard explained. "It is also the brigade headquarters. . . ." He mentioned the number of the brigade. "Why
don't you go in and ask: maybe something important has happened?" Tamarin suggested. "We can all go in—no one will stop
us." Tamarin glanced with amazement at the German, who
laughed and derisively waved his hand.

They ascended the stone steps and entered a large, crowded
room with a domed ceiling and a stone floor. The din was terrific;
people were talking in loud voices, the loudspeaker was rasping, typewriters were clattering, and telephones ringing. Newcomers wearing mantles, cloaks and smartly polished boots en-

tered the room in a continuous stream. Tamarin could not take
seriously these men who wore officers' uniforms, just as he could
not take seriously this bedlam as the headquarters of a military
organization, no matter how small. The smoke was so thick that
Tamarin felt groggy. The bodyguard returned after asking some
questions and announced that a great victory had been won, but
that he was unable to get the details. *"Quatsch!"* the German said
firmly. "Let's go!" Tamarin ordered. He was amused, and at the
same time his military instincts were offended. "I suppose this is
an out-of-the-way place, and we are a long way from the
front. . . ."

The café was all that Tamarin had expected to see in Spain.
It was more a cheap roadside inn than a café. The right half of
the building apparently was intended for livestock. "Even now
they probably come here riding donkeys and mules. Certainly
Don Quixote and Sancho Panza have spent more than one night
under this roof. . . ." To the left was the kind of kitchen that
is described in novels, with a large open fireplace, and with ropes
and pulleys hanging from the beams of the ceiling. "That is
where they hang the quarters of beef. . . ." Adjoining the
kitchen was a large dining-room with wooden tables and old-
fashioned chairs, and with a small table on a slightly elevated
platform for the proprietress. The proprietress, a venerable woman
with a mustache, looked uneasily at the military guests. After a
conversation with her the bodyguard sadly reported that there
was no food with the exception of . . . He used a long, difficult
word. "What on earth is *avellanos?* If that is the only thing we
can get, let's try it," Tamarin suggested benevolently. "How about
wine? Have they any sherry?" The question seemed to surprise
the bodyguard. He again consulted the proprietress and returned
saying that sherry was available, and that it would be served immediately. The German nodded vigorously, indicating that this
was also his choice. Both men stood looking at the general,
apparently waiting for an invitation. "Sit down," Tamarin suggested. He almost added "citizens," but his tongue stumbled on

the French *"citoyens."* Somehow in Russian and in Moscow the word had a more natural sound, especially since 1920. Though in the early days of the revolution Tamarin had always felt that he was being ridiculed when he was addressed as "citizen."

They chose a corner table. Tamarin sat on the bench, and his companions on two chairs facing him. The bodyguard deposited one of his guns on an empty chair, and stood the rifle in the corner. He used the second gun to occupy his hands, like a singer toying with a rose or a handkerchief while rendering a number on the concert stage.

"Why not put away the other gun? There seems to be no immediate danger," Tamarin was in an indulgent mood. The young man smiled self-consciously. The German unwrapped a small package, took out some bread and sausage, and stuck the string in his pocket. Tamarin opened the basket. His companions gave an involuntary exclamation when they saw its contents. There was ham, fried chicken, fruit, and a pie: there was even a fork, a knife and some mustard. "He is an extremely thoughtful person!" Tamarin decided, feeling gayer than ever. He felt a slight pang when he noticed how hard his companions tried to keep their eyes averted from the basket. "Our fellows at least have plenty to eat, God bless them—not like these! . . ."

"We can divide this into three equal parts," the general said with exaggerated casualness as he tore the paper which stuck to the ham. The bodyguard blushed. "And you can give me some of your sausage, which looks very tempting," Tamarin added considerately.

The proprietress brought the sherry, some glasses and a thick, heavy drink which tasted like chocolate. Tamarin filled the glasses with wine. "Please, not so much for me!" the bodyguard exclaimed with obvious sincerity. He took one sip and pushed the glass aside. The German looked at him with contempt, emptied the glass in one gulp, and examined the label on the bottle. Tamarin immediately refilled his glass. Two elderly Spaniards entered the café and bowed politely, first to the proprietress and then to the general and to his two companions. The driver and the body-guard quickly finished their share of ham, chicken and pie. "They haven't tasted food like this for a long time. . . ."

"At Kempinski's in Berlin they always had excellent sherry," the German said. Tamarin filled his glass again. "I was not hinting," the driver explained, and thanked Tamarin, speaking with much greater deliberation than he had used until then. "In the old days before Hitler I often ate at Kempinski's and I always began with a glass of sherry, or with some caviar. '*Caviar im Eisblock*' . . . A wonderful hors d'oeuvre!" he added with a slight bow, evidently intending it as a compliment to a Russian. "I know of nothing better, unless it is *Rheinlachs* with mayon-naise? . . ."

The driver told them that he was born in Magdeburg, that he was the son of a civil servant, that he held a doctor of philos-ophy degree from the University of Berlin, that he had occupied an important position in the socialist party, that he had worked for the party organization and had written for the socialist papers, and that he had had an excellent chance of being sent to the Reichstag at the next election.

"My candidacy already had been approved by the party councils. But because of Mr. Hitler I had to leave the country, though I am a hundred per cent Aryan. There is not a drop of Jewish blood in my veins. . . . Don't misunderstand me—I am not anti-semitic," he added hurriedly. "Some of my best friends are Jews. I merely am stating a fact."

"You are a sergeant?"

"I was wounded, recommended for a decoration, and was supposed to receive an officer's commission three months ago. But the way things are done here, there was the usual delay," the German answered glumly. The tone of his voice indicated that he had a low opinion of Spanish efficiency. Tamarin shook his head sympathetically and asked the Spaniard in French:

"I suppose you don't speak German?"

"Not a word!" the German angrily interrupted the young

man. "Fortunately I know a little French, though I am forgetting it rapidly. We had a Swiss governess when I was a boy."

"That's excellent—at least we have one language in common," Tamarin said and changed the subject to military matters. The bodyguard asserted that there could be no doubt about the ultimate victory.

"What makes you think so?" Tamarin inquired cautiously.

"The people hate the fascists. Our enemies are fighting for selfish class interests, while we fight with real spirit! A magnificent spirit!" the bodyguard exclaimed passionately. "We are hungry, we have few weapons, we perish from bullets, hunger and sicknesses, but we will win."

"Certainly," Tamarin said. "I wonder what sicknesses he means? Could it be typhus?" Remembering the civil war in Russia, he unconsciously made a mental note to make some further inquiries. "If I have to die, I hope it will not be from typhus lice. . . ." The Spaniard was talking about the war in a disconnected way, partly because he was awed by the presence of a Soviet general, and partly because he could not find enough French words. He spoke French fluently and with an amusing accent which was much more pleasant than the accent of the German. It developed that he was the son of a factory worker in Irún, that he had worked in a machine shop since he was twelve, that at first he had joined the anarchists, but that later he had realized that he had made a serious mistake. The anarchists were a party of the middle-class and not of the proletariat.

"Am I not right?" he asked the general deferentially.

"Certainly."

"I joined the party only two years ago," the Spaniard continued. After that, he referred to the communists simply as the "party," just as British cabinet members, when they say "His Majesty's Government," refer to the British government, and not to the government of any other monarch. "After leaving the anarchists I joined the Trotskyists. This also was a mistake."

"Fighting spirit is unquestionably a great thing, but you cannot fight tanks and airplanes with spirit alone. You must have weapons, organization, and discipline," the general said, speaking with a slight trace of acerbity.

"*Das sag ich ja eben*," the German agreed and nodded his head emphatically.

"I also realize it, but the discipline here is very easy-going," the bodyguard answered apologetically and began to talk about the splendid fighting qualities of the loyalist army. The driver listened with a smile of contempt.

"And what is your opinion?" Tamarin asked him.

"My opinion?" the driver asked in German. "My opinion is that Madrid or Franco cannot affect the outcome. Everything will be settled in Berlin. If Mr. Hitler sends German troops, they will win without any trouble. But if they [he nodded at the Spaniard] should continue fighting against the Italian gentlemen, then . . ." Once again he made a derisive gesture with his hand.

"You really think so?" Tamarin said, inwardly sharing the German's opinion. "You may be a socialist, but you still speak about Herr Hitler in a different tone of voice from that in which you speak about '*den italienischen Herren*'," he thought, pouring the last of the wine into his glass. Without any warning the Spaniard asked Tamarin whether he had ever known Chapayev, and was obviously disappointed when he received a negative answer. He had enjoyed the film very much.

"And I also liked *Michael Strogoff*. . . . Is it true that the Tsar tore out the beards of the Russian boyars with his own hands?"

"Only when the offense was very serious, and even then not oftener than twice a month," Tamarin answered, cursing inwardly and instantly regretting his joke. Rolling his eyes, the bodyguard recounted the atrocities committed by the Spanish fascists. He mentioned tortures, burning people alive, and putting out their eyes.

"Have you ever witnessed anything of that kind?"

"No, I never have, but I have seen bodies with their eyes

gouged out," the young man answered in an offended tone. Suddenly Tamarin remembered the performance which he had seen in Nadia's company at the theatre of horrors in Paris. "He may not be lying, at that," he thought uncertainly. "Nothing seems impossible. . . ."

"How about your soldiers? Are they in the habit of torturing prisoners?"

"Never, our enemies lie about us," the bodyguard answered without much conviction. The driver shrugged his shoulders. "We only shoot spies," the bodyguard added, staring at the German. "Probably both sides are lying," Tamarin consoled himself. "There you have a real theatre of horrors! No one has to bother about buying tickets. . . ."

Suddenly there was a commotion at the table where the two Spaniards were sitting. Both old men sprang to their feet and shouted at one another in a continuous torrent of words. "What's this? I am glad they have no daggers. . . . What on earth are they angry about?" Tamarin wondered. The bodyguard listened curiously to what they were saying. The proprietress also looked in their direction, but without any sign of concern. Flailing their arms the old men screamed wildly at each other; their faces were disfigured with passion. Unable to understand a single word Tamarin had the impression that momentarily they would be at each other's throat. "Go to it, boys!" he thought, feeling mellow with the sherry. But, instead, they gradually lowered their voices, the insane shrieking dropped to an ordinary argument, and then to a normal conversation. Their angry faces brightened with smiles, they sat down, and resumed their discussion in a friendly and easy manner. One of them turned to the proprietress, raised his hat, and ordered two more cups of *avellanos*. "Just a literary argument," the bodyguard explained without registering any surprise. The driver shrugged his shoulders and glancing inside the basket, said wistfully:

"Nothing left for supper. . . ."

"We will have supper in Madrid," Tamarin answered. He was

pleased with the lunch. Conversation on a footing of equality
with the two men gave him an unaccountable sense of satisfaction
that surprised him. Despite the revolution and the Soviet regime,
his experience told him that cameraderie between generals and
enlisted men was not sound, and that it constituted a danger to
the efficiency of the army. "I suppose they are Spaniards and
rational beings. . . . But then, in 1917, as soon as my soldiers
became rational beings, everything went to hell. . . ."

The driver asked Tamarin whether he had known Lenin.
The general had a strange sensation that the German had an
irresistible impulse to bestow a title on Lenin, and to word his
question: "Your Excellency, did you ever know His Excellency,
Lenin?"

"No, I never did."

"And Stalin?" the bodyguard asked excitedly, his eyes glowing.

"No," Tamarin answered. His companions appeared to be
disappointed. The conversation lagged. "Should I drop Nadia a
card from this place?" Tamarin wondered. "Is there a mail box
somewhere near?" he asked. "I doubt it," the German answered.
"Usually you will find mail boxes on street cars in the larger
towns." "Certainly there are mail boxes here. There is one right
across the street from the café," the bodyguard said indignantly.
He obtained from the proprietress a post card with a view of the
town. Tamarin took out his fountain pen and wrote several lines.
"Shall I mail it for you?" the driver asked. "Yes, please," Tamarin
accepted without too much eagerness: he always felt safer when
he mailed his letters himself. The German took the card, quickly
glanced at the address, saw the word "Mademoiselle," and smiled
with an air of gentlemanly understanding. "All right," the driver
said in English. Like all Germans he was an "anglophile":
while he never missed an opportunity to abuse the English, he
considered them the finest race of people in the world. Returning
a minute later, he said with an ironically glum expression that
the box was sealed and handed the card back to the general.

"I believe you wrote it in Russian?" he asked. "If you write it in French the chances will be better that it will reach its destination. Anyway, it is safer to mail it in Madrid."

"Why can't I write in Russian?" Tamarin asked angrily. "Let's get started. I suppose we will not reach Madrid before seven?"

"If nothing goes wrong we should be there by eight. That damned fellow in the garage would not give us enough gasoline. He swore that he had no more. We will be lucky if we find any along the way. . . ."

"What if we can't find any?"

"Probably we have enough, unless we have to go on a detour near Madrid."

"Why a detour?"

"There is a dangerous stretch of road there. Let me show you."

The driver took out a notebook on the cardboard cover of which were the neatly and beautifully lettered words: "Diary of a Revolutionary Fighter." He looked inside, but decided against tearing out a page. Instead he picked up the piece of paper in which the ham had been wrapped, and drew several crooked lines and a circle.

"*Da haben wir Madrid, Puerta del Sol,*" he said placing a bread crumb in the center, and began to call off other names: Morata-Tajuna, Serro Rojo, Caranbancel Bajo. Tamarin had a vague mental picture of the front around Madrid, but he had not realized that they would have to pass so close to the enemy lines. "Their lines of communication are, to say the least, precarious! . . ." It occurred to him that, if he were taken prisoner he would be shot without any waste of words. This was a most unpleasant and disturbing thought: so far, in the wars in which he had taken part, generals who were taken prisoners were never shot.

"It will be dark when we get there. Luckily I know the road. I was wounded near Madrid. . . . If I had been on any other front, I would be a commissioned officer now. That's the way things are done in Madrid!" the German said and again waved his hand. The bodyguard rose to his feet, and, while he was adjusting his belt with the dangling hand grenades, he upset the salt dish. His face turned white. Hurriedly opening the window, he picked up his glass and splashed out the water that was left in it. Tamarin watched him with amazement.

"They consider it a bad omen. If you spill salt, you must spill some water. He is as superstitious as a peasant woman. He even carries a charm around his neck. . . . A fine Marxist!" the driver said in German, his voice ringing with contempt.

XVIII

DARKNESS WAS settling when they heard the rumble of artillery in the distance. Tamarin had not expected that he would find the sounds so exciting: "to think that after twenty years I should see another war!" More than once of late the thought had occurred to him that, perhaps, he was not a military man by nature, and that if, instead of graduating from a military academy, he had attended the regular schools, he would have made a good professor of physics or history. This thought gave him a sense of futility, but now, hearing the hollow, distant, unmistakable rumble, Tamarin felt a joyous exhilaration.

When they reached the top of a hill the German mentioned that from this spot one could get a clear picture of the Madrid front. Tamarin climbed out of the car and pulled out his field glasses and notebook. He could not see very much. Still he was able to make a rough sketch. The bodyguard watched him with the same deferential expression with which the young aides must have watched Napoleon on the eve of Austerlitz. A conviction was written on his face that he was witnessing the birth of a brilliant idea. The driver measured the gasoline in the tank and cursed under his breath.

The number of military patrols increased. The inspection became more and more thorough. At every cross-road and bridge officers in khaki uniforms scrutinized the road pass more and more minutely. Frowningly they asked the bodyguard questions which he apparently resented, because he blushed, and glanced back at the general, explaining apologetically that they were asking all sorts of nonsense.

At one of the crossings the driver stopped, looked at the map, and asked several questions of the soldiers, who were mounting guard without an officer. The soldiers eagerly supplied the information and shaking their heads, pointed at something on the road. The driver looked at his watch, for a second became lost in contemplation, glanced back at Tamarin, settled behind the wheel, began to say something, changed his mind, and started the car. The guards shouted at him, but he merely increased his speed. Tamarin, who had been dozing, his head full of pleasant reveries, felt the cold wind and shifted his position. "I must be catching cold!" he thought in a peculiar daze. A minute or two later the cold and the striking change of speed woke him again. The car was careening wildly along the road. They had not traveled at such speed before; as a matter of fact Tamarin never remembered traveling so fast in a car in his life. Shivering and blinking his eyes, he tried to gather his wits. The driver was leaning over the wheel like a jockey riding in a race. Next to him the bodyguard with a rigid, white face also was leaning forward clutching his knee with one hand, and a hand grenade with the other. "What's wrong? What has happened?" Tamarin felt that this was not the time to tell them to travel slower and not to take unnecessary chances. Suddenly—like a bolt out of the blue—the thought of treason occurred to him: what if these men were kidnapping him and taking him across the lines to the fascists? At that moment the road became flanked by hills, and the driver cut down his speed. He exchanged several words with the Spaniard, laughed, and holding the wheel firmly in his hands leaned against the back of his seat. The bodyguard unclenched his hands and with youthful delight turned to the general. *"Ça c'est bien,"* he said. *"Ça c'est bien. . . ."* Obviously pleased with himself, the German explained that they just had passed a very dangerous stretch of the road. "From now on we are safe. The other way we would have had to make a long detour, and we are almost out of gas," he said. Tamarin felt the urge to reprimand him: he had no right to take such risks without first asking his permission. But because of his fleeting suspicions the general was ill at ease, and decided against admonishing the driver. "Victors are never wrong," he began, but found it difficult to translate the sentence into French or German. Instead he curtly nodded his approval.

Darkness had settled when they arrived in Madrid. The firing had died down. Zigzagging sharply, the Buick slowly made its way through a narrow passage in a street barricade. Tamarin, who while he was still in Paris had carefully studied the map of Madrid, tried to get his bearings, but he could not see any landmarks in the darkness. He was excited chiefly because of an unusual military situation: a besieged capital. "Terribly dark! I never have seen a city so blacked out! . . ." Street lights were far apart, the car slipped through tiny pools of light, and immediately was swallowed by darkness. The driver managed to see the way in some mysterious manner. "Where are we? Are we in the suburbs, or are we near the center of town?" Groups of men, most of them in uniforms, stood around the street lights. Muffled voices reached them from behind closed shutters of the houses. Through one partly closed shutter he saw men sitting around tables in a lighted room, and for some reason this glimpse of a café had a reassuring effect on Tamarin. "I will see everything tomorrow. There is no sense in trying to look at things tonight. All I need now is some food, a warm blanket, and a chance to rest. . . ." Tamarin was not well and the travel had tired him. "It's all so ridiculous! I could not ask for anything better: traveling alone in an excellent car, and here I am more worn out than if I had been traveling in a freight car. . . ." He immediately reminded himself that when he had traveled in Russian freight cars he had been twenty years younger.

The car stopped in a short, narrow street faintly lighted at one end. Tamarin saw a long, three-story, somber-looking building. Bags of sand were piled on the sidewalk along the wall. "That's the place," the bodyguard said, alighting. He ran up the steps of the porch and knocked on the door. A bluish light flickered behind the glass, and a woman appeared with a flashlight in her hand. The bodyguard took off his cap, bowed, and showing her a paper, explained something in a lowered voice. The woman nodded and, smiling, began to speak very rapidly. "Thank God! I suppose this means that she has a room?" Tamarin asked, stepping out of the car. Something cracked and clinked under his feet. The sidewalks were strewn with broken glass. The empty window frames were covered with cloth and paper. In two of the windows the broken panes were dangling loosely in the wind. Tamarin again was about to lift his suitcase, but the bodyguard rushed at him as though intent on forestalling a disaster. "Everything will be brought to your room," he said. "Fortunately, one of her best rooms is vacant. I hope you will not mind the third floor?" "Certainly not! What nonsense!" "She has other rooms on the second floor but they are taken now. There are other Russians here," the bodyguard informed him happily. Tamarin frowned. "Probably Gay-Pay-Oo men," he thought. "And where will you sleep?" "There is no room for us here. We will sleep at the garage. . . ." The Spanish woman tried to carry the suitcase, but with an awkward movement she let it fall on the broken glass. The driver angrily shouldered her out of the way and carefully carried the suitcase and the typewriter inside the house. "They can't even sweep up the glass!" the German grumbled indignantly, returning to the porch and scraping pieces of glass off his boot against the top step. "At what time will you want the car?" he asked Tamarin. "At seven sharp. . . ." Tamarin said good night to his companions, both of whom, especially the Spaniard, seemed reluctant to part with him.

Raising the flashlight above her head the Spanish woman let Tamarin lead the way. He crossed the threshold and stopped, not knowing which way to turn in the darkness. Closing the door

behind her the woman snapped the switch. A single bulb flashed
on in a huge chandelier. "Looks like a mansion that belonged to
some wealthy family. . . . This place was never intended for an
hotel." The general hurriedly looked around with surprised eyes.
Paintings, statuary, and immense vases filled the large hall. On
the right an armed guard stood watch over a wide door. "In
there?" Tamarin asked, indicating the door with his hand. With a
frightened expression the woman shook her head, pointed at the
stairs, and began to chatter faster than ever. Tamarin spread his
hands hopelessly, and began to wonder whether he had let his
companions leave too soon. "I have no idea what she is trying to
say. . . . She is not bad-looking. . . . More like Micaela than
like Carmen. . . . I believe that girl's name was Micaela? . . ."

Another leather-jacketed armed guard who looked like neither
a soldier nor a civilian stood on the next landing. He glanced
indifferently at the general's uniform, and mechanically gave the
clenched fist salute, apparently not in the least concerned with
the military aspect of his gesture: he merely bobbed up his arm.
From the hall on the second floor came the measured clatter of
typewriters. "What sort of a place is this?" Tamarin wondered,
glancing uneasily around. The third floor landing was empty.
They turned left down the hall. Here, too, the clatter of typewriters reached them from behind closed doors. The Spanish
woman stopped opposite the last door, opened it with a key, and
turned on the light. With great relief Tamarin saw a small but
comfortably furnished room. "Excellent. *Merci. Gracia*," he said,
trying to remember how he should thank her in Spanish. The
woman continued to talk rapidly, the harsh "r" and "h" sounds
dominating everything she was saying. "I wish she would stop.
. . . It is ridiculous to stand here and listen without being able
to understand a word," he thought, smiling helplessly. "Kutuzov
would immediately have chucked her under the chin. . . ."
Probably any other time Tamarin would have behaved like
Kutuzov, but now the only thing he wanted was to see "Micaela"
leave. His head was aching.

There was not a sign of a pillow or a blanket anywhere. A metal bed covered with a bare mattress stood in the corner of the room. As soon as he was alone Tamarin examined them carefully and was satisfied with the results. "Evidently there is no reason to fear insects—that's most important of all. . . ." He walked to the window and pulled aside the black curtain. There was no glass—only the jagged edges of the pane. The window opened on the same dimly-lighted, narrow, slightly inclined street. He could hear people engaged in conversation on the first floor of the house opposite. There was something restful about the peaceful murmur of voices. "It may be odd, but it is life. Imagination always is worse than reality. They lead their lives like the rest of us. . . . The wind is blowing hard. That's unfortunate . . ."

Without taking off his coat Tamarin sprawled in an armchair, dropped his chin on his chest, and, shivering all over, rested for several minutes, contemplating with horror the work ahead of him. "I shall have to open the suitcase and the overnight bag, unpack my things, pull off my boots, wash . . ." A basin and a pitcher filled with water stood on a bench in the corner of the room. "I would give anything for a hot bath!" he thought with a sigh, knowing well that a besieged city was not the place to think in terms of hot baths. With the exception of the improvised wash-basin everything in the room looked substantial: a desk with several drawers—"they will come in handy"—shelves, a cupboard with a mirror in the door, and a full-length mirror on the wall opposite the cupboard. There even were pictures hanging on the walls. With an effort of will he undressed and began to wash, trying not to waste any water. As soon as he had covered his face with soap there was a knock on the door. Her teeth flashing, "Micaela" coyly stepped over the threshold and handed him a sheet, a blanket and a bolster which was to serve as a pillow. *"Merci. Gracia . . . Multo, multo gracia,"* Tamarin improvised, mustering his recollections of Spanish, as he covered his throat with one hand and squinted his eyes which were smarting from soap. He finished washing and made up the bed—the result was not bad. His teeth chattering from the cold, he hung his clothes in the cupboard, arranged his underclothes on the shelves, and deposited the sausage and the books on the dressing-table. Except for the strong breeze coming from the curtained window, the room was cozy.

Again there was a knock, and "Micaela" appeared, carrying a heavier load than before. In her right hand she held a steaming hot pan, in the left—a small piece of bread, a fork, a spoon, and a glass which she carried by sticking one finger inside and pressing it against the bread. Under her left arm was a bottle. Bowing and thanking her, Tamarin spilled some of the liquid out of the pan. "Why should you go to all this trouble? I am extremely grateful," he said, speaking in Russian ("what difference does it make what language I speak: she does not understand French anyway!"). "*Tortillas,*" the Spanish woman said proudly. "*Tortillas,*" the general repeated, not knowing what else to say.

The pan was filled with some sort of a rice sauce in which floated a few pieces of meat heavily seasoned with pepper. Tamarin found it amusing that he should make a meal out of a dish which bore the exotic name of "tortillas." The food was quite palatable, but he was not hungry. "Now I know I am ill. . . ." The wine, too, had a pleasant flavor. There was no label on the bottle. "Probably it also has some exotic name. . . . First thing you know, I shall turn into a toreador. . . ." A coronet was engraved on the fork and on the spoon. "So that's it! The house must have been the property of some marquis or duke? . . . My father, God bless his memory, would have known which it was; he knew how many leaves and how many pearls belong on each coronet. If I am not mistaken, eight leaves indicate a duke . . . I wonder where the duke and the duchess are now? . . . They never would suspect that a Tsarist general is a guest in their house! . . . Strange . . . But there is nothing ducal about this room. Probably the housekeeper or the governess slept here. . . ." With an inward satisfaction he surveyed the writing-desk and peered into the inkwell, which looked as though it had been dry for a long time. "The first thing tomorrow morning I must buy some ink and fill my fountain pen." He glanced at the titles of the books which lined the shelves. Most of them held no appeal for him. *"La influencia militar en los destinos de España......."* *"De octubre rojo a mi destierro" por Leon Trotsky. . . ."* "I suppose we can be thankful that he is not here, in Spain! . . ." *" 'De octubre rojo'*—'From the Red October'; that much is clear." He looked in the dictionary. *" 'Destino . . .' 'destierro'*—'exile.' *From the Red October to my Exile.* Spanish is not so difficult. . . . Someone else must have lived in this room after the governess. . . ." Tamarin studied the picture over the dressing-table, which struck some vaguely familiar chord. Distinguishing the letters with difficulty in the dim light, he read the inscription: "Vulcan's Forge by Velasquez." He tried to understand the meaning of these ferocious naked people with bare feet, but he could not remember anything about Vulcan. "I believe he was a god. . . . He forged something. . . . A god and a forge. No, my memory is not working tonight. . . ." Once again he peered out of the window. "A rope ladder, a señorita, a duchess with castanets . . . How can there be castanets on a ladder? . . ." The dark, narrow street offered nothing that might stimulate his imagination. "This is no time for duchesses and señoritas anyway!" he thought dejectedly.

Tamarin slipped on his pajamas and stretched out on the bed, which was harder than he had expected. He pulled the blanket over himself and with a sensation of delight relaxed his muscles. "When a man is old he can experience moments of bliss without any señoritas." As a matter of habit he wanted to read a little, but he had forgotten to move his volume of Clausewitz from the dressing-table to the chair which he had placed near the bed. He had no desire to crawl from under the blanket: the air was too cold. Instead he turned the light switch, which luckily he could reach without rising.

Tamarin was awakened by a terrific noise. He sat bolt upright in bed. "What was that?" Shouts and the sound of many running feet came from the street below. Tamarin felt along the wall until he found the switch and turned it—nothing happened. His eyes could see nothing in the darkness, which was blacker than it had been in the evening. The shouts in the street grew louder. Suddenly there was a loud explosion. "An air raid! . . ." His heart began to pound. "I had forgotten how it feels! . . ." With a shaking hand he determinedly turned the switch several times more, as though the urgency of his effort could be transmitted to the bulb. At last he realized that the current was cut off at the power station. With his feet, Tamarin tried to find his slippers, but gave up the attempt, and, walking with bare feet on the stone floor, cautiously made his way to the window, holding his left hand in front of him and guided by the current of cold air. He stumbled, almost fell, but finally reached the curtain, and pulled it aside. The darkness outside was almost as black as it was in the room. The shouting came from somewhere on the left. Apparently people were running in search of shelter. Somewhere near, there was the sound of another tremendous explosion, and blending with it came a long, rolling rumble, followed by a woman's shrieks, which changed to agonized moans and sobbing. Tamarin realized that a house had collapsed not very far away. "Maybe my time has come at last! . . ." He made the sign of the cross, looked at the ceiling, and calmly tried to anticipate what would happen. "Will it crush me? . . . No, I doubt it—this is the top floor. . . ." There was a third explosion, then a fourth, and a fifth. The blows followed one another in breath-taking succession. It seemed impossible that any living being could move through space with such speed. "Only a minute has elapsed, and he may already be miles away. . . . Gone like a whirlwind! . . ."

The shouting in the street changed and became less loud. An occasional jubilant note broke through, as though the people who were safe were exchanging congratulations. Another dull thud came from somewhere in the distance. Suddenly the bulb in the room flickered and went on, while other pale blue lights appeared in the street. A relieved: "ah-ah-ah!"—came from the crowd. The street was rapidly being filled with people. A large, somber automobile sped past. Tamarin wanted to learn where the bombs had fallen, and how near the house was that had been hit, but there was no one he could ask. "They have a certain amount of organization: first aid is functioning, and the current was turned off during the raid."

Familiar voices called to him from the street: his two companions were standing on the sidewalk trying to attract his attention. "What are you doing there?" Tamarin called back cheerfully and invited them to come up. While he waited for them he took his bathrobe out of the cupboard and put it on, wondering how proper it was for a general dressed in this fashion to talk to enlisted men. The Spaniard wore sandals on his bare feet, and he had left some of his lethal weapons behind. The German was dressed according to regulations, and his manner was as punctilious as ever. "What was it? What happened?" Tamarin asked. The bodyguard excitedly told him that a heavy bomb had fallen not more than seven hundred and fifty feet away; a large house had collapsed, killing twenty women and children, and wounding many others. "The fifth column is signaling to them," he added mysteriously and, seeing that the general was not familiar with the expression, elucidated: fascist sympathizers in Madrid were signaling to the flyers. "They found one of them just now: he had a signal lantern." "What did they do to him?" "They threw him out of the window," the German said with glee. "This seems to be the rule around here when they catch a spy above the sixth floor." "We already have carried out your orders," the bodyguard was anxious to change the subject. "We have gasoline, we went to headquarters, registered, and received a pass good for any section of the front." He handed Tamarin a piece of cardboard. "Thank you. I shall look for you tomorrow at seven," the general said, no longer surprised at the way things were done in Spain. "I have heard that an important action has been planned for tonight," the bodyguard said, lowering his voice. "We will attack the Clinic in University City. The fascists are holding it. This is a military secret." "I will not tell a soul. Isn't University City a stone's throw from here?" "Yes. Street cars marked 22 and 12 take you there from Puerta del Sol." Tamarin heaved a sigh of despair: clinic, an important action, street cars running to the front lines. . . . "Of what earthly use can my military education be in storming a clinic? . . ." The bodyguard gave him an anxious, compassionate look. "I hope you are not ill?" he said. "It is very easy to catch cold here. There is a saying in Madrid: warm clothes should be worn until the forty-first of May." Tamarin smiled weakly and let them go. He was feeling much worse.

The general looked at his watch in amazement: it was not yet midnight. A long sleepless night lay ahead; he knew it would be sleepless because his rest had been broken. "Should I take a sedative?" Tamarin always traveled with a medical kit. In the old days he had carried a nicely made box with partitions, compartments and an assortment of bottles; now he used an old candy box. The contents, too, had changed: no one ever spoke about phenacetin or antipyrene, which were the standard drugs when he was a young man. "Veronal? . . . I better wait; I will take some if I see that I cannot go to sleep. . . ."

Tamarin placed the heavy bathrobe over the blanket and stretched out again. He wished he had something warm to put on his feet. The feverish sensation itself was almost pleasant, provided he were sure that he could lie like this for a long, long time —forever. Mentally and physically Tamarin was so exhausted that he felt as though he were a hundred years old. "I hope to God I am not seriously ill! I haven't a soul I know here!" he thought and rolled his throbbing head on the pillow. "I am glad I was not frightened. The sound is what frightens you, especially the rumble of a collapsing house. Artillery is very different: the danger is greater, but the sound is not so frightening." The realization that he was taking an active part in another war was also pleasing, though this reaction was not as acute as it had been several hours earlier. "I see, I see . . . Hurl people out of windows, maybe gouge out their eyes. . . . The others do it in the name of Christ, and these do it in the name of liberty. . . .

Shameless liars, all of them. . . . Liberty! Can it be as great a
source of strength in the souls of men as the 'honor of the uniform'
was in the souls of my father and of his contemporaries? Then,
our fathers took for granted that under no circumstances could
one be false to one's uniform, that certain things were impossible
because they were incompatible with the uniform, and that when
the time came to die for one's uniform one died simply, without
any rationalizations. But among these people is there anything
that is incompatible with the uniform of liberty?. Among them
the percentage of deserters, betrayers and traitors is not ten times,
but ten thousand times greater than it was among the others. . . .
And if they should win, what brand of liberty will they establish?
Probably they will stop gouging out eyes, though I would not be
too certain even about that. . . . Obviously there are wars that are
justified, but this one is senseless. . . . And the most senseless
thing about it is that I should find myself here. Why should I, a
Russian, a former landowner in the State of Orlov, a Russian
general—I cannot tell myself whether I am a former or an active
general—why should I take part in this civil war in Spain? . . .
And what is my attitude? Essentially it makes no difference to me
who wins: Miaja or Franco. As far as I am concerned they are
both musical comedy generals. . . ."

Tamarin was disturbed by the thought that if he were killed
this first night in Madrid no one would ever learn what had
become of him. "What sort of records can they have? Who will
go to the trouble of making inquiries about a stranger without
relatives or friends? Unless those two young men should make a
report and Moscow be notified. . . ." From the windows of the
first floor below came the sound of calm and gay voices. People
were joking, as they settled for the night. Today they had been
spared—no one knew what would happen tomorrow. . . . "It is
all so stupid. . . . Strange that stupidity should dominate everything. . . . Stupidity and boredom. . . ."

Suddenly the sound of music reached him from downstairs.
Tamarin listened in amazement. "A guitar?" They were playing

something familiar. A pleasant voice was singing in Russian to
the accompaniment of the guitar. ". . . I always was home at
dawn, I always was carefree, and I always drank vodka," the
tenor sang. "What miracle is this? . . ." ". . . Among the gypsies
I received my formal education. . . ." A burst of gay laughter.
"They are Russians! I thought they were Gay-Pay-Oo men, but
they cannot be anything except Russian officers!" Tamarin was
transported with joy. ". . . Riding half-drunk behind a troika, my
thoughts will turn to you again, and out of my besotted eyes a
tear will roll slowly down my cheek. . . ." Unexpectedly Tamarin's eyes also became dimmed with tears. "What a sweet tenor!
And he sings it, just as we sang it in our day. . . ." Suddenly he
remembered another night, long, long, almost fifty years, ago—the
annual holiday of the Alexandrisky Regiment. . . . ". . . And
who are you in a black mantle, whose eyes are filled with magic
charm? The army knows you as immortal, Alexandrisky Black
Hussar! . . ." Tamarin saw the officers' mess hall, the long table
lined with bottles, the gay crowd of singing officers, the animated
face of the future Tsar, waving his hands and leading them in
song. "If some malevolent eye could have seen into the future!
. . . What was the sense in it? What is the sense in anything? . . ."

The singing stopped, and was followed by a long Russian
curse, a peal of laughter, and the sound of breaking glass. "They
are sure to know me! . . . Shall I drop in on them?" Tamarin
wondered. "No, that's impossible. . . . I am supposed to be on a
secret mission. . . . They would know my name. In another
three years no one on earth will know it. . . . No one on earth!
'. . . The army knows you as immortal! . . .' Nothing of the
kind! . . . No one is immortal, and everything is a muddle. . . .
Why should this and that other be spanned by one life? . . .
What had my mind and my will to do with it? . . . Very little.
. . . And the same holds true of most people, unless there is something exceptional about them. A person sets out for an objective
and reaches something entirely different. . . . No, I cannot drop

in on them. Perhaps only as a last resort, if I am desperately ill?
. . . But I am ill now! . . . Could it possibly be typhus? No,
typhus has an incu . . . incubation period. . . ." He had difficulty in visualizing the word "incubation." "What other word
begins with 'incu'? 'Incuba?' 'Incunabula?' Absurd! . . . I am
terribly thirsty. . . . It cannot be typhus. Someone told me that
there is a local fever which is hard on newcomers. . . ."

Tamarin rose, with a shaking hand poured some wine into a
glass, and drank it in one gulp. "Maybe I shall be able to sleep
now? This wine is strong. Or shall I try reading? . . ." He
glanced at the books on the dressing-table: the Clausewitz, a self-
teacher and a Spanish dictionary, a Madrid city guide, and a
volume of Pushkin which he had bought in Paris. "I am glad I
brought them along!" He stretched out, waited for the chill to
pass, and, feeling that his body would never again be warm, with
an effort opened the book. Rather, the book opened at the marker
of its own accord. With greater emotion than ever before Tamarin
read:

> *"He said to me: 'Be at rest,*
> *Soon you will reach*
> *The Kingdom of Heaven.*
> *Soon your earthly wanderings*
> *Will draw to an end.*
> *The angel of death is waiting*
> *With your martyr's crown.'"*

XIX

FOR A long time—for three, or possibly four hours—Tamarin lay
in bed, breathing heavily and shaking with alternating chills and
fever. At intervals he turned on the light, stared intently at the

hands of his watch, tried to decide what time it was, and was never certain. The light hurt his inflamed eyes, and he turned it off. "I am ill, very ill," he repeated dismally to himself, trying to think of something he could do. "I have no one close to me left anywhere in the world. Back home there is a cemetery full of people who were my friends. Here I haven't even casual acquaintances who might have some idea of who I am. . . ." Toward the end of the long night his thoughts became more and more confused. He realized that he was running a high temperature. "Maybe thirty-nine, or even forty? . . ." For a while he concentrated his entire mental energy on trying to remember whether this was according to Celsius or Réaumur, but his memory refused to help him and this in turn disturbed him more than ever. "And who was Celsius? . . . I have no idea. . . ."

The stale odor of food left in the pan nauseated him. With a supreme effort Tamarin rose and put the pan in the hall, outside his door. The clatter of a lonely typewriter downstairs reached his ears. "So they type here all hours of the night?" Tamarin, who was accustomed to the regular habits of the French, was surprised. "Perhaps I ought to work? If I take some medicine, I should be able to do some typing. . . ." He found his improvised medicine kit; two of the little boxes had been crushed and their contents spilled. "I believe this is aspirin," he thought, swallowing three tablets in rapid succession and washing them down with wine. "What was in the other box?" He remembered that they were compressed powders recommended as a stimulant by a druggist. He had bought them in Paris when he had noticed that he was tiring too easily. "Have I made a mistake? The two look very much alike. But these should be taken cautiously, not oftener than once a day—at least that is what the old man on the corner of the Boulevard St. Michel told me. I must have made a mistake—these pills have a very bitter taste. . . ." He drained what was left of the wine into his glass, and drank it. "It has a nice bouquet, but it is much stronger than the French wines. . . ."

The typewriter stood on the dressing-table. For some reason, looked at from the side, it reminded Tamarin of a model battle-ship. "Franco has several battleships—I must remember to mention it in my report. . . . In my book I said that thus far it is too early to judge the relative superiority of sea and air power: we have not had sufficient experience. . . . Anyway, why should it make any difference to me?" Tamarin said aloud, though ordinarily he was not in the habit of talking to himself. The typewriter ribbon was old and worn in many places, but he had several extra spools. He decided to change the ribbon. "It makes no difference to me," he grumbled. "Franco, or Miaja—they are all alike. . . . The ones on this side are a trifle more decent and scrupulous: the only harm they have done is to debase liberty. But then only people who are too lazy to do anything have not debased or degraded liberty. To hell with it anyway! They can debase and degrade it all they want! Instead of using liberty as camouflage for their dirty game the fascists use religion, which is much worse because it is blas-phemy. . . . No true believer can consider it anything but blasphemy! . . ."

Tamarin managed to fasten the end of the ribbon to the spool with great difficulty, though he was familiar with the operation and ordinarily enjoyed it. Extravagance was not one of his fail-ings, but whether in Paris or Moscow he changed typewriter ribbons frequently: he liked to see clear, black type. His fingers were covered with black ink. The pitcher was almost empty. He poured the remaining water into the basin, but only succeeded in smearing the ink all over his hands which left black streaks on the clean towel. "I shall feel badly about this when I see 'Micaela.' . . . No, I cannot write like this! Maybe I will feel better if I take a walk? . . ."

The idea of fresh air appealed to Tamarin, and he hurriedly began to put on his clothes. "I have a pass, and I can go anywhere I please and see anything I want to see. The door downstairs was bolted from inside, so I will not have to look for a key. . . . Per-haps I shall see the attack, and a night attack at that!" The pos-sibility delighted him. The tired feeling vanished, but his thoughts were still confused. "The wine has warmed me. . . . It is excellent wine. . . . I must not forget to mail the post card!" Nadia's post card was still in his coat pocket, ready to be mailed. Tamarin slipped on his coat and tiptoed out of the room. The typewriter downstairs had not stopped. "Maybe I am having hallucinations? No, nothing of this sort has ever happened to me, and besides why should I be pursued by the clatter of typewriters? . . ."

An armed soldier was dozing on a divan in the first-floor hall. Just as Tamarin reached the bottom step a car stopped in front of the house. A tall, grey-haired man in a dark, shabby civilian suit entered the hall. "He is from Moscow! I think I have worked with him on some commission? He is a Lett," Tamarin felt an intense dislike for the man. With a terrified expression the soldier jumped up from the divan. The second guard by the door also straightened up and looked frightened. Pretending that he had not seen Tamarin, the civilian disappeared behind a door.

Outside, the night seemed weird. Perhaps that Greek who transplanted himself to Spain—that strangest of all the great masters—during the last years of his life, when he was threatened with the loss of his mind, watched and studied these queer spots and designs in the Spanish night sky. A brisk wind was chasing the clouds, and ever so often the huge, reddish moon peered from behind them. Tamarin looked up and remained motionless for a full minute, gazing with amazement at the sky. The thought occurred to him that perhaps he was delirious and should return immediately to his room and go to bed. "Absurd! . . . It's all so strange," he said to himself, and buttoning his coat, started to walk down the street. "It is Spanish, so very Spanish! I never have seen a night like this anywhere else." The air was cold, the streets empty, and the street lights far apart. Near one of them his gaze fell on an odd-looking, high pillar. He did not realize at once that it was a mail box. But when he dropped the post card inside— "certainly it is a mail box; what else could it be?"—he felt very much relieved. Even under normal circumstances unmailed letters preyed on his mind. But tonight his feeling of relief was so great that finding a mail box in a large city seemed an extraordinary piece of good luck. "At least I have left a trail behind me! . . ."

A fieldpiece went off not very far away, then a second, and a third. Tamarin felt an exhilaration. "That's it! That's where I want to go!" he said, hurrying toward the sound. Crumbled and gutted houses became more and more frequent. "Surprising that there are not more of them! If the Germans were to take this war seriously, there would be nothing left of the city." A tall column with a ball at the top loomed on the left. "A monument? No man ever deserved it, and erecting them is a waste of time. No one will miss it if they destroy it. Then, in their turn, these can tear down the monuments which are treasured by the others. The world would be the better for it," he mused as though he were giving advice. Tamarin was even more delighted when through a half-closed door he caught a glimpse of a lighted café. He entered, mumbled something unintelligible, and pointed his finger at the first bottle he saw. The light came from a stove on which fresh fish was sizzling in a pan. The old man in the café filled the customer's glass without so much as looking at his uniform. "If Hitler in all the splendor of his parade uniform were to walk in on him, probably he would not be any more impressed," Tamarin thought. "A real philosopher!" He swallowed the drink, called for another, and paid the bill. The field guns were firing again, this time accompanied by the rattle of machine-guns. "University City?" Tamarin asked cheerfully, trying to remember how the bodyguard had pronounced the name in Spanish. The old man nodded indifferently and shook the pan on the stove. Only then Tamarin became conscious of the strong, disagreeable odor of fish, and with the violent nausea of a sick man rushed outside.

At that moment, as though nature wanted to surprise him for the last time, the moon appeared from behind the clouds shedding a red glow on the devastated city. Tamarin emitted an involuntary exclamation. "Magic! It's simply magic!" he muttered. "I believe 'magic' is the appropriate word. . . . With the street lights and the moonlight I can even read the signs. . . . The street lights are more frequent around here. *'Pelluqueria'*—that's a barber shop!" he was pleased with himself. " *'Confiteria,' 'Camiseria'*—I can understand every word! *'Carpinteria!'* What on earth is a *'Carpinteria?'* *'Assegurada da incendios'*—insured against fire. Every house is insured against fire. . . . What effective insurance! . . . Russia also was *'assegurada da incendios.'* So were we all."

A soldier standing on the corner made a motion to stop him, but, recognizing his uniform, saluted, and let him pass. Tamarin emerged on a large square. Crumbled buildings, bathed in moonlight, were on all sides. To the right a tall building was going up in flames. Tamarin laughed. "Velasquez lighted the scene with a fire from a forge. An artist's trick. But here life is playing tricks! . . . 'Cine las Flores.' This also is probably insured!"

Ahead, a narrow road led down into a gully with several winding footpaths branching from it up the opposite side. Only then did Tamarin notice an uneven row of buildings along the ridge. He guessed that this was University City, and hurrying across the road he began to climb up the footpath. A shell exploded over his head. "I must be just in time for the attack . . ." he thought. Men with rifles in their hands were running ahead of him toward the building. "What fools! Look at them! . . . The machine-guns will mow them down! . . ."

A man in a leather jacket was leading them. Tamarin could see his movements as though he were watching him on a screen. In contrast to the others he seemed to know what to do. Having crossed about twenty feet on the run, he glanced over his shoulder, shouted something, and dropped to the ground. Not many of the men followed his example. At the same moment the machine-guns opened fire. Having waited a full minute, the man in the leather jacket rose, doubled up and, zigzagging, rushed ahead, his right arm poised to hurl a hand grenade. Some of the men behind him were falling. Tamarin gave an exclamation and darted after them, pulling out his sword as he went. "Boys! . . . *Todos para uno!* . . . *Lenin dos dos!*" he called in a voice cracking with excitement. Something powerful exploded just in front of him, Tamarin swayed to one side, dropped his sword, lifted both hands, and fell. The dying rumble of the explosion merged with the rattle of the machine-guns.

XX

THE NIGHT WISLICENUS disappeared Kangarov arrived at the sanatorium well after eight. He was intentionally late, so he would not meet Nadia's guest under any circumstances. He was in a very bad humor. To show Nadia that he had will power, he intended not to speak to her for at least two days. This did not mean that there would be complete silence. A curt "good morning," or "Have you enough money?" or "Is that the dinner bell?"—were permissible and would not in any way weaken his case. But he meant to avoid any full-fledged conversations. "She must be made to realize that I am really angry, and that she behaved atrociously when she invited that bastard to see her! I am not in the least jealous. It would be ridiculous if I were to be jealous of her at any time, and especially in relation to this old man. I know very well that she is not in love with him. She asked him because she does not know any better, and because she wanted to assert her independence: I am free, white, and twenty-one and I can invite anyone I please. As yet, I am not in a position to tell her what she can do, or whom she can invite," he thought with a tender flutter of the heart. "But she should sense that this 'status quo' will not last much longer: our relations are gradually becoming clarified."

On the way from Paris Kangarov's resolution weakened, and as the car stopped in front of the sanatorium he decided to cut down the length of Nadia's punishment to one day: "After all, the punishment will be harder on me than it will be on her." But his mood was not brightened. "Something extremely disagreeable may come of this visit from Wislicenus. . . . Probably they are watching me already!" At first he could not take this seriously himself, then he saw that it was possible and became frightened, then once again he decided that he had no reason to worry. "Absurd! . . . What have I ever done? And who cares about Nadia? . . . But the situation is dangerous. . . . Very, very dangerous! . . ."

Kangarov's thoughts turned to his health. He had put on weight, and he consumed prodigious quantities of food, telling Nadia that he was suffering from a spurious appetite. The doctor at the sanatorium told him that though it was not serious he must watch his weight: his nerves were the important thing. "I should like to see how his nerves would react, if he were to find himself in my shoes," Kangarov wondered with a bitter smile, thinking about his thwarted political ambitions, his wife, who was certain to refuse him a divorce, and the condition of his health. His latest obsession was a sickly fear of cancer: he examined himself daily looking for some indication of a swelling. "Why are you so afraid of cancer?" Nadia asked. "Probably you have never heard about it, my dear child, but forty-eight is the cancer age. It is the most susceptible year for cancer in a man's life." "No, I never have heard about it, but then you are not the only man who is forty-eight? [I bet he is older than that!]" "You are such a baby! . . . It's impossible to talk seriously to you. I shall have to buy you a doll instead." "No, it would be unworthy of both of us for me to be jealous of her: she is nothing but a child," Kangarov decided as he entered the door. "I may as well talk to her, just as though nothing had happened."

"Has everyone finished dinner?" he asked the door man. "Yes, Your Excellency, but the cook is keeping your dinner for you." "I hate to put him to that trouble: anything cold would do just as well," Kangarov said curtly. Inwardly he had hoped to hear: "Yes, everyone has had dinner except Mademoiselle Nadia who is waiting for you." The girl at the cashier's desk slid some papers into the drawer, gave him a friendly smile, and asked: "I hope you are not wet, Monsieur l'Ambassadeur? The weather is very bad, but I am sure that we will get our share of good days before the month is over." "No, I am not wet [what were those papers she was in such a hurry to hide when she saw me?] Any letters for me?" "No, only newspapers." Kangarov sighed with a certain amount of relief. Of late he found that he dreaded opening letters: there always was something unpleasant in them. "Is Mademoiselle Nadia in her room?" "No, I believe she is in the sitting-room listening to the radio. Would you like me to call her, Monsieur l'Ambassadeur?" "No, no! I will have my dinner first. But please tell them to serve just the main course, and tell the cook to close the kitchen." "Don't give it a thought, Monsieur l'Ambassadeur! He has been waiting for you. Monsieur l'Ambassadeur is late so seldom."

The universal respect accorded his person at the sanatorium never failed to mollify Kangarov. In the beginning, like all Soviet people abroad, he constantly expected some awkward situation to arise. But not only were his fears rapidly dispelled, the Soviet ambassador even came to feel that he was the guest of honor at the sanatorium. Kangarov entered the dining-room, avidly ate everything that was placed before him, drank half a bottle of wine and mellowed even more. "Why should she have waited for me? The poor thing probably was hungry." After dinner he wandered into the sitting-room. Nadia was listening to the radio, so that conversation was impossible. The ambassador nodded to her with a polite smile which was intended for the benefit of the public—several other guests were in the room. To Nadia the smile was supposed to convey a coolness and the realization that he was angry with her. For a second, Nadia had a desire to tell him that Wislicenus was more of a lout than ever, that he had failed to keep the appointment, and that he had not even bothered to call her. But she too decided to show her will power: "if he does not intend to talk to me, I will not talk to him! Let's see who wins at this game! . . ."

Nadia won. Next morning Kangarov dropped a casual: "How

are we?"—and then added: "After breakfast we have a little work to do." The friendly opening seemed to have no effect on Nadia. She played the rôle of a conscientious employee who is aware of her duties and who is ready to carry out the orders of her superior. To re-establish normal relations between them Kangarov was forced to dictate an unnecessary letter. From business their conversation turned to general subjects, but there was no mention of Wislicenus.

That evening the cashier presented the ambassador with the weekly bill. In checking over the extras he was puzzled to notice that there was no charge for afternoon tea. "You haven't forgotten anything? I believe yesterday afternoon Mademoiselle had some people for tea?" he asked casually. "No, Monsieur l'Ambassadeur. Yesterday the weather was so bad that we did not have a single visitor from outside," the cashier answered, her curiosity instantly on the alert. She was very much intrigued by the relations between the ambassador and Mademoiselle Nadia. "So the goose did not come to see her after all? Perhaps she called him and told him not to come? Perhaps she saw that I was angry and changed her mind? . . ." Kangarov's heart overflowed with joy. He decided not to ask Nadia any questions, and he became as tender with her as he had ever been.

One morning, two or three days later, Kangarov after breakfast stretched out on the couch in his room and unfolded the paper. Though he frequently complained about overwork, he had very little to do, and out of sheer boredom he acquired the habit of reading the papers word for word. On the fourth page his glance accidentally fell on a small news item: "The Disappearance of a Russian." The proprietor of an hotel (the name and address were given in full) had notified the police that a Russian who had been a guest at the hotel for some time had disappeared (the exact date was given) without a word of warning. His things had been left behind in his room. The name was misspelled, but Kangarov remembered that Wislicenus had been staying there. For some reason the ambassador was terribly upset by the news. He even had something approaching a palpitation of the heart, and this time there was nothing imaginary about it. "That is the date on which he was coming to see Nadia!" (Kangarov checked the date, though the very moment he had seen it in the paper he had a premonition that it could not have been otherwise.) "But where is the connection? The date has nothing to do with it. . . . Why should it worry me, anyway? He has disappeared and that's that. Probably he went on a business trip without leaving a forwarding address. That would be just like him. . . . In his type of work an unexpected trip of several days' duration is a common occurrence. But why hadn't he mentioned it to the proprietor? There could be any number of reasons. . . . Perhaps he didn't have time. There could be hundreds of reasons! . . . Or maybe he skipped the bill! Very likely everything he owned consisted of an extra pair of pants. . . ."

This exercise in logic did not satisfy Kangarov. He went downstairs, picked up two other morning papers, returned to his room, and for some reason locked the door. One of the papers described the incident in exactly the same words, except that the name was misspelled in a different way. The other made no mention of it at all. This had a calming effect on the ambassador. He paced the floor of his room. "Probably there is nothing to worry about. Very likely he has gone somewhere. What else could it be? Nothing sensational about it. They would handle the story in a very different way if it were a . . ."

Kangarov could not wait until the afternoon papers arrived at the sanatorium. He wanted to send a boy after them to the station where they were available earlier, but at the last moment he changed his mind and went himself. On the way back, having glanced around to see that he was not being watched, he unfolded the paper. He could not find any mention of the disappearance. "The whole thing is ridiculous!" Kangarov returned to the sanatorium, looking anxiously at the few people he met on the way. He watched to see whether there was anything unusual about the cashier's manner—"she seems to have a peculiar smile. . . ."

Going to his room, he put the papers with the story of the disappearance in a drawer, but then he decided to destroy them. He tore them in small pieces and flushed them down the toilet. Ordinarily, toward evening Nadia glanced hurriedly at the first and third pages of the paper (he never could understand how a person could go through an entire day without knowing what was happening in the world).

Kangarov had a habit of complaining to Nadia that he hadn't closed an eye all night. She sympathized with him without taking his words too seriously. But that night he actually was unable to sleep. He thought a great deal about his position, about the past, and he felt a chill when he remembered his old newspaper article: "Come to Your Senses, Renegades!" Next morning, without knowing why, he went to Paris. Even a mention of this affair ("why call it an affair?") to anyone was unthinkable. Kangarov hoped that someone would say something indirectly, or, perhaps, drop a hint. No one said a word. This might indicate a number of things. One thing was definitely reassuring. Evidently the disappearance had failed to become a sensation. Neither the papers, nor the police showed any interest in the case. "And why should anyone be interested? . . . But I must give the situation some serious thought." Actually, there was no situation to consider, and the series of disorderly impressions and suspicions that flitted through Kangarov's mind could hardly be called thoughts. Suddenly he came to a decision: it was time for him to leave France. This depended entirely on him; he had been granted sick leave, and no one could object if he cut it short.

"I have something very important to tell you, my child," Kangarov said to Nadia that evening. "We are going back tomorrow."

Nadia looked at him with surprised eyes, and he was transported with delight.

"Tomorrow?"

"Yes, I am afraid we have to leave tomorrow. Why?"

"Oh, nothing. . . . Why the sudden rush? . . . You still

have ten days before your leave expires, and you were planning one more consultation with Fouquot before we left."

"No, I changed my mind, and I really had no intention of seeing him again. He has told me everything he knows, and he has not helped me at all. Besides, there are certain things I have to do, and my work is falling behind. . . . You didn't want to sit here with me anyway? I thought you said that this place bored you?"

"My feelings are not important. You know what you have to do. But do we have to go tomorrow? I should like to make another trip to Paris."

"What for? If you are planning to buy glad rags, you can buy them anywhere, or else you can wait until we are back here again."

"Yes, I wanted to do a little shopping, and I wanted to see some people."

"Whom, for instance?"

"For instance, Wislicenus of whom you are so fond," Nadia said to annoy Kangarov.

"Wislicenus? They tell me he has left," the ambassador said casually. Inwardly, he was delighted to learn that she apparently had not seen anything in the papers.

"Left? Where did he go?"

"Some assignment or other. . . . I don't know."

"Probably he also has galloped away to Spain."

"Why 'also'?"

Kangarov suddenly was overwhelmed with joy. "Why hadn't I thought of that myself? That's what it is—he has galloped away to Spain! That, more or less, explains everything!"

"Because it seems that Tamarin is in Spain. Today I unexpectedly received a card from him post-marked Madrid. He went away without bidding goodbye and without saying a word about it."

"You little simpleton! We are not supposed to advertise any of our business trips, and especially an assignment to Spain. You are right! I have heard that Wislicenus went to Madrid, but please don't mention it to a soul. And that other foolish old man had no right to send you post cards from Spain. You better not let it be known. You might get him into trouble!"

Kangarov felt vaguely that the explanation was not altogether adequate. Even if Wislicenus had gone to Spain, there was no reason why he should have left in that way. He could have told the proprietor that he was going, without telling him where. He could have taken his things and paid his bill. But now Kangarov's mind was definitely at rest: he was firmly convinced that Wislicenus was in Spain. Not a trace of his former misgiving remained; instead, his entire being vibrated with joy, energy, and happiness. "Nadia is with me. . . . Nothing else matters!" Once again his mind turned to a place in the country, and he began to dream of trees and tulips.

"My child! My dear child!" he was beaming. "The orders are signed and delivered: we are leaving tomorrow. Tonight we have to pack. We might as well get started. I will attend to everything. And if your heart is set on any knickknacks that we can buy in Paris without wasting time, and without wandering from store to store, we can pick them up tomorrow on the way to the station. I will go with you. I love to watch you shop! If you need money, I can arrange a small advance. But you better make a list, ahead of time, of the knickknacks your heart desires."

"I am not interested in knickknacks," Nadia answered angrily.

As a matter of fact the sudden change made little difference to Nadia. She was tired of the sanatorium, but Kangarov bored her even more, whether they were in Paris or anywhere else. Everything now depended on the answer from the editors: would they accept the novelette? She had sent the manuscript to Gene with an accompanying letter which had a casual sound, but in which every word had been carefully considered (she had twice re-written the original draft). Nadia made it sound as though she had no idea that the story would be accepted. "Believe me, Gene, when I say that I am not fooling myself. I know that it is very slight and lacks distinction, but, to use your old-time expression, I am sending it to you on a fluke. I am sure that they will turn it down, and that their judgment will be right. It will make no difference to me, and I shall not be in the least disappointed. I wrote it because I had nothing better to do. . . ." This opening was followed by detailed instructions about what he should do and what he should say to the editors (Nadia knew that she had a much more practical mind than Gene). The manuscript had been sent by registered mail. She was told at the post office that it would be cheaper to send it *"imprimé."* Nadia had hesitated: she had little money left (she simply could not understand what happened to her salary). But finally she decided to seal the envelope: it made it look more impressive.

Now Nadia was waiting for the answer. She felt that this was a ridiculously common experience. "I believe reams have been written about it: a beginner waiting for the verdict of the editors. But it could not have been as vitally important to the others: my entire future depends on this." Not enough time had elapsed for an answer, even if they were to send it by telegraph. Nadia had not mentioned telegrams because that would not have been in keeping with her complete indifference to the fate of her story. But she was confident that if the story was accepted Gene would wire her immediately. "He will do everything he can: he was in love with me, and he told me all kinds of things" (the mention in her letter of the old days in Moscow had not been accidental; she had done this deliberately, though she was not too comfortable about it). In her letter she had asked him not to mention the story to anyone. But she realized that she was asking the impossible and that it was too much to expect from any human being. "If I were in Moscow I would have told everybody about it. I don't care! It will not be the first story to be rejected! . . . Nina will make fun of me." Nadia tried to imagine the most insulting things Nina could say about her failure. "In the first place, she makes fun of me no matter what I do. That's just the nature of the beast, and everybody knows it. In the second place, there is no disgrace in having one's first story rejected. [Nadia already knew that there would be a second story.] This has happened to some of the greatest writers. In the third place, the subject or the style may not fit in with their present editorial plans. In the fourth place, even if the first story is not very good, does it prove anything? In the fifth place, Nina could not write an intelligent letter, let alone a novelette. In the sixth place . . ." In the sixth place, no matter how indifferent she pretended to be, she knew that she would not enjoy having anyone laugh at her and make fun of her misfortunes. "If you dance, you have to pay the piper." She knew what the payment would be like, but she was not certain how much pleasure she would derive from the dancing. If the editors accepted the novelette Nadia intended to give up her job, return to Moscow, and become a real writer—"a professional." She had come across this expression in a newspaper and it had struck her as tempting and strange: somehow she associated it in her mind with the words "professional prostitution."

Sitting at her desk, Nadia wrote: "Dear Gene, a few words to add to my other letter. We are leaving tomorrow, much sooner than we had expected. You know my permanent address, but I remember how careless you are, and I am repeating it just in case" (the address was given in full). "You should hear something soon about my opus. While I am not worried about it, still I . . ." (She repeated all the instructions she had given him in the preceding letter.) "I know that they would not accept it without you. But with your connections and your influence, I have some hope. Stranger things have happened." She thought that the mention of his connections and influence was a masterly stroke. The "few words" became four full pages. When Nadia sealed the letter she paced the floor for a long time, and it was very late when she began to pack.

Nadia expected that Kangarov would talk to her about love during their long railroad journey. The prospect was boring and ridiculous, and she was at a loss. She felt that she was not being honest, and her conscience bothered her. "I should be frank with him." But Nadia did not know how to go about it. She had drifted into this situation with Kangarov, and now she could not find a way out. Besides, she had become a little afraid of Kangarov. She noticed certain peculiarities about him. "I believe he is losing his mind. He drinks a great deal more than is good for him. And his appetite! Good Lord, how he eats! There is something pathologic about it. I feel sorry for him. After all, he is not such a bad person. The worst thing anyone can say about him is that he is hysterical. His hysteria must be catching, because I seem to be developing a similar case merely by associating with him."

At the railroad station Kangarov continued to behave in a most peculiar fashion. On the stairs and on the platform he kept glancing nervously in every direction, he looked searchingly at every person they met, and as soon as they were on the train he quickly walked the entire length of the car peering into every compartment. "What is the matter with him? Is he afraid of being followed?" Nadia was puzzled by his behavior. Apparently Kangarov found nothing to arouse his suspicions. When finally the train moved out of the station he became very gay, assumed the devil-may-care pose which she knew so well, pulled out a flask of cognac and a folding cup, and offered her a drink. Nadia knew that he would say: "Now I shall know all your thoughts"—would take a couple of drinks, and then would exclaim: "Cognac is a great invention!" Running true to form, this was exactly what Kangarov said and did. "Too bad there are no hors d'oeuvre to go with it. But for you, my child, I have some sweets. . . ." He took out of his suitcase a large, beautifully packed box of candy, selected a small, cylindrical piece of chocolate, broke it in two and put one half in her mouth while he ate the other. This also was part of the usual procedure which bored her so much. But then, suddenly, with unexpected strength he lifted her and perched her on his knee. "Have you lost your mind? Leave me alone! Let me go!" she said and immediately became aware that involuntarily she had lowered her voice. "Let me go! Do you hear me?" "What makes you so cruel? . . ." He did not release her at once, waiting to see whether she meant what she was saying. Nadia tore herself free and moved into a far corner. "This is becoming impos-

sible! . . ." "You are such a little simpleton. . . ." "Simpleton?
. . . You are a damned fool!" she said and realized at once that
her violent outburst was a milestone—it marked the beginning of
a new chapter. In the past, Kangarov in a fatherly tone frequently
had called her a little simpleton, but this was the first time that
she had ever called the minister plenipotentiary of a great power a
damned fool to his face—"even if it is the truth." The minister
plenipotentiary also was somewhat surprised, but with a strained
and affected laugh he patted her on the knee. "Offended again!
You are so funny. . . . Better listen to what I have to say." "You
will never say anything worth hearing, so better keep quiet."
Nadia decided to have it out—after calling him a damned fool she
had no hope of keeping her job. "You are an impudent girl!"
Kangarov said in a whisper. "How dare you talk like that to your
superior who is about to offer you . . ." "Offer me what? What
are you offering me?" "To use a high-flown expression—who is
about to offer you his heart and hand." "You don't say!" Nadia
exclaimed with heavy irony. "That is exactly what I am saying!"
"But if I am not mistaken you already are married?" "You know
very well that I intend to get a divorce. . . . Don't think that I
am getting a divorce on your account—I shall insist on it anyway.
But what is your answer?" "I am so overcome with this sudden
honor that I am absolutely speechless." "Please be serious! You are
an intelligent girl, Nadia, and you must know that I am in love
with you. Will you be my wife?" he checked himself as he was
about to draw on the literary recollections of his younger years and
add: "in the eyes of God and of the people." "Answer me: yes or
no?" "No." "You say no, but I feel that you are saying yes!" "I
cannot do anything about the way you feel." "You don't like me?"
"I like you very much, but . . ." She was tempted to use the
expression which had been so popular when she was in school:
"but at a distance." "You want to say that you like me as a friend?
I can be both: your friend and your husband. I know that I am
twice as old as you are ["wouldn't three times be more like it?"
she made a mental correction], but I don't feel my age! ["how

very consoling!"] I am in love with you like a young boy! I will do anything for you, Nadia!" She wanted to keep the conversation in an ironical key, but she understood that this was no longer possible. "I am deeply touched." "And there is something to be said on my side," he said in a convincing whisper. "No one can deny that you are clever and beautiful, but until now no one has proposed to you . . ." Nadia turned a deep red. "What I want to say is that you would not occupy such a brilliant position marrying anyone else," he hurriedly corrected himself, sensing that he had blundered. "If you . . ." "No, no! Understand. . . . Please try to understand what I mean. I only ask for one thing: don't say no, don't deprive me of hope. Simply say: 'let me think it over.' Don't worry about the divorce. I mean to have it anyway!" "You can mean to have anything you choose!" "Nadia!" "And please don't worry about my sad fate as an old maid!" "I see I was wrong when I said that you were clever. You are a little simpleton! You take exception to one unintentional, silly word! Darling! Nadia! Think about it! Say: 'let me think it over.'" "Let me think it over," she repeated tauntingly, imitating his voice. "But do say yes just as soon as you can." "Yes, sir." "You are very cruel! I simply must know the answer!" "So you can proceed with the divorce? I thought you meant to have it anyway?" "I do mean to have it!" he asserted happily. "Now everything is fine! We understand each other at last. Not a word about it! Sh-sh-sh! If you want to read, here is your paper. . . ." Nadia shrugged her shoulders. "But don't torture me too long, my dear! I know you are not telling the truth when you say that you are surprised." "Stop it! You said yourself: not another word about it! Sh-sh-sh!" "Sh-sh-sh! Sh-sh-sh!" he hissed with glee. "Just one little kiss. . . . No, no, your hand! . . . Sh-sh-sh! . . ."

Hiding behind the newspaper, Nadia in her bewildered mind went over every detail of the scene. "I don't believe that there ever was a man who told a woman that he loved her in a more idiotic way! I never believed that he seriously intended to get a divorce—I thought that all he wanted was an affair! . . ." Nadia realized that this was the consideration that had made her so ashamed of herself. "As long as I thought that he intended to have an affair I found it ridiculous and disgusting. Has this new angle changed my attitude?" She was not sure. "One thing is obvious: he has taken my 'no' for a 'yes,' and all his absurd 'sh-sh-sh' and 'not a word' sound like the cry of a conqueror! I certainly told him 'no,' and he can put any interpretation on it he pleases! But how did I, myself, intend it? Was it an absolute 'no,' a hundred per cent 'no,' or only a ninety per cent 'no'?"

Nadia was horrified. "Have I for a single minute seriously considered the possibility of marrying him? Certainly not! As they say in old-fashioned novels, he is a 'brilliant match,' he is in love with me, and, strange as it may seem, I don't find him repulsive, but the very thought of marriage is absurd! I must make it clear to him so he can get this foolish notion out of his head. He really may try to get a divorce. . . . But, after all, that's his worry: I told him 'no' and that's that. If he actually gets a divorce from her, all I can do is offer him my sincere congratulations. I can imagine her face! . . ." This vision of Helen Kangarov's face was the only bright spot in the entire situation. "And what is most unpleasant about it? The most horrible part of it is that he was right when he said that no one had ever proposed to me, and that there is no one in sight who would. Basil never has given me a second thought. There were boys who fell in love with me: Sasha, Gene—but that was puppy love. Men under thirty do not exist for me. . . . And not over forty—certainly not over forty-five at the most! But why am I clogging my brain with all this ridiculous nonsense?" Nadia was surprised at herself. "But it really is horrible! If no one has fallen in love with me until now, the chances of it happening from now on will be less and less. Then there will be no one! . . ." Nadia buried her face deeper in the paper. "If he sees me crying, he will think that I am carried away with happiness. . . . What shall I tell him? I must give up my job and leave at once. But how will I exist? How can I live? If only the answer would come! Any answer at all, so long as they take it! Should I leave before the answer arrives? He never would let me go. . . . In Moscow Nina will say that while I was abroad I failed to catch a viscount. Let her talk her head off! So far, she herself has not married a viscount or anyone else, for that matter!" Nadia felt a violent surge of anger, and sighed.

A bell tinkled in the corridor, and someone knocked on the door of their compartment. A man in a blue jacket inquired whether they wanted to make reservations for the dining-car. "Yes, yes! A table for two. We want to eat early," Kangarov said gaily, coming instantly to life. "You and I will have to have some wine. How about some champagne? To celebrate the occasion. . . . I beg your pardon! . . . I know, I know: there is no occasion to celebrate. You have not given me your answer! . . . I know! . . ."

XXI

THE SECRETARY, who was their only friend among the embassy staff, met them at the station. He gave Nadia a proper and happy smile, and his expression clearly said: "I fail to see anything unusual about your trip."

". . . You have gained weight, but the journey must have been tiring." "I am tired all the time," Kangarov said curtly. "How are things? Has anything gone wrong? You may as well tell me now." Apparently nothing had gone wrong—just the routine worries associated with state and diplomatic affairs of the utmost importance. ". . . *Eo ipso*, during the first days you will have a great many matters to consider," the secretary said, his face assuming an appropriately concerned and dignified expression. Evidently he had no intention of discussing state affairs in Nadia's presence. "What a bore!" Nadia thought. She did not dislike the secretary. She knew that fundamentally he was a decent person—

the most decent among all her colleagues: he would not tell on her, he would not gossip behind her back, and he would not try to trip her up. But his appearance, his voice, and the things he said exuded boredom. After talking to him for two minutes at the station, Nadia had a feeling that she never had been away, that she had listened to the secretary all her life, and that nothing would ever change. ". . . What did you say about my wife? . . ." The secretary had not mentioned Helen Kangarov's name. For thirty seconds or so, with an air of not wanting to interrupt his superior, he politely waited for a more definite question. Convinced that he would not be given a more concrete lead, he finally said with punctilious restraint: "Your wife is very well. None of us were sure about the exact time of your arrival." His manner indicated that his innate tact made it painful for him to dwell on unpleasant subjects—it was the same pained expression which he assumed when in the course of a conversation some foreigner made accidental mention of communist propaganda. After a brief pause, he relayed the latest news from "well-informed circles." ". . . And the king is planning a ball with all the trimmings. They haven't held such a brilliant affair at the palace for a long time." "I wonder what makes our dear king so happy?" The secretary shrugged his shoulders with a meaningful, diplomatic expression. "And how are you? Are you still breaking as many women's hearts?" "Thank you, but I already have had my daily laugh," the secretary answered.

Next morning when Nadia entered the embassy office Bazarov was giving his colleagues a detailed account of the meeting between the ambassador and his wife. ". . . There were no peals of thunder, but Helen is adamant on the subject of divorce." "You are lying—you could not have overheard a word of their conversation." "Certainly not! He has no idea of what was said, but there is no doubt that the situation has reached the breaking point." "No doubt whatever! . . . But Helen cannot expect any real money out of the ambassador. The alimony she can squeeze out of him will hardly be worth the effort. After all, he has to have something for little Nadia. . . . Ah! Nadia! Welcome home!" Bazarov greeted Nadia as she entered the room. She sensed that they had been talking about her and blushed. "They are so mean and so disgusting! . . . Is there a single human being among them? But what difference does it make? Maybe I shall soon be able to leave all this behind. . . ."

Helen Kangarov listened with calm, cold fury to her husband's plea. Kangarov spoke in a low, excited voice, trying to make his words sound respectful and even tender. The approach he had chosen was extremely simple. A catastrophe had befallen two people who had been deeply in love with each other: suddenly they had discovered that they loved no longer. To continue living together under these circumstances was senseless and unthinkable. The only decent thing they could do was to grant complete freedom, and at the same time preserve their friendship and mutual respect.

During her husband's soliloquy Helen Kangarov's face remained expressionless. She listened to him calmly, without interruptions, even with a light smile which, however, did not augur anything pleasant. As far as she was concerned Kangarov's words were not at all unexpected. She had no doubt that her husband was having an affair with Nadia. "He has an awful lot of nerve!" she thought. "Over my dead body!"

"What do you mean by 'complete freedom'? Do you mean a divorce?" Helen Kangarov asked with a smile.

"My dear, I leave it to you! If two people know . . ." the ambassador began, reassured by her calmness: he had expected that his words would be greeted with an hysterical outburst. Helen Kangarov interrupted him.

"If two people know that you are living with that little bitch, I have no intention of giving you a divorce."

"Helen! You should be ashamed of yourself! I realize that you are upset, but you must try to understand. . . ."

"I am not in the least upset. Why should I be? I am not so desperately in love with you."

"That's exactly what I said. Under these circumstances the obvious thing . . ."

"Under these circumstances the only obvious thing is that you are a damned fool," Helen Kangarov said in an icy voice. The ambassador again was somewhat surprised. Within two days independently of each other two women had told him the same thing. His eyes turned yellow with anger.

"I have no intention of listening to abuse!"

"This is not abuse—this is gospel truth. You are well past fifty, you are virtually falling apart, but you let an intriguing, flat-faced little bitch make you lose your mind, or what you flatter yourself by calling a mind. What else can I call you, except a damned fool?"

"I have no intention of listening to abuse," Kangarov repeated, making an effort to restrain himself: "I must not irritate her whatever I do." But his low, excited voice seemed no longer adequate to the occasion. "I will not attempt to answer groundless insinuations which are not worthy of you, of me, or of our past," he said forcefully. "I merely ask you to tell me what is the logical conclusion to be drawn from your own words? Considering the way you feel about me, can we remain man and wife? Can we . . ."

"You can spare me your eloquence. I will not give you a divorce!"

"But why, my dear?"

"Because."

"That is not an answer. Let us look at it like two reasonable beings. If two people . . ."

"I will not give it to you, and that's that! Nothing you can say will change my mind: ever! . . ."

"Allow me to remind you that I can get along without your consent. After all, we are living in a socialist and not in a bourgeois world! Just because a man is married we do not consider him a slave. And . . ."

Helen Kangarov emitted her finest, demoniacal laughter.

"I should like to see you do it! I believe that it would be better for you to avoid a scandal. They don't pat you on the head for that sort of thing in Moscow."

"For what sort of thing? What scandal? What are you talking about? Please understand, Helen, that I have no desire to quarrel with you. Why do you insist upon insulting me? Am I to blame that . . . Is there anyone to blame?"

"Apparently you have the idea that if you were to have the right to see the little bitch, instead of sneaking to her room at night, you would be carrying out God's will? God's will has nothing to do with it! She doesn't give a damn about you! You must be a complete idiot to think that you can be attractive to a woman, even if she is a little bitch! She wants to be the wife of an ambassador—that's all she wants. She will trim you like a sheep and leave you within a year."

"Further conversation seems useless!" Kangarov said, barely able to control himself. His eyes were two pools of fury. "But as long as you have mentioned my official position, I have one other confession to make which also concerns you. I did not want to mention it until now, but I will not be silent any longer. My position in Moscow is not secure."

"Why? You are lying!"

"I have no idea why. You may not trust me in personal matters —that is your privilege! But I have never given you any grounds to doubt my political judgment," he said with conviction: he felt that he was making a dent at last. "Probably my enemies have told him something about me. You know very well what is happening in Moscow. I have heard certain things in Paris."

"What have you heard?"

"I am not at liberty to say, but I can tell you frankly: my position is not secure. You can draw your own conclusions. I may be recalled any moment, and that is not the worst that can happen. You know me: if they recall me I shall start for Moscow the same day, no matter what may await me. I will not forget the honors that have been bestowed on me, and I will not betray the trust placed in me by the party and by the Soviet government," Kangarov said, sounding like Cato suffering from a mortal wound.

"What have you heard about Moscow? You know you can trust me."

"I cannot repeat it even to you, but it was quite grave. . . . Let us suppose for a second that I am right. I am not saying that my position is hopeless," he added to make his words sound more plausible, and thinking that unfortunately it was not altogether his imagination. "But let us suppose that it is, and that I am recalled to Moscow. In view of the situation which has risen between us, would I be justified in linking your fate with mine?"

"What about her fate?"

"Whose fate? Helen, be sensible!"

"You are not trying to tell me that you are asking me for a divorce without intending to marry her? If that is so, why do you want a divorce?"

"Let us not wander away from the subject. I am not interested in bickering. I merely am asking you: would I be justified in linking your fate with mine? Are you prepared to take the consequences?"

At that moment the unexpected happened. Helen Kangarov rose, excitedly walked the length of the room, and stopping in front of her husband placed her hand on his shoulder.

"You can think anything you want about me, but I will not desert my husband when he is in trouble!" she said with deep feeling. Helen Kangarov was no longer thinking of any part she had ever played, unless it was the public reading she had given in Moscow of the poem called "The Russian Women." She was sincerely moved. "I shared your good fortune with you, and I will share your misfortune with you."

"Believe me, Helen. . . . But have I the right to accept such a sacrifice from you?"

"There is no question of right. This is my duty, and no matter what you think of me, I am not like other women. . . . Let us not say another word about it!"

"I am deeply touched, Helen, but I want you to understand . . ."

"Let us not say another word about it!" Helen Kangarov repeated and walked out of the room. The Queen's dramatic parting with the Earl of Leicester—it was the best scene in her repertoire.

"This is a catastrophe!" Kangarov thought in despair, dropping to the couch. "A major catastrophe! . . . I had expected anything but that. . . ." After sitting there for a minute or two he put his head on the pillow, started to stretch out, but changed his mind, switched on a wall light, and turned it off again. "What shall I do? I can always get a divorce without her consent. Shall I risk going to Moscow? Would they let me out again? And what will I do with Nadia in the meantime? If I take her to Russia with me, she will never come back. She will leave me if I as much as tell her about it! And if Nadia leaves me I shall be at the end of my rope!" He stared at the bracket, shaped like a question-mark, on which the wall light was hanging. "She virtually has refused me as it is. Not exactly refused me, but her answer is suspended in mid-air! I bluff when I am with her, and I bluff when I am alone, but deep in my heart I know that she is likely to leave me at any moment. Helen is right; I am old, my life is drawing to a close, it is the beginning of the end! Who was ever in love with an old man? 'You are virtually falling apart,' " he remembered her words. "Yes, she is right! Perhaps it is a crime to think of linking a youthful being with my declining life?" In desperation Kangarov felt that he could not imagine life without Nadia: she was the meaning and the object of his being. "But what if she loves someone else? Wislicenus? No, he is as much of an ass as I am. No, it would be someone else, one of the Moscow crowd, some young Ivan or Peter? Or that pug-nosed Basil whose picture she keeps on her table? I suppose she will belong to him!" With horror and bitter hatred he imagined their meeting in Moscow—a reunion in Basil's apartment. "But if that is true, what do I care about my life? To hell with it!" His heart was pounding. "An attack? What do I care? I had some medicine somewhere. . . . To hell with the medicine!" In front of the couch stood a serving-table loaded with liqueur bottles. Kangarov poured himself a glass of something out of a decanter, swallowed it, refilled the glass, emptied it again, and walked across the room. From the couch a pug-nosed man who was not a day over thirty gave him a condescending ironical smile as he embraced Nadia's naked body. "I must end it all this minute! I have no gun, but I can go to the gunsmith and buy one. Do I have to have a permit? I can show him my papers instead. . . . No, it is too far to go, and it will take too long. . . ." Suddenly his bloodshot eyes became fixed on the lamp hanging on the wall over the couch. "That bracket looks strong enough. It should hold two hundred pounds. I must test it. . . ." His breathing was heavy. He remembered his friend who had hanged himself thirty years ago in an hotel in Geneva where they had been living. "Did he use his suspenders? No, I believe he used a rope. I can find a rope. . . . There is one over there. . . . An international scandal? What do I care? Someone will see me from the street? To hell with them all! I can draw the curtain." With a shaking hand he pulled the curtain across the nearest window, hesitated about the other, decided not to bother, took another drink, and, swaying from side to side, walked over to the wall, his eyes fixed on the bracket. He squeezed himself between the wall and the couch, pushed the couch toward the center of the room, reached with one hand for the bracket, and tested it. The bracket seemed firmly imbedded in the wall. Kangarov grabbed it with both hands, and pulling up his legs hung his entire weight on it. His coat bulging absurdly at the bottom gave a tearing sound as the sleeves ripped under the arms. The bracket gave and broke out of the wall, followed by a cascade of plaster and shattered glass. Kangarov stumbled, fell on his knees, quickly jumped up and stood staring with glassy eyes at the floor.

With a perfunctory knock the secretary opened the door and froze in amazement on the threshold. "What has happened? Has the lamp fallen off the wall?" "The lamp has fallen off the wall," the ambassador repeated, speaking like a man in a trance. "I will give orders right away to have the place cl ned up." The secretary had intended to ask Kangarov about his health, but something about him made him change his mind. "The workmanship here is not very good. The other day I stood on a chair reaching for a book, and one of the legs cracked. . . . Am I interrupting you? I wanted to give you this from the king," he said, handing the ambassador a large envelope with an air of devotion and respect, as though the king had personally entrusted him with it. "May I open it for you?" Kangarov nodded. "The light is not very good in here. It is an invitation from the king, addressed to you and to your wife. . . . When you have no further use for it, I hope you will give it to me for my collection. . . . They say that this affair will surpass all former receptions! They know how to put on a show here even better than we put them on in Moscow." "Even better than we put them on in Moscow," Kangarov repeated like an automaton.

XXII

"THEY CANNOT be expecting many people tonight." Cerisier was puzzled as he looked around the empty hall of the de Bellancombre mansion. "I wonder why she insisted that I should come?" The famous lawyer for several weeks now had been a member of the inner circle in the salon of the Countess, and her invitations no longer thrilled him. All his acquaintances had been made aware that he was one of the regular attendants, and this generally recognized fact became a part of his social reputation. In some way he had gathered the impression that tonight was a special occasion, and he had worn a dinner-jacket. "This would make a wonderful scene in a cheap novel or in a moving-picture scenario:

'A brilliant reception in the palace of the Countess de Bellancombre. Ladies in evening dress, music, and champagne. As
soon as the reception is over the famous attorney, Cerisier, drives
straight to . . .'" He shuddered and decided that tonight of all
nights it was callow and hopeless to try to cultivate an ironic manner. On his way over he was unable to make up his mind whether
he should even mention to anyone where he expected to be at
dawn.

Slightly irritated by the realization that he already was suc-
cumbing to the aura of the house, Cerisier ascended the stairs
with a heavy waddle. He was more conscious of this aura than
most people. Ordinarily Cerisier made no effort to adjust himself
to the tone set by the households in which he was a visitor. He
was an independent-minded man, and subservience was foreign
to his nature. But in spite of this when he was in the de Bellancombre mansion he spoke and behaved differently from the way
he behaved in the salon of a wealthy banker, where in turn his
manner was very different from his manner with professors or
journalists. He felt that in different surroundings he was a different person. Among the elect who frequented the drawing-room
of the Countess de Bellancombre, Cerisier was a left-wing socialist
and a defender of collectivism and of the Great Revolution. He
could not help it if some of the elect were charming people who
were fond of him. Serious arguments arose only on rare occasions,
and he had to rely on his wit to defend the great principles he
represented.

The old Count met Cerisier in the first of the four drawing-
rooms. He greeted him with an expression which implied that
he expected to hear something witty and amusing. The host had
assumed that expression by mistake: ordinarily he reserved it for
Vermandois. Before dinner the Count de Bellancombre had played
bridge at the club, compensating himself ahead of time for the
wasted evening. In the course of the game he had made a play
which all the onlookers had acclaimed as a classic, as history-making, and as a stroke of genius. But, like all great artists, he was

forever critical of his own achievements, and in looking back he realized that his play had not been perfect; fate had come to his rescue just as it had come to the rescue of Napoleon at Marengo. Thoughts about the history-making play stayed with the Count throughout the evening. At dinner his answers showed that he was not listening to the conversation. This was unusual. The Count's remarks were never distinguished for their brilliancy, but as a rule he listened to people with adequate attention, and he expressed simple, universally acceptable, wholesome opinions which never placed him in an embarrassing position. The Count had no desire to be original. Besides, in his own salon which was one of the most brilliant in Paris, and that meant in the world, he had noticed that nine out of ten famous men in nine out of ten cases spoke in commonplaces. When the Count met Cerisier in the first drawing-room he was thinking about another possible variation of the history-making play, and as a result he used the wrong smile. As soon as they entered the next room he immediately directed it at the right person.

The great writer occupied his usual place in the music-room. A good part of the space was taken up by a grand piano, an organ, and an immense radio—the Countess approved of the radio only for the purpose of listening to good music. "I am so glad you could come! Tonight no one is here except our friend. I called you simply because I wanted to see you before we leave. I hope you did not have anything more interesting planned for this evening?" the hostess said graciously. "I am very grateful that you thought of me. When are you leaving?" Cerisier asked, settling cautiously into an armchair. He knew that these six ugly and fragile armchairs, along with the Nattier, Largillière, and Rigaud paintings and the Lefebvre Gobelins which hung on the walls, constituted the chief attraction of the second drawing-room. The armchairs unquestionably contributed to the atmosphere, but he was always afraid that they would collapse under his weight (the Count wearily watched his movements out of the corner of his eye). "Tomorrow morning. The reading has been set for Tuesday." "What reading?"

"Haven't you read about it in the papers? Our friend has been asked to give a reading of a fragment of his new novel. One of the most distinguished literary societies has made the arrangements. It is sponsored by the royal family." "I hadn't heard about it." "It was in all the papers," the Countess explained in an offended tone. "Our friend very seldom condescends to give a reading abroad. He is not too generous about it even in Paris." ("Why should he be? They could not find enough fools in Paris to fill an auditorium," the thought occurred simultaneously to Cerisier and to the Count.) "How very interesting! I regret terribly that I shall not be able to hear you." "You will not miss anything. I cannot understand why anyone should be interested," Vermandois answered somberly. ("Probably no one will be," the other two were in silent accord.) "If the European intellectual aristocrats were not interested, the papers would not write about it, and the manager never would have made you an offer which would flatter any prima donna," the Countess said with a smile, passing a cup of tea to Cerisier. "It is not very strong, one lump of sugar, and no lemon—I remember." She made a ritual of pouring tea, and the fact that the Countess de Bellancombre knew how the lawyer liked it was another feather in his social cap. "We just were talking about you. Last time you were here you called Turner the Baudelaire among painters. I admire the depth of your perception!" Vermandois, who apparently was in a bad humor, glanced darkly at the lawyer. "Baudelaire is just the man," the Countess repeated with a pensive smile. "Or was there something of Keats about him? . . . Do you like Keats, my friend?" "Only the English are qualified to judge English poetry, just as only the French can judge French poetry. I would go further and say that perhaps only writers have the right to judge literature," Vermandois said. The Countess laughed nervously and Cerisier impatiently shrugged his shoulders. "People who presume to judge writers in a foreign language are hypocrites and poseurs." "But, my friend, you cannot deny that X. [she mentioned the name of a well-known French writer] has understood the soul of England,

and that he knows English literature?" "I never have read any of his books, and I never will. I haven't read all of Voltaire, and I have forgotten half of Montaigne. Do you suppose that at my age I spend my time exploring the genius of Monsieur X.? And, besides, the synchronization of literary fashions in different countries is very inadequate. In London they consider the last word of literary fashion French books which to us have become nothing if not funny. Probably this works both ways." The Countess sighed and turning to Cerisier changed the subject to politics. "Yes, I was depending on the fact that my opponent would find himself in a dilemma. It was an exceptional combination of circumstances," the Count was thinking about bridge. ". . . But who, besides Hitler, is responsible? . . ." "No one can deny that British policy is at least partly to blame for the situation. They should have taken one of two courses. Either they should have declared war on Hitler . . ." "Anything is better than war!" the Countess exclaimed, closing her eyes in horror as though to shut out the vision of bloody bodies. "We all agree that war is horrible, and that it cannot solve anything. But how can we avoid war? I believe that a firm policy toward Hitler . . ." "Unquestionably that is the crux of the matter: how far is it safe for us to make concessions to Hitler?" the Count concurred absent-mindedly, thinking how much pleasanter it would be to be playing bridge instead of participating in these repetitious and hopelessly boring conversations. "Evidently it is my fate to listen until the end of my days to this talk about Hitler," Vermandois thought. With an effort he rose to his feet. "My dear, may I use your telephone? That gentleman hasn't called me? Has he?"

"No, he has not," the Countess answered hesitantly. "I imagine he misunderstood you."

"You are expecting a call from your publisher?" the Count's manner made it difficult to say whether he was being thoughtful, or sarcastic. "Come, my friend! Let me show you to the telephone."

"I am terribly worried about him," the Countess said in a frightened half-whisper as soon as she was alone with Cerisier.

"He is in a terrible state of mind. How does he look to you? His face has an expression that belongs to another world."

"I have no idea what expressions faces have in the other world, but he does not look well. He seems to be breaking. What is the matter with him?"

"Everything in general. You know that he never has been an optimist, as I have," the Countess smiled gently. "But the recent course of world events has made a devastating impression on him. He says that his pessimism cannot keep up with reality, that people are more rotten and stupid than he had ever imagined. According to him this is the end of civilization, of freedom, and of all the ideas which we hold dear. Sometimes he even says that there never has been any civilization, that it was a myth—one of the many myths created by people to console themselves. You may say that he contradicts himself? But contradictions are no surprise to him, he knows that he contradicts himself at every turn. Obviously, it is impossible for me to repeat everything he says. According to him during the last century a certain semblance of rational civilization had appeared, but now the primitive nature of man has once again reasserted itself, and this semblance of civilization is rotting, decomposing, and polluting the air. . . . I cannot remember everything he says! . . . Besides, he has no money. . . ."

"You mean his income is not large?" Cerisier asked curiously. "So that's it! That accounts for his pessimism," he thought.

"I can be frank with you because I know that you like him. His publisher is exploiting him. And our friend is so punctilious about money matters! We should be only too happy to help him, but I cannot even broach the subject to him. It seems so terrible to think that a man of his genius needs money! At the age of seventy he has to work like a horse ["he is older than that," Cerisier thought]. And literature owes him so much! . . . I arranged this invitation abroad. The manager is paying him ten thousand francs for this reading and he is promising all sorts of things: world-wide lecture tours, radio broadcasts . . ."

"That does not sound bad. Our friend's financial distress seems to be relative," Cerisier said. "Ten thousand francs for an hour and a half of drivel," he thought angrily.

"Though he abhors readings, perhaps the change will help him. I suppose there will be banquets and speeches in his honor? Isn't that true? Our ambassador there is a personal friend. . . . I have written to him, and we shall be invited to the king's Ball. . . . That should amuse him? What do you think?"

"I think that it is wonderful to have a friend like you," Cerisier said with sincere feeling. "If the occasion should ever arise, I should like to go somewhere with her. Nothing can stop her!" he thought. "But considering his communist leanings, how will our friend feel at the king's Ball?" he asked with a laugh.

"His communist leanings! . . . I know what they are! . . . I find that even I am somewhat disappointed in the Soviets. . . . Did you get him?" the Countess turned to Vermandois, who had entered the room looking gloomier than ever. "He was not at home? I was afraid of that."

"But didn't the publisher himself set the hour? Such atrocious manners!" the Count said cheerfully, but wilted immediately under his wife's indignant stare.

"You can talk to him as soon as we get back. When he hears about your reading, believe me, he will be in a much more receptive frame of mind! . . . Who will have another cup of tea? So you believe that geography will be the deciding factor in the Spanish war?" she asked Cerisier. The political discussion was resumed.

Vermandois made no pretense of listening. Apparently the publisher was unwilling to advance the new sum he needed. A smaller advance would mean a serious financial loss and a blow to his self-respect. Again he thought bitterly that he was the only famous man in France without money. "I should have written moving-picture scenarios, or the kind of novels that Emile writes. They all are like that! Money is the most important thing in the life of this hack, of this Narcissus of a shyster, despite his protestations and belief that 'ideals' are everything—his cheap, catch-penny, political ideals." At that moment (this happened to him frequently) he violently hated the rich. "If there should be another world war, or if the communists should come into power, God willing they will lose everything. It is an ill wind that blows nobody good," he gleefully imagined the picture of Cerisier without money. "The old fool, too, will shed her communist sympathies!" But the old fool, as he called the Countess, irritated him much less than the others, or, rather, being irritated with her had become a habit. The Count was simply a nobody. "But the appearance of this legally-minded gentleman affects my nerves as much as the sight of a drill in a dentist's office. The most disgusting thing about him is this combination of a venal mind with 'political idealism.' And most ridiculous of all, his 'political idealism' is almost sincere. When these gentlemen ascend the rostrum they forget their shyster tricks and their log-rolling. A capacity to change their personalities is part of their character. That is why when they become ministers of state they can assume any personality at any given moment. Danton? He can be a Danton. Machiavelli? He can be a Machiavelli. Cavaignac? He can be a Cavaignac. Though probably there was something of Cerisier in the real Danton. But the men of seventeen-ninety-three did everything on a grand scale, and there was less of the mercantile spirit about them, and then they were playing to a first-night audience and not merely giving the three hundredth performance in a successful run. Though in some ways Cerisier is a direct descendant of Danton. Every great tragedy in history, beginning with the French Revolution and ending with the San Francisco earthquake, has had the trivial ending of a moving-picture scenario. . . ."

". . . But France is not ready for war." "Hitler will never risk a war. Believe me, it is nothing but bluff. And even if he is serious you do not for a moment think that Germany and Italy can fight a successful war against the coalition of France, England, and Russia?" "I still hope that Mussolini is fooling Hitler. He is a product of Latin civilization, and he has a more subtle and bril-

liant mind. . . ." As usual, Vermandois felt the urge to argue—
that urge for which later he always berated himself.

"In Europe today there is only one man who knows what he
wants," he said in a voice which precluded any possibility of a
dissenting opinion. "And this man Hitler is a dull fanatic whose
objectives are incredibly stupid, rotten and horrible. If he is successful we shall have to do away with the expression 'homo sapiens,'
because apparently it is nothing but intolerable bragging. And
if that is so, what is the basis for democracy? In the minds of
the classicists of democratic mythology it was faith in human reason. But now it has become obvious that the people are incapable
of governing themselves, because of their shortcomings, one of
which is that they are too stupid. This does not mean that gentlemen who wear evening clothes are more intelligent than the mass
of people." He looked out of the corner of his eye at Cerisier.
"These gentlemen are as much to blame for Hitler being in power
as are the people who entrusted them with the affairs of state.
Unfortunately, among the social and political programs which
exist in the world today those that are ambitious are stupid and
disgusting, while those that are reasonable are absurdly vague
and petty. Confronted with the choice between Hitler and a five-
cent increase in his income tax the German 'homo sapiens' chose
Hitler. In this era of 'government by the people' a new, or perhaps a long unused weapon has been discovered. We have had
infantry, artillery, and cavalry, and now we have mysticism. Or,
if you prefer, you can say that cavalry has disappeared and has
been replaced by mysticism. And we have overlooked its possibilities, just as in 1914 we had overlooked the possibilities of
heavy artillery! We made a point of rationalizing everything, including what little faith was left in France. This was a mere
oversight, but it happens to be extremely important. The Germans
have made a cult of a small man with a mustache. We could have
found something to offset it without any difficulty. For instance,
we might have made a cult of the wife of the President of the
Senate. . . . Two or three years of preparation, a billion francs

for bribing the press, and we should have had a very good cult. That's how we should have spent our money instead of wasting it on the Maginot Line. But we overlooked the value of a cult, and that is unfortunate, because on account of this oversight we shall lose the war."

"Why do you make such an issue of the mustache? Hitler has a mustache, but your Stalin has one that is even longer and more luxurious," the Count remarked. He detested Vermandois not for his communist leanings, but because he had transformed the de Bellancombre household into a political salon which interfered with the Count's bridge.

"Mohammed knew the value of a cult when he appropriated ninety-nine flattering epithets," Vermandois continued. "But in the first place, that is not enough. Why only ninety-nine? In the second place, the technique of deifying men has progressed since the days of Mohammed. Radio has dealt a terrible blow to the cause of liberty. The conquests of science have served to prostitute civilization. You will live to see the day when the reproductions of Velasquez will be much more beautiful than the originals."

"I cannot quite understand what Mohammed and Velasquez have to do with it," Cerisier said, shrugging his shoulders: this was a rare opportunity for a serious argument. "Only men who are blind, or who have no wish to see, persist in the assumption that democracy has given the people nothing more than an extra 'five cents.' My friend, have you ever heard of President Roosevelt, and of his program? I am glossing over the intellectual arrogance of juxtaposing oneself to humanity—of saying that while man in general is stupid, I am not. . . . Besides, to say that man is stupid means nothing. If he is stupid, let us try to improve his mind. In order to progress, this stupid 'homo sapiens' must be free for a certain minimum length of time. Slavery and ignorance will not improve his mind. Man can learn the art of self-government only by exercising his rights."

"That may be true. Unfortunately the course in self-government usually is discontinued long before the end of the term. Men with mustaches do away with this course before the people have had an opportunity to learn. Strangely enough, though morally and mentally these dictators are the dregs of society, their pedigree is always democratic. They all sprang from the people. Hitler is a house painter, Mussolini—the son of a blacksmith, Stalin —the son of a shoemaker. Our gracious host, I believe, is the twelfth count in his distinguished line. In his presence I dislike to put forward the theory that aristocracy no longer produces dictators."

"Two corrections," the Count said. "First: I am the sixteenth, and not the twelfth count in my line . . ."

"My dear, you have missed another opportunity of letting something pass in silence," the Countess said with a smile, though inwardly she was pleased with her husband's remark.

"Secondly, Pilsudski belonged to the nobility, even if he was not an aristocrat in the strictest sense of the word." The Count retreated into silence. For at least five minutes after such an outburst he did not have to bother about the conversation.

"If man is bad, we have to create a society which will make him better," Cerisier said. "The words about the divine spark in the human soul are as true today as they ever were."

"What good is the divine spark if man cannot do anything half-way decent with it?" Vermandois interrupted him angrily. "I am tired of hearing about this divine spark! The less of it a nation has, the more powerful it becomes. According to the laws of history—incidentally, that is an expression which always turns my stomach!—the rate of speed at which a people travels toward its own destruction is in direct ratio to the growth and development of its civilization. The Spartans conquered the Athenians, the Romans conquered the Greeks, the Barbarians conquered the Romans."

"But in the last war the victors were the free, democratic nations."

"They were victorious not because they were free, but in spite of it. At a certain level of cultural development a people loses interest in war, in soldierly qualities, and in military glory.

Human duplicity immediately provided an ingenious explanation: love of soldiering and of military glory does not necessarily mean love of war. That's ridiculous! Without a love of war there cannot be any enthusiasm for a military career. A general who has not fought in a war is a paradox. A good soldier cannot be sincere in hoping that he will go through life without fighting a single war. Obviously, that is one of the most important factors underlying all wars. The situation of the world would be hopeless if it were not for a lucky accident: the most powerful country in the world, the United States, happens to be a democracy, and it has as an ally the Atlantic Ocean. But what would the classicists of democratic mythology have said if by some accident Germany had had the greatest number of men, and the greatest reserve of natural resources and factories? A free man was a better soldier than a slave as long as the slave was armed with a bow and arrow, while the free man was armed with a gun. But when the material progress of the two is approximately equal, the free man and the slave are, at best, equals as soldiers."

"All this is very stimulating, but experience has taught us that ominous prophecies never come true," Cerisier remarked. "De Tocqueville predicted the downfall of the United States. Edgar Quinet predicted the downfall of England. You are predicting the end of civilization. My friend, you are looking on the dark side!"

"My dear friends, I want to make a motion," the Countess hurriedly interrupted. "I believe that is the proper parliamentary procedure? . . . Tonight in London N. [she mentioned the name of a famous conductor] is giving Mozart's 'Requiem.' The concert will begin in a few minutes. Would you like to listen? Does anyone object?"

"At this moment I cannot imagine anything that appeals to me more than listening to the 'Requiem,'" Vermandois said. Cerisier nodded. The Count felt that even the 'Requiem' was better than this silly conversation. He walked over to the radio and began to turn the dials.

"I wish you would make your views more explicit," Cerisier said. "The masses are stupid, but the men who wear collars and ties are not any better. Democracy is no good, but neither is dictatorship. Can you tell us what it is that you advocate?"

"*Mesdames et Messieurs, vous allez entendre . . .*" the announcer began in a deep-throated voice. The Countess impatiently waved her hand, and the Count turned down the radio.

"I know this fellow. He will take five minutes to tell us the history of the 'Requiem'—stories every child knows by heart!"

"Yes, about the manservant who had been sent to Mozart for the 'Requiem' which his master had ordered. And about Mozart, who believed that the manservant in his grey livery was a messenger from heaven, or from hell," Vermandois said darkly. "Mozart's death was not due to sad forebodings, but to some prosaic internal disease which was aggravated by a chronic lack of money. ["He dwells too much on money; he even judges Mozart in the light of his personal experiences," Cerisier thought.] The words of the 'Requiem' are connected with a legend which is much more plausible. The poem *'Dies Irae,'* remarkable for its rhythm and for the force and weight of its words, according to the legend was written in prison, in the thirteenth century. A criminal who had been sentenced to die wrote it on his last night. . . ." The muscles in Cerisier's face twitched. Vermandois looked at him with surprise and continued: "You can guess the end of the story: next morning the criminal was being led to the gallows; on the way he recited his poem, and the deeply moved inquisitors pardoned him on the spot. . . . Too bad that the Gay-Pay-Oo and the Gestapo are not as sensitive to the charms of poetry. . . . You better turn on the radio, my friend, or else we shall miss the beginning."

". . . *Et le plus grand musicien de tous les siècles expira dans les bras de ses amis inconsolables après avoir entendu les sons de son immortel chef-d'oeuvre que vous allez entendre maintenant. . . .*"

XXIII

"'. . . *Quid sum miser tunc dicturus*. . . . *Cum vix justus sit securus*. . . .' If the court is so strict that the innocent barely escape punishment, why shouldn't we sin a little?" Cerisier said with a smile. The Countess shook her finger at him. "Yes, after this masterpiece there should be silence and more silence. Don't you agree, my friend?" he turned to Vermandois who with his eyes closed was sitting in an armchair. He had not taken part in the first exchange of impressions. "He has aged terribly—he looks at least eighty!" the lawyer thought. Vermandois gave a start and opened his eyes. The Countess watched him nervously.

"I am so excited," she said. "You non-believers cannot possibly understand what it means."

"Mozart was a Mason," Cerisier corrected her immediately. "His lodge worked to his music. . . . But we should not argue after listening to the 'Requiem'! . . ."

"The argument has been settled for us," Vermandois said, looking gloomier than ever. "Mozart's pupils have worked on the 'Requiem' and have changed it to suit themselves. But *'Dies Irae,'* *'Tuba mirum,'* *'Rex tremendae maiestatis'*—that's Mozart. That's one of the highest peaks ever reached by art. It bares everything, it is the ultimate self-revelation, even so false a being as man finds it difficult to lie for two or three hours, after hearing it. . . . And, as usual, truth carried to an extreme became self-contradictory! Subjective truth so easily and so imperceptibly becomes an objective lie. In contrast to Balaam, Mozart wanted to pronounce a benediction, but he sounds as though he is invoking a damnation. Mozart probably loved life as no one else ever loved it. And suddenly the unexpected! It seemed that he was going to die! How could it be true? Good Lord, how could such things be? How could they be possible? No more Vienna—Vienna with its churches, its Prater, its boiling hot coffee, and its delicious red wine! No more Salzburg with its mountains and its skies! No

more women! No more sun! And—a thought too horrible to contemplate—no more music! Gracious God, how can that be? . . .
Something had to be done! . . . So he did it. Last straws can
always be found, and each year they save an amazing number of
people in this world from drowning. In his day there were two
strong faiths in the world. One faith was still in the bloodstream
of the people; it was old, tried, ageless, and mellowed by a
thousand years of stormy existence. The other faith had just
come into being and was new, young, and aggressive. Both
offered him their consolations. You say he was a Mason. Yes,
Mozart was a Mason, but he also was a Catholic. The old faith
promised him eternal life in a better world, it promised him love
—a higher, eternal spiritual love. 'Oh, God! That is not what
I need. That is not the love I am crying for! To me that is a
mere abstraction! . . .' The old faith promised him music—
the eternal music of eternal life. 'But I shall miss the other music
—my kind of music! What shall I do with the toneless music of
souls for which I, Mozart, perhaps have no ear and no talent.
I know my kind of music! The music which is the chief object,
and the main joy of my existence! The music which I helped to
create and to which I still can give more than anyone else! . . .'
Then there was the other—the enlightened, freethinking Masonic
consolation. It was weaker, much weaker. Faith in reason, faith
in justice, hope of an earthly existence which in its comforts
would equal paradise. 'But what does it mean to me? I shall never
live to see it! . . .' Enlightened faith smiled modestly. Men—
intelligent men—for its sake were willing to face barricades and
certain death. Mozart reached for that straw too. In the end he
became resigned—what else could he have done? We all become
resigned. But unlike the others he told us everything in his
immortal masterpiece. He told us the whole truth and advised
others not to lie. Vaguely he began to believe in the 'Rex tremendae maiestatis' . . . Everything that existed in Mozart's day
still existed when I was beginning my life. Now life has been
drained of everything; little is left of the first faith, and the

second also is fading. Nothing exists that can fill the chasm:
there is no third faith! What can you offer in place of those
two? What can you give us in place of a 'Requiem'? Offers are
seldom lacking. But they all are warmed-over dishes, cheap
seventy-seventh editions, flat and anemic variations of a dying faith.
. . . No idiot will want to be burned at the stake in the name
of universal suffrage, or of the gardens of paradise around the
glass houses built by the Gay-Pay-Oo—or at least no one but
an idiot. Besides, people generally have lost the spirit of martyr-
dom. Too many fires have burned too many fools! . . . Don't you
agree with me, my friend?" he tauntingly asked Cerisier. "You,
for instance! . . . Not only would you never volunteer to be
burned at the stake, but you would not even risk defending a safe
Parisian barricade against a possible attack by harmless Parisian
policemen. First, because policemen may become rough, secondly
because erecting barricades is an offense carrying a ninety-day
prison sentence, and finally because in your absence no one can
take care of your clients. That being the case, how can we believe
in the permanence of the democratic order anywhere, and especially in our senile country? I should have imagined that at
least the first faith would have had more courageous defenders,"
he said, glancing at the Count, who seemingly was not paying any
attention to Vermandois' words. Cerisier shrugged his shoulders
and glanced at his hostess as though to invite her to bear witness
that he was not challenging anyone, but that on the contrary
he was very calm under severe provocation. The Countess watched
them nervously, ready on the instant to interrupt an argument.
"Don't worry! I attach no significance to his words—I refuse to
take them seriously," the reassuring smile of the lawyer tried to
convey to her.

"Allow me to refute your argument about the barricades,"
Cerisier said. "Perhaps I will not defend them—though how can
you be so sure? I will fight if I am driven to it. . . . But even
if I don't, others who are younger will defend them. You are wrong
when you say that the ideal of liberty no longer will generate

enthusiasm in this world. I assure you that it will arouse emotion to a high pitch. And so will the ideals of equality and of the brotherhood of man. . . . No matter what you say, civilization is indestructible. It will not and cannot disappear: what would become of it? You are worried because you have been unable to find a third faith, but, personally, I still am perfectly satisfied with the second."

"And I am satisfied with the first," the Count said coldly. "You have disposed of it much too soon, my friend. It will outlive the second, and the third, and the thirty-third."

"I am so happy for both of you," Vermandois answered. "Mozart was right: resign yourself and choose a fairy tale that pleases you. Whether it is rational or irrational, earthly or spiritual, you still can wait for your particular *'Rex tremendae maiestatis.'* But you, my friends, will have a *'Rex tremendae maiestatis'* on this earth, and he will be a man with a mustache and with incredibly stupid ideas. Humanity is marching toward a dumping ground. You can run after it with a torch in your hand, you can run ahead, proclaiming that the dumping ground is in reality a crystal palace. Either is more pleasant than standing on the side-lines and being vaguely conscious of one's questionable righteousness. The temptation is great to say: 'Reason exists no longer—we can get along without reason!' But somehow I cannot do it. Apparently I am bound too strongly by my ties with the nineteenth century and with the century which preceded it and was even more naïve. Occasionally I am flippant about them, but they are my life, I live in them, and I shall die with them. . . . And one other thing," he added suddenly to the surprise of his listeners. "I often have been accused of internationalism. Conceding for the sake of the argument that it will be a crystal palace and not a dumping ground, I still have no desire to see a better and happier world, if France does not play a leading role in it. A world without French culture and without the French language does not interest me! And we are a tired and a senile country, we are the most ancient among all the living nations, our civilization has lasted longer and has been fully as fruitful as the Greek civilization. I only hope that I shall die without hearing France's 'Requiem'!"

The others stared at him in amazement. Leaning heavily on the arm-rests, Vermandois rose and began to take leave of his hostess.

"You should not excite yourself like this. Why are you leaving so early? But I suppose you must get a good rest tonight."

"I am certain that no one here has any intention of burying France," Cerisier said in a puzzled voice, warmly pressing Vermandois' hand. "I wish you luck. I am terribly sorry that I shall not be present at the reading. *Bon voyage.*" He too made a motion to leave, but the Countess detained him.

"I am so afraid for him," she said again as soon as Vermandois, accompanied by his host, had left the room. "I don't want to mention it, but I know how much you love and appreciate him. His health is bad—very bad. Besides, he seems to have placed himself in the hands of some idiot or criminal. Can you imagine it, the last time he examined him he told our friend that his blood pressure was a hundred and ninety?"

"That is not necessarily fatal. People have higher blood pressure and live. They have effective ways now of lowering it," Cerisier replied. Lately, he too had become interested in the subject of blood pressure.

"But who on earth would ever tell a patient a thing like that? . . . Believe me, I made a veritable scene when I talked to this doctor on the telephone. . . . It never occurred to me that the 'Requiem' would upset him so. . . . Did you remind our friend that we shall stop for him tomorrow on the way to the station?" she sternly asked her husband, who had just entered the room.

"Yes, I reminded him," the Count answered. He had been terribly bored, but he was happy to see that his guests, who had interfered with his bridge, had suffered from boredom even more. The Countess gazed pensively at Cerisier. "What kind and beautiful eyes she has! This writer who no longer can write is a poseur incapable of thinking straight, but she adores him! She is a generous and wonderful woman!" Cerisier thought. Suddenly he remembered where he had to be at dawn, shuddered, and took his leave.

XXIV

"Yes, probably there is a modicum of truth in what the old Narcissus said," Cerisier thought with an uneasy feeling, as he ascended the steps to his house. "The 'Requiem' bares the soul, and after listening to it one has at least to be honest with one-self. . . . But how am I to blame? I have done everything I could to save the unfortunate young man. No one paid me, and I defended him as though I were receiving hundreds of thousands." He checked himself and was satisfied that it was true—he was a conscientious lawyer. "I am going there in a few hours in case I can give him some moral support. Is it my fault that I am alive, and that I shall remain alive after he is executed? The reason I went to see the Countess was because I wanted to avoid offending her with a blunt refusal, and because I could not face this evening alone. Of course, the moving-pictures could make another sensational caption out of it: 'After the brilliant reception at the Countess de Bellancombre's the famous lawyer returns to his spacious, luxurious apartment, and goes to sleep in his snow-white bed. . . .'"

Self-analysis for Cerisier, as for most people, was a difficult, unpleasant and unusual occupation. He entered his study, turned on the desk-light, took off his dinner-jacket and vest, and hung them on the back of the armchair. Usually, before going to bed he made himself a cup of camomile tea. He saw no reason why tonight should be an exception. "Why should it be? I may as well continue in the honest key sounded by the 'Requiem,'" Cerisier searched his mind and decided that he would be lying if he were to say that he could not drink his camomile tea on the eve of his client's execution. "Yes, I know, five hours from now a young man who has committed a horrible crime will die an awful death. . . . Why call it awful? Tuberculosis and cancer, from which thousands of people will die tonight, are much worse. He will die an unusual death. I would be a hypocrite to think that because of this I shall not be able to continue living as I have lived before. No matter what happens I shall have to go through with the appointments that have been made for tomorrow. . . ." With a frown he remembered that tomorrow he had two business appointments in his office and a business lunch. They could not be cancelled, or at least it would be very inconsiderate of him to do so, especially since one of the clients was coming all the way from Fontainebleau to see him. With an uncomfortable feeling he realized that at lunch tomorrow his friends, having seen the papers, would know where he had been the night before. "For the sake of appearances they may not at first ask anything about it. And again, they may begin asking questions as soon as we meet. Be that as it may, the conversation is certain to touch on the subject. How should I behave? Shall I pretend that I cannot eat? Shall I give vent to my outraged humane feelings? Shall I shudder and give them all the gruesome details? Man is a hypocrite and the effect of the 'Requiem' wears off quickly. . . ." He was relieved when he realized that the Countess and Vermandois would not have time to read the account: they would leave in the morning, and the morning papers would not have the story, though very likely they would carry some cautious and disgusting hint about the *"Bois de justice"* ("what a revolting expression!"), about the executioner who. . . . "They never write about an execution ahead of time, but they consider hints permissible: we are informed that. . . . Next day they can go in for all the blood-curdling details: reporters are paid by the line. They view such things with professional indifference, and I have no right to talk about them because my attitude is much the same. That is the most horrible thing about it: the complete indifference men show for other men. As a general rule, human nature is not cruel or vicious, but it is indifferent and weak. . . ."

Having filled his cup, Cerisier returned to the study and frowned again when he remembered that he had to think about the proper clothes. That day, before putting on his dinner jacket, he had worn a brown, or rather a light tan suit with a dark red tie. No established rules existed about the clothes a lawyer should wear at the execution of his client. "Certain things go without saying. Obviously, I could not wear a dinner jacket, or a light suit! I should dress the way I would dress if I were going to the funeral of an acquaintance. . . ." He took out of the cupboard a black suit and a dark blue tie. "It's disgusting! . . . Everything is disgusting! . . . What shall I do now? . . ."

Four and a half hours remained until the time set for the execution. "No use trying to go to bed: I could not close my eyes. Shall I spend the rest of the night in an armchair? I must find something to read, or I shall lose my mind." But 'the honest key' of the "Requiem" made him admit that nothing of the sort would happen. "People lose their minds from brain injuries, from apoplexy, from syphilis, but never because they are excited, especially if the excitement concerns the fate of someone else. What shall I read? Something philosophical? Some light novel? . . ." Cerisier considered this a moment: no, he did not feel like it. He remembered that in some scientific work he had seen a detailed description of an execution. His excellent memory helped him to locate the right book. He found the well-bound, shiny volume in his large, neatly arranged library and settled in an armchair. For some reason he did not feel like wearing a bathrobe. Instead he unbuttoned his trousers and his shirt collar, moved the desk light over, and placed the cup on the little table by the armchair.

"Dès qu'un homme est condamné à mort, sa vie devient sacrée. . . . L'homme est vivement depouillé de tous ses vétements, qu'on jette bien vite loin de lui, afin qu'il ne puisse les atteindre, car peut être y a-t-il caché une arme ou du poison; rien ne trouve *grâce, pas même les souliers, pas même les bas. Quand il est nu, comme Dieu l'a créé, on lui fait endosser le costume de prisonniers, la dure chemise, le pantalon, la vareuse de grosse laine grise, les forts chaussons feutrés: il a l'habillement complet, sauf la cravate, sauf le mouchoir, car il pouvait essayer de s'étrangler. . . ."*

"How horrible, but then I always was opposed to capital punishment," Cerisier thought. "Such horrors will not exist in a socialist society. We cannot be held responsible for the atrocities committed by the Russian socialists. We support them—up to a certain point—because they are conducting a great social experiment and because our course is dictated by various tactical considerations. Does that make us responsible for them?" he asked himself. With an unpleasant sensation, Cerisier shook his head, took a sip from the cup, and turning the page, continued to read:

". . . La tête, separée vers la quatrième vertèbre cervicale, est lancée dans le panier, pendant que l'exécuteur, d'une seule impulsion de la main, y fait glisser le corps sur le plan incliné. La rapidité de l'action est inexprimable, et la mort est d'une telle instantanéité qu'il est difficile de la comprendre. Le glaive oblique et alourdi de plomb agit à la fois comme coin, comme masse et comme faux; il tombe d'une hauteur de 2ᵐ,80; il pèse 60 kilogrammes, ce qui, en tenant compte de l'action de la pesanteur, produit un travail équivalant à 168 kilogram-mètres. La chute, calculée mathématiquement, dure ¾ de seconde (exactement 0,75.562)."

"The man is a scientist, but what an awful way to use science! . . ." Cerisier thought, still under the spell of the "Requiem." "How can one fail to be ashamed for humanity? . . ." Cerisier glanced at his watch and decided that Alvera still must be asleep. "Provided a man in his position can sleep at all. In three hours they will enter his cell. Their steps and the sound of their voices will awaken him. . . . 'Courage, Alvera! The hour of retribution is at hand! . . .' A glass of rum, a cigarette . . . " He remembered his call on the head of the state, which had been so unpleasant for both of them. "I could not tell him anything new. He was familiar with the case—he is a conscientious man. But why should this distinguished engineer have to consider the question of pardoning a convicted criminal? What a burden it must be to know that in the final instance a man's life depends on his decision! The jury rendered the verdict, the judge pronounced the sentence, but he has to decide whether the man is to remain alive. The only risk he runs is that his decision may be criticized by the rightist or the leftist press. Decision is made too easy for him. . . . No telling in what position life—present-day life—may place him some day. . . . He told me that he would take the matter under advisement, and I bowed, indicating my faith in his charity. . . . The President refused the pardon, but he can still enjoy his coffee and liqueurs after dinner." He continued to read and discovered that beyond a certain point the horror of the scientific description had no effect on him.

"*On traverse les allées pleines de cyprès, où les tombes amoncelées semblent manquer de place et se pressent les unes contre les autres, on franchit une vaste palissade en planches, et l'on pénètre dans la partie réservée aux supplicies: c'est le Champ de navets. Rien n'est plus désolé: la terre grise et laide est bosselée çà et là; de larges tranchées sont ouvertes et attendent leur proie. . . . Le cadavre a les yeux ouverts ou fermés selon que le glaive l'a frappé pendant qu'il ouvrait ou fermait les yeux. On enlève au corps les entraves qui lui liaient les jambes, les poignets et les bras; s'il porte quelque vêtement qui ne soit pas absolument hors d'usage, ceux qui l'ont amené s'en emparent; puis on traine le panier près de la fosse, on le penche, et l'on verse le cadavre, qui tombe avec des mouvements étranges, sinistres, car il a conservé son élasticité, et il semble faire des gestes que l'absence de tête rend grotesquement horribles. On peut remarquer sur le cadavre le même phénomène physique que produit la mort par suspension ou strangulation. . .*"

. . . He awoke with a start. The desk light on the table by the armchair still was burning, the book which had fallen out of his hands was lying on the rug. Cerisier glanced at his watch and smothering an exclamation, jumped to his feet. "Five minutes of four. I am too late!" His heart was pounding. He put on his slippers, rushed into the bathroom, and ran a comb through his hair. He would not get there in time, even if he were lucky enough to find a taxi without any delay. "Should I phone the garage? No, that would take even longer! . . ." Hurriedly he tied the blue tie, slipped on the vest and coat, and suddenly realized that he had on the trousers which belonged to the dinner jacket. With a curse he pulled them off, tearing out a button with the suspenders, mechanically picked it up, pulled on the other trousers, slipped on his overcoat, and rushed outside. Remembering that he had forgotten to turn out the light, he made a move to go back, but changed his mind, and ran down the steps. "No, I shall never make it! . . . Perhaps I should not try? . . . I can say that I was ill, or I can blame it on my convictions. . . ."

A taxi appeared from around the corner. In a desperate voice Cerisier called to the driver: "Versailles! I will give you the address when we get there!" The driver seemed to hesitate. "An extra twenty francs if you make it in a hurry! Drive as fast as you can! . . ." The running and excitement made him pant. Cerisier leaned back and buttoned his vest and overcoat. Passing under a street light, he caught a glimpse of a clock: two minutes past four. "This might have happened to anyone," he tried to reassure himself. "It's not my fault that the days in the office wear me out. . . . It's shameful and inexcusable, but it could have happened to anyone. . . ."

They heard the distant rumble as soon as they reached the city limits of Versailles. Cerisier listened, trying to hold his breath. The rumble grew more distinct. The driver, who realized at last where they were going, glanced suspiciously at the lawyer. "They will not let us by!" he said. "They will let me by—I am the lawyer," Cerisier answered, taking the ticket out of his pocket. "Go as far as you can. . . ." People were running along the sidewalks. "Curiosity seekers. . . . Every one of us has a streak of morbid curiosity. . . . The crowd is just as the newspapers describe it: prostitutes, gangsters, and society women," he thought, staring at the people. He could not see very clearly in the dimly lighted street. "What kind of people are they? For instance, who is this? The man by the street light—is he a gangster? No, just an ordinary shopkeeper, and the woman with him is his wife and not a prostitute. . . . I too have a streak of morbid curiosity, but I have improvised a legitimate excuse: what moral assistance can I possibly give to a man who is about to lose his life? . . ."

The car diminished its speed. The rumble grew louder and more terrifying. The driver turned his head and shouted something, but Cerisier could not hear a single word. Suddenly bright lights appeared on one side, and the taxi came to a stop. Around the corner stood a detachment of gendarmes, beyond them a huge, noisy crowd, and still farther a row of men on horseback. The square was flooded with lights. With few exceptions all the windows in the surrounding houses were brightly illuminated. "Keep going! . . . I will show them my ticket. . . . You can tell them! . . ." Cerisier shouted. The driver shook his head hopelessly, without counting stuck the money in his pocket, and climbing hurriedly onto the seat, stared with avid curiosity, over the heads of the crowd and the police, at the lighted square. Cerisier jumped out of the car and ran toward the police line. Suddenly the rumble changed to a wild, terrifying howl, which just as suddenly was cut short. A silence followed. Then again the noise began to grow in volume, but now the sound was entirely different.

The police cordon still stood at the corner, but now they were letting people pass without looking at their tickets. The crowd was streaming out of the square. The mobile guards rode by with drawn faces. The street became darker. One after the other the lighted windows were darkened. Some of the street lights too were being extinguished. Slowly Cerisier made his way through the crowd, which was moving in the opposite direction. Snatches of conversation reached him from every direction. ". . . No, he was not afraid! No use talking, he was a brave man. . . . They will need men like him in the next war." "The two have nothing in common. . . . Courage in war is something entirely different. I remember. . . ." ". . . He refused to see a priest, and he refused a cigarette. All he wanted was a glass of rum. . . ." ". . . I did not realize that it would be over so quickly. Thirty seconds!" "No, no! It took much longer than that: at least two or three minutes. . . ." ". . . No matter what you say, it is horrible! His lawyer virtually proved that he was insane!" ". . . It is a gruesome spectacle! And did you notice the morbid curiosity of the mob? . . ." "I suppose you, Pierre, are the only one who has a healthy curiosity!" ". . . I saw everything as plainly as I see that policeman! But I arrived here at ten o'clock. . . ." ". . . If he was insane, this was a terrible injustice! Insane people should be treated. . . ." "You never could do anything with him! He would have lived for years and years at our expense! . . ." "Money has nothing to do with it! We should not think of money when human lives are involved! . . ." ". . . They awakened him at four. . . . Just imagine how long the wait must have seemed to him! . . ." "Why all these formalities? We are great ones for that. . . ." ". . . The man whom he killed must also have suffered. . . ." ". . . After all, it is an easy death. . . . If it were not for the disgrace, I should not mind dying like that. . . ." "Soon we shall be fighting another war, and hundreds of thousands of people will die from gas, which is much more painful than the guillotine." ". . . They should not admit so many foreigners to France!" "Many foreigners make fine citizens, and many Frenchmen are killers. . . ." ". . . Good Lord! I have to get up tomorrow at seven! . . ." "Tomorrow? You mean today." "What is the sense of going to bed? Let's go to a bar— they will be opening soon. . . ."

Beyond the first cordon of police was a second, and almost in the center of the square a third. Swaying on his feet, Cerisier approached the last line and stopped, leaning heavily against a street light. Most of the guillotine had already been dismantled:

only one post remained upright. Someone was pouring water on the pavement out of a watering can. Beyond the police cordon a man in uniform was sitting on a folding chair. He was writing rapidly with a fountain pen on a sheet of paper spread out on a briefcase in his lap. A man in civilian clothes who looked like a newspaper reporter was talking to an elderly commissary. "So he showed no sign of being excited?" "He was very calm. During the last few days he acted like a man who has lost his mind. Many of them put on an act, but once in a great while along comes one who is crazy. . . . The prison guards told me that something happened to him on the night before his trial. Nervous shock, probably. . . ." "Why hadn't the guards mentioned it to their superiors, or to his lawyer?" The commissary shrugged his shoulders. "I don't know. It would have been too late anyway. Besides, he may have been acting." "I suppose most of them do put on an act. I never can understand such people. . . ." "They are people like you and me," the commissary said indifferently and glanced at Cerisier.

"What can I do for you?" he asked. The lawyer silently handed him the ticket. "It's all over. Can't you see that everybody is leaving?"

"I . . . I . . ." Cerisier began. His head was spinning. This was the second or third time in his life that he had felt dizzy. A dignified, elderly man in a dark grey coat approached them, glancing from side to side as though he was searching for something. From the photographs he had seen of him in the papers Cerisier recognized the Paris executioner. Speaking in a low voice, he addressed a question to the man sitting on the chair. Without looking up, the man pointed his finger to the left and rose to his feet. Cerisier's eyes followed the direction of his finger, and he saw several men carrying something heavy toward a black wagon drawn by a black nag, standing under a street light some distance away. The commissary peered anxiously at Cerisier's face, glanced hurriedly at his ticket, and said:

"Are you ill, Monsieur? Would you like some water? Quick!

. . . Some water!" he shouted to the policeman as he gently steadied the lawyer on his feet. Someone brought the folding chair. Cerisier rested his weight on it, and fainted.

XXV

THE READING was not a success.

Vermandois had a premonition that everything would go wrong. On the way from Paris he caught cold, and his voice was hoarse. "The entire performance will be terrible! I shall be absolutely ridiculous!" he morosely warned the Countess while they were driving in a car from the hotel to the auditorium. He had a superstitious belief that this might help: whenever he warned anybody ahead of time that a reading would be bad the result was usually passable. "You could not be ridiculous! It is simply the cold you have caught in this terrible weather," the Countess answered with determination, as if he were blaming his cold on malignant supernatural forces. Her voice was vibrant with excitement. The Count bleated something unintelligible.

The audience was large. By stretching a point one might say that the auditorium was filled to capacity, but the point definitely had to be stretched. Along the wall on the stage, back of the speaker's table, stood two rows of chairs reserved for guests of honor and patrons of art in the eventuality that all the regular seats were sold out. In the side room opening on the stage the manager, looking alternately worried and frightened, whispered to the Countess that many of the seats in the front rows were still empty. "Perhaps they will arrive at the last moment?" the Count suggested with a note of glee in his voice. "That's not important! But don't you think the extra chairs on the stage should be removed?" the Countess asked nervously. "I told you that they would not be necessary!" To remove the chairs under the watchful eyes of the audience seemed awkward. "It really is not important! . . . The very cream of smart society is here tonight. Don't you think so?" The manager cheerfully named several important people in the audience. None of the members of the royal family or of the cabinet were present.

His stiff shirt shining, the prominent critic who was to preside over the meeting entered the room. He shook hands with Vermandois and said that it was time to begin. "We make it a point to begin on time. My introduction will not take more than fifteen minutes." "Yes, yes! Let's begin!" the Countess said firmly and left the room with a farewell smile of encouragement such as a trainer gives to a fighter when he pushes him into the ring. With quick, short steps she walked toward the front row. "Too bad they left those chairs on the stage," the Count said, settling down next to her. "There are more than enough seats in the auditorium." "That does not mean a thing!" the Countess whispered angrily. She tried not to look at the empty seats. Usually, only people who appreciated finer things occupied the front rows.

The prominent critic pulled back the curtain over the door and invited Vermandois to enter first. The audience gave him a warm reception. While the applause was not tempestuous, it was more than adequate—by stretching a point it even could be described as an ovation. Smiling and inclining his head to one side, the prominent critic also clapped several times and fixed his eyes on the guest to show that his own presence was not in any way responsible for the applause.

The critic took his seat behind the table and proceeded with the introduction. He repeated all the generalities which Vermandois had heard and read about himself during the last half-century (the only variable quantity were the adjectives which became more extravagant as he won new literary laurels and as his years of service grew longer). "The brilliant Epicureanism blended with the great artist's thoughtful and sensitive awareness of contemporary problems vital to mankind" were mentioned; so was the "warm and generous heart beating behind the brilliant paradoxes"; so was the "crystal pure style which carries on the tradition of the grand century"; so was everything else. The critic spoke with such affectionate interest in his own figures of speech that the audience hung breathless on his words. With a supreme effort Vermandois fixed a gentle, self-conscious smile on his face which was intended to convey his protestations: "Really, I did not expect all this! . . . This is too much! . . . I do not deserve it! . . . But every word he says is so clever and so brilliant! . . ." ". . . He has been called an Epicurus, but he is an Epicurus who, over the thousand-year-old aromatic flame of a great civilization, has been fused with a Gracchus!" the critic said emphatically, and inclining his head to one side again, smiled at the guest. With an unprintable word ringing in his mind, Vermandois responded by making his smile even a shade more modest and self-conscious. "Ladies and gentlemen, there is little else I can say. Allow me to extend on your behalf, as well as on my own, a warm welcome to this great writer who has come to us as an ambassador of French thought to which mankind owes so much." His concluding words were followed by applause which grew in volume as the ambassador of French thought shook hands with the critic, changed places with him, adjusted the reading light, and opened the cardboard file which he held in his hand.

Vermandois began with a brief introduction of his own. His voice ringing with emotion, he thanked the critic for his brilliant and far too generous words. With an emotion just as deep he thanked the audience which had filled the auditorium—he had been told that he had the distinction of addressing the finest minds, as well as the élite, of capital society. He said that he realized only too well that their presence was not intended as a compliment to him, but rather to French letters, which he represented in a very modest capacity. He referred in the most flattering terms to their capital where he was a guest, to its beauty, and to its charming hospitality. Then he continued with a brief résumé of his new novel, and playfully asked them not to become alarmed at the thickness of the file. He was not a ruthless man, he said, and he would read only one chapter, "The Return of Aristippus," which unfortunately was long, but, perhaps, less boring than the others. He said everything just right, exactly as he had said it hundreds of times before. But almost at once he became conscious of a false note and of the hoarseness of his voice, and knew that the reading had not gotten off to a good start. To top everything else, in turning over the pages of the manuscript he noticed in a conspicuous place, at the end of a paragraph the words: ". . . *l'or et les pierres précieuses dont elle lui fit don*. . . ." "What is the matter with me? Have I forgotten how to write?" Vermandois was horrified. "I have read it hundreds of times! If I missed this, there must be other passages like it! . . ." With a nervous stroke of the pencil he made a note in the margin. He always held a pencil in his hand during a reading—this occupied at least one of his hands. After he had finished the introduction someone in the audience began to applaud, but the others remained silent, apparently considering that before the reading a third burst of applause was superfluous. "Perhaps I was not sufficiently complimentary? . . ." Vermandois blew his nose and cleared his throat. The Countess watched his every move with approving and frightened eyes. He began to read: "Aristippus was returning to Athens . . ." (Aristippus was the new name of Lysander, who still earlier had been Anaximander). The first sentence struck him as being unbearably trite for any audience—even for this audience. "He was not returning anywhere, he is an imaginary figure, and at my age I should be ashamed to spend my time inventing stories about a non-existent Aristippus. . . ."

Vermandois read very badly—much worse than usual. He knew that he was reading without expression, and that the audience was not reacting properly. His cold and his hoarseness made it difficult for him to speak. He joked apologetically about it, but like everything else that evening the joke fell flat, and besides it came at the end of the best passage in the chapter, completely destroying its effect. But he doubted that the audience was capable of appreciating it anyway, just as he doubted that it would have noticed the *"dont elle lui fit don."* The people who were supposed to appreciate the finer points occasionally exchanged glances and smiles, but invariably at the wrong moments and, as time went on, less and less frequently.

After reading for forty minutes Vermandois stopped for an intermission. The applause was not as loud as it had been when the guest had first appeared on the stage. One possible explanation was that the greatest ovation was being reserved for the very end. The prominent critic announced in stentorian, almost threatening tones, that the intermission would last ten minutes. Overwhelmed by a painful sensation of awkwardness and shame Vermandois hurriedly retreated behind the curtained door. A minute later with a broad smile and with both hands outstretched, the Countess appeared in the room. But the expression on her face and the manner in which she praised him told him that he had not been a success. "My friend, what an amazing chapter even for you, and I assure you that your way of reading it was equally amazing!" the Count said and his beaming face left no further doubts: the evening was a failure—a complete fiasco.

The prominent critic entered the room accompanied by three local authors, whom he treated in a cavalier fashion. Realization of his firmly entrenched power was written on his face. "I am delighted! . . . I have been looking forward to this meeting! . . ." Vermandois said, firmly shaking hands with the local authors and registering pleasure on his face. "If I could only remember what in the devil they have written!" Vermandois thought angrily. "But to hell with them!" The three young authors behaved like tourists from the provinces who have been visiting the Louvre and suddenly find themselves face to face with the Gioconda. The critic made several valuable remarks about the novel. The local authors spoke chiefly about their love for French literature. Toward the end of the intermission the manager came in. His expression reflected sorrow for humanity in general, and with a strange, almost furtive movement he weakly pressed the hand of Vermandois. The Countess continued to extol the merits of the novel.

The intermission was over. The number of empty seats in the auditorium appeared to have increased—or was it his imagination? The row of chairs on the stage looked derisive: *memento mori.* Vermandois' attempt to get into the right state of mind by artificial means had not succeeded. Of late he had not been successful in anything he had undertaken—his last success seemed to date back to the days before the World War. At the moment, his sense of frustration was aroused by an important-looking man who, with eyes closed and mouth wide open, was asleep in the front row, not very far from the Countess. The Count watched the sleeper with an approving eye. The Countess glared at the old man with scorching hatred. If she could have strangled him and carried the body out of the auditorium without being observed, she would have done so then and there. Sensing more clearly than ever that if there was any subject that was a matter of complete indifference to the audience it was the return of Aristippus to Athens, Vermandois continued to read in a flat voice. About five minutes before he finished someone in the center of the auditorium rose, cast a furtive look at the chairman, doubled up, and with his coat over his arm tiptoed toward the exit. His example encouraged others, and five or six more followed him. The eyes of the Countess were terrible to behold.

The end of the reading was not followed by a stormy or any other kind of ovation. Vermandois rose, bowed to the audience, folded the manuscript, and stuck his pencil in his pocket. He was applauded. The prominent critic said a few more words, but without inclining his head to one side. The manager had vanished. In the car, after a long silence the Countess made unguarded mention of the stupidity of the audience and its lack of appreciation of the finer points. The Count's smug expression bordered on the indecent.

As soon as they reached the hotel Vermandois said that he had a headache and went to his room, though the Countess vacillating between despair and adulation suggested that they celebrate with champagne. "Certainly! Tonight of all nights we must have champagne!" the Count insisted brazenly. "You remember that we have to go to the museum tomorrow, my friend?" "By all means! . . ." "They have a Melchior d'Hondecoeter here with which I am not familiar!" "We will take a look at this Melchior d'Hondecoeter! . . . You cannot afford to miss it! . . ." Vermandois said with quiet hatred.

Vermandois spent a restless night. Public opinion made virtually no difference to him. The audience had been bored, but it would have been equally bored if Racine in person were to rise from the grave and read: *"Il suivait tout pensif le chemin de Mycenes . . . "* Quickly Vermandois climbed out of bed, found the place in the manuscript, and drew a line through *"dont elle lui fit don."* "Perhaps some parts are repetitious. But it is better to use 'Paris' three times on one page, than to resort to journalistic expressions such as 'The City of Light,' or 'The Capital of the World.' Besides, that is a minor point. The public is not aware of such technicalities. . . ." The concrete results of his failure were not pleasant. In Paris the manager had spoken enticingly about a series of lectures in various European countries and of a grand tour across North and South America. The very idea of a "series of lectures" horrified Vermandois, but the amount of money mentioned would have provided him with a comfortable cushion for the rest of his days. "I should have to suffer for half a year, but then I would have no more worries about having to earn a living. . . . At seventy 'the rest of my days' has a strange sound! . . ." Now all these plans would have to be discarded: the manager certainly would not renew his offer. Thoughts about honest poverty, and even about dying on straw as a free man, passed through his mind. Rembrandt and Beethoven had been poor. . . . But Raphael and Voltaire had been rich. One could be a free man on straw, but it was more comfortable to be a free man on something else. . . . "I hate rich people. . . . But there is no use fooling myself—I am not fond of paupers either. . . . The thing to do is to plunge heart and soul into some great collective undertaking. Without that, life has no meaning. It has little meaning even with it. . . . Should we follow Flaubert's advice and live like fakirs—

with worms in our bodies and with our heads in the clouds? But wouldn't it be more pleasant to get along without worms? . . ." He took a sedative and fell asleep at half past two.

When the telephone rang late next morning, Vermandois awoke with a heavy head. "The manager!" he thought hopefully for a second. "My friend, is there anything wrong? I thought you were to call me at nine," the Countess said with gentle reproof in her voice. "I called you at nine on the dot, but no one answered. I thought perhaps you were still asleep." "How odd! I could not close my eyes all night!" He realized that his lie had not been adroit. Nothing could be more insulting to the Countess than the supposition that she was sleeping, and sleeping soundly. "I will be down in thirty minutes," Vermandois promised, horrified at the thought of spending the entire day in the company of the old fool.

XXVI

WEARING FULL dress Kangarov knocked on the door of his wife's boudoir. "*Entrez, entrez!*" Helen Kangarov called. A French hairdresser was arranging her hair for the ball. Unable to turn her head she smiled at the ambassador's reflection in the mirror. For the benefit of the hairdresser the smile conveyed tenderness, but also a certain uneasiness. Helen Kangarov worried more and more about her husband. "He does not look well, even in evening clothes!" she thought nervously. The hairdresser bowed respectfully to the ambassador and wished him a good evening. But though he used the word *"Excellency"* which ordinarily had a soothing effect on him, Kangarov merely nodded to the hairdresser and curtly asked his wife to hurry.

"We have plenty of time, my dear," Helen Kangarov said meekly. The words "my dear" had no connotation of tenderness—her husband did not deserve it—but neither did they imply hostility. Before the ball she was in excellent, almost exhilarated spirits.

Helen Kangarov was pleased with her coiffure (the hair-dresser was not the famous one who was recognized the world over as the master—his prices were out of the question—but the second best, whose position in relation to the master was like that occupied by Marlowe in relation to Shakespeare). She also was pleased with the dress which was spread over the boudoir arm-chair: turquoise trimmed with silver. Only the complete absence of jewelry annoyed her. On this question she had had a slight en-counter with her husband soon after she had been presented at court. Kangarov had told her positively that she "could not, should not and would not" wear any jewelry. This triplicating form of speech was supposed to indicate that the ambassador's mind was made up and that nothing could change it. Thus after Stalin's victory he had told everyone in Moscow that he "never was, never could and never would be" a follower of Trotsky. "We have no money to throw away on jewelry, Helen. As it is, your wardrobe just about ruins me. You know the modest budget on which an ambassador has to live." "Jewelry as such does not interest me," she answered with dignity ("as such" was one of her favorite expressions). "But I have to dress like the others." "What others do you mean? Who at court will notice your jewelry? Do you imagine that you can impress the queen with a two-hundred-franc diadem?" Kangarov had the haziest notion of the value of diadems. "Our position makes any show of this kind indecent. After all, you are the wife of a man who represents a proletarian state, and not some bourgeois republic!" "That has not stopped you from ordering two full dress suits," Helen Kangarov became sar-castic—the idea of a two-hundred-franc diadem was not in the least alluring. "There is a great deal of difference between jewelry and full dress. It is not my fault that extra long tails suddenly came into fashion." "And is it my fault that I cannot appear three times in the same dress?" Helen Kangarov responded bitterly, though until then there had been no mention of dresses, but lacking the diadem she at least had to have the last word in the argument. Their rambling conversations were never distinguished for their logic.

This had taken place a long time ago, before the appearance of the trouble maker, as Helen Kangarov called Nadia whenever she refrained from referring to her as "that little bitch." She based this devastating description of Nadia on moral grounds, as well as on her physical attractiveness. Now a conversation of this kind between Helen Kangarov and her husband would have been impossible. After she had refused to give him a divorce they spoke only in the presence of others, adhering to a policy of a minimum of politeness.

"On the contrary. But we have very little time, my dear. You must hurry," Kangarov answered. The manner in which he emphasized "my dear" was pregnant with meaning. The most likely interpretation was: "you may as well stop trying, everything is at an end between us, as you will soon find out!" Helen Kangarov was reasonably certain that her husband would not attempt a divorce without her consent, but his tone and his manner worried her. "What is he plotting now, and what will I find out?" In order not to lose her festive mood she did not answer. Instead she reassured her husband with a friendly wave of her hand around which was draped the loose sleeve of her dressing gown. The ambassador left the room with another curt nod to the hairdresser, who had been waiting for the end of the Russian conversation in an attitude of respectful resignation. Any abrupt movement by his client was likely to undo all the results of his painstaking labors.

Kangarov returned to his study. He disliked everything about the room, especially the wall light which reminded him of his attempt to take his life. He stopped in front of the beautiful writing desk which he had inherited from his predecessor. During the last quarter of a century nothing had changed in the ambassador's study, except that the portraits of the Tsar and the Tsarina had been replaced by portraits of Lenin and Stalin. The envelope that had upset him so much two hours ago was still lying in the lower tray with the rest of the incoming mail. Among the letters which had arrived from Moscow there was one addressed to Nadia. "I cannot open it, I cannot hide it from her, and besides what's the use?" he thought as he reached for one of the two contrastingly colored telephones which stood on his desk. The head of the government to which he was accredited had the same type of telephones on his desk, except that he had three, while Kangarov was unable to find any possible use for a third one. When he had first arrived at his post the two gaily colored telephones had given him a great deal of satisfaction. Before the revolution a private telephone never occurred to him in his wildest dreams. But now the telephones no longer interested him. "Is Nadia still here? She is? Will you please tell her to come to my study."

Kangarov again picked up the ordinary-looking, yellow envelope, bearing a Soviet stamp. "It's from one of her Ivans or Peters. . . . Or perhaps from that pug-nosed fellow? . . . The letter is not important. . . . But what on earth shall I do if the slut will not give me a divorce? . . ." On that day when he had attempted suicide Kangarov had called his wife the first vile word that came into his mind, and since then in his thoughts he always referred to her as "the slut," as though it were her given name, or party alias. "If necessary I will get a divorce in Moscow without her consent! I will explain everything to them! Debauchery is one crime with which they cannot saddle me!" he said to himself with conviction and, pulling up the tails of his coat, settled into an armchair. The stiff white shirt, decorated with pearl studs which because of their modest size could not be considered jewelry, bulged in front. "I will get a divorce! I will get a divorce! . . ." he repeated mechanically several times.

An unmistakably diplomatic knock sounded on the door. "Am I intruding?" the secretary asked as he fixed his frightened eyes on the pale, tired, puffy face of the ambassador. "Your wife asked me to tell you that she will be ready in twenty minutes," he said with a mild show of disapproval. He was on the best of terms with Helen Kangarov (as he was with everyone else), but he felt strongly that messages of this kind should be entrusted to the servants and not to the diplomatic staff of the embassy.

"What did you say? You speak so indistinctly that I cannot hear a word of what you are saying," Kangarov said angrily. The secretary sighed. "Just to think what women can do to a man!" He repeated the message and changed the subject to more important matters.

"Should I remind you of the instructions we received yester-day?"

"What instructions? Oh, yes . . . Let's postpone discussing them until tomorrow."

"I thought that perhaps the matter should be considered before the ball. . . . Louis-Etienne Vermandois will be at the palace. You may want to begin with him?"

"Begin with him," the ambassador repeated absent-mindedly and suddenly came to life. "What terrible manners! After I have dined and wined them in Paris, this Vermandois and his friends, the Count and Countess de Bellancombre, have not even bothered to leave cards at the embassy!"

"They have been here only two or three days. I am sure they will pay us an official call. Incidentally, I went to the reading that Louis-Etienne Vermandois gave last night, but unfortunately it was a fiasco. I went because I wanted to hear a famous writer who unquestionably is one of the outstanding advanced thinkers in the bourgeois world," the secretary explained impressively. "Can you imagine my surprise? The auditorium was half empty, and the applause was very half-hearted, especially toward the end. He chose a remarkable but somewhat boring chapter, and he read very indifferently, though not without originality."

"I am glad to hear it. He had it coming to him."

"May I suggest that you consider speaking to him tonight at the ball? . . . In connection with our instructions," the secretary explained. "He has a big name, and his opinions are respected by

leading left-wing, middle-class circles in Europe and America.
. . . In both the Americas," he corrected himself. Kangarov
nodded, indicating that he considered the suggestion a sound one.

The entire problem was most unpleasant. In the diplomatic mail received at the embassy the day before was a letter—
the secretary insisted on calling it "instructions"—mentioning the
Moscow trials and directing the diplomatic representatives abroad
to do everything in their power to mobilize European public opinion for a protest against the moral support which the international
bourgeoisie was lending to subversive forces in the U.S.S.R.
Having read the letter, Kangarov had handed it silently to the
secretary, from whom he had virtually no secrets. The secretary
had taken a long time to read the letter, carefully studying each
word. His whole appearance had borne mute witness to the
high degree of his mental effort. "I feel that there cannot be any
doubt about the purport of these instructions," he had said, glancing over his shoulder at the door. He could not lower his voice
because the ambassador's hearing was not as good as it had been.
"Please come to the point without any subtleties." The secretary
had looked at the ambassador, with silent accusation in his eyes
—he was sincerely devoted to him—and had expressed an opinion
based on a careful reading of the letter. A new public trial was
in the making in Moscow. The color of Kangarov's face had
changed, and he had re-read the letter. "Yes, probably you are
right," he had said, thinking: "If I were on the suspect list, they
would not have sent these instructions to me. . . ." The secretary
had understood the thoughts of his superior, and Kangarov had
known that he had understood them. The silence that had followed had been so meaningful that it became almost eerie. "How
can I mobilize public opinion?" Kangarov had asked angrily.
"They refuse to make any special appropriations. I suppose they
think that we can buy it with caviar!" "Money is not everything in
this case. Just as important are tactfulness and . . . and dexterity," the secretary had said softly, unable to find the right words
at once, but finally overcoming the difficulty. "Tactfulness and
dexterity are most important. They are not so stupid!" he quickly

corrected himself: "They know what they are doing when they come to you with a matter of this kind." "Dexterity! . . . God-damn dexterity! . . . What we need is money and plenty of it, and to hell with dexterity!" Kangarov had answered, though he had been pleased by the compliment of the secretary, who was not addicted to flattery. For a few minutes he once again had become his normal self. "How stupid, how monstrously stupid are the things he is doing in Moscow! Why all this terror, these executions and repressions, and against whom are they directed? Against the comrades of Lenin! This is worse than a crime, this is a mistake!" the ambassador had thought, feeling like a combination of Fouché and Talleyrand. He had exchanged glances with the secretary. Obviously the same thoughts were running through the secretary's mind, but nothing could have forced him to voice them.

"Did you call me?" Nadia asked, entering the study. She had stayed later than usual in the embassy because she had some unfinished work, and also because she wanted to catch a glimpse of Helen Kangarov's dress, which already served as a subject for jokes, enthusiastic comments, and speculations as to the price, among the staff. Nadia, too, was considering a new dress. "I would be irresistible in the one with the 'dentelle cirée,'" she thought, with sad irony remembering a dress she had seen in the window of a Paris shop. "But who do I know here who is worth going after? Certainly not the secretary! . . ." Anyway, that particular dress was out of the question. "Even if I never took any dessert, I could not in a year save enough to buy it! . . ." Of late she had developed a taste for candied fruit, and her resolution not to eat any sweets was being postponed from day to day. The thoughts about the dress and about the necessity for saving turned her mind to Kangarov. The week before, she had told herself definitely that she would not marry him under any circumstances. "But I will continue working for him until I find another job. What else can I do? As far as he is concerned, 'As Such' can have him!"

The secretary bowed and left the room. In the last few days

his diplomatic bearing had undergone a slight change. Before, whenever he was in the company of Nadia and the ambassador his expression seemed to say: "I have not seen, heard, or noticed anything improper." The new and additional shade of meaning was: "But even if there is room for gossip, I have no intention of delving into people's private lives; in any event, I propose to observe strict neutrality as between the two parties." The "two parties" were Nadia and Helen Kangarov. The secretary was willing to extend to both of them the benefit of what is known in diplomatic parlance as "the most favored nation" policy.

"Why are you here so late, my sweet?" Kangarov asked, brightening noticeably. Addressing her as "my dear" no longer satisfied him, and he had been calling her "my sweet," or even "sugar." "Are you working?"

"Yes, I typed the memorandum you dictated to me yesterday. I have just finished it."

"You are becoming very ambitious. . . . There is a letter for you. From Moscow," the ambassador added, watching her with suspicious eyes. Nadia blushed: she immediately recognized the handwriting of Gene, from whom she was expecting to hear about her story.

"Thank you . . . Is there anything else?"

"No, nothing else. I just wanted to tell you . . . But if you are impatient, open the letter and read it. I will wait."

"No, I can read it later."

"May I inquire who it is from?" Kangarov asked in a casual way. At that moment the telephone on his desk began to ring. With an inward curse he picked up the receiver. Pretending that she did not want to be in his way while he was talking on the telephone, Nadia slipped out unobtrusively, and ran to her room. Her heart was pounding. "My fate will be decided in another second!" she thought, though apparently her fate had been decided and sealed some time ago. "Help me, oh Lord! Help me, oh God!" Nadia prayed. She locked the door, tore open the yellow envelope, and with shaking hands unfolded the letter and glanced at the first lines: ". . . good news . . ." She emitted an involuntary exclamation.

"Nadia, my dear, my great Russian writer, I hasten to let you have the good news. Your novelette is appreciated muchly; it has been accepted, and it will appear in one of the first forthcoming issues of our magazine. . . ." Nadia was so excited that she unconsciously pressed her hand against her heart. "I want to be the first to congratulate Nadia Gorky, the great writer. So, if Your Honor remembers, a certain Gene was not so stupid when he advised you to write? Apparently the same Gene, on occasion, can be of some use, even though ages ago, in a certain city known as Moscow, he met with disfavor and with haughty contempt? Both specialists who have perused your story are unanimous in stating that its literary merits are more than satisfactory, and that its ideology is above reproach. The opinion of these two men is shared fully by a third who in point of time was your first reader and admirer, who has some say on the magazine, and whose name, my dear Nadia Dostoyevsky, will have to remain unknown to you. Certain faults have been noted, and certain minor changes and cuts in the *magnum opus* will have to be made. But you can rest assured, Nadia, that nothing important will be omitted" (first he had written: "we will not omit," but had crossed it out). "In addition, the editorial office plans to do away with the word 'novelette,' an intention to which I, the undersigned, fully subscribe. Why a 'novelette,' my dear? What is a novelette? You have written a splendid realistic story, and that's that. If you, my dear Nadia Shakespeare, care to have my personal opinion, I feel that your characterization of Eugene is the weakest link in the story. But that is a minor point. By far the most important are the ideological content, the setting, and the restraint with which you write, and which, remember my words, very soon will bring you into the front ranks of Soviet literature. My only advice is: write, write, and keep on writing! You have a good chance of equaling" (the preceding word which began with the letters "overshad . . ." had been crossed out) "the popularity of Gorky! If that should ever come to pass, don't forget, my dear, that a certain Gene . . . But not another word about it now. . . ."

"A new life! An entirely new life! A beautiful new chapter is under way!" Nadia thought (even her thoughts were now couched in literary terms). "Now I am not afraid of anything: I am a writer —a Russian writer . . ." Nadia was not the first or the last person to be enraptured by the sound of those two words. Her imagination associated them with adjectives from reviews which were certain to come: "the gifted Soviet writer," "the talented Russian writer," "the well-known writer." Her imagination lacked the courage to go as far as "famous," or beyond.

At intervals Nadia re-read the letter and paced the floor of her room. "Yes, now I can go back to Russia and create!" This was a word that also had magic in it. Nadia was not certain whether she created when she wrote. She was honest with herself, and she could not pretend that God was guiding her hand. "They say that the minds of great writers are crowded with images. . . . But isn't my Kartalinsky an image? . . . I wonder what makes Gene say that my characterization of Eugene is weak? . . . No, I don't believe he said that it was weak," she glanced at the letter again. "'The weakest link,' but not necessarily weak. . . ." The matter of remuneration was mentioned toward the very end of the letter; the amount was much larger than she had expected. Nadia was happy—happier than she had ever been in her life. Her thoughts were confused. She had an urge to discuss with someone the sudden break in her life, but she knew no one with whom she could talk. Tamarin was better than the others, but she had not heard from him since she had received his post card from Madrid. With an uneasy feeling she remembered Wislicenus. Obviously, something strange had happened to that man. His name was never mentioned at the embassy. On one occasion, in the course of a casual conversation with the secretary, Nadia had referred to Wislicenus. She had a fleeting impression that for an instant the secretary's eyes had reflected terror, and he immediately had changed the subject. "Shall I tell the secretary?

He is stupid, but he is not a bad person. And not so stupid, at that," Nadia mused. She felt that under the circumstances she could not be too critical of anyone. But she visualized the boring, solid, appropriate and involved sentence which the secretary would deliver when she told him the news, and she gave up the idea. Suddenly she experienced a passionate desire to let Helen Kangarov know about her success. "This will spoil the ball for her!" she thought. And though Nadia told herself that as a Russian writer she should be above settling scores with a dull, flighty woman who had such limited interests, the temptation was more than she could bear. She simply had to let Helen Kangarov know. Dropping the letter in her desk drawer, Nadia went to the ambassador's study.

Kangarov stood motionless by the divan under the wall light. Nadia was struck by his wooden expression and by the blank stare of his eyes. "Most people look heartier in their graves!" she thought with sincere compassion, knowing she was responsible for his condition. "But what can I do? How am I to blame? . . ."

"Yes? Who? What?" Kangarov asked, fixing his bloodshot eyes on the door. Even in her compassionate mood she barely resisted an impulse to answer: "No. Nobody. Nothing. I came to ask whether you needed me any more?" But Nadia felt that such an answer was now out of the question. Frivolity was at an end, and such a tone would be out of keeping with their new relationship. In the future he was to be her superior, and she was prepared to take his orders in the line of duty, but that was all. She remained silent. He gave a start, as though he had just become aware of her presence.

"What happened to you?" he asked in a hoarse voice, settling in an armchair. "Sit down, my sweet! I thought you were reading your letter, but the first thing I knew you had left the room."

"You were talking on the telephone and I thought that perhaps it was a private conversation," she said in a mild tone. "I finished your memorandum. . . . Here is the carbon copy. . . ."

"Thank you . . . I meant to ask you about the letter. Anything interesting? Any news?" Kangarov asked. Recently he had acquired the habit of asking questions in an oddly brusque manner such as is affected by character actors taking the part of Napoleon, and gradually it had come to be one of his mannerisms. "If it is not a secret, who was the letter from?"

"Nothing secret about it. It was from Eugene Golubovsky," Nadia answered, becoming irritated. Her patience was quickly exhausted. "I realize that I should not forget that he is a sick man. But what did he care about my reputation? And what does he care about his 'As Such'?" To her amazement Nadia found herself for no apparent reason siding with Helen Kangarov. "He is the young writer I told you about." Suddenly she felt the urge to talk running away with her, and she knew that she would blurt out the news.

"A writer? I have never heard his name. . . . Anything interesting?"

"Nothing very exciting. Interesting only as far as I, personally, am concerned. . . . I doubt that you would be interested. Not having anything better to do ["what a stupid way of putting it!"] I recently wrote a story and sent it to . . . [she mentioned the name of the magazine]. The editors liked it and have accepted it. It will be published soon."

Kangarov stared at her with bulging eyes. He had a vague premonition that in some way this was bad news.

"What did you say?"

"Didn't you hear me?" ("That again is the wrong tone to take!")

"You wrote a story? What kind of a story?"

"A realistic story, which in a way is symbolic. I hope you will read it when it is published."

"My sweet is a writer! . . . Just look at her! . . . But why didn't you show it to me? You have never even mentioned it!"

"Why should that surprise you? . . . You know about it now, but I would rather you didn't mention it to anyone else. Naturally, if you want to say something to your wife or to the secretary I have no objection," Nadia said indifferently. Kangarov watched her with puzzled eyes. He still was not clear in his mind why this should be bad news, but he was uneasy. In any event this gave him a pretext to kiss her.

"Congratulations, my sweet! With your permission . . ."

"Leave me alone!" Nadia said, angrily pushing him away. "Leave me alone! I simply must have a serious talk with you. I insist that you get all this nonsense out of your head."

"What nonsense? Get what out of my head? You little simpleton!"

"Simpleton or not, I feel I must tell you that you seem to be laboring under a misapprehension. Up to a certain point I thought you were joking. But if I was mistaken I want you to understand once and for all that I have no intention of marrying you. And I would advise you not to divorce your wife. But that is your business, and I apologize for even mentioning it. . . . I also wanted to tell you that I have definitely made up my mind to return to Moscow. I should like to go as soon as possible. You will have no difficulty in finding someone to take my place."

"You have lost your mind!" Kangarov said, his face taking on an apoplectic hue. With a single movement he rose to his feet. His features were contorted, and his yellow eyes completely insane. "What if he has a stroke? Or what if he tries to hit me?" she thought, and watching him with terrified eyes she retreated several steps. Kangarov followed her. Even had he not been wearing evening clothes, he would probably not have struck Nadia, but he certainly would have clutched her hands or her shoulders. But the full dress and the bulging stiff shirt made any impulsive gestures impossible.

Just then the door opened quietly and Helen Kangarov entered the room. Nadia's face turned a deep red. More as a matter of habit Helen Kangarov looked her over disdainfully from head to foot. She tried to be calm; all her thoughts were on the evening ahead of her. She seemed not to notice her husband's condition, or at least she pretended not to notice it.

"Good evening," she said drily, and turning to her husband

added: "You see I am right on time. After you were in such a hurry I suppose I shall have to wait for you, as usual."

Nadia left the room. She was very upset. For the first time she felt that there was something cheap—very cheap and degrading about it all. She would have had difficulty in defining what "it all" was: her relations with Kangarov, her feud with his wife, her own trivial thoughts, conversations, and emotions, or the general atmosphere of the embassy. "I really deserve something better!" she thought. Her eyes filled with tears. "It is time for me to go home! I need to live differently. . . ." Years later, Nadia came to consider this the most important day in her life, and not only because she had learned that her first story had been accepted. Suddenly, at first dimly and vaguely, her life, the people around her, Russia, and the purpose of her own existence began to take on a new meaning. She ran to her room, locked the door, and for a long time paced the floor. Tears were streaming down her cheeks.

XXVII

ON THE day set for the ball the chamberlain had little more work than usual: the century-old palace mechanism was functioning without any confusion. As on any other day, the chamberlain rose around ten. For a quarter of an hour after opening his eyes he lay in his absurdly huge, canopied bed that looked like a bier, and considered a variety of pleasant matters: the ball scheduled for that evening (to his amazement even in his old age he derived a great deal of pleasure from court balls), the conversation he had had the day before with the charming young princess, and above all the newest and finest treasure in his stamp collection. Two days ago, after a great deal of painful hesitation, he had finally violated his budget and all his calculations, and had acquired a British Guiana, 1856, "black on magenta, the famous error." This was insane. But he felt that without the British Guiana life lost for him most, if not all, of its charm.

The chamberlain was ready at a quarter past eleven. He had no respect for statesmen who began their day, or who went to bed, at five in the morning. If they could be believed, many ministers of state worked as much as eighteen hours a day. For many years the chamberlain had known intimately all the cabinet ministers in his own country, as well as many foreign statesmen. As a result of his observations he was convinced that nothing tragic would have befallen the world if they had devoted less time to their work—"if they had followed the example of Bismarck, who never rose before noon." He also took for granted that it was a physical impossibility to work eighteen hours a day; to tell a lie was much easier.

In the chamberlain's own department there was no need for an eighteen-hour working day. After finishing breakfast, he made an inspection tour of the palace, ascertaining that all his orders had been carried out to the letter, and then went for his daily canter through the park. He never rode less than an hour, and the figure cut by the handsome old man on a thoroughbred had a reassuring effect on the most confirmed pessimists. He seemed to be a living proof that nothing could be wrong with the world. After lunching with the royal family, he retired to his apartments, rested, worked on some report or other, and wrote a page in his diary. That day he could not spare any time for his stamp collection, but no matter what he was doing his face brightened every time he remembered the British Guiana, 1856, which at last was in his possession.

The chamberlain ate dinner in his own apartments, which were assigned to him in the royal palace as part of the perquisites of his office. He had his own cook. The king's cook the chamberlain considered quite mediocre, and whenever circumstances made it possible, he ate dinner at home. At seven-fifteen, a little earlier than usual, though he was dining alone, and though he would have to change again immediately afterwards, he put on a dinner jacket. The wits in the royal entourage insisted that when he was sick and in bed, he put on a dinner jacket or full dress every evening before taking his medicine. The chamberlain went into the immense drawing-room filled with old-fashioned furniture, with large portraits of the kings adorning the walls. In this room everything belonged to history; a historic, seventeenth-century murder had even been committed in front of the fireplace. He settled in an historic armchair and slowly sipped a glass of 1878 sherry which was served to him on a heavy silver tray by a giant butler. Then he proceeded to the historic dining-room and sat down at an historic table lighted by wax candles in historic candelabra.

Unlike the old prince, the chamberlain was not by any means hostile to all innovations. But he had occupied these apartments for over twenty years—they were as magnificent as any of the rooms in the king's suite—and he considered it unnecessary and unseemly to make any changes in the mode of life established by his predecessors. Every place had to have a fitting style, and here nothing had been changed. The dinner was served exactly as it had been served to his predecessors, with a menu written out in French longhand, with a multitude of courses, and with four different wines, each served at just the right temperature.

As a rule the chamberlain preferred not to read at the table, but that night he glanced at the headlines in the evening papers. Some idea of the latest news was almost necessary before the ball. The headlines instantly killed his desire to read any further. All the events were of such magnitude or threatened to assume proportions of such magnitude, that their very immensity became tiring. "Fortunately, God willing, enough is left for our lifetime," the chamberlain vaguely consoled himself. "Things like that never happened in our day," he said to himself, in the past tense. "We must preserve what we can, everything we can, and as long as we can. '*Je maintiendrai*' is an excellent motto."

Sad thoughts could not spoil the chamberlain's dinner. He enjoyed eating alone—guests interfered with his appetite. Having finished, he retired to the drawing-room where he lingered over his coffee, sipping cognac served in a large glass, and pondering the arrangements for the ball and the newspaper headlines. On the wall facing the armchair hung the portrait of a king who three hundred years ago had won the sobriquet of Ferocious. "In any issue of an historical magazine we can always find parallels to present-day events. But taking into consideration the number of atrocities committed, and the fact that these contemporary gentlemen believe that their form of government is advanced and enlightened and they, themselves, even more so—a delusion from which the Ferocious never suffered—the comparison is hardly in their favor. In our case the ferocious ones were an exception, a kind of skeleton in the closet. For obvious reasons the majority of kings were like my king. In contrast to these contemporary gentlemen they had no need to worry about their careers, because their birthright was their career."

The chamberlain made a mental note of this comparison for future use in his memoirs. He had his own system of memorizing. He had no notebook and he never had used a fountain pen in his life. Instead, he committed to memory one or two key words. "Ferocious. Career . . ." He remembered that the famous French writer, Louis-Etienne Vermandois, would be at the ball. His invitation had been a rather serious breach of court etiquette. Without having been presented previously at court, people were not invited to any of the court functions. But in the matter of etiquette the chamberlain knew no rules or precedents: he created them himself, depending on circumstances. The chamberlain was anxious to meet Vermandois; he believed that Voltaire must have held the same attraction for Frederick and Catherine. "Too bad I cannot read my memoirs to him. They say he is an anarchist, or a communist, or something of that sort. Should I invite him for dinner, and read him a chapter or two? I would rather have an intelligent anarchist for a listener, than some stupid court functionary. But probably he would be bored: he knows none of the people I speak of. Memoirs are a form of self-deception anyway:

actually, except to himself, a man's life is of no interest to anyone . . ." With an eye to the introduction to his memoirs, he
made a mental note of this thought, too. "Self-deception. Ferocious
—career, self-deception . . ."

Glancing at the historic clock, the chamberlain went to dress.
He put on his ornate coat which, even among other court uniforms, was distinguished for its quantity of gold braid. Without
it his position at court would have been just as unthinkable as a
dance without music. The chamberlain had no objection to
changing uniforms five or even six times in the course of a single
day. To his friends he was in the habit of saying that he preferred to be dressed like Solomon rather than like the lilies of the
field.

The orchestra struck up a march. The doors of the ballroom were
thrown open wide, and several pages crossed the threshold. At a
proper distance behind them walked the chamberlain. A light
smile, or rather the trace of a smile played on his face—one-fifth of
his usual smile. A full smile would have been inappropriate during the entrance ritual, while a sterner expression would have
detracted from the festive spirit of the ball. His movements were
majestic and, at the same time, almost natural. "This is an art,"
thought Vermandois, standing in a long line of guests. The chamberlain looked neither to the right nor to the left, as though the
whole affair were no concern of his. But imperceptibly he was
directing the entire ceremony, which without him would have
been impossible, just as impossible as it is for an orchestra to play
without a conductor, regardless of how often it has rehearsed a
program. He saw to it that the pages kept in step, that the guests
stood in a reasonably straight line, and that the music was neither
too fast nor too slow. The king and queen appeared in the door
at just the right moment. The guests greeted them with a curtsey
and a deep bow. For obvious reasons precision could not be expected during this part of the ritual, but the ripple of movement
did not in any way mar the beauty of the pageant. Struggling to
overcome his self-consciousness and graciously bowing in all

directions, the king, with a gentle smile, moved forward. "He is walking a little too fast," the chamberlain thought, seeing every-thing that was happening behind him in the mirrors on the wall toward which they were marching. Undiscernibly he slackened his pace. The king and the queen instantly followed his lead. The space between them and the chamberlain decreased not more than a foot.

The march came to an end at the very moment when the pages were about to collide with their own reflections in the mirrors. The king and the queen turned around. The orchestra struck up the opening chord of a polonaise. The lady nearest the king was the ambassador's wife, with whom he was supposed to open the ball. They moved in the direction opposite to that from which they had marched, followed by the queen and a foreign prince. The other couples were drawn into the polonaise line not quite so smoothly. But the chamberlain realized that with sixty couples dancing the polonaise nothing better could be expected. Everything was progressing nicely. From his long experience he knew that state entrances, parades and maneuvers were always a success. But inwardly he felt that the balls which had been given at the palace forty years ago had been much more impressive. "Then the guests were different. Only real people were invited," he thought, moving toward the doors of the white drawing-room where the third act of the play—the *"cercle"*—was about to take place. He was intercepted on the way by acquaintances and by people who considered themselves his acquaintances (he did not recognize many of the faces around him), who pressed his hand and praised the beauty of the pageant in the same way that people compliment a hostess. After all, they could not very well say these things to the queen.

As though by pre-arrangement, the king, queen and the princes were followed to the white drawing-room only by the guests who had the right to be there. The chamberlain stood to the left and a foot or so behind the king, and now his face was adorned with three-fifths of a smile: the *"cercle"* did not require the same degree of solemnity as was expected during a state entrance. Avoiding anything that sounded like a formal introduction, he casually, almost incidentally, mentioned the names of the people whom he had reason to believe the king was likely not to remember. But the king remembered everyone. He had inherited an excellent professional memory for names and faces. Generally speaking, the chamberlain was well pleased with the king. Some time ago—also in connection with his memoirs—he had copied an excerpt from Renan: *"Il faut pardonner aux rois leur médiocrité: ils ne se sont pas choisis."* "The more mediocre the king, the better it is for the state, and the more he is loved by his subjects," was his own elaboration of Renan's thought, and he regretted that for obvious reasons he could not use it in his memoirs. "I am very happy to see you, my dear ambassador," the king said to Kangarov, who was next in the line of guests. "I hope you are comfortable in our capital." "Very comfortable indeed, Your Majesty. What amazes me most about this city . . ." the ambassador began, but the disappearance of another fifth of the chamberlain's smile warned him that the guest line must move along. "I am happy to see you. I trust you are well?" the queen said drily to the wife of the Soviet ambassador, who sank down before her in a deep curtsey which she had rehearsed numerous times before her mirror. "But the red blotches no longer appear on her face— she has resigned herself to the idea. . . ." the chamberlain thought watching the queen, and with an inward relish remembered that the old prince had not come to the ball: "to avoid talking to all kinds of riff-raff!" The face of the chamberlain suddenly lighted up with all the five fifths of a smile.

"Yes, this is an art," Vermandois was thinking. "Even if it is second-class art, something like the ballet. Years of civilization have been necessary to create it. Dancers have to be taught for years, but these people seem to have it in their blood. They certainly have not rehearsed the entrance? . . . The music is good too—it's Mozart's 'Turkish March.' Émile would have described it in his novel: 'Vienna of the carefree Mozart days, Vienna of the minuets, masquerades, swords, silks, and gold.' Here they are imitating Vienna. Amusing, when you think that in turn Vienna was imitating Stamboul or Baghdad with its 'curved sabres, harems, and hanging gardens bathed in the sun.' That's the origin of all those Turkish marches. They could not be natural any more than we can, and they invariably imitated something, usually Versailles. . . . A pretty march . . ." Vermandois remembered the opinions he had voiced in the salon of the Countess about Mozart's "Requiem," and smiled: "Try to appraise an artist on the strength of his creations! He creates 'Requiem' but he also creates the 'Turkish March.' Someone ordered a march, and so he wrote it. It always has been that way: even the creations of the most independent and spirited artists depend on the market. If Racine had written an immortal tragedy in seventeen instead of in five acts, the contemporary market would have made it impossible to stage it. Wagner adjusted the length of his operas to the free evening hours of his delightful fellow-countrymen. . . . But it is more than just a matter of an immediate market. Mozart believed in the ideals of the 'Requiem' on Thursdays, and in the ideals of the 'Turkish March' on Fridays. This does not prevent the critics from demanding that in our novels we draw 'clear, precise, and consistent characterizations.' These never-ending absurdities of the critics affected Wagner so much, that childishly he introduced *Leit-motifs* for all his characters. Actually, I alone should require at least one hundred seventy-five such *motifs*, depending on the state of my health, on the progress of my work, or on whether the man who has just talked to me got on my nerves. . . . Even our best, our most closely approximating definitions, such as 'a decent person,' take no account of the animal and subconscious foundations, or of the fortunate combinations of physiological and spiritual characteristics that go to make a decent person. But we have faith in such classifications, and we love and hate them with the childishness of David who in his psalms sicked the Almighty God on his personal enemies. . . ."

The secretary of the French embassy informed Vermandois
of the names of the more important people dancing the polonaise. For the most part they were the historic names implanted
in the memories of men during their school years. But among
them were also names not in any way associated with history.
"There is Madame Kangarov, the wife of the Soviet ambassador,"
the secretary said with an ironic smile, indicating the sixth lady
from the head of the column—the third couple behind the princes
of the blood. "Which one? Kangarov is a very good friend of
mine," Vermandois unexpectedly said, principally in order to
annoy the secretary, who for some reason irritated him. "Who is
she with? What ambassador?" The secretary named a notoriously
reactionary power, and with the same smile explained: "That's
one of the chamberlain's favorite pastimes—he loves to bring
together people like that." "I must say that the Soviet ambassador's
secretary is much more attractive than his wife. I wonder if she
is here tonight?" "I have no idea who she is," the secretary
answered hurriedly, and walked away. He had hopes of getting
into the white drawing-room. The Count and Countess de Bellancombre also disappeared behind the doors. Vermandois could not
find a soul he knew in the ballroom. He had not been invited to
the white drawing-room, and he was ashamed to admit that this
lack of attention piqued him. "I am an old fool! . . ."

The orchestra changed to a waltz. Vermandois wandered into
a long room where tables covered with shining white cloths were
lined along the walls. Already guests were gathering around them.
Vermandois drank some champagne which, to his amazement,
was excellent. The old silver and china were beautiful beyond
words. He peered into the next drawing-room, which adjoined
the brilliantly illuminated winter garden. Here the temperature
was much pleasanter, and the armchairs more comfortable than
the straight chairs in the ballroom. "I can enjoy a rest here."
He had stood in line for a long time waiting for the royal entrance.
A stream of men in gold-braided uniforms and of women in striking dresses flowed in and out of the winter garden. "There is no

denying that the picture is colorful . . . These people irritate me much less than the waiters in knee-breeches in the house of a Paris banker. But actually only Émile, Paul Bourget and others like them can detect any essential difference between the two. In one instance the fathers were robbers, in the other—the great-grandfathers. That is so. . . . I believe that a good and rather reasonable monarchist has been lost in me. As a matter of fact, it is still not too late for me to join the royalist camp. . . ."

The imagination of Vermandois began to explore this possibility. "I could visit the pretender, return and write a book—a sort of *Genius of Christianity* of the monarchist philosophy. That would be a world-wide sensation. The right-wingers would groan with delight: 'Vermandois is one of us! . . .' They would forgive me everything, and put me on a pedestal. The left-wingers would indulge in some biting remarks and then forget me. That would be one way of joining a 'great collective enterprise,' the very consideration which prompted me when I almost joined the communist party. I should shelve any intelligence I possess, and join in the 'great undertaking of liberating humanity.' The liberation of cooks can be reconciled with monarchist as well as with communist philosophy. Merely a question of resourcefulness. True, communism is more of a novelty, but 'only that is new which has been forgotten,' and at present monarchy stands first on the forgotten list. Who was it who said 'you cannot turn back the clock'? That is one of the silliest aphorisms in the entire political phraseology of the world. Specialists devote their entire time to turning the clock any way they choose. As a matter of fact that is the only philosophical achievement which can be credited to Hitler. He was the first to demonstrate that the clock can be turned back for several centuries, and that at least half of the world's population is willing to believe that back means forward. The conservatives and the reactionaries made the greatest mistake when they admitted that they were conservatives and reactionaries. They should have insisted that they were the most advanced socialists and democrats. Who can deny that Hitler was brought

into power by the will of the people, and that his rawness, his dull-
ness and his cruelty have their roots in the people? The present
condition of the world is due to the aura of the people—people in
the real sense—which for the first time is making itself felt in two
major countries: Russia and Germany. A butcher has burst in on
history, and to justify his appearance new mysticism, metaphysics
and philosophies are being manufactured at special rates. All the
so-called élite hurriedly disappeared underground. But the élite
of mind never was, is, or will be in power, which is just as well
because then everything would go to the devil. And among the
lesser élites the 'élite of upbringing' is probably the least offensive. . . . This ballet actually for a long time maintained order
and stability in the world," Vermandois thought. He knew that
he would not visit the pretender and that he would not join the
royalists, but he no longer feared for his mind because he changed
his opinions several times a day. "All 'great political ideals'
without exception are so insignificant, so elementary and so universal that the difference between them cannot be very great.
The arguments for and against each one are the same, and the
originators are possessed with the same craving for fame and for
the pleasures which life and power can give them. . . . Anything may serve as an anchor for salvation. . . . 'Our thousand-
year-old traditions. . . .' 'The forty kings. . . .' 'Stability of the
social system. . . .' 'The history of France. . . .' 'The well-being
of the English people. . . .' 'The prosperity of the Scandinavian
countries. . . .'" Vermandois recited in his mind all the arguments
ordinarily put forth by monarchists. "At least there is beauty in it
—beauty which cannot be equaled by any other form of government. Thought? Naturally, they opposed thought. But under
Louis XIV there was a Racine and a Molière, and monarchy did
not interfere with the development of a Descartes or a Pascal.
So far, minds of such calibre have not appeared under Stalin and
Hitler. Possibly after going through the various stages of democracy, bolshevism, fascism, and racialism, humanity will develop a
yearning for this type of mysticism, and the twentieth century will

go down in history as the century of the overthrow and restoration of kings. They all left with return tickets in their pockets. . . ."

Having fortified himself with champagne and with these fleeting thoughts (he called them "thoughts for a railroad journey, or just before falling asleep"), Vermandois returned to the ballroom. There the fifth or sixth waltz was in progress. The wife of the Soviet ambassador was dancing again with the ambassador of the reactionary power. A bald-headed, stocky man with an ominously apoplectic neck, the ambassador loved dancing with a passion which would have been natural in a very young or a very old man, but which in a middle-aged man was almost pathological. The royal family physician sitting in the corner undressed all the guests with professional curiosity, in his imagination. He felt that this particular guest should at once leave for Royat or Nauheim and begin taking salts of iodine. The ambassador went out of his way to be pleasant. In his conversations with the Soviet ambassador's wife he hoped to pick up some morsel for a private letter to the minister of foreign affairs, who was a personal good friend, and who enjoyed international gossip. But, contrary to the general rule, Helen Kangarov was on her guard whenever she was happy, and the ambassador was unable to pick up anything spicy. With the exception of her French, which was not as good as his, her responses were on the same level with his compliments. "She really is very charming," the ambassador thought mechanically, reciting a madrigal. He belonged to the school which still recites madrigals and even composes epigrams.

"You dance like the divine Pavlova," the ambassador said, and immediately was assailed by doubts: "Was Pavlova a White Russian?" "All Slavs have a natural talent for dancing. The Russian ballet is the finest in the world."

"You are too generous, but I adore our ballet. We simply raved about it in school!"

"In this ballroom . . ." the ambassador was saying. "I wonder what she means by school? Could she mean some reformatory?" he asked himself, at the same moment answering with the knowing smile of a fellow-conspirator the smile of the chamberlain, who was leading Vermandois into the white drawing-room. "Do you know who that is? That is the famous French writer, Vermandois . . . I have forgotten what he has written! . . ."

"And I never even knew! . . ." Helen Kangarov answered just as casually. She was happy almost to distraction. Among the ladies at the palace ball she was conspicuously popular. She had danced a third waltz with the young prince, and now dancing with the bald-headed ambassador was to her a minor, insignificant incident. Out of curiosity, or out of snobbishness, or out of a desire to display their broadmindedness the most conservative officials of the highest rank were exceptionally nice to her. Helen Kangarov had never felt closer to the pinnacle of glory. She was turning the heads of the young princes—she was in the seventh heaven. . . .

The ritual of presentation was very brief. "Allow me to present to Your Majesty Monsieur Louis-Etienne Vermandois," the chamberlain said and hurriedly added: "The famous author of the novels which you, Sire, enjoy so much." He knew that before famous foreigners were presented to him the king ordinarily consulted reference books, though he did not like this to be generally known. "Perhaps he has not had time? He might think that this was a Swiss missionary, or some famous composer. . . ." But the precaution was unnecessary. The king uttered several appropriate words. "I hope you are here for a long visit," the queen said. "Not very original, but adequate for the occasion," the chamberlain thought. He hurriedly completed the introduction and led Vermandois into another room.

"The king is one of your ardent admirers," he said, taking an armchair at a corner table. "But His Majesty prefers not to discuss literature."

"I am very flattered."

"He is in a difficult position," the chamberlain said and laughed. "When I was a young man, I was secretary of our embassy in Vienna. At the palace receptions there the late Franz-Josef for seventy years invariably asked the same question: 'How

long since the last hunt, Count?' or 'How was the shooting, my
dear ambassador?' He did not vary them even if the count or
ambassador in question had never held a gun in his life. If the
ambassador happened to represent an emperor or some very good
king the old man would inquire about His Majesty's health. But
the emperor never said anything else to anyone. I remember the
excitement when on one occasion he did say something else. It
was a veritable sensation."

With a chuckle the chamberlain took a glass from the tray
offered to him by a waiter, sipped the champagne, and wondered
whether he was committing treason to his class when he discussed
an emperor in this informal way with a man without background
or family.

"Yes, times have changed," Vermandois said, listening to the
strains of a new waltz. "Lord Byron, who was ready to tear down
the entire existing social structure, expressed an opinion that the
waltz, which was just coming into its own, was a lewd and
indecent dance."

"How interesting! I have never heard this about Byron." The
chamberlain felt that this bit of information would fit nicely into
his memoirs. He began to talk about Paris, where he visited frequently, and about various famous people whom he knew personally. Among them were a few writers, but the mention of their
names seemed to evoke no enthusiasm in the French guest. "I
believe literary celebrities have even less regard for one another
than rival statesmen," the chamberlain thought, and changed the
subject to politics. They discussed the debates in the French
chamber, each had an anecdote to tell about them, then cautiously
they mentioned Stalin, and after a brief pause began to talk about
the war in Spain. Though both had demonstrated that they were
accomplished drawing-room conversationalists, being absolute
strangers they found it difficult to maintain a steady flow of
conversation. The chamberlain, displaying his liberal views and
his impartiality, said that the atrocities perpetrated by both sides
had shaken his faith in the noble character of the Spanish people.

"But then, Lope de Vega, their greatest writer, presided over *auto-da-fé* ceremonies," the chamberlain said. "Perhaps southern peoples have a streak of cruelty in them. Or, perhaps, the newspapers are exaggerating."

"I doubt that. History teaches us that we should lend a credulous ear to reports of cruelties and atrocities. On the other hand, we should be amazed whenever we hear tales of kindness and knightly virtue," Vermandois said, fortuitously taking a misanthropic stand. Now he was forced to continue in the same vein, though he found it entirely out of place in a palace, and in a conversation with a high-ranking official whom he had just met. The chamberlain's face reflected the appropriate degree of sorrow. In his mind he considered several suitable answers. "History teaches us that it does not teach us anything" ("too bookish, and not conducive to further conversation"). "I know that you are a disciple of Schopenhauer" ("I know nothing of the kind, and he may well detest Schopenhauer"). "I admit that current events give solid grounds for pessimism, but we should avoid looking at the dark side." His vocal cords mechanically made the choice without recourse to reason, or to cause and effect.

"Current events are reason enough for being pessimistic, but we should avoid looking at the dark side. We are imbued with a knightly conception of warfare."

"I hope you don't expect the Spanish loyalists to call out to Franco's soldiers: '*Messieurs les fascistes, tirez les premiers*'?"

"Hardly, but I should welcome a return to the conventions of the Battle of Fontenoy," the chamberlain answered, immediately recognizing the quotation ("the quotation is well known, but I doubt that he gives a chamberlain credit for even a rudimentary education").

"You hope for the impossible: a return to something that never existed. Count d'Hauteroche never called to Lord Charles Hay: 'Gentlemen, we are waiting for the English to shoot first!' And Lord Charles Hay never called to the Count d'Hauteroche: 'Gentlemen, we are waiting for the French to shoot first!' But, apparently, they had an identical instinct and motive for lying,

because without pre-arrangement they invented the same phrase.
. . . The Battle of Fontenoy was one of the most brutal slaugh-
ters in history. More lies are told about wars and military valor
than about anything else under the sun, including bolsheviks.
People of the eighteenth century held a childish belief that the
masses love peace. Unfortunately, it is not so."

"Every definition has to be qualified," the chamberlain
answered, sorrowfully shaking his head. (" 'I fully agree with you,
but for God's sake not so loud! The palace is full of democrats! . . .' No, that would have been too indiscreet. . . . 'every
definition has to be qualified' is much safer"). "I never for a moment believe that everything was perfect in Athens under Pericles,
but it was glorious, for all its imperfections ["excellent!"]. The
French people, through the mouths of their great thinkers, proclaimed new ideals. . . ."

"Not the people. The thinkers proclaimed them of their own
accord. And speaking of new ideals, the ideals of fascism and
communism are inferior to our ideals ["communist ideals are
inferior? What on earth is he?" the chamberlain was puzzled],
but their ideals are pragmatic. The fascist ideals are slanted
toward war, and the communist ideals are slanted toward revolution. Our ideals are without a slant. As long as communists and
fascists did not exist, history, like an old nag, somehow managed
to drag through several decades, and we should be grateful for
that much! But now the nag is galloping, and I am waiting for the
outcome with fear and trembling. Probably our relatively young
century will be known as the most loathsome century in history.
The young thing has already justified these brilliant expectations.
It has only one good quality: it is obvious and frank."

Unexpectedly, Vermandois experienced the same feeling that
the chamberlain had experienced earlier: a feeling of committing
treason to his class. But this awkward sensation was overcome
quickly by a habit of many years' standing. He received invitations because he was expected to talk, and he could no more refuse
to talk than a tenor can refuse to sing after he has accepted a

fee from his host. To talk simply and unassumingly, without re-
sorting to aphorisms and quotations, required much more effort.
("How cheap! . . . That is the supreme ordeal, by social inter-
course and smart chatter, which no one can undergo without
harming himself.")

"Speaking of the young thing," the chamberlain said. "Just
this morning I noticed in the 'Figaro' a news item about the execution of the young man who was your secretary, and who committed that horrible murder. I have been watching his strange case,
and I cannot . . ."

"Has he been executed?" Vermandois exclaimed in a shrill voice.
The chamberlain, who was not accustomed to interruptions, raised
his eyebrows.

"Haven't you heard? I see that you don't read the papers. I
believe Goethe and Tolstoy also followed that rule. . . ." He
rose to greet a foreign prince who was emerging from the white
drawing-room. "I am delighted to have had this chat with you,"
the chamberlain said, but his smile was already focused on the
prince.

"When the time comes all these gentlemen will have to face
the hangman," Vermandois thought, glaring furiously at the men
in gold-braided uniforms who were walking past him. "They may
as well enjoy themselves while they can! In days gone by turkeys
were fattened like that, before their throats were slit." Not without relish he changed abruptly from royalist to communist. "This
society is doomed. That other miserable lunatic has been executed,
but these are still at large." He stared at a fat man standing at
one of the tables. Through some dim association with his journey
to Versailles to attend Alvera's trial, he decided that this man unknown to him was a banker who thus far had not been caught steal-
ing. Somehow, to consider this man a banker, rather than a duke
or a count, fitted in better with his mood. "He may have bought
a title for himself. . . . But the gallows as the culmination of this
gentleman's career would indicate that an intelligent guiding
force exists in this world. That force which in the old days was

known as the design of the universe, or as supreme and divine justice. Michelangelo tried to picture this force as a flying, bearded old man. . . . To admit the existence of a supreme intelligence, would to me mean a denial of the existence of reason, the one valuable attribute in this world, and the only one that justifies its existence. . . . They will all perish, and most of them will not be given a chance to fight. They will perish stupidly, passively, as cattle locked in a barn perish in a fire." In the distance Vermandois saw Kangarov, and changing as abruptly from a bolshevik to a revolutionary democrat, thought that no harm would be done if the Soviet ambassador were hanged along with the others. "He is a Gay-Pay-Oo agent, or at least partly so. In their entire revolution one part idealism is mixed with ninety-nine parts lust for power, ambition, and brutality. For them revolution is a career, and not a bad career at that. He told me that for many years, like Lenin, he wrote articles living in exile, where he was absolutely safe. Where, except in a revolutionary world, could a man become a general at the age of thirty, without having done anything to win his spurs? . . . Old age has crept upon me so blindly and so ruthlessly! I see all this splendor for the last time in my life. . . ."

Vermandois remembered that the manager had declined to make arrangements for a lecture tour. "The expenses will be larger than the receipts, and so until the end of my days I am doomed to write articles and ask publishers for advances. And what if I am taken ill? What if I no longer can work? . . . The fact that Beethoven and Rembrandt were paupers is reassuring to an extent. Idiots (naturally only rich idiots) say that this stimulated their creative genius: 'the money goad,' 'bitter experiences,' et cetera. But I should like to consult Beethoven and Rembrandt about it. . . . Cézanne dreamed in terms of tremendous paintings, but he painted as he did, partly because he had to economize on paints and canvas. . . . At least I have never sold my independence, and I have never lent my name to advertise pens or wines, something most people seem to be doing today. I have followed the narrow path of honest art, and not the broad highway which is so much used today," Vermandois thought disjoint-edly, quite moved by the nobility of his own character—a frame of mind unusual for him. "Yes, all this is beautiful. . . . I have seen few such magnificent pageants in my life. . . ." Suddenly he had a vision of a guillotine, of a thin, pale, demented man, and of a head covered with blood—his instinct of an experienced writer made the vision almost real. "How deeply Shakespeare and the moving-pictures are rooted in our minds! . . . Yes, this is the beginning of the end," Vermandois told himself as he watched the Soviet ambassador approach him. "What is the matter with him today? He looks like the Metro-Goldwyn lion. . . ."

After eleven the king re-appeared in the ballroom. He was tired, but he was also relieved to know that the most trying part of the evening—the state entrance, the polonaise, and the informal reception—was over. Not to disturb the guests the king immediately settled in an armchair by the wall, and with a tired, benevolent, and regal smile watched the dancing couples. Now, at last he was able to derive a certain, infinitesimally small amount of pleasure from the affair.

The chamberlain, who sat a little to the left and behind the king, appeared to be entertaining him with a lively conversation. Actually, very little was said. The chamberlain understood that the king had talked enough for one night, and that silence and rest appealed to him most. Conversations with so many different people were more tiring than any of his other duties. That is why at intervals the chamberlain, leaning forward and slightly to the right, said a few words which did not require an answer. But his expression, his beaming smile, and his alert posture gave anyone who observed them the impression that the king and the chamberlain were engaged in a most animated and pleasant conversation which just that moment had been interrupted.

The chamberlain was very happy. He had had two interesting meetings that evening. One with Vermandois, the other with a foreign prince, who had told him a most amusing story (absolutely new) about Edward VII—a story that was good material for his memoirs (the key word for remembering it was "Carlsbad"). That, along with the picture of the Soviet ambassador's wife flirting with the ambassador of a reactionary power, made him feel that his memoirs had progressed another five or six pages. But there had also been something unpleasant. "The newspaper headlines. . . . Something threatening the security of all this?" he remembered, and almost frowned (actually, the chamberlain could not possibly frown at a palace ball, with thousands of eyes watching him).

A waltzing couple drew near to where the king was sitting: a tall, handsome captain of a guard regiment, and a young girl who was the daughter of one of the chamberlain's friends. He knew that they were passionately in love, and that their engagement was soon to be announced. Both belonged to the small circle of wealthy and titled families. "What a handsome couple! They could not look better if they had been made to order. She is simply charming," the chamberlain thought. "Our breed is not so bad after all. . . ." The couple glided past the king. The girl had not even noticed him. But the officer, absorbed though he was in silent exchange with her, saw the king, and a slight, almost imperceptible change took place in his movements and in the expression of his face, indicating that he waltzed past the king's chair differently than he waltzed past all other chairs. The king, who also knew the secret, smiled tenderly at the girl, but she was not aware of the royal smile. He turned to the chamberlain. "I know you envy them," the king said jokingly. The chamberlain, whose eyes had been following the girl, beamed even more. "Every age has its own pleasures, Sire," he answered, not worrying too much about the finesse of his remarks in his conversations with the king.

The Soviet ambassador, whose full dress stood out among the sea of gold-braided uniforms, came into the chamberlain's line of vision. The sight of Kangarov once again stirred sad thoughts in his subconscious mind. "Nonsense, nonsense," he reassured himself cheerfully. The chamberlain surveyed the majestic ballroom aglow with lights, gold, and diamonds, and saw the couple once again. "No, our breed can still hold its own. We are made of sterner stuff than Vermandois. We have enough to last another century. Or even two or three centuries!" And suddenly warming his soul, festively illuminating his whole life, reconciling him to evil, and climaxing everything good, in the chamberlain's imagination arose the vision of the British Guiana, 1856, "black on magenta, the famous error. . . ."

Kangarov was sitting at a small table with Vermandois. He already had made the necessary preliminary remarks about Paris, about their mutual friends, and about the lecture, but the real purpose of the conversation had not as yet been broached. He still was stunned by the blow which had fallen on him so unexpectedly. After the brief conversation with the king, Kangarov had gone to the buffet, taken several drinks, moved to the winter garden, and wandered back. "Yes, without a doubt everything is now at an end!" his thoughts were as disjointed as if he were delirious or asleep. "I feel that this is her final decision! There was hatred, real hatred in her eyes. . . . If that is true, what have I to live for? . . . Divorce no longer has any purpose. The slut will not give me a divorce, and without her consent I shall have trouble getting it. And why should I bother about it now? . . ." Acquaintances, with whom he shook hands and exchanged a few words, stared at him in amazement and left him— they actually hurried away. He continued to drink wine, champagne and cognac, moving from table to table in order not to attract the attention of the waiters. Kangarov made an effort to focus his thoughts. "What else in life is there for me? The party? . . ." Like Nadia, that evening he began to see strange and unexpected things. For the first time he realized clearly that the party had no meaning for him, that he never had served the party, but like most people had made a career of it, concealing this fact, even from himself, beneath a coating of ideology. But now e en this discovery was not important. He had lost all interest in his profession. "What is there for me to do? I shall go on like this until the end of my days. . . ." At that moment he saw Vermandois. "I had something to tell him. . . . Oh, yes, the instructions. . . . I may as well carry them out. . . ." Because of his mental state he went about it much more crudely than he should, or would have at any other time. Kangarov told Vermandois that the State Publishing House wanted to publish his works in Russian: not just a few of them, but his collected works.

"An excellent idea," Vermandois said with a smile, looking at the ambassador with pleased surprise. "Some of my books appeared in Russia under the old regime, but only a few of them. Unfortunately, I never received anything for them: Russia was not a party to the Berne Convention."

"Our government also is not a party to it," Kangarov said curtly. "But we make exceptions for friends of the Soviet Union. We pay them in foreign exchange—in dollars. These exceptions are made only for our true friends."

"Really?" Vermandois asked. At first the ambassador's words had delighted him. Perhaps fate was rewarding him for the failure of the manager to make him an offer. "Fate really owes me a reward. . . . And without lectures, without traveling, without idiotic speeches! . . . How marvelous it would be! . . ." But after the second emphasis on the word "friends," he again was on his guard.

"Nothing would delight me more. You know my old feeling for Russia and everything Russian . . ." Vermandois began. Kangarov interrupted him.

"Incidentally, my dear friend, right now you can render a real service to the Soviet Union," he said. Any other time his instinct would have guided the ambassador through this difficult situation. But at the moment nothing interested him. "He can be bought like any other bastard. . . . They are all alike. . . ." Without any preliminaries, without any diplomatic overtures, without that dexterity for which the secretary had praised him with good reason, Kangarov broached the matter of the telegram. "Yes, her decision is final. . . . She is leaving. . . . She is leaving . . ." he thought while he continued to talk without looking at the Frenchman. "She will marry that pug-nosed fellow! . . . This is the end. . . . And without her what does life hold for me? . . ." Suddenly, lifting his eyes, he saw that Vermandois' face had turned purple. "Have I said something I should have left unsaid?" he thought. "I know I am doing a dirty business, but it's not my fault. I am not a bad man, I never spilled blood, I hate cruelty, but life which is so cruel to me is a dirty thing. . . ."

"So you want to publish my complete works, if I send a telegram to those . . .?" Vermandois asked. The blood continued to surge to his face. Suddenly he was possessed with fury. He felt that all free thought had been insulted in his person. The shadows of Descartes, Pascal, Montaigne, and Beethoven seemed to crowd around him, waiting for his answer.

"You misunderstand me. We are discussing two separate and distinct matters. The publication of your works is one, and the telegram is another . . ." Kangarov began, but he did not finish. Heavily Vermandois rose to his feet. ("Yes, of course I hate Hitler more than I hate the bolsheviks. But if freedom and human dignity are to be defended, they must be defended honestly: against all tyrants and all corrupters . . .")

"Merde! . . ." he said. His face was convulsed. People who heard him, cast glances in his direction. Kangarov also rose. He was completely at a loss for something to say. Shaking with fury, Vermandois kept repeating the same word—only one word—a word which had never been heard in the palace of the kings throughout the centuries of its existence.